Dreams can come true with

Jenny COLGAN

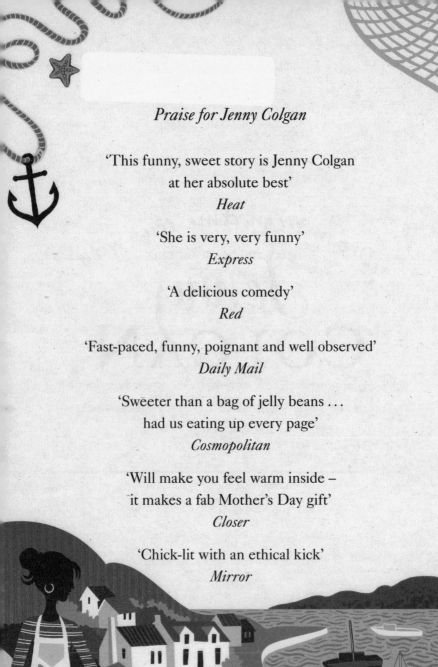

Praise for Jenny Colgan

'This funny, sweet story is Jenny Colgan at her absolute best'
Heat

'She is very, very funny'
Express

'A delicious comedy'
Red

'Fast-paced, funny, poignant and well observed'
Daily Mail

'Sweeter than a bag of jelly beans . . . had us eating up every page'
Cosmopolitan

'Will make you feel warm inside – it makes a fab Mother's Day gift'
Closer

'Chick-lit with an ethical kick'
Mirror

‘A quirky tale of love, work and the meaning of life’
Company

‘A smart, witty love story’
Observer

‘Full of laugh-out-loud observations . . . utterly unputdownable’
Woman

‘Cheery and heart-warming’
Sunday Mirror

‘A chick-lit writer with a difference . . . never scared to try something different, Colgan always pulls it off’
Image

‘A Colgan novel is like listening to your best pal, souped up on vino, spilling the latest gossip – entertaining, dramatic and frequently hilarious’
Daily Record

‘An entertaining read’
Sunday Express

‘Part-chick lit, part-food porn . . . this is full-on fun for foodies’
Bella

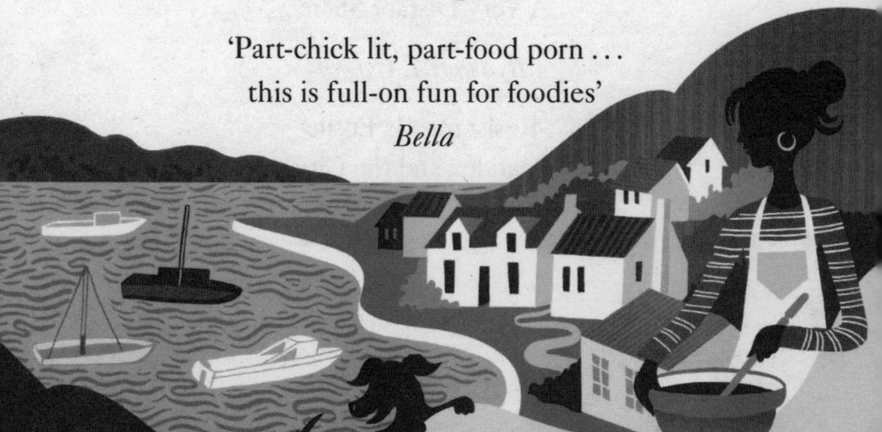

Also by Jenny Colgan

Amanda's Wedding
Talking to Addison
Looking for Andrew McCarthy
Working Wonders
Do You Remember the First Time?
Where Have All the Boys Gone?
West End Girls
Operation Sunshine
Diamonds Are a Girl's Best Friend
The Good, the Bad and the Dumped
Meet Me at the Cupcake Café
Christmas at the Cupcake Café
Welcome to Rosie Hopkins' Sweetshop of Dreams
Christmas at Rosie Hopkins' Sweetshop
The Christmas Surprise
The Loveliest Chocolate Shop in Paris
Little Beach Street Bakery
Summer at Little Beach Street Bakery
Christmas at Little Beach Street Bakery
The Little Shop of Happy-Ever-After
A Very Distant Shore

By Jenny T. Colgan

Resistance Is Futile
Spandex and the City

Jenny Colgan is the author of numerous bestselling novels, including *The Little Shop of Happy-Ever-After* and *Summer at the Little Beach Street Bakery*, which are also published by Sphere. *Meet Me at the Cupcake Café* won the 2012 Melissa Nathan Award for Comedy Romance and was a *Sunday Times* top ten bestseller, as was *Welcome to Rosie Hopkins' Sweetshop of Dreams*, which won the RNA Romantic Novel of the Year Award 2013. Jenny was born in Scotland and has lived in London, the Netherlands, the US and France. She eventually settled on the wettest of all of these places, and currently lives just north of Edinburgh with her husband Andrew, her dog Nevil Shute and her three children: Wallace, who is eleven and likes pretending to be nineteen and not knowing what this embarrassing 'family' thing is that keeps following him about; Michael-Francis, who is nine and likes making new friends on aeroplanes; and Delphine, who is seven and is mostly raccoon as far as we can tell so far.

Things Jenny likes include: cakes; far too much *Doctor Who*; wearing Converse trainers every day so her feet are now just gigantic big flat pans; baths only slightly cooler than the surface of the sun and very, very long books, the longer the better. For more about Jenny, visit her website and her Facebook page, or follow her on Twitter @jennycolgan.

Jenny COLGAN

the Summer Seaside Kitchen

sphere

SPHERE

First published in Great Britain in 2017 by Sphere

1 3 5 7 9 10 8 6 4 2

A CIP catalogue record for this book
is available from the British Library.

ISBN 978-0-7515-6480-8

Typeset in Caslon by M Rules
Printed and bound in Great Britain by
Clays Ltd, St Ives plc

Papers used by Sphere are from well-managed forests
and other responsible sources.

MIX
Paper from
responsible sources
FSC® C104740

Sphere
An imprint of
Little, Brown Book Group
Carmelite House
50 Victoria Embankment
London EC4Y 0DZ

An Hachette UK Company
www.hachette.co.uk

www.littlebrown.co.uk

To nurses. Because you're amazing.

A Word from Jenny

Hello! If this is your first book of mine you've read – hello, and welcome! I really hope you enjoy it. And if you've read my books before, a huge and heartfelt thank you; it is lovely to see you again and, wow, you're looking great, did you change your hair? It *totally* suits you.

Welcome to *The Summer Seaside Kitchen*! It's the strangest thing that often you can go away on holiday to lots of different places, but not spend much time getting to know your own country very well (I know as I type this that my dear friend Wesley will be sniffing and rolling his eyes, because we have been friends for over twenty years and not once have I visited him in Belfast). *Anyway*, moving swiftly on: when I moved back to Scotland last year after decades of living abroad, I decided to rectify this.

I'd never really spent time in the Highlands and Islands before, being a 'lallander' by birth (which means being from the south of Scotland), so I took every opportunity to visit and explore, and I will say that I fell in love with the Islands straightaway.

The vast white beaches; the ancient strange monuments; the flat, treeless places (trees often can't grow in the strong winds) and those endless summer nights when it never gets dark. Lewis, Harris, Bute, Orkney and particularly Shetland, one of the strangest and loveliest places in the UK as far as I'm concerned, all cast their own particular spell.

I wanted to set a book up in the very far north, but here, I have made up an island which is kind of an amalgam, as there is nothing worse than writing about a real place and getting it wrong and everyone gets really very cross with you. Trust me, I have learned this from bitter experience 😃.

So, Mure is a fictional place, but I hope carries the essence and the feel of those amazing islands of the far north, which are so strange and beautiful and wonderful to me – although of course, to the musically-voiced people living there, they are simply 'home'.

Here you'll also find traditional recipes for pies and bread which I love to make and hope you'll enjoy trying out – you can let me know how that goes at @jennycolgan on Twitter or come find me on Facebook! (I am theoretically on Instagram but can't really work it.)

I so hope you enjoy *The Summer Seaside Kitchen.* It is a very personal book to me as, after a long time away, last year I finally came home to the land of my birth, as Flora does – and found that it had been waiting for me all along.

With love,

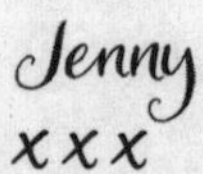

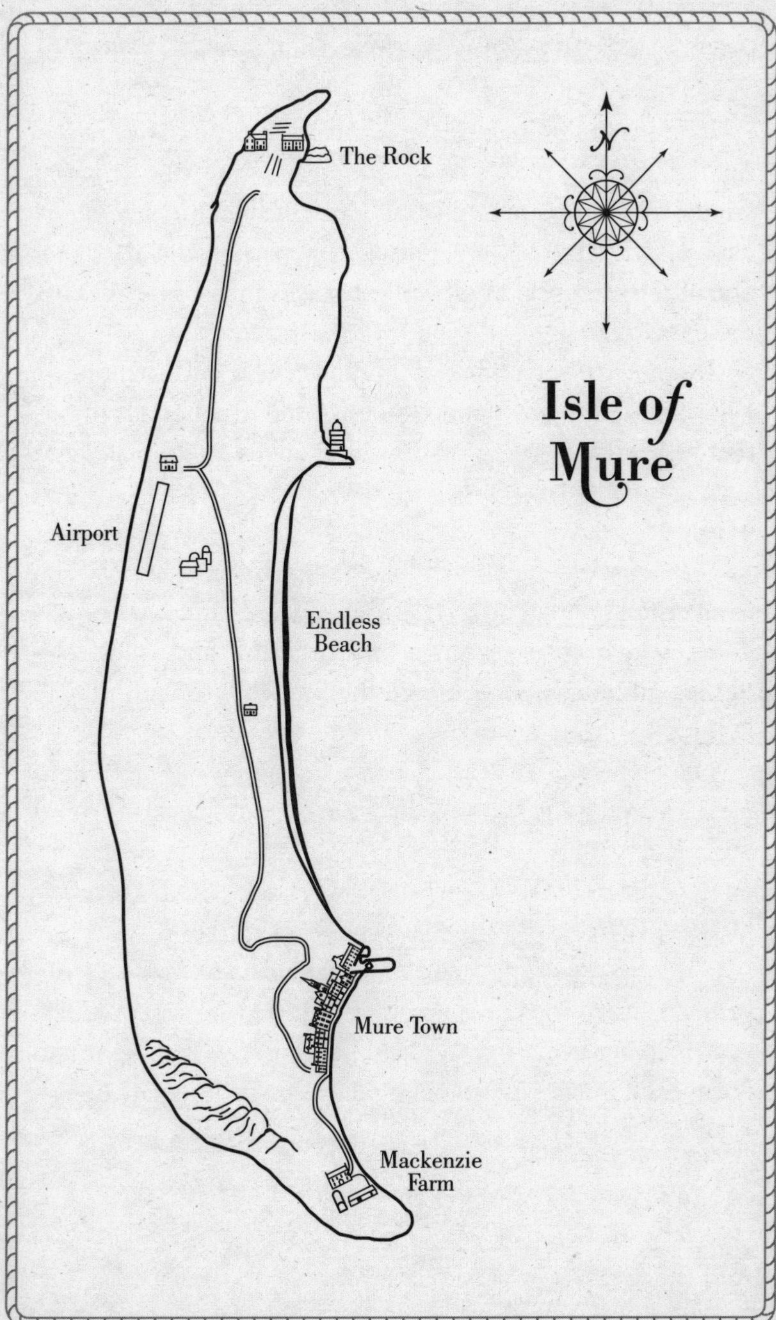
Isle of Mure
N
The Rock
Airport
Endless Beach
Mure Town
Mackenzie Farm

hiraeth (n): *a homesickness for a home to which you cannot return, a home that maybe never was; the nostalgia, the yearning, the grief for lost places in your past*

Chapter One

If you have ever flown into London – I did originally type 'You know when you fly into London?' and then I thought, well, that might be a bit presumptuous, like hey-ho, here I am flying about all the time, whereas the reality is I've always bought the cheapie discount flight that meant I had to get up at 4.30 a.m. and therefore didn't sleep at all the night before in case I missed the alarm and actually it ended up costing me more to get to the airport at an ungodly hour and then pour overpriced coffee down myself than it would have done just to buy a sensibly timed flight in the first place ... but anyway.

So.

If you've ever flown into London, you'll know that they often have to put you in a holding pattern, where you circle about, waiting for a landing slot. And I never usually mind it; I like seeing the vast expanse of the huge city below me, that unfathomable number of people busying away, the idea that every single one of them is full of hopes and dreams and disappointments, street after street after street, millions and millions of souls and dreams. I always find it pleasingly mind-boggling.

And if you had been hovering over London on this particular day in early spring, then beneath you you would have seen the massive, endless sprawl; the surprising amount of green space clustered in the west, where it looks as if you could walk clear across the city through its parks, and on to the clustered, smoky east, the streets and spaces becoming ever more congested; the wheel along the river glinting in the early-morning sun, the ships moving up and down the sometimes dirty, sometimes gleaming water, and the great glass towers that seem to have sprung up without anyone asking for them as London changes in front of your eyes; past the Millennium Dome, getting lower now, and there's the shining point of Canary Wharf, once the highest skyscraper in the country, with its train station that stops in the middle of the building, something that must have seemed pretty awesome in about 1988.

But let's imagine you could carry on; could zoom down like a living Google Maps in which you don't only go and look at your own house (or that might just be me).

If you carry on down further, it would pretty soon stop looking so serene, less as if you were surveying it like a god in the sky, and you'd start to notice how crowded everything is and how grubby it all looks, and how many people are shoving past each other, even now, when it's not long past 7 a.m., exhausted-looking cleaners who've just finished their dawn shifts trudging home in the opposite direction to the eager suited and booted young men and women; office jockeys and retail staff and mobile phone fixers and Uber drivers and window cleaners and *Big Issue* sellers and the many, many men wearing hi-vis vests who do mysterious things with traffic cones; and we're nearly at ground level now, whizzing round corners, following the path of the Docklands Light Railway, with its passengers trying to hold their own against the early-morning crush, because there is no way around it, you have to stick your elbows out, otherwise you won't get a place, might not even get to stand: the idea of possibly getting a seat stops miles back at Gallions Reach, but you might, you might just get a corner place to stand that isn't pressed up against somebody's armpit, the carriage thick with coffee and hungover breath and halitosis and the sense that everyone has been somehow ripped from their beds too soon, that even the watery sunlight tilting over the horizon in this early spring isn't entirely convinced about it; but tough, because the great machine of London is all ready and waiting, hungry, always hungry, to swallow you up, squeeze everything it can out of you and send you back to do the entire thing in reverse.

And there is Flora MacKenzie, with her elbows out, waiting to get on the little driverless train that will take her into the absurd spaghetti chaos of Bank station. You can see her: she's just stepping on. Her hair is a strange colour; very, very pale. Not blonde, and not red exactly, and kind of possibly strawberry blonde, but more faded than that. It's almost not a colour at all. And she is ever so slightly too tall; and her skin is pale as milk and her eyes are a watery colour and it's sometimes quite difficult to tell exactly what colour they are. And there she is, her bag and her briefcase tight by her side, wearing a mac that she's not sure is too light or too heavy for the day.

At this moment in time, and still pretty early in the morning, Flora MacKenzie isn't thinking about whether she's happy or sad, although that is shortly going to become very, very important.

If you could have stopped and asked her how she was feeling right at that moment, she'd probably have just said, 'Tired.' Because that's what people in London are. They're exhausted or knackered or absolutely frantic all the time because . . . well, nobody's sure why, it just seems to be the law, along with walking quickly and queuing outside pop-up restaurants and never, ever going to Madame Tussauds.

She's thinking about whether she will be able to get into a position where she can read her book; about whether the waistband on her skirt has become tighter, while simultaneously and regretfully thinking that if that thought ever occurs to you, it almost certainly has; about whether the weather is going to get hotter, and if so, is she going to go bare-legged (this is problematic for many reasons, not least because Flora's skin is paler than milk and resists any attempts to rectify this. She tried fake tan, but it looked as if she'd waded into a paddling pool full of Bisto. And as soon as she started walking, the backs of her knees got sweaty – she hadn't even known the backs of your knees *could* get sweaty – and long dribbling white lines cut through the tan, as her office mate Kai kindly pointed out to her. Kai has the most creamy coffee-coloured skin and Flora envies it very much. She also prefers autumn in London, on the whole).

She is thinking about the Tinder date she had the other

night, where the guy who had seemed so nice online immediately started making fun of her accent, as everybody does, everywhere, all the time; then, when he saw this wasn't impressing her, suggested they skip dinner and just go back to his house, and this is making her sigh.

She's twenty-six, and had a lovely party to prove it, and everyone got drunk and said that she was going to find a boyfriend any day, or, alternately, how it was that in London it was just impossible to meet anyone nice; there weren't any men and the ones there were were gay or married or evil, and in fact not everyone got drunk because one of her friends was pregnant for the first time and kept making a massive deal out of it while pretending not to and being secretly delighted. Flora was pleased for her, of course she was. She doesn't want to be pregnant. But even so.

Flora is squashed up against a man in a smart suit. She glances up, briefly, just in case, which is ridiculous: she's never seen *him* get the DLR; *he* always arrives looking absolutely spotless and uncreased and she knows he lives in town somewhere.

As usual, at her birthday party, Flora's friends knew better than to ask her about her boss after she'd had a couple of glasses of Prosecco. The boss on whom she has the most ridiculous, pointless crush.

If you have ever had an utterly agonising crush, you will know what this is like. Kai knows exactly how pointless this crush is, because he works for him too, and can see their boss clearly for exactly what he is, which is a terrible bastard. But there is of course no point telling this to Flora.

Anyway, the man on the train is not him. Flora feels

stupid for looking. She feels fourteen whenever she so much as thinks about him, and her pale cheeks don't hide her blushes at all. She knows it's ridiculous and stupid and pointless. She still can't help it.

She starts half reading her book on her Kindle, crammed in the tiny carriage, trying not to swing into anyone; half looking out of the window, dreaming. Other things bubbling in her mind:

a) She's getting another new flatmate. People move so often in and out of her big Victorian flatshare, she rarely gets to know any of them. Their old mail piles up in the hallway amid the skeletons of dead bicycles, and she thinks someone should do something about it, but she doesn't do anything about it.
b) Whether she should move again.
c) Boyfriend. Sigh.
d) Time for Pret A Manger?
e) Maybe a new hair colour? Something she could remove? Would that shiny grey suit her, or would she look like she had grey hair?
f) Life, the future, everything.
g) Whether to paint her room the same colour as her new hair, or whether that would mean she had to move too.
h) Happiness and stuff.
i) Cuticles.
j) Maybe not silver, maybe blue? Maybe a bit blue? Would that be okay in the office? Could she buy a blue bit and put it in, then take it out?
k) Cat?

And she's on her way to work, as a paralegal, in the centre of London, and she isn't happy particularly, but she isn't sad because, Flora thinks, this is just what everyone does, isn't it? Cram themselves on to a commute. Eat too much cake when it's someone's birthday in the office. Vow to go to the gym at lunchtime but don't make it. Stare at a screen for so long they get a headache. Order too much from ASOS then forget to send it back.

Sometimes she goes from tube to house to office without even noticing what the weather is doing. It's just a normal, tedious day.

Although in two hours and forty-five minutes, it won't be.

Chapter Two

Meanwhile, three miles to the west, a blonde woman was shouting, loudly.

She was gorgeous. Even annoyed and spitting after a sleepless and exceptionally energetic night, her hair roughed up and tumbling about her shoulders, she was still leggy, clear-skinned and utterly beautiful.

Outside there was the low hum of traffic, just discernible through the triple-glazed glass of the penthouse apartment. The early-morning clouds were low, settling on the thrusting towers of the City skyline and over the River Thames – it was an incredible view – but the forecast threatened a damp, muggy day, hot and uncomfortable. The blonde was yelling, but Joel was simply staring out of the window, which didn't help matters. She'd started out nice, suggesting dinner that night, but as soon as Joel had made it clear he wasn't particularly interested in dinner that night, and that in fact three meetings was probably very much enough possibly for his entire life, she'd turned nasty pretty fast, and now she was shouting because she was not used to people treating her like this.

'You want to know your problem?'

Joel did not.

'You think that you're all right underneath. That that makes it okay to behave like an absolute bastard all the time. That there's a soft side to you somewhere and you can turn it on and off at will. And I'm telling you, you can't.'

Joel wondered how long this was going to take. He had a psychiatrist who generally wasn't as direct as this. He wanted a cup of coffee. No: he wanted her to leave, then he wanted a cup of coffee. He wondered if looking at his phone would speed matters up. It did.

'Look at you! All you are is how you behave. That's it. Nobody gives a crap what's going on inside you, or what you've been through. All you are is what you do. And what you do is a disgrace.'

'Are you done?' Joel found himself saying. The blonde looked like she was going to hurl a shoe at him. Then she stopped herself and began to pull on her clothes in an affronted silence. Joel felt he shouldn't look, but he'd forgotten how gorgeous she was. He blinked.

'Screw you,' she spat at him. Her skirt was incredibly short. She was very clearly going to be doing the walk of shame on the tube home to west London.

'Can I get you an Uber?' he said.

'No, thank you,' she replied stiffly. Then she changed her mind. 'Yes,' she said. 'Get me one now.'

He picked up his phone again.

'Where do you live?'

'You don't remember? You've been there!'

Joel blinked. He didn't know London very well.

'Yes, of course . . . '

She sighed.

'Shepherd's Bush.'

'Of course.'

There was a pause.

'What goes around comes around, Joel. You'll get yours.'

But he was already up, heading for the coffee machine; checking his emails; getting ready for the day. Something was nagging at him about a case but he couldn't quite remember what it was. Something good. What was it?

Seven hundred miles due north, the men were coming down from the fields, stretching their muscles, the dogs scampering around their feet, rabbits scattering before them, the wind blowing in off the water as fresh as lemon ice under the soaring bright white sky. The first of the morning's work done, they were looking for breakfast, as below them on the stones of the harbour the fishermen hauled in the catch and sang in the clear morning light, their voices carrying up the hillside and into the open air:

> And what do you think they made of his eyes?
> Sing aber o vane sing aber o linn
> The finest herring that ever made pies
> Sing aber o vane sing aber o linn

Sing herring, sing eyes, sing fish, sing pies
Sing aber o vane sing aber o linn
And indeed I have more of my herring to sing
Sing aber o vane sing aber o linn

Chapter Three

Joel walked into his office with a look of concentration on his face. He knew what had been nagging at him: he had an early-morning meeting with Colton Rogers, another American. Famously wealthy, he'd made his money through tech start-ups. Joel had heard of him but had never met him before. If he was coming to London and bringing his money, then Joel was very pleased indeed to hear this. All thoughts of the unpleasant incident that morning had completely gone from his head.

He nodded at his assistant, Margo, to go and fetch Rogers' people, and looked cheerfully out of his office window. They were just over Broadgate, in the heart of the City, overlooking the Circle and on to the towers beyond; he could see all the way down to the river. The streets were full of bustling people; black cabs in a line, even this early in the day. He loved the city, felt animated by it, enjoyed being a part of the big money-making machine. From up here it felt like his domain, and he wanted to own it. He was half smiling to himself when Margo turned up, ushering Colton Rogers and his team in and indicating a tray of bagels and Danishes, even though they both knew that nobody ever took one.

'Hey,' said Rogers. He was tall and rangy and wore the classic West Coast tech-guy outfit – jeans, a polo neck and white sneakers. He also had a slightly greying, exceedingly tidy beard along his jaw. Joel wondered if his own suit looked as strange to Rogers as Rogers' outfit looked to him. 'Nice to meet you, Mr Rogers.'

'Colton, please.'

He came over and looked at the view.

'God, this city is crazy. How can you stand it? So many goddam people everywhere. It's like an ants' nest.'

They both peered down.

'You get used to it,' said Joel, indicating a seat. 'What can I do for you, Colton?'

There was a pause. Joel tried not to think of how much this man was worth. Bringing a client this size into the firm . . . well. It would go down very well.

'I've got a place,' said Colton. 'A really beautiful place. And they're trying to build wind farms on it. Or near it. Or next to it or something. Anyway. I don't want them there.'

Joel blinked.

'Right,' he said. 'Whereabouts?'

'Scotland,' he said.

'Ah,' said Joel. 'You'll probably need our Scottish office.'

'No, it's got to be you guys.'

Joel smiled even more broadly.

'Well, it's nice that we've been recommended—'

'Oh Christ, no, it's nothing like that. I think you vicious bloodsuckers are all the same, and trust me, I've met a lot of you. No. I gather that you've got a local lawyer up there. Someone who can come and fight for me who's actually visited the damn place.'

Joel squinted and racked his brains. He'd never even been to Scotland; didn't actually know what Colton was talking about. He didn't think they had anyone like that. Someone from Scotland. He didn't want to admit it, though.

'It's a big firm . . . ' he began. 'Did they give you a name?'

'Yeah,' said Colton. 'But I can't remember it. Something Scottishy-sounding.'

Joel blinked. He normally saved displays of impatience for his staff.

Margo started in the corner of the room and Joel turned to her.

'Yes?'

'Might be that Flora MacKenzie? The paralegal? That's a Scottish name, isn't it?'

This rang absolutely no bells with Joel.

'She's from up there . . . somewhere really weird.'

'Weird?' said Colton, a smile playing on his lips. He gestured once more to the throbbing landscape on the other side of the glass. 'Living all jam-packed on top of each other in a place where you can't breathe or drive or get across town is probably what I'd call weird.'

'Sorry, sir,' said Margo, going bright red.

'She's just a junior, though, right?' said Joel.

Colton lifted his eyebrows.

'It's all right, I haven't actually murdered anybody. I just want somebody local who actually has a clue what's going on before they start charging me eight hundred dollars an hour. It's called Mure.'

'What is?' said Joel.

Colton looked frustrated.

'The place I'm talking about.'

'Yes,' muttered Margo. 'That's her.'

'Well, get her then,' said Joel irritably.

'Yes, but anywhere we go, if it's nice we won't be able to sit outside and it'll be overbooked and—'

'That's al fresco living in London,' said Kai, who sat at the next desk. 'You just have to squeeze in.'

Flora frowned. It always seemed to be such an effort to plan a get-together – everyone would bid out or in at the last minute or hang around for a better offer – but it was so hot. It seemed to her that being outside, rather than trapped in her stifling little bedroom at the end of the DLR, was the right way to go tonight. Plus, it was so hard to sleep when it was hot like this. She might as well go out . . . She glanced at the large pile of files in front of her and sighed. They'd sort it out at lunchtime.

The internal line rang and she picked it up, unsuspecting.

'Flora MacKenzie.'

'Yes, it is you, isn't it?' came Margo's clipped, very formal voice. Flora had studied her carefully, given that she got to spend so much time at close proximity to Joel, and was utterly terrified of her: her immaculate clothes and the way she would look at you as if you were an idiot if you ever asked her for anything. 'You're the Scot.'

She somehow said this like somebody might say, 'You're the Martian with the four heads.'

Flora swallowed nervously. 'Yes?'

'Could you come upstairs, please?'

'Why?' said Flora before she could help herself. She didn't work for Joel, she worked for various other partners, far further down the ladder.

Margo paused. She obviously didn't appreciate being interrogated by some nothing hick junior from the fourth floor.

'Whenever you're ready,' she said icily.

It quickly ran through Flora's head to say that she actually required a blow-dry, a wax, a fake tan and a full makeover to make her ready, but she thought better than to risk it just then.

'I'll be straight up,' she said, replacing the phone and trying not to panic.

Flora's career so far had involved her keeping her head down at H&I, the University of the Highlands and Islands, doing a law undergraduate course and making up for what she lacked in natural ability by working her socks off, then going for job interview after job interview, polishing her shoes and her CV and clattering around a huge, unfriendly and unfamiliar London, asking for advice, trying to make connections, competing against a million other young people trying to do the same thing. And when she scored a job at a big firm, with the opportunity to move up, maybe even one day convert her degree, she'd soaked in everything, tried to hold on to everything, learn as much as she could, asking everyone for advice.

Never once in all that time did anyone say to her: don't fall for your boss, you idiot. And never once did she think it would happen.

Until it did.

It had been such a brief interview. At various stages of the process, she'd been quizzed by cadres of terrifying women who barked questions at her and old men who sighed as if thinking it wasn't fair that they couldn't ask her whether she was planning to get pregnant. She'd met HR, bumped into other grads, many of whom she recognised trailing round the same, slightly dispiriting trail – there were, as ever, far more people qualified for the jobs than places for them to go.

But she had done her research, knew her area down to the ground, was utterly prepared by the years at the kitchen table with her mother constantly asking her if she'd done her homework – could she do more? was she ready? was the exam passed? There were smarter people than Flora, but not many who worked harder. Then right at the end she'd been asked to step into the partner's office. And there he was.

He was yelling at someone at the end of the phone. His accent was noisy, unapologetically American, and he was gesticulating with his free arm, hollering something about district impartiality and how they had another think coming, and Margo – although Flora didn't know who this glamorous woman was then – had indicated briefly that this was the new junior, and he'd waved his assistant away crossly, then paused, jammed the phone down and stuck out his hand, a faint smile breaking across his face as he almost paid attention.

'Hi,' he said. 'Joel Binder.'

'Flora MacKenzie.'

'Great,' he'd said. 'Welcome to the firm.' And that was it. That was all it was. She'd stayed gazing at him – his chestnut-coloured hair, strong profile and oddly full lips – until Margo had ushered her out. Flora hadn't noticed the look the woman had given her as they'd left the room.

'He seems nice,' she said, feeling herself blush hot. He didn't look like most of the lawyers she knew – stressed, overworked; dandruff on their shoulders; skin that didn't see the outdoors anything like enough; yeasty paunches.

Margo simply hummed and didn't say anything.

He didn't speak to her again for about six months. Occasionally she watched him in meetings as she sat there shyly trying to take notes and miss nothing; he was commanding, rude, aggressive and an overwhelmingly successful lawyer, and Flora, to her utter shame and embarrassment, had a crush on him beyond belief.

'So, tell me about Joel,' she'd said faux-casually, out for a getting-to-know-you drink with some of the other slaves – junior paras who were expected to work twenty-hour days for practically no money and basically have no other life at all. 'You know, the partner?'

Kai turned to her and burst out laughing.

'Seriously?' he said.

'What?' said Flora, feeling herself go pink and staring at her large glass of white wine, so pale it was almost green. She hadn't known what to order and had let the others go for it, and was now slightly worried about how to pay for it. Living in London was horrifyingly expensive, even with a salary.

Kai had been there all summer as an intern, and was on the fast track to becoming an actual lawyer, so he was well up on office gossip. He rolled his eyes.

'Christ. Another one.'

'What? What do you mean? I didn't say anything.'

Where did they get this self-confidence? Flora wondered all the time, particularly about people who'd been raised in London. Did it just arrive? She knew she ought to be doing extra classes – maybe, who knows, even training to be a full lawyer. But after what had happened … She couldn't. Not just yet.

And work seemed so … well. It was what she had always wanted. A proper professional, smart job. But after she'd got over the novelty factor of having a season ticket and a salary and smart shoes and lunch breaks, it had started to seem a little … Hmm. Repetitive. The paperwork cascaded and never ended, and just as she felt she was getting on top of things, a case would be settled or called off and then it would all start again. She knew she should be studying on top of everything else. But she rather felt she was failing with the 'everything else'.

'You'll get over it, babes,' Kai had reassured her when she'd complained (repeatedly) about her workload. It didn't matter how late she stayed or how efficient she was with filing. It was a shame, she reflected, that being shit-hot at filing wasn't actually all that sexy. Probably just as well she'd kept it off her Tinder profile.

'Seriously, didn't you notice that he's horrible?'

Oh yeah. He was horrible, Flora reminded herself. Tall, sharp-suited, brusque, American. He strode through the building as if he owned it. He treated the juniors with disdain, could never remember anyone's name and never complimented anyone.

'He's a negger,' said Kai.

'A *what*?' said Flora, horrified.

'A negger.'

Flora blinked.

'It means he's mean to people so they notice him and want him to say something nice. It's like dog training or something.'

'I don't understand.'

Kai saw it as his mission in life to educate the shy, odd-looking girl from the Islands and leapt on every opportunity to expound his accumulated twenty-six years of sophisticated knowledge.

'Like you'll just hang on for a tiny word of kindness, a crumb of recognition, and that makes people fall for him. Well, people with low self-esteem.'

Flora frowned.

'Maybe I just think he's hot.'

'Yeah. *Cruel* hot. Never go there. Also, he's your super-boss. Try not to shit on your own doorstep. Also—'

'There's another also? I don't think I need another also.'

'No, listen, Flors, I'm not sure you're his type . . . OMG, speak of the devil. And I think he might literally *be* the devil. Uh, I'll let you make your mind up about the type.'

Flora had glanced up then, and sure enough, crossing

Broadgate Circle, at the very heart of the City law firms, there he was, confident and commanding-looking, his nut-brown hair shining in the sun, smoothly escorting a giraffe of a blonde girl who clopped across the slate wearing bright pink, a colour that would look bizarre on anybody else but simply made her look like the most ravishing thing ever. Nothing like Flora could ever be in a million years. She was a bird of paradise; a completely different species.

Flora watched them and groaned.

'No,' she said. 'You're right.'

'You are very good at filing, though,' Kai had said encouragingly. 'I mean, that's got to count for something.'

She'd grinned, and they'd ordered another bottle.

That had been a couple of years ago, and Kai's career had come on in leaps and bounds. While hers ... hadn't. Of course she'd got more used to London, more cynical about her office, and she'd had dates and dalliances and various misadventures with chaps here and there, not all of which she could recall without getting embarrassed, and one nice boyfriend, Hugh, who had lasted a year and who had wanted to take it further but she hadn't felt ... well. It. Whatever it was meant to be. She'd never been there. She'd known, even as they parted (with wonderful manners; Hugh was a darling), that in about ten years, when everyone else was settled and happy and she was still bouncing about being single, she might entirely regret doing this. But she'd done it anyway. She had had long dry spells too. And she was fine. Mostly. It was just a crush, a daft thing that had faded into the background as she'd got on with building a life in this huge machine of a town, getting away from everything that had happened before.

Except that now, at 10.45 a.m. on a broiling Thursday in early May, her crush, for the first time in history, suddenly wanted to see her in his office.

Chapter Four

Flora had to rush, but she had to nip into the bathroom too and redo her make-up. Flustered, she realised she was bright pink. That was the problem with being so pale. Well, that and not being able to go out in bright sunlight without turning the colour of a lobster and starting to smoke slightly.

She stared at herself and sighed. She hated looking so washed-out; she felt completely colourless, even as her friends talked about how unusual she was. She wasn't at all unusual in the island she'd come from: tall and pale, like the Viking ancestors who went back hundreds of generations. Her mother's hair was almost pure white. It was only down here, where people would let her talk and then at the end say, as if it was a compliment, that they hadn't been listening to a word, they just liked the way she spoke. She was learning, slowly, to say 'now' instead of 'noo' and 'you' instead of 'dhu', but sometimes she forgot even that.

She tried to quell her racing heart. Margo had sounded

frosty, but she always bloody did. Flora hadn't done anything wrong, had she? Even if she had, Joel's office wouldn't be in charge of dealing with that. Her time with Joel was limited to when she was minuting for Kai, who was studying for his legal exams and was being encouraged by the firm as a prospect for the future. Kai was pretty great to work for, and Flora would often take notes for him and do all the follow-up.

But Kai hadn't mentioned anything this morning; he was due in court, in any case, leaving Flora with the usual mound of paperwork to sort out.

No, this morning it was just her.

She took a deep breath and headed for the lift.

Joel's vast corner office was incredibly impressive, filled with flashy-looking artwork that didn't seem to mean anything apart from proving that he was successful enough to be surrounded by flashy-looking artwork. He nodded as she walked in. He was wearing a dark grey suit, a fresh white shirt and a navy tie that contrasted with his hair. Flora felt a blush starting even before she was through the door, and cursed herself for it.

There was also a tall man with an oddly light beard – by the casual way he dressed, he was obviously very important – and a couple of other people milling in the background, taking calls and more or less pretending to be busy. Flora wasn't sure if she should sit or stand.

'Hello,' she said, trying to sound brave.

'I can tell where you're from before you say a word!' said

the bearded man, coming forward to shake her hand. 'Look at that hair! You're Mure stock, that's for sure.'

Flora wasn't at all sure she liked being referred to in the same way her brothers referred to the cattle, and simply stood there.

'Where are you from, um . . . ' Joel glanced down at his notes, 'Flora?'

Flora's heart started to beat faster. Why did this matter? Why was it important? Why were they talking about her home? That was the last thing she'd expected. Or wanted.

'Oh, it's a small . . . I mean, you won't have heard of it.'

She didn't want to talk about Mure. Never did; always changed the subject whenever it came up. She lived in London now, where the world came to reinvent itself.

'She's from Mure,' said the bearded man proudly. 'I knew it. I've heard all about you.'

Flora looked at him.

'Excuse me?'

'I'm Colton Rogers!'

There was a long pause. Joel was looking at her, bemused.

'You know who I am, right?'

Flora hadn't been home for some time. But she knew. She nodded quietly.

Colton Rogers was the American big shot who'd bought up a lot of the island and was, according to rumours that changed daily, about to concrete over the entire place, turn it all into a golf course, throw everybody off so that he could make it his own private sanctuary, or take over their homes in order to breed wild birds.

The rumours had been huge and mostly unsubstantiated,

mainly because nobody had ever met him. Flora now felt very, very nervous. If he wanted the firm to represent him, what had he done?

'Um . . . ' She glanced at Joel, unsure what he wanted her to do, but he was looking as confused as she felt, drumming a pen against his teeth.

'Well, people say things . . . I don't pay much attention,' she said.

'You don't, huh?' he said, looking displeased. 'You've not heard I'm restoring the Rock.'

The Rock was a tumbledown old croft on the very northern tip of the island, with an extraordinary, unparalleled setting. There had been rumours that conglomerates and moguls were coming in to transform it since Flora had been a little girl.

'Are you really?'

'Sure am! It's nearly finished!' Colton Rogers said proudly. 'You not seen it?'

Flora hadn't been home for three years. And she'd vowed then never to go back.

'No,' she said. 'I've heard about it.'

'Well, I need your help,' said Colton.

'Shouldn't you have a Scottish lawyer? Or Norwegian?'

'Norwegian?' said Joel. 'How far away is this place?'

They both turned to look at him.

'Three hundred miles north of Aberdeen,' said Colton. 'You don't get out much, do you? Still doing eighty billable hours a week?'

'Minimum,' said Joel.

'It's no way to live, man.'

'Yes, well, you've made your billions,' said Joel, half smiling.

'Right, listen,' said Colton, turning back to Flora. 'I need you to go up there. Do some work for me. Speak to your friends and neighbours.'

'I need to tell you, Mr Rogers, I'm not a laywer,' said Flora. 'I'm a paralegal.'

'Colton, please. And so much the better,' said Colton. 'Cheaper. And I need local knowledge. I know how you lot all stick together. *Hvarleðes hever du dað?*'

Flora looked at him in shock.

'*Eg hev dað gott, takk, og du?*' she stuttered out. Joel looked at them in astonishment.

Flora suddenly felt the need to lean on something. She grabbed the back of a chair. She wasn't sure she could speak. She felt her throat constrict and she was worried that, although she had never had a panic attack before, she might be having one now.

Memories, crashing in from everywhere. All at once, like the huge rolling waves that attacked the shore; like the crystal winds that swept down from the Arctic and flattened the crab grass, reshaping the dunes over and over, like a giant's fist playing in a sandpit.

And there was a huge hole at the centre of it, and she didn't want to look at it.

No. No. She was arranging a night out with Kai. She was typing up minutes and thinking of getting a cat.

She felt everyone's eyes on her, and wished she could simply vanish; disappear into nothingness. Her cheeks were burning up. How could she say no? No, I don't want to go home. No, I don't. Never again.

'So,' said Colton.

'What's the job?' said Joel.

'Well,' said Colton. 'You really need to come and see it.'

'Oh, she will,' said Joel, without asking Flora.

'Can I stay in the Rock? Is it done?' said Flora timidly.

Colton turned his grey eyes on her and she saw why, despite his apparently mild nature, he was such a feared businessman.

'I thought you were a Mure girl. Have you no family there at all?'

Flora breathed a long sigh.

'Yes,' she said finally. 'Yes, I do.'

Chapter Five

There is a legend in the islands Flora comes from, about selkies.

Technically, 'selkie' means seal, or seal person, although in its original language, Gaelic, it's the same word you would use for mermaid. Selkies lose their ocean shape for as long as they are on land.

If you're a woman and want a selkie as a lover (they are notoriously handsome), you stand by the sea and weep seven tears.

If you're a man and take a selkie lover and you want to keep her, you hide her sealskin and she can never go back to the seas again.

Flora often thought this was just a roundabout way of saying, man, it's so hard to meet people up north, you have to nick a boyfriend from the wild. But it hadn't stopped lots of people saying her mother was one.

And after Flora had left, lots of people had said it about her too.

Once upon a time . . . once upon a time . . .

Flora had assumed she would never get to sleep that night. She'd sleepwalked through the rest of the day, even managing to join in with someone's birthday song, nibble a horrible shop-bought cake and neck a couple of glasses of warm Prosecco, but she'd skipped the after-work drinks and headed home by herself, hoping her flatmates would be out. They all seemed to be freelancers who worked in start-ups, were in and out at odd hours of the day and viewed her as unimaginably square. Flora liked being unimaginably square. It was better than being the strange girl from the strange island any day.

As always, she considered cooking, looked at the filthy, borderline dangerous gas hob in the kitchen and decided against it. She ate a Leon salad on her bed watching Netflix and followed it with half a packet of Hobnobs, which was more or less a balanced meal, she considered. As she ate, she stared at her phone in fear. She should call home and tell them she was coming. She should. Oh God. She was going to have to see everyone. And everyone would be staring and judging.

She swallowed hard and, like the world's worst coward, sent a text. Then, like an even worse coward, she hid her phone under her duvet so she didn't have to read the reply.

Maybe she shouldn't stay at home?

But she couldn't stay at the Harbour's Rest, the only other hotel on the island. For one, it was horrible; for two, it was awful; for three, the firm wasn't expecting to cover her hotel costs; and for four … well. It would shame her dad, and the farm.

So. She was going home. Oh God.

Some people, she knew, loved to go home. Kai ate round his mum's about three times a week. That wasn't an option she had, though. She lay there, wide awake, wondering what on earth she was going to do.

She blinked. And then she realised somehow that she was asleep, and somebody was trying to tell her a story. *Once upon a time*, they were saying, and then again, *Once upon a time.* And she was begging them to carry on, it was important, she needed to know what was happening, but it was too late, the voice faded out and, bang, she was awake again; and it was another morning in noisy London, where even the birds sounded like mobile phones ringing. And the traffic rumbled and rumbled past her window, and she was already running late if she wanted to get into the shower before any of her flatmates and at least get a shot at the hot water.

She glanced at her phone. *Aye* was the return message. Not 'great' or 'welcome' or 'we can't wait to see you'. Just: *Aye.*

Chapter Six

Geneva. Paris. Vienna. New York. Barbados. Istanbul.

Flora read the airport departures board with a sense that a hundred per cent of everyone else around here was heading for a much more exciting day than she was. And also, although everyone was wearing T-shirts and some of the men were in shorts, she was almost certainly the only person with a parka in her hand luggage in May. She'd even resurrected a Fair Isle hat she'd had for years and been somehow unable to throw away. Just in case.

She headed towards the Inverness flight with a heavy heart. The last time she had made this journey . . . Well. She wasn't thinking about that.

She would just focus on the job. Once she knew what the job was, properly. She'd wanted to ask Joel but had been oddly shy about it, even when Kai had stood over her and instructed her to write an email.

'Don't put kisses on it!' he'd said.

'Shut up!' she had replied, but her very timid message about whether he could brief her any more on the Rogers case hadn't been deemed worthy of a reply, so she was still in the dark.

She reckoned Colton Rogers wanted to do something the islanders didn't like, and he wanted the firm to front it. The problem was – and he didn't know this – the islanders didn't like her either.

Flora sighed, watching London swirl beneath her as they took off, gazing at the bumper-to-bumper traffic on the M25 and wishing, as very few people ever have, that she was in it.

The second plane ride was bumpy. It was generally bumpy; the plane was tiny – a dozen seats, mostly given over to scientists, ornithologists, hardy walkers and a few curious tourists. Flora looked down as they sped low over the water. The fleet was out; in one of her last conversations with her father – brief as always – he'd mentioned that their catch was up and permissions were up, but they'd been told to stop killing the seals. She leaned her head against the window. The land had dropped far behind and she was, as always, stunned by how very far away from the rest of Britain the island was.

It hadn't felt like that when she was a child.

Mure, with its little high street and its soft rolling hills, had been her world: her father out in the fields, with the boys as soon as they were old enough; her mother cooking in the kitchen, her long mane of white hair swishing behind her; Flora doing her homework at the old wooden table. The mainland felt like a myth, going on a train an annual treat at Christmas, and everything else moved to the rhythm of the seasons: the long white summers with endless evenings and the door open to the fresh sea breeze; the cosy dark winters when the fire burned high all day in the range and the kitchen was the only warm place to be.

Flora wondered if anyone would come to meet her at the airport, then told herself to stop it. It was the middle of the farming day. They'd be busy. She'd catch the bus.

She dismounted last, the tourists stumbling around, and walked through the little tin shed they called an airport.

The bus was filled with excited early holidaymakers, joyful that it wasn't raining, equipped with bicycles and walking canes and guidebooks. The sun was glinting through, even though the morning haar – the sea mist – hadn't yet lifted, and as they approached the little town, it made the place look as though it was rising out of a cloud of smoke, like a mystery, or a magic trick. The deep green hills sloped down to the bright white sand you found in this part of the world; the long beaches seemed to stretch on for ever.

It was easy to see why the island had been so tempting to the Viking hordes who had claimed it and named it, and whose blood ran in its citizens' veins even now. No Westminster politician ever visited Mure. Very few Edinburgh ones did. It was a little spot unto itself, up at the very northern tip of the known world.

As they drew into the harbour, the fog started to lift, revealing the cheerfully painted buildings that lined the port and formed the main street. Closer to, Flora noted that they looked a little dilapidated, paint peeling from the fierce northern gales. One shop – she searched her memory and remembered it finally as a little chemist's – had closed down and sat, empty and sad.

Stepping off the bus, she felt nervous. What would people make of her? Because she knew she hadn't behaved well after the funeral. Not well at all.

It wasn't for long, she told herself. She was only here for a week. Soon she would be back in the city, enjoying the summer, sitting on the South Bank among the hordes, having bad dates, drinking overpriced cocktails, taking the night tube. Being young and in London. Surely it was the best place in the world.

Of course the very first person she'd see was Mrs Kennedy, her old dancing teacher, who'd already been ancient when Flora was a girl but whose eyes were still a piercing blue.

'Flora MacKenzie!' she stated, pointing her walking stick at her. 'Well, in all my days.'

I am a big serious London paralegal, Flora told herself. I am perfectly busy and professional and normal and absolutely a hundred per cent not fourteen.

'Hello, Mrs Kennedy,' she sing-songed automatically. Flora had sat next to big lawyers in court; taken part in serious cases with very seriously bad people. She wasn't scared of them. But Mrs Kennedy was a holy terror. Flora hadn't forgotten a single step even now, although she could only be prevailed upon to perform at parties when people had had too many drinks to appreciate it, and she'd rather lost the finesse.

‘So are dhu back, is it?’

‘I’m . . . I’m just working,’ said Flora, knowing that this piece of information would be round the entire island in less time than it would take her to walk to the farmhouse.

‘Good,’ said Mrs Kennedy. ‘Glad to hear it. They need looking after.’

‘That’s not what I meant,’ said Flora. ‘I mean, I’m actually working. Like, I have a job. In London. It’s a Big Six firm.’

Inwardly, she cursed. Who on earth did she think she was trying to impress here?

Mrs Kennedy sniffed.

‘Oh, would that be right, would it? Well, very fancy and nice for some, I’m sure.’

And she swept off down towards the little pier as fast as her arthritic legs would carry her.

Oh Lord, thought Flora. She’d known, after the funeral, that her name wasn’t exactly respected on Mure, but she hadn’t imagined it would be this bad. She felt a sudden flash of homesickness for her horrible little London room and the comforting rumble of the tube, the carriages full of nobody she knew.

The fishermen glanced up as she passed. A reticent bunch on the whole, they nodded at her and she nodded back, feeling conscious of how loud her small wheelie suitcase sounded on the cobblestones. She felt someone come silently to a doorway behind her, but when she turned her head, they’d gone. She sighed.

Just past the western end of the high street, the road parted and one fork headed up towards the hills. Most of the buildings were concentrated at the eastern end of the port; here, the pathways led to farming country.

The sun was lying bright on the fields as she walked up the old roadway, pitted and bumpy, towards the house, its sturdy square shape standing out against the hills; its grey stone looking smart in the clear light, belied by its messy interior. Her childhood home.

As she crossed the muddy courtyard, she took a deep breath. Okay. Calm. Professional. Collected. She wasn't going to let anyone wind her up. Everything was going to be—

'SIIIIS!'

'Oh man, is that Flora? How fat has she got? Is she recognisable?'

'Widen the doors!'

Flora shut her eyes.

'Shut up, you guys!' she said, horrified and yet relieved at the same time. If they were being rude to her, they couldn't be too furious. Right?

First, her brothers Innes and Fintan came tumbling out of the door; Innes tall and pale like her mother, broad-built and handsome. He'd been married, briefly, and spent as much time with his young daughter as he could manage. Next to him was Fintan, slender, dark and nervous. And finally, behind them, Hamish, who was utterly huge and did most of the heavy lifting. Innes covered the heavy thinking, more or less.

Her father wasn't there, Flora noticed.

The boys mock-embraced her, and she mock-cuffed them. They were as awkward as she was, she noticed.

The farmhouse was old and rambling, its dark passageways leading to small rooms here and there. With a good sledgehammer, it could have been absolutely exceptional, with uninterrupted views down to the sea across their own land – sheep and cows were their main concern: hardy little short-tails that weren't great for eating but produced strong, soft wool that went to the looms of the other islands and the mainland alike, making high-quality knitwear and blankets and tartan; and the cows were wonderful milkers.

On a good day, both the bright blue sky and the deep green fields looked to be full of little fluffy clouds. Closer to the sea, the land turned sandier, and there was seaweed and a few ropes of mussels.

Flora took a deep breath before she followed the boys inside.

For a second, her heart felt heavy. Then, as she stepped into the cold hallway, she was almost knocked over by a huge, hairy, slightly croaky woofing thing.

'BRAMBLE!'

The dog had not forgotten her; he was utterly thrilled beyond belief to see her, leaping up and down, weeing slightly on the flagstones and doing his best to engulf her in his delight.

'Someone's pleased to see me, at least,' said Flora, and the boys shrugged, 'Yeah, whatever,' then Innes asked her to put the kettle on and she gave him the Vs and put her bag down and looked around her and thought, Oh Lord.

Chapter Seven

If anything, it was worse than she'd expected.

The large kitchen was at the back of the house, overlooking the bay; it got any rays of sun there were to catch. Inside, it was as if a clock had stopped. Dust lay on the surfaces; spiders frolicked happily in the corners. Flora put her handbag down on the kitchen table, the same huge table that had seen fights (sometimes physical if the boys were in a mood); Christmases with grandparents and aunts and uncles from all over the island; schoolgirl dreams; tear-stained homework; big games of Risk when the weather stopped anything but basic animal care; tinned soup when the storms came and the snow sat and the ferries couldn't get over; impassioned debates about Scottish independence and politics and anything else that crossed their minds; their father sitting quietly as he always did, reading *Farmers Weekly* and demanding to be left in peace with his bottle of ale in front of the fire after tea, which was always at 5 p.m. They went to bed early.

When Flora had left, she had been perfectly happy to leave that table behind, with its timeless rhythm of her mothers' stews and casseroles and roasts and soups and breakfasts and ploughman's lunches. Her brothers grew ever bigger and noisier, but life never changed, never moved on. The boys stayed at home, more or less, the dinners kept appearing, and Flora had felt so stifled; stifled by the pheasant that popped up around November; by the same chipped blue and white mugs on the mantelpiece; the spring daisies and the Christmas peonies.

She had flown, not wanting to be weighed down as her mother was by the seasonal thrum of being a farmer's wife; the endless staring at grey skies and wheeling birds and dancing boats.

Now she looked at the table, piled high with dirty cups and old newspapers, and felt the grains of her life written into it, unerasable; simply there.

When her mother had come home for the last time, the boys heaved one of the beds out of the spare room downstairs into pride of place by the big window in the kitchen. The legs squeaked on the heavy flagstones, but at least that room was always warm and cosy, and she could see everything that was going on. Nobody said, as they carried it in, what it was: a deathbed.

The previous day, Flora had returned, flying up from her probationary year alone and practically friendless in a scary new city; horrified at the speed of the diagnosis her mother had kept from her own family all year.

Saif, the local GP, had popped over that morning to make sure she was organised with drugs – it was only palliatives now, painkillers. There was meant to be a strict regime as to when she could take them, and how many. Both the local nurse and Saif quietly asked Flora not to quote them on this, but to give her as many as she wanted, whenever she wanted them.

Numbly, Flora had nodded her head, as if pretending she understood; as if she had the faintest idea what was happening, staring at them in horrified disbelief. Then she had stood, shoulder to shoulder with the boys as they brought her mother home for the last time.

That evening, her mother had woken up, or seemed to, briefly, as the sky was beginning to turn a fulsome pink, and Flora sat next to her and gave her some water, although she was close to choking, and her medicine, which relaxed her mother right away, up to the point where she was able to stroke Flora's hand; and Flora leaned her head against her mother's and they breathed together, in, out, and everyone came over; and who even knew exactly when the last breath came or who noticed it first or how it was taken, but it came; in the place where she had taken nearly every breath she ever took, and they were incredibly grateful to have her there, at home, not connected to things that beeped, or in a sterile ward, or surrounded by people shouting and trying useless manoeuvres, but where the old blackened kettle on top of the oven was still set to whistle; where Bramble's tail slowly thumped a rhythm on the rug as it always did; where the ancient pile of unused keys – the house was never locked – sat in the bowl with mysterious bits and bobs of screws and handy things; where the curtains still hung that Annie had made herself when she'd first moved in there, so many years ago, a young bride full, Flora imagined, of cheer and hopefulness: orange flowers on a blue background, which had been fashionable, then hideous, and were now on the point of tipping back into being fashionable again.

There had been babies on the rug in that room, then children tearing around, the endless comings and goings of the farmhands; how many vegetable soups, and apple pies; how many scraped knees, and tears wiped away, and muddy footprints in various sizes of wellingtons; how many birthday cakes – chocolate for Fintan and Hamish, lemon for Innes, vanilla for Flora – how many candles blown out and Christmas presents wrapped, and how many cups of tea . . .

And it had all vanished in the blink of an eye when Flora had been twenty-three years old, and she had run away as far and fast as she could; couldn't bear to think of it, never ever wanted to come back; wanted nothing of a life that had been ripped from all of them; didn't want to assume the mantle of the family's pain, come home as they'd all expected. As the entire island had expected.

She stood there now, in the dark, dusty, unloved kitchen, braced herself on the back of the chair and simply let the tears flow.

Chapter Eight

She heard her father – or rather, his dog, Bracken, woofing hello at the intruder – before she saw him, and rubbed her face quickly

Eck MacKenzie had always been strong-looking. But his blue eyes were sinking now; there were broken veins on his cheeks from decades of high winds on the moorland, and his hair was thinning under his omnipresent tweed bunnet.

'Flora,' he said, nodding.

They had spoken, of course, since the funeral. But only briefly. She'd invited him down to London and he'd said, 'Aye, maybe, maybe,' which they both knew meant never, never.

'You're no back to stay?'

Flora shook her head. 'But I'm working up here,' she said eagerly. 'I mean, I'll be here for a bit. Maybe a week?'

He nodded. 'Aye.' Her father's ayes, she well knew, could mean many things. This one meant, well, that's fine as far as that goes.

After that, everyone stood around. If Mum had been there, Flora thought, she'd have been bustling, making tea, thrusting cake on everyone whether they wanted it or not; making everything cosy and nice and not strange.

Instead, everyone looked a bit awkward.

'Mm, tea?' said Flora, which helped a bit.

They sat around the kitchen table bleakly. There was almost no food in, and everything felt like a gap.

'So, how's work?' said Fintan eventually, as if it had to be dragged out of him.

'Uh, good,' said Flora. 'I'm up here to talk to Colton Rogers.'

'Good luck with that,' snorted her father.

'That bastard!' said Innes.

Uh-oh, thought Flora.

'Hang on. He's nice!' she said.

The boys exchanged glances.

'Well, we wouldn't know,' said Fintan.

'He doesn't have anything to do with the local people,' said Innes. 'Doesn't employ us, doesn't buy from us.'

'He's building some fancy-pants place over on the north of the island,' said Fintan. 'For rich idiots to fly in by helicopter and have "experiences".'

'Idiots,' said Innes.

'And he gets arseholes up here to hunt grouse. They come in the Harbour's Rest and behave like English wankers,' said Fintan.

'Well, I expect you're very friendly and give them the benefit of the doubt,' said Flora.

'Not nice people,' said Hamish, shaking his head and giving a biscuit to Bramble, who was standing there, poised for exactly that eventuality.

Her father wasn't even at the table with them. He was sitting by the fireside, stoking up the grate and sipping a large glass of whisky, even though it was early in the day. Flora looked at him, then back at her plate.

'Are you guys eating ... I mean, are you looking after yourselves all right?' she asked.

'We tidied up for you coming,' frowned Fintan.

'Seriously?' said Flora.

'What's that supposed to mean?' Fintan was on the defensive immediately.

'No, no, I was just saying ... '

'We eat sausages,' said Hamish, frowning. 'Also sometimes bacon.'

'You'll kill yourselves!'

Her father was looking thinner. Flora wondered if he was eating much at all, or if it was all just whisky. It had been two years; surely they must be starting to get over it.

Not that she was.

'Yeah, thanks for the life advice you've flown all this way to give us, Flora,' said Innes. 'We'll just stop working twelve-hour days ... How long is your working day again?'

'It's plenty long,' snapped back Flora. 'And I commute.'

'Do you cook?'

'No. But there's M and S, and Deliveroo ... '

Flora looked at their faces and decided this was not the time to attempt to explain Deliveroo.

'So,' she said, glancing around, 'how's the farm doing?'

There was a very long pause. Innes stared at his plate.

'Why? You going to come back and lawyer it up?' said Fintan shortly.

'No,' said Flora. 'That's not what I meant.'

'Not well,' said Innes shortly. 'Not all of us are pulling our weight.'

'What do you mean by that?' said Fintan.

'You heard.'

'I do my bit.'

'You do the absolute bare minimum. Thank God Hamish picks up your slack.'

'I like cows,' said Hamish.

'Shut up, Hamish,' said Fintan. 'You like everything.'

Without looking at him, Flora passed Hamish her last biscuit. He ate it in two bites.

'How are things, Dad?' said Flora.

'Och. Fine,' said her dad without turning round. He kept staring at the fire, Bracken's head in his lap.

'Right,' said Flora. 'Great.'

Innes switched on the TV. This was the only new thing in the house; it was huge, and tuned to Sky Sports 9, which showed the shinty. He turned it up loud and handed round a bag of horrible, greasy sausage rolls he'd brought up from the village. And Flora sat and watched in silence with the others, the gap inside her so vast and hollow she could hardly breathe.

Chapter Nine

At 9 p.m., Flora got a message from Colton Rogers' office that he would be caught up tomorrow and wouldn't be able to see her after all, which was even more useless. She texted Kai about it, who got back to her straightaway.

> Hey babe. How is it?
>
> 
>
> Are they thrilled you're back?
>
> 
>
> Well this will cheer you up. Joel is concerned about what's happening. He's coming up.
>
> 

Get some sleep.

Eventually Flora gave up on the shinty and went to bed, but she couldn't sleep. She felt the slightly musty pillowcase under her head, the thin duvet, the sagging mattress, and wondered when was the last time anyone had slept in here. It wasn't as if her father encouraged guests particularly. Why would he when everyone he knew in the world, more or less, lived within walking distance? And with a large family, the house had always felt full and lively enough anyway; if anything, too noisy.

Now she could hear a tap dripping in a distant sink. She frowned, realising that it had dripped when she had lived here; that nobody had thought to fix it for years.

She missed, suddenly, the noisy streets of east London: the shouting, the parties and occasional fights that erupted on hot nights, the sound of police helicopters whomping overhead; all the things that normally made her stressed and irritated now felt familiar. Here, there was so much silence, apart from that damned tap. A faint drift of wind in the sea grass. No cars, no neighbours, no music, no people. It felt completely empty, like the end of the world. She felt utterly alone.

Oddly, it also felt like her first night in London had: starting a new life, everything strange. But then she'd felt enthused; full of possibility and hope and excitement. And even though she maybe hadn't gone as far as she might have, she'd done it. She'd been building a life for herself; trying, working hard. Controlling her own destiny.

Only to end up right back here where she'd started. She'd shed plenty of tears for her mother. But these ones were just for herself.

She listened to the tap, hating it, and at 3 a.m. got up to try and turn it off, without success. As she tiptoed through the kitchen, the dawn already well under way, Bramble looked up hopefully with a flap of his tail on the flagstones. She paused for a second, checking the damped fire in the grate. When she headed back to the bedroom, Bramble got up silently and followed her, and she let him. She climbed back into the slightly chilly bed, and he crawled up on top of her and arranged his large bulk around her legs. His heavy warmth felt very pleasant, and as his breathing slowed, so did hers, and eventually she fell asleep.

She woke up as though she'd been given an electric shock as the boys headed out for milking. Joel! Joel was coming!

She had plenty of work to do but couldn't settle. The house felt oppressive and the sun was shining; she wanted to make the most of the lovely day and get rid of some of her excess energy, so she called her old school friend Lorna. They weren't the same school year, but that never mattered in Mure. There were only two classes: wee and big.

And now Lorna had returned to become first a teacher and now headmistress at the local primary school. It was the school holidays, so she was free for once.

Lorna, a sweet-faced, russet-haired girl who worked like

a fiend, had been very good about the fact that Flora barely contacted her (apart from the occasional like on Facebook) while she lived her exciting London life, then expected her to be the receiver of all her woes when she turned up on the island. Flora had offered to buy the coffee, and Lorna prepared herself to listen politely to her complaining about how undrinkable it was compared to whatever fancy stuff she was used to in London.

When she saw Flora, though, she was so shocked by the absence of her customary sparkle that she put all that out of her mind.

'Come on!' she said, grinning. 'It can't be *that* bad to be home!'

Flora attempted a smile.

'Everyone's giving me sideways looks, like I've betrayed them,' she said.

'You're imagining things,' said Lorna. 'And they're worried about the boys, up there alone on that farm. It's strange.'

'It's not my fault, though.'

'I mean, you'd think one of them would be married off by now.'

'Well, you couldn't marry Hamish,' said Flora. 'He can't find his own head with both hands.'

Lorna sighed.

'I know. Shame – he's such a hunk.'

'And Innes gave it a shot.'

'Have you seen Agot yet?'

Agot was Innes' daughter. He had custody at funny times, as his ex, Eilidh, had moved back to the mainland.

'No, not yet.'

Lorna smiled.

'Why? What?'

'You'll see,' said Lorna. 'Can you ask Eilidh to send her to my school, please? The rolls are horrifying.'

'I know,' said Flora.

'Too many people are leaving. Going off to find jobs.'

'I saw the empty shops.'

Lorna grunted as they carried on down the path from the farm.

'Come on,' she said, gesticulating towards the harbour, where the seagulls were swooping to see if anything was left behind from the previous night's fish and chips, and light was bouncing off the waves. The forecast had been ominous, but in fact a quick bout of rain had appeared to clear everything away. It was strange, but it sometimes happened like that: the mainland, all the way down to London, would be cold and grey, but the weather front missed them completely, leaving them in bright, clear sunlight. You wouldn't swim in it, but you could definitely sit outside (in the sun, with a jumper on). 'How bad can it be on a day like today?'

'I know,' said Flora. 'Sorry. It's just . . . you know.'

'I do,' said Lorna. She had lost her mother too. Sometimes, Flora thought, it was enough just to be with someone who understood.

'How's your dad?'

'Shit.'

'Mine too.'

Flora kicked a stone.

'Argh. You know when they said I had to come here for work . . . honestly, I got such butterflies in my stomach. Such nerves. Because it's here, all the time. And it's turning me into a *misery*. I hate it. I hate being grumpy all the time. I'm sure I'm a fun person really. I'm sure I used to be.'

Lorna smiled.

'To be fair, you've always been quite irritating.'

'Shut up!'

'Anyway,' said Lorna. 'It's okay, you know. It's okay to grieve. You're meant to. It's a period of adjustment.'

Flora sighed.

'I like it in London. I'm too busy to grieve there. I don't actually have to look around and see her all the time, or think about her or be interrogated about her.'

They'd reached the Harbour's Rest, cheerfully run by a tall Icelandic girl called Inge-Britt. It dealt mostly with tourists, didn't have to worry about repeat visits and cleaned its cutlery accordingly. They ordered coffee and sat down in the shabby lounge.

Lorna looked at Flora.

'Is it really so awful being back here? I mean, plenty of us … we live here all the time. It's nice. It's fine. Some of us like it.'

Flora stirred her coffee. A faintly grey scum rose to the top from the powdered milk.

'I know,' she said. 'I don't mean I'm different or special … '

'Your mum thought you were.'

'Everyone's mum thinks they are.'

'Not like yours. "Oh, Flora did this! Flora got this in her exams!" She always wanted more for you.'

Lorna paused.

'Are you happy down there?'

Flora shrugged.

'We should have had this conversation at night. With wine instead of . . . whatever this is.'

'I'll go halfers on a custard bun with you.'

'Shall we ask for it without a plate? Might be cleaner.'

Bun carefully divided, Flora thought again.

'I feel I didn't fit in here. Then I went away and I don't fit in there. So I don't know. Why is it so easy for you?'

'Ha!' said Lorna. She'd always loved teaching. She'd gone to teacher-training college on the mainland and had a wonderful time, then she'd been perfectly happy to come home again where her friends and family were, eventually (to be fair, there wasn't a lot of competition for her tiny posting) becoming headmistress of the island's little primary school. Its falling roll was a worry, and she'd like to meet a nice man, but apart from that . . . 'No,' she admitted. 'It's no bad.'

'I just feel sometimes that I'm not sure I belong anywhere.'

Lorna tutted and stood up. Flora followed her obediently outside and across to the edge of the harbour.

'Look,' said Lorna.

Flora didn't know what she meant. It was just the same as usual, wasn't it? Same old waves beating against the harbour walls. Same old boats bobbing around the place, same old seagulls clattering away at the bins, same old coloured houses, and round the headland, the farms and the fish processing plants.

'Yeah?' she said. 'It's just the same.'

'No!' said Lorna. 'LOOK! Look at the clouds scudding

across the sky. How much sky do you get in London anyway? When I went there, all I could see were buildings and more buildings and pigeons and that was just about it.'

'Hmmph,' said Flora.

'Take a breath,' said Lorna, stepping up onto the wall. The air was fresh and clean, tinged with salt; the wind whipped her hair. 'Taste it! The last time I was in the city, I thought I'd choke from the fumes. This is awesome.'

Flora grinned. 'You're nuts, you are.'

'BREATHE! There are so few places in the world where you can breathe like this. It's the freshest air in existence. Breathe it in! Take your stupid yoga classes and shove them up your bum! Nothing's better than this.'

Flora was laughing now.

'SERIOUSLY!' Lorna was wobbling across the top of the wall now. 'You're mad, Flora MacKenzie. It's *awesome* here.'

'But it's freezing!'

'Buy a bigger coat. It's not rocket science. Look! LOOK!'

Flora followed her up on to the top of the wall, where they used to sit when they were teenagers, eating chips and swinging their legs. She followed Lorna's pointing finger. Below them she could see the elongated neck, the extraordinary beauty of a tall heron. It stood on one leg, poised like a ballerina, as if totally aware of how lovely it was, a halo of sunshine around its head; then, as if waiting for them both to be watching, it spread its glorious wings and sped, fast and low, over the bouncing, gleaming waves, the echo of the other, coarser birds yelping off the walls of the brightly painted pastel buildings behind them as the bird headed for the white horizon.

'You don't get that in London,' said Lorna.

And Flora had to admit, as they watched the heron scoop a glistening fish from the sea without so much as slowing down, that Lorna was right.

As they stood together gazing out to sea, Lorna leaned over towards her.

'It's going to be okay,' she said quietly, because she was the very best type of friend to have, the type who could never hold a grudge; and out of the blue, Flora found herself blinking back tears again, and cursed herself. She realised, suddenly, that that was the first time anybody had said that. Her father couldn't say it, because it wasn't true for him. He'd lost everything; things weren't going to be okay. But the boys: they all seemed so trapped. And the island seemed to think she barely deserved to come back.

'Do you think?' she said, with a quiver in her voice. Lorna looked confused.

'Of course it is!' she said. 'Of course it is. It won't be the same – it's never the same. You're in a different world when you lose a parent.'

'I should have done more,' said Flora, turning suddenly.

Lorna shook her head. 'Don't worry,' she said. 'You weren't to know. Nobody does. Not until you cross that river. Not until you live in that world. Then you understand.'

'And it gets better?'

'It does.'

The heron had stopped on a rock, gazing fervently at the horizon. It was so still and perfect, it looked like a photograph. Flora stared at it as she blinked her tears away.

'So,' said Lorna. 'What are you going to do today?'

Flora sighed.

'Do you know what the boys could really do with? A proper home-cooked meal.'

'Oh yes!' said Lorna. 'Your mum was the best cook I ever knew. She taught you, didn't she?'

'She did,' said Flora. 'I'm very rusty, though. God, the food in London—'

'DON'T START!' said Lorna. 'I was just starting to like you again.'

Chapter Ten

Margo popped her head round the door. Joel had pulled an all-nighter working on another case, and there were shadows under his eyes. She did wonder about him sometimes. She saw his emails; took his incoming calls. Apart from the occasional distraught girl who'd thought she was on to something, there was nothing personal. Ever.

Of course, that didn't mean anything. But sometimes she wondered if his rudeness was covering something else. And sometimes she just thought he was a tool.

'Coffee?'

He shook his head irritably.

'Are you going to get to Scotland today?'

He twisted his face.

'Do I have to go? Really? Can't I just deal with it from here?'

She shrugged.

'Colton seems very fond of the place. So it might make sense for the future, if you're trying to get him on-side.'

'Yeah yeah yeah. Well, let me know when he calls. I want to stay out of the godforsaken hellhole for as long as possible. Have you seen where it is on a map?'

Margo shook her head as he showed her how far north of the British mainland it was.

'If they've got more than one eyebrow between them, I'll be amazed,' he said. 'God. Right. I've changed my mind about that coffee.'

Margo scuttled off.

Flora stomped around the very small supermarket, feeling exasperated. She'd had plans to make something different for dinner, something they wouldn't have normally, that wasn't like the food her mother used to make. She didn't think they were ready for her mother's recipes yet.

She thought back, briefly, to when she and Hugh were dating, and they'd go down to Borough Market, just next to London Bridge. It was a foodies' paradise, and extraordinarily expensive, and they'd dally there on a Saturday morning, planning something wonderful to make that night – squid ink risotto or hot and sour Thai soup – and trying lots of things she'd simply never tasted before: kimchi and ceviche and all sorts of other delicacies. She was still a traditional cook, but Hugh knew a bit about food and he'd pushed her taste buds.

She was thinking that for that night she'd make some little chive dumplings with a spicy chicken broth, and some garlic and chili kale. Perfect for the boys if they were hungry coming in from the fields; the day was bright and clear, but there was still a wind coming down from the north and it would be good to have something warming inside.

'Hello,' she said to old Wullie, who worked, as far as anyone could tell, about twenty hours a day running the island's only grocery shop. He might not even be that old. He might actually just be a very tired thirty-five.

'Flora MacKenzie,' he grunted. Flora felt oddly disgruntled. She'd have quite liked someone to have taken a look at her smart clothes and nice boots and gone, 'Flora MacKenzie! Look at you!' But nobody had.

'Hi there!' she said. 'I'm back! Well, for work, you know. I work in London.'

Wullie stared straight ahead without interest, as he always had.

'Aye,' he said.

'So,' she said. 'Um. Have you got any . . . rice wine?'

'Neh.'

'Lemon grass?'

He looked at her and blinked slowly.

'Soy sauce?'

'Aye,' he said, and pointed out a tiny, very dusty, sticky-looking bottle.

'And what about vegetables?' she said brightly. Wullie gestured at a shelf full of tins and Flora felt very cross. They grew all sorts of good stuff on the island: carrots, potatoes, tomatoes that loved the long summer evenings as long as you could keep them warm enough. Why was none of that here?

'Isn't there a farm shop?' she said.

'A waut?' said Wullie with a faint air of menace in his voice.

'Nothing,' said Flora, scampering away.

In the end she made it, out of all things, from an old Pot Noodle sachet and some harsh local onions she found in the pantry at the house. In her anxiety – as well as trying to clean the filthy kitchen at the same time – she horribly overboiled the chicken on the unfamiliar Aga, and the dumplings were hard as bullets.

Innes regarded the food carefully when they came in from the fields, washing up at the big sink.

'Is this a feminist position?' he said as they took their familiar places at the table: Innes and Hamish on the window side, Flora and Fintan on the other, her father nearest the range. 'Is being terrible at cooking all the rage in London these days?'

'Well, we could pebble-dash the barn with it,' suggested Fintan, poking at his plate dubiously.

'Or there's that dry wall needs putting up,' said Innes. 'We could use it for putty.'

'Stop complaining and just eat it,' said Flora.

'But it tastes like dishwater,' said Innes, in what he clearly thought was a reasonable tone.

Flora wanted to throw a plate at him. She knew it was ridiculous – the whole thing was absolutely horrible – but she felt incredibly embarrassed and angry at the same time. She was so rusty about everything up here.

'I like it, Flora,' said Hamish, who'd practically licked his plate clean. 'What is it, please?'

'Oh for Christ's sake, Hamish,' said Fintan. 'You're worse than Bracken and Bramble.'

'Is there anything else?' said Innes sadly.

'Not unless any of you thought to make anything.'

They all looked at each other.

'Well, you can starve then,' she said, crossly.

'Toast!' said Innes joyfully, and they all got up.

'What?'

'Mrs Laird,' explained Fintan. 'You know, who used to look after the vicar? She can actually make stuff. She makes bread for us.'

Flora went pink.

'I can do all that.'

'Come on, love,' said her dad from the fireplace. 'We're only messing with you. Nobody gets it right first time.'

Flora took a deep breath and looked round at the filthy kitchen.

'I'm going for a walk,' she said.

'To the chippy?' said Hamish hopefully.

'No!' said Flora, tears stinging her eyes as she marched out of the house. She'd have banged the door behind her, but it never got shut in the summer and had warped a bit, and nobody had thought to oil the hinges, which also made her furious. Had they all just given up?

And now they were doing the big ha ha has, teasing her, just like they always used to. With no one to stick up for her.

Well, she wasn't putting up with it. She was going to head out, go somewhere ... but where? The pub would be full of her dad's friends and she didn't want to get into *that*.

Everything else was shut. Oh for God's sake, this place. But she couldn't go home either.

She decided instead to take a walk up the Carndyne fell and clear her head.

The great fell, from which you could see across to the mainland, and to the islands behind if you went that side, was a beautiful hill – more of a mountain, really. People came from all over to climb it, and in the winter it got very snowy. It was unexpectedly dangerous; it could be mistaken for an easy summer walk when in fact it was unusually tricky and could get perilous in bad weather. There wasn't a season passed when Mountain Rescue wasn't called out to one idiot or another who thought they'd take a quick wander up the lovely green hill and got themselves into trouble far faster than they could imagine, even though there were plenty of signs and the guidebooks were very clear.

Murians, who often made up Mountain Rescue in the summertime, scoffed at this kind of thing and had little truck with girls who marched up in flip-flops and T-shirts, or boys who thought they could traverse a col without a rope and were very grateful for the dog rescue and the wry remarks of the locals.

Flora, of course, knew it like the back of her hand; had first climbed it at the age of nine. It was also the alternate-year school trip, which always provoked loud groans. The other class got to go to Esker, a little village on the mainland that hosted a pathetic excuse for a summer funfair, with rackety rides and straightforwardly fradulent stalls that nonetheless provoked wild excitement in the stimulus-hungry island boys and girls, who would come back laden with enormous lollies and cheap felt toys, sneering at the climbers, who had nothing but empty lunch boxes from sandwiches eaten at 10 a.m., sore feet and, occasionally, hoods full of rainwater.

It was late in the day, but the evenings were so long now, and as Flora climbed higher, she began to breathe deeply and take in the sights all around her. After another ten minutes, she turned round in surprise to see that Bramble was following her, panting cheerfully.

'Oh no!' she said. 'No, go back down. Honestly, I need some alone time.'

Bramble completely ignored this and waddled up to her, licking her hand gently.

'Dog! You are too old and fat to walk up this mountain! What if you get stuck?'

Bramble wagged his tail gently. Flora looked behind her. If she took him all the way down, she'd have to walk back into the kitchen, into the weird silence she was sure would have descended on everyone, and apologise for her outburst, or just generally look foolish. She sighed and marched on.

'You'd better keep up with me, then.'

Bramble moved forward, his claws clicking on the stones. If it wasn't for the chubby wobble of his haunches, he'd have looked quite noble.

Flora passed on up over the ridge and on to a long grassy mid-section. The air was clean and cool, and as she turned to look back, she saw the late-evening sun glittering and dancing off the sea, which unusually was as calm as a pond. In the distance she spotted the ferry carving out its familiar path across the bay. It must be, she thought, a pleasant night to be on board a boat. Then she could catch the sleeper from Fort William and be back in London . . .

Mind you, it was 31 degrees in London right now. It would be horribly sticky, with that nasty smell of overheated bins and cars blaring music everywhere and a slight undercurrent of noise and menace and people living too close together. London in the summer was . . . it was great, but it was just so crowded. So many people cramming onto the South Bank, jammed into overheated tubes and sweaty buses, searching for a tiny patch of scrubby grass in a park or a garden somewhere; hot pavements and cooking smells, and dope hanging over everything.

Up here, undeniably, she could breathe.

But that's not the point, she argued crossly with herself. It wasn't the point at all. Nobody was denying it was beautiful up here. Of course it was; it was gorgeous, everyone knew that. The question was whether it was right for her. For everything she wanted to accomplish; for everything she wanted to do with her life, whatever that was.

And now she was back in that stupid farmhouse, chained at that bloody sink, just like her mother had been. She kicked a stone bitterly. This had not been the plan. This hadn't been the plan at all. And if everyone was going to keep taking the piss, making fun of her after the sacrifice she'd made, well, she didn't want to deal with them in the slightest.

She carried on climbing, hoping the vigorous exercise would calm her down a little, but instead she found herself having quite long arguments inside her head about things, which wasn't helping at all. Blinking, she realised she'd come higher than she'd meant to, and could see right across to the hills on the mainland. The sky was filling with little pink clouds scuttling here and there, and the harbour below was barely more than a dot; likewise the ferry reaching the port. She marched on.

Nearing the top, she finally felt tired enough – it was a tricky scrambly bit, up some scree – for her head to start to clear. She found the waterfall she knew was tucked behind a wall of rock, and she and Bramble drank deeply of its freezing, utterly refreshing water, like liquid crystal on her tongue. She had just decided that this would be far enough when suddenly she heard a yelping.

She glanced round.

'Bramble? Bramble?'

The dog whined in response, but didn't run up to her as he normally would.

'BRAMBLE?'

The sun was starting to dip behind the mountains, and the chill was instant and noticeable. Concerned, Flora made her way across to the dog. To her horror, he had got one of his paws trapped in between two rocks. His back legs were desperately scrabbling against the wet stone as he tried to right himself.

She waded into the water and carefully freed his paw from the hole it had got stuck in, while he writhed in panic in her arms.

'It's okay! It's okay. It's okay,' she whispered in his ear as she heaved his enormous bulk onto the nearest patch of soft earth. 'You're going to be fine.'

Bramble was whimpering now, and trembling hard. They

were both completely soaked, and with the sun gone, it was becoming increasingly chilly. The dog's front right paw was hanging at a very unpleasant angle; Flora felt slightly sick even to look at it. Bramble yelped and looked at her as if it was all her fault, and she made soothing noises, all the while feeling panicked inside. She didn't have her phone; she'd stormed out without her bag, too annoyed to pick anything up. Even if she had had it, there wasn't a signal up here at the best of times, and this was beginning to look very much not like the best of times.

It was at least ninety minutes down the fell. The poor creature couldn't walk, and he weighed more than she did; she couldn't possibly carry him. But she couldn't leave him here either; he'd just try and follow her, and who knew what would happen then? She didn't have anything to tie him up with – and the idea of tying up and leaving an animal in pain, even if it was to get help, was just unbearable. Plus, it would be dark up here shortly, and how was she going to get anyone to come back up in the pitch black to look for an animal? It was far too dangerous; it would put human lives at risk.

Flora swore loudly. For God's sake. The most awful thing about it was that it would just confirm everything her family already thought: that she'd become soft with her city-living ways; that she didn't even know how to walk up the bloody fell. Oh God. She looked down at the dog.

'There you go, shh, don't worry,' she said. She could hear his heart beating through his chest, very fast. His breathing was shallow, and he was shivering miserably.

'My poor Bramble,' she said, burying her face in his fur. She realised that she was very cold. Too cold. The sun had misled her; it was still spring in the very north of Britain, which meant it was still dangerous.

Well, at least she had the dog to keep her warm, if they cuddled together. But she couldn't spend a night out here; that was a mad idea.

Her life, Flora decided crossly, was a mad idea.

She saw the clouds coming in. Of course she did. It was the oldest saying in the world: if you don't like the weather in Scotland, just wait five minutes. The rain darkened the hills across the bay, hiding them from view. Soon the coastline had vanished too under its dark sheet. The wind brought the fresh, unearthly smell of forthcoming rain. Bramble whimpered as if he knew something bad was about to happen. Flora reflected that at least he had his fur. Otherwise things looked pretty grim.

She tried hoisting the dog up. He weighed a ton soaking wet. It absolutely didn't help that he was panicked with the pain in his paw and scrabbled desperately to escape her arms, which meant the entire thing would be impossible.

The first drops of heavy rain started to fall. Flora realised she was wearing her London coat, which was absolutely fine for popping out in a light shower, but utterly useless for being up on top of a Scottish mountain in the middle of a storm.

When would the boys start to worry about her? she wondered. They'd probably assumed she'd gone to meet Lorna in the pub and wouldn't expect her back for hours. Dogs were allowed in the pub, so it wouldn't worry anyone particularly that Bramble wasn't there, even if they noticed.

Flora took her jacket off and put it over her head – it

didn't even have a hood – but the water was running down her neck regardless. She said every single swear word she knew, over and over again, but it didn't help. In fact, it precipitated a rumble of thunder somewhere in the distance.

Shelter, she thought. She needed to find shelter. She thought about the layout of the mountain in her head, from her childhood running up and down its paths, picking wild flowers for her mother, who would glance at them distractedly before looking around for a vase, which they didn't have, and dunking them in a mug.

There was, she remembered, a cave about two hundred metres downhill and round the other side, facing inland. She had drunk cider and snogged there with Clark when they were at school – he was now the island's policeman, which showed how things had changed – and cigarette butts and bottle tops had littered the ground then. She wondered if it was still like that. Probably. There weren't that many places on their tiny island where you could get away from prying eyes. If she could make it there, they could shelter until . . . well. Until she thought of a better idea.

She took a deep breath. Once she was down this mountain, she was going to tell the boys . . . well, she was going to tell the boys to stuff it. They could get on with everything themselves, eat beans out of a tin if they wanted, she no longer cared. She hated this stupid place and its stupid mad weather and its stupid tiny bunch of people who all knew each other and had opinions all the time. She was done. She was out.

Bramble nuzzled her foot.

Maybe she would take Bramble with her. Mind you, moving a huge, ancient dog into a tiny London rental … Well. Okay, maybe. Maybe she could come visit. Maybe …

Bramble whined.

'Stop that, dog,' she said. 'Oh God. Right. Okay.'

The best way, she worked out, after some slightly muddy and ungraceful scrambling in the soaking undergrowth, was to lift Bramble over her shoulder, like in a war film, trying to avoid his damaged paw. He struggled to begin with, then seemed to realise she was trying to help him.

Now utterly drenched from head to toe, with mud covering her almost completely, she made a growling noise at the sky and started skidding and slipping back down the hill.

'For CHRIST'S sake, you STUPID dumb dog!' she shouted, marching ferociously, using her anger to propel her forward. 'If you weren't so DAMN greedy and always wuffing up all the leftovers, I wouldn't be nearly KILLING myself carrying you. And you probably wouldn't have been trapped in that waterfall if you were a proper HEALTHY dog.'

'Aoww,' agreed Bramble mournfully, lifting his head and covering her face with another layer of mud.

If she hadn't known it so well, she would have missed the cave altogether, given that it was out of the way round the back end of the hill and had a hefty spray of early-season heather growing in front of it. She staggered towards it through the sheeting rain, continuing to lecture the dog as she went, her feet in their utterly unsuitable – and now ruined – Converse becoming ever more sodden. She nearly dropped poor Bramble as she pushed her way through the trailing greenery into the relative safety of the cave.

'BLOODY BLOODY BLOODY HELL,' she said, depositing him as gently as she could manage on the sandy floor. She was puffing and sweating now as well as utterly drenched and furious. It was not a good look.

'Hello,' came a quiet voice.

Chapter Eleven

Flora could barely see. The darkness inside the cave plus the stream of water plastering her hair over her head and across her eyes meant she couldn't focus at all. She blinked, then rubbed her hands over her face to try and clear her vision.

Then she did it again, in the hope that what she had seen would go away.

Staring straight at her were about a dozen twelve-year-olds and a large, pink-faced man, all wide-eyed and gazing at her in bemusement. Some of the children seemed quite frightened. Flora wondered if she looked very peculiar.

Probably. She was plastered with mud from head to foot and had just dumped a gigantic whining dog on the floor.

She tried to think of a way to pass all this off in a casual fashion, as if it was the kind of thing one did all the time on Mure, but Bramble was whining pitifully, and the eerily quiet children were staring at her like she'd been deliberately torturing him.

'Uh. Hi,' she said. The man stepped forward carefully, in the calm way you might approach a dangerous animal.

'Are you all right?'

Outside, the rain pounded the hillside.

'Of course I'm all right,' said Flora, then realised she could hardly breathe and bent over.

'I was talking to the dog,' said the man. His accent was local, but when Flora lifted her head, she found she didn't recognise him.

She blinked the last of the water out of her eyes.

'Sorry . . . are you guys some kind of lost tribe?'

But the man had already knelt down and was making soothing noises, gently stroking Bramble's panting flank.

'It's his paw,' said Flora. 'Don't touch it. He got it caught in some rocks.'

'He's out of shape,' said the man, scratching behind Bramble's ears.

'Don't insult my dog,' said Flora sharply.

'Right. Sorry.'

He looked up at her. He was large, broad shouldered and heavy set, with thick hair; his eyes were a penetrating blue and he didn't look very pleased.

'So why have you got him marching all over a mountain in a storm?'

'I could say exactly the same about you and your albino dwarf army,' muttered Flora.

'Do you always climb mountains in shoes like that?'

'Yes,' said Flora. 'I like to feel the mud between my toes.'

The man's face lost its stern expression for a moment.

'You're from round here?' he said.

'Not really,' said Flora, lying. 'What are you doing?'

'Charlie MacArthur,' said the man, sticking out his hand. 'Outward Adventures. We're on a trip.'

'And this is meant to be fun, is it?'

A ragged cheer went up from the little band.

'Of course,' said Charlie. 'We've been far too hot today.'

'What's wrong with your dug?' said one of the boys shyly. His accent was rough and westerly; Glaswegian, Flora would have said.

'I don't know,' said Flora. 'I think he's broken his paw.'

There was a general murmur of sympathy from the assembled group. As Flora focused on them a bit more closely, she noticed they were a wary-looking collection; not noisy and confident like the large groups of children she saw marching up and down on the harbour wall, shouting and yelling at each other cheerfully, hurling chips for the seagulls and generally acting like they didn't have a care in the world, which they didn't, because they were twelve.

This lot were different. She'd been right: they were pale; they were scrawny too, swamped by their huge, obviously borrowed waterproofs. She glanced up at Charlie again.

'Can the lads pet your dog?' he said. 'We'll get him home for you. If you want. You know. If you don't have a plan sorted.'

Flora straightened up and looked at him with narrowed eyes, not wanting to let her sudden relief show too much. She had enough annoying males patronising her around here; she certainly didn't need another one.

She shrugged.

'If you like,' she said.

'Oh, if I like. If I like. Well, that's very gracious of you.'

He looked outside.

'We'll wait till the sheeting rain stops, I think. No point in giving us all hypothermia.'

He glanced over to where the children were gently patting the dog. Bramble had finally settled and was stretched out, his breathing slowing. He looked like he was going to sleep. Flora's brow furrowed.

'He'll be all right,' said Charlie. 'Looks more like a bad sprain than a break; it hasn't swollen. He's just falling asleep, don't worry.'

'I knew that,' said Flora. There was a silence. Flora knew she was behaving badly towards someone who was clearly trying to help her, but somehow her bad mood today was infecting everything and she didn't know how to get out of it.

They sat staring at the rain.

'So, what, you do Outward Adventures for children in howling storms?' said Flora eventually, when it became clear that Charlie was perfectly happy with silence for as long as it took for the rain to stop.

He shrugged. 'Weather's all part of it, isn't it? We'll put our tents up in here if it doesn't let up, although I'd rather we were outside. Can't light a fire in here.'

'Isn't it a bit miserable?'

'You think we should all be in five-star hotels?'

'For holidays, I would think so.'

Charlie shook his head. They were well out of earshot of the children, who were still being unusually quiet.

'Neh. Not for these ones.'

'Who are they?' said Flora. They looked like such mites, some of them.

Charlie shrugged. 'They've all got a parent in prison. At least one. This is a chance for them to get away from everything … well. A lot of them have all sorts going on. There's a charity that sends them to us.'

Flora was incredibly taken aback.

'Oh,' she said quietly. 'I didn't realise.'

'Why should you?' said Charlie. 'They're just kids.'

Flora blinked.

'They look like they've had it tough.'

'Some of them, aye. Very tough. A few nights under canvas, even if it is raining, isn't the worst thing. This is their first night. Wait till you see them in a few days. You won't recognise them. They're not sure what's going on yet.' He smiled. 'Once we get the fire lit, things warm up.'

'Is it just you?'

'Oh no, I've got a partner. She's gone down to get extra waterproofs. Normally I'd send the kids to help, but I don't want anyone with bronchitis.'

'Oh,' said Flora, wondering who this saint was out in the rain getting waterproofs for underprivileged children when she herself had been having a temper tantrum about nobody liking her dinner. 'I'm Flora, by the way.'

'Charlie.' He reintroduced himself. 'Nice to meet you.'

They shook hands again. His hand was rough and weathered, and large, like the rest of him. There was something solid about him. She could see if you were a child far from home, you'd trust him straightaway.

‘So how come you get to be the one sheltering in the cave?’

Charlie shrugged

‘We take turns. Plus, this is a lads’ session. They need a bit of time with a chap. They tend not to see very many.’

‘What do you mean?’ said Flora.

‘Ah. A lot of them have no dad at home. Female teachers, female social workers; sometimes the first time they come in contact with a man is through the police service. Or a gang.’

He got up then and headed back to see what the children were doing with the dog. Quickly he sent two of them out to gather branches, and when they came back, wet and giggly, he showed them how to make a makeshift field stretcher, using a tarpaulin from his backpack and giving them all pieces of rope to practise knots on. In no time, they’d rigged up something entirely passable; now the only challenge was getting Bramble onto it. Finally relaxed, he had fallen asleep licking his paw.

Charlie opened up his first aid kit.

‘What are you doing?’ said Flora.

‘Trying to work out the right dose of ibuprofen for a dog. He is quite fat, you know.’

‘You said,’ said Flora. She frowned. ‘You do this all the time?’

‘Oh no. We take lots of management dickheads too, don’t worry. Helps us afford to have this lot.’

Flora smiled. Charlie peered outside.

‘I think it’s clearing up.’

‘It is *not* clearing up!’

'Anything that isn't stair rods is still fighting weather, I reckon.'

He turned round to the group of lads.

'Who's hard enough?'

The boys all cheered.

'Who reckons they can get the dog down the hill to the vet's?'

'ME! Me, sir! Let me! I'll do it!'

'Don't let *him* do it, he'll drop the bloody dog like he dropped his sandwiches!'

'I didn't drop my sandwiches!'

The group collapsed in laughter at some hapless freckled soul up the front, who had turned bright pink.

'Settle down,' said Charlie in a voice that brooked no argument. 'Right, lad, what's your name again?'

'Ethan,' whispered the boy. He had a drawn look, and shadows under his eyes that didn't belong in one so young.

'Did they taste all right, those sandwiches?'

'Yeah, if you like mud!' shouted someone.

'Oi!' said Charlie. 'Enough!'

He bent down to the little fellow.

'Look,' he said. 'It's going to get dark soon. This animal is injured and we have to rescue him. It'll be wet and heavy and difficult.'

He paused.

'Can you help me?'

The boy nodded fiercely.

Charlie knelt by the dog's head with a couple of ibuprofen.

'He won't eat those,' said Flora, who had long memories of her mother attempting to worm Bramble.

'He will in this,' said Charlie, crushing them into a Kendal mint cake. Sure enough, Bramble snoozily opened a bloodshot eye and lazily licked up the treat without even noticing.

'That'll help him out. Okay, lads.'

Charlie pointed out a few others to help Ethan – none, Flora noticed, of the ones who'd made fun of him – and the chosen group moved carefully to line the stretcher.

'Come on,' said Charlie, and he and Flora knelt down to roll the dog on to the tarpaulin.

'This dog is—'

'Too fat. Yes, you *said*,' said Flora. 'Thanks *once again*, Captain Do-Gooder.'

He eyed her up.

'That's a new one. Normally people are generally quite grateful when I help them out up a mountain.'

'Are they?' said Flora, who was cold and hungry and thoroughly ungrateful. She thought about it. 'Thanks.'

'Don't mention it,' said Charlie drily.

Bramble scuffled a little on the stretcher, but Flora soothed him. Charlie took off his belt, and Flora watched in astonishment as he put it gently round Bramble's rotund middle to attach him to the stretcher.

The rain was definitely moving on now, and it was possible to see down the mountain to the little harbour nestled in its embrace; the fields that led almost down to the dunes; the water chopping up in the firth.

'Time to go,' said Charlie. 'Right, boys. On my count, lift gently and slowly . . . '

Just as the boys were readying themselves, a shadow

fell across the cave entrance. Flora blinked. There stood a large woman – not fat, just a presence; a suggestion of broad shoulders and a strong chin. Her waterproof hood was pulled and knotted tight around her head; a stray drop of water was hanging off her nose.

'All done,' she announced cheerily. 'Tomorrow you'll all be helping, rain or shine. We're only taking pity on you because it's your first day. And it's nearly time for mud rounders!'

The boys cheered. The woman blinked as she caught sight of Flora.

'Who are you?' she said. 'We don't have any parental accompaniment, I think we made that quite clear.'

'Oh no, I'm—'

'And if you're an inspector, we need two weeks' notice in writing, not that it would matter when you turn up, because our standards of service are perfect.'

Flora blinked again.

'No, I'm—'

'She's just a daft lassie whose dog's hurt its paw,' said Charlie. 'Look at her shoes.'

The woman did so, and burst out laughing.

'Oh, right,' she said. 'Are you helping out?' Her tone changed when she talked to Charlie or the boys.

'Yes, Jan!' they shouted.

'Well, that's great,' she said. 'You head down the mountain, then come straight back up; we have a lot of sausages to eat!'

She didn't look at Flora again.

Chapter Twelve

The boys were, Flora had to admit, incredibly helpful and careful as they threaded the stretcher down the trickier parts until they once more reached the dirt path. Bramble obviously realised they were trying to do right by him, as he didn't thrash about too much, and didn't seem to mind the belt. Flora gently skritched his ears when she could and whispered sweet nothings, mostly about sanctimonious Outward Adventures teachers who thought they knew everything. Her wet shoes squelched on the path.

As they approached the farm, she yelled to Fintan, who was crossing the path to feed the chickens, and he waved back and came towards her.

'What the hell happened to Bramble?' he said, his expression concerned. 'What did you do to him, Flora?'

'I didn't do anything to him!' said Flora indignantly. 'He tried to climb a waterfall, despite being the dog equivalent of seventy-five years old! He's an idiot!'

Fintan looked at Charlie, slightly bashfully, Flora noticed.

'Hi, Charlie,' he said. 'Sorry about this. What did my sister do?'

'She's your sister?' said Charlie. 'God. You look nothing alike.'

'I'm right here,' said Flora.

'Thank God you were up there,' said Fintan. 'Did she really wander up in sandshoes? Poor Bramble.'

'I think it's just a sprain,' said Charlie. 'He'll probably be right as rain in the morning.'

The boys had gently laid the stretcher down.

'Thanks, lads,' said Fintan. 'Do you want a . . . ?'

'A what?' said Flora.

Fintan's face creased.

'Oh,' he said quietly. 'I was going to say "a piece of cake", but we don't have any.'

There were very few days when there hadn't been a fruit cake standing underneath its covering, waiting for passing guests. The boys looked up expectantly.

'There's a packet of Hobnobs in my room,' said Flora reluctantly. She'd been hiding them to keep them out of her brothers' clutches; she still didn't trust them. 'Hang on.'

'No worries,' said Charlie. 'We've got a nutritious supper up the mountain for them. They live off sugar as it is.'

'Awww,' said one of the boys, but even as he said it, Flora could see he was missing a tooth.

'Okay then.'

'Want a cup of tea? Or a wee dram?' said Fintan.

'Not while I'm working,' said Charlie. 'No, I'd better get these guys back up the hill. It's getting pretty late.'

'It is,' said Fintan.

'I'm sorry,' said Flora. The men nodded.

'Bye now,' said Charlie, but he was talking to Bramble. He patted the dog gently, then he and the boys turned and headed back up the mountain through the softly falling twilight rain.

'You calmed down from your little paddy then?' said Fintan.

Back in the kitchen, everything was still a complete tip; nothing was washed up, and food was congealing on plates and in saucepans. Flora looked at it and closed her eyes briefly. She put Bramble in his bed next to the range, where, exhausted from his ordeal, he immediately fell asleep. Then she headed off to her bedroom.

Fintan shouted after her.

'If you were looking for those Hobnobs, me and Hamish ate them.'

'I like Hobnobs,' said Hamish. 'Buy more Hobnobs, Flora.'

Chapter Thirteen

'How is this your job, though?' Lorna groaned the next day. 'You sit around and get paid for literally absolutely nothing.'

'I'm waiting for the client,' said Flora. 'I'm at his beck and call. And at the moment it's all beck and no call.'

'Can you get this coffee on expenses?'

'I can,' said Flora, looking down at the Harbour's Rest's offering in disgust. 'I don't think I will, though. Out of respect to the concept of coffee.'

She looked around.

'Does Colton Rogers ever come in here?'

Lorna snorted. 'Seriously, I don't think he's here at all. Nobody sees him.'

Old Maggie, who was a stalwart of Mure's social scene and sat on the town council, leaned over.

'He sucks money out of this community,' she sniffed, 'and gives nothing back. He takes all our beauty and our natural advantages . . . and he spends no money here.'

Lorna glanced at Flora, who shook her head fiercely. She didn't want Maggie to know Colton was her client.

'He's like the invisible man,' said Lorna. 'You'd think he'd pop in for a pint.'

'I don't think Americans do that,' said Flora. 'I think they just like wheatgrass shots.'

Maggie blinked.

'Well,' she said.

She leaned over again.

'It's good to see you back, dearie. For the summer?'

'Um, no, just . . . just popping in,' said Flora.

'Your dad will be pleased.'

'You'd think,' said Flora mournfully.

'Oh well,' said Lorna, wary of Flora getting morose again. '*We're* happy to see you.'

'Quite right,' said Maggie. 'And will you be dancing again? I'm sure Mrs—'

'No,' said Flora shortly.

Maggie and Lorna exchanged looks.

'Hello!' a loud voice called from the door.

The girls turned around. Standing there was a large, hearty-looking woman Flora didn't recognise at first.

'LORNA!' the woman boomed.

'Jan,' said Lorna, with none of her normal bouncy friendliness. Flora realised it was the woman from the hill in the rain. 'How are things?'

'Not bad, not bad.'

Lorna looked rather dejected, Flora thought.

'Jan, have you met Flora?'

'No,' said Jan.

'Actually, hi, we met yesterday?' said Flora tentatively.

The woman squinted.

'Oh YES!' she bellowed. 'You're the sulky one! Can you believe she marched up the fell without any proper shoes?'

'Well, she's lived on it for nearly thirty years,' said Lorna mildly. 'I think she's probably allowed.'

'Would have died if we hadn't found her.'

'I *so* wouldn't have,' said Flora crossly.

'Those mountains are dangerous.'

'Yes, I know that, thanks, seeing as I was born and bred here.'

Jan sniffed.

'Really? Because you look like a city-dweller to me.'

'Oh thanks,' said Flora, then was annoyed because she'd taken it as a compliment.

'Are you having a good trip?' said Lorna quickly.

'Well, obviously we have huge responsibilities to our less fortunate friends,' boomed Jan. 'Which of course is why we were thinking . . . have you thought any more about taking some of the children on at the school?'

'I've explained before,' said Lorna. 'We'd be absolutely delighted to have any of your children. But they need to live here. Their parents or guardians need to apply.'

'They can't!' said Jan. 'They don't have the capability!'

'Well, how can I take them, then? Be reasonable. I can't run a boarding school.'

'It would do them the world of good.'

'I'm sure it would. But Scotland doesn't have state boarding, and even if it did, we don't have the facilities, and even if we did, we can't find the staff . . . '

Lorna was looking increasingly dismayed.

'Jan, any time you want to bring them over for a week in term-time, we'd be more than happy to welcome them.'

'They need more than that,' said Jan.

'I'm sure they do,' said Lorna. 'I'm just sorry we're not able to provide it.'

'Another door slammed in their faces,' said Jan, and left with an aggrieved sniff.

'She seems mean,' said Flora.

'Oh, she's all right,' said Lorna. 'Runs Outward Adventures for underprivileged children. Thinks it gives her the right to bully everyone who doesn't do that.'

'I know, I met her other half.'

'Charlie? He's all right. And pretty hot for a Wester. Jan just feels that anyone who isn't trying to save the world all the time is morally lacking.'

'That must get tiresome.'

'She's good at what she does, though.'

'Maybe I should get her to take the boys,' said Flora gloomily. 'Teach them how to look after themselves for a few days.'

'Are you making the tea again?'

Flora sighed.

'If I don't do it, nobody does,' she said. 'They just eat sausages every night. They're all going to die of coronary artery disease. So. Can't say I'm looking forward to it, though.'

Lorna smiled. Her own mother had tended towards the Findus Crispy Pancakes end of things. The best present she'd ever received was a chest freezer. Lorna had always loved going to the MacKenzies', Flora's glamorous, other-wordly looking mother pottering about with steaming dishes on the go; perfect pies turned out of glass tureens; always a little bit of shortbread to go with the warm, frothy milk that came straight from the dairy.

'I don't know,' said Flora. 'I thought maybe I could try a pie.'

'When's the last time you did that?'

Flora laughed.

'Don't. I'm sure it will come back to me. Mind you, I thought that last night.'

'Do you want me to come up?'

'And cook for my family and show them how much better you are at everything than me? Not likely. They already like you better than me as it is. Are you *sure* you can't marry one of the boys and move in and just take over? Come on, everyone fancied Fintan at school.'

Lorna smiled.

'Not bloody likely. No offence – I love them dearly.'

'Plus you're still trying to cop off with that doctor.'

'Sod off.' Lorna blushed deeply. She had a huge crush on the local GP: so big, it was actually mean of Flora to tease her about it, and she apologised immediately.

'Sorry. And I do know what it's like, I promise. My boss . . . you might meet him, actually.'

Even saying this much made Flora extremely pink.

'What?'

'I think he's going to come up, try and chivvy Colton along.'

'You like him?'

'He's . . . he's attractive. That's all.'

'You do! Is he single?'

'Hard to say,' said Flora. 'He always seems to be with a tall, skinny blonde, but I can't tell if it's the same girl. Like Leonardo DiCaprio.'

'Hmm,' said Lorna. 'Doesn't sound like your type.'

'He isn't!' said Flora. 'In fact, when you see him, tell me how disgusting you think he is.'

'Okay.'

'Do you want me to do the same thing with the doctor?'

'Don't you dare,' said Lorna loyally, and Flora laughed.

'God, it's nice to meet someone worse than me. Right. I'm off to buy pie stuff. Wish me luck.'

'Humble pie stuff, more like.'

'Yeah yeah yeah,' said Flora.

But as she trudged off, the sun warm on the back of her neck, the breeze lifting her hair, she felt undeniably cheered by spending time with her friend; not a work friend, or a passing friend, but someone she'd known as long as she could remember.

Chapter Fourteen

Flora worked up a sweat marching up the hill carrying her shopping bags, and was hungry again by the time she got home, but with that nice tiredness that comes from exercise and the feeling you always get when you wake up after a bad day – that things can't be quite as bad as they were yesterday. And there was still no word from London. She wasn't sure quite what was going on. It was utterly peculiar not being at work and yet not being on holiday either – neither feeling she ought to be filling up her time better nor feeling slightly sunburnt and hung-over (it took Flora about fifteen minutes slathered with factor 50 to get sunburnt, and not much longer to get hung-over).

Bramble looked up as she came in, and his heavy tail beat a rhythm on the old flagstones. Obviously he'd forgiven her for his terrible day. She checked his bandage – it had gone on pristine, but was already getting gnawed. He was going to need one of those cone-shaped collars, she thought. She always thought dogs looked embarrassed in those things.

The house was empty, of course; the boys would be out at all four corners of the farm.

She tuned the internet into Capital FM – which downloaded at a speed that would have made a snail sad – so she could cheer herself up with the London traffic reports. The trains had all been cancelled again. The Blackwall Tunnel was closed. It helped knowing that not everyone was having a fabulous time all the time.

'And be careful, temperatures will hit the high twenties by four p.m., so it'll be a sticky commute home for you guys,' said the smug mid-Atlantic DJ, and Flora rolled her eyes.

She looked around the kitchen. The pots and pans she'd used to absolutely no effect the day before were still sitting in the sink and had been joined by the porridge pot, an ancient brown and orange thing that was only ever used for the morning oats. Flora had the faintest memory of her mother saving up something – was it stamps? – to buy the set of different-sized pans. This was the only one left. Its screws were coming loose.

She followed the line of sunlight that danced in and out of the dirty kitchen windows. This place was utterly filthy. It wasn't the boys' fault exactly – they worked hard – but it certainly wasn't going to get any better on its own. And there was something about mess and dirt that made it hard to relax. Flora wasn't a clean freak, not by any means, but this was so dispiriting and couldn't be doing any of them any good. And that was before they all caught amoebic dysentery.

No. It wouldn't do.

She cracked open the ancient dishwasher and emptied its filthy filter. As it ran through a cycle with the dishwasher cleaner that had obviously never been used, she started washing everything by hand, using a vast amount of the cleaning products she'd gathered up along with the pie ingredients in the supermarket; filling and refilling the sink with hot water and making the creaky old boiler start up over and over again. She didn't just wash the dirty dishes; she washed every single smeared bit of crockery, piling a load up in the corner to be taken to the island's sole charity shop. When, after all, did they ever have thirty-five people round who all needed a saucer? How many freebie mugs from fertiliser companies could conceivably be useful?

Then she started scrubbing the shelves, thick with dust and sticky rings; she made herself filthy crawling into cupboards, and swilled bowl after bowl of grey water down the drain. She threw away piles of old advertising leaflets and used envelopes; gathered up bills and bank statements and divided them into piles that she could go over with her father – she would have to get him into internet banking; it would make his life a lot easier. Possibly. Or Innes, at least.

She threw out all the old packets of half-eaten pasta and out-of-date rice – it was amazing they didn't have mice, truly – and tidied up the contents of the cupboards. She didn't know what to do with them, but it was nice to know that such peculiar items as cornflour and suet were all in there.

The work was tiring, but it was satisfying to see results as she refilled the mop bucket again and again. Just to be doing something felt like a triumph in itself, lifting her from the slightly panicky morass into which she'd steadily felt herself sinking since she'd known she was coming back. She thought of Jan the night before, out in the hosing rain, putting up tents for poor kids from the inner city. Well, Jan wasn't the only person who could do good things, she found herself thinking, then realised this was ridiculous.

She'd filled the oven with noxious chemicals – she made a note to dispose of them carefully, in case they got into the duck pond – but it had to be left on for a good couple of hours. She might as well put the kettle on. She was pleased to see it gleaming, having been left to soak in limescale remover. She rinsed it under the tap about a billion times, feeling the satisfaction of watching the little white flakes disappear, then boiled up some water. She'd refilled her mother's little tins with 'Tea' 'Coffee' and 'Sugar' written on them, although she had vowed to herself that as soon as there was any money – and she'd have to take a look at that with her father too: *was* there any money? – the first thing she was going to do was get a proper coffee machine so she didn't have to drink the powdered stuff she'd weaned herself off long ago.

Then she realised that thinking like that made it seem as though she was going to be staying longer than a week.

Which she wasn't. Job done. In and out and home again. Back again. Home again. Ugh. The terminology was confusing.

Reaching up to run a finger along the newly polished dresser top, she knocked over the pile of recipe books that stood there. She had bought her mother lots, whatever was fashionable, figuring that if she spent that much time in the kitchen, she might want to try cooking different things. So there was Nigella, Jamie, anything Flora had thought looked interesting but not too technical or weird. Anything with courgetti spaghetti was absolutely out.

She looked at them now as they cascaded on to the floor. Pristine. Utterly untouched; practically the only tidy things in the room. Her mother – who had always thanked her profusely – must have politely put them up on the shelf then never, ever opened them. Not even for a look.

Flora shook her head, half smiling. No wonder her father said he knew where she got her stubborn side.

As she picked the books up, wondering if she could sell them, she came across an old notebook tucked in between them. The kettle boiled on as Flora stared at it. It was at the same time both new to her – she couldn't exactly recall seeing it – but on the other hand as utterly familiar as the back of her hand, like seeing a stranger in a crowd then realising she'd known them all her life.

She crouched down, and tentatively picked it up.

It had a dark hard cover with red binding, coming slightly loose, and a matching red bookmark string inside it. There were grease spots on the cover. She opened it up, knowing even as she did so exactly what it was. No wonder her mother had never needed to use any of those other books she'd bought for her.

She had her own recipe book.

Chapter Fifteen

How could she have forgotten? But then Flora had never really thought of meals being designed as such; her mum just cooked, that was all, as natural as breathing. Dinner appeared, steady as clockwork, 5 p.m. on the dot, when the boys got in from the fields or from school; great big slices of apple pie to finish, with farm cream, of course, sluiced out of the old cracked white jug with the blue cows round the rim (which had survived the purge). Puddings and jellies; thick hams and delicate potatoes; and always pie. As a small child, Flora would help her, sitting at her elbow and absorbing everything. She was particularly good at licking the spoon but reasonably good at passing the baking powder and kneading and mixing. As she'd grown older and was studying for exams, she still worked to the rhythm of her mother's wooden spoon and rolling pin. And here it all was.

She suddenly felt a slight hiccup of excitement.

She poured water into the huge old enamel mug her

mother had kept topped up all day long; there were deep brown tannin lines scored into it. It felt a little strange, a little intimate, to be drinking from her mother's cup. She regarded it curiously, then decided to go ahead, even if it was spooky. She was being superstitious, that was all. She dunked the tea bag and let it steep for longer than she normally would, smiling wryly as she did so. Her mother had liked tea you could stand the spoon up in. Then she took the cup and sat down in her mother's armchair; the one nearest the fire, the one she almost never used. Sitting down wasn't really the kind of thing her mother did. It only happened on her birthday, and Mothering Sunday and Christmas Day, when they all made a great fuss of her, imploring her to relax while they fetched and carried and did everything for her.

Flora wanted a biscuit, but there were none; instead she settled back to look at the notebook, this little piece of her mother, years on.

It gave off a faint smell, like a concentrated essence of the kitchen: a little grease, some flour; simply home, built up like a patina across the years, from tiny fingers sticky and desperate to touch the jam ('HOT! HOT! HOT!' Flora could faintly hear the echo of her mother's voice shouting at them all as they jabbered and pushed to get closer to the jewel-coloured liquid she stirred in a huge vat for days in the autumn, filling jars and sending them out to the village fair, the kirk harvest festival and the old and infirm anywhere). She sipped her tea and turned to the first page.

The first thing she saw was a note in her father's cramped handwriting, the ink faded now. *Love you, Annie*, it said. *Hope you write some lovely things here.* And it was dated, faintly,

August '78, which meant it must have been around her mother's birthday.

Flora squinted at it. It was a notebook – a handsome one – not a recipe book. Why had it turned into a recipe book? What else would her mother have written in there? She smiled as she thought about her father, never the most imaginative of gift givers. But perhaps her mother had loved it anyway.

She turned the page. All the recipes had her mother's funny little titles and annotations. Here was vegetable broth. As soon as she saw it, she could conjure up the sharp smell of the boiling stock her mother made on a Sunday after the roast; the thick, rich soup that resulted; the steamed-up windows of the farmhouse when she came back from school on dark winter Monday evenings, the warm room lit up and cosy as she sat and did her homework, complaining mightily that all the boys fancied Lorna MacLeod which they did, while her brothers set the table and her mother refilled her teacup, and Flora's too, and busied herself at the stove.

Over another page and it was another soup recipe, oxtail this time, but the writing was different. With a start, Flora recognised her Granny Maud's hand – Maud was long dead now; a northern witch, like her mother – a beautiful copperplate inscribed in fountain pen. At the top she'd written, in small flowing letters, a Gaelic phrase Flora couldn't decipher straightaway; she had to fetch the old dictionary from the sitting room before she could figure it out: 'It will be of the longest time ... until it is as good as mine.'

There was something about that simple, gentle phrase that made Flora smile. As she pulled her legs up under herself – the weather had turned, as it always did, and now rain was slamming gently against the windows – Bramble looked up, then struggled to his feet and limped carefully across the room. He flopped his head and promptly fell back to sleep again.

'I hope this is you recovering, and not just being a lazy arse,' murmured Flora.

She didn't remember Granny Maud that well, as by the time Flora had come along, she'd had rather enough grandchildren and was starting to slow down quite a lot. She'd come and help Annie shell peas and they'd drink tea and gossip in Gaelic, which Flora couldn't follow, and occasionally Granny would make a slightly sarcastic remark about Flora having her head stuck in a book, which would make Annie narrow her eyes a little and the matter would be dropped.

It had been, though, a straightforward loving relationship, Flora thought. Annie, fourth of Granny's seven living children, had simply left school at seventeen and married her dad the next day, in a kirk service, wearing a plain white cotton shift, barely a wedding dress at all.

Flora remembered when her friend Lesley had got married. Her mother had practically begged to attend, and had swooned over Lesley's Empire antique lace and narrow train and wild-flower bouquet, even as Flora and Lorna had rolled their eyes and got drunk quietly in a corner and shown the English friends of Lesley's nervous-looking new husband how to dance like island girls.

It would have been nice, Flora knew, if she could have got married before she lost her mother. She'd probably have liked that. She'd have liked that so very much. She hadn't really thought about marriage a great deal; only in the abstract, as something that might happen one day but was a long way off.

She wondered if her mother would have liked to have seen it.

Tears sprang to her eyes. Well. There was no point in crying about something that had never even happened, she told herself sternly, rubbing Bramble's chin. There had been no wedding; no boyfriend had ever asked her, not even Hugh, and she hadn't liked anyone enough to be more than slightly upset when they didn't. That was just how life was. She turned the page quickly.

As she did so, engrossed in the hard-to-make-out spidery handwriting, with its ink smudges, food spots and random Gaelic words interspersed with the English text (not to mention the strange old imperial measurements she had never even heard of – what the hell was a 'gill'?), she heard a noise at the door.

She looked up, startled. Her dad was standing there, looking like he'd seen a ghost. Surprised, she let the huge enamel cup drop from her fingers, and they both watched it rattle to the floor, making the most extraordinary noise.

'Dad . . .'

'Jesus,' he said, putting his hand to his chest. 'Sorry, love. Sorry. I didn't mean to frighten you. I didn't . . . I just . . . You look so like her. You just look so like her sitting there. Sorry.'

Flora had jumped up to get a cloth from the sink, where it was soaking in bleach. She mopped up the spilt tea.

'I was just . . . '

Her father shook his head. 'Sorry, lass, sorry. I got . . . I just got a shock.'

'Shall I put the kettle on?'

He smiled. 'That's exactly what she'd have said if I'd seen a ghost.'

There was a pause. He looked around the kitchen, and his eyes lit up.

'Oh, well look at that,' he said. 'Oh, Flora.'

Flora felt a bit irritated. She didn't particularly want praise for scrubbing a floor.

'You've made it so much better.'

'Well, don't mess it up again,' she said, her voice coming out harsher than she'd intended.

'Oh . . . no. You filled up the tea bin!'

'I did.'

'It's . . . ' He shook his head. 'You know, I hadn't really noticed how disorderly everything was.'

'Well, maybe try and keep it straight now?'

'Aye . . . aye,' he said. 'I'll tell the boys. I just came back to get my . . . ' He looked confused.

'What?' said Flora, worried. The last thing she needed now was him getting forgetful.

'My . . . my . . . '

'Stick? Sandwiches?'

She made him his tea as the lazy old dogs nudged around him.

'Ach, no,' he said, smiling. 'I thought you might still be out. I thought I might have a wee nap.'

Flora smiled.

'Of course you can have a nap, for God's sake; you've been up since five!'

'I might just . . .'

The Aga was still warm, of course, as it always was, and he pulled up the other chair – his chair – next to it.

'Don't let me disturb whatever you're doing,' he said gravely.

Oddly, Flora found she had spirited the notebook away into her bag. She didn't want to upset him, obviously, by letting him see it. She felt, too, somehow, as if this were something private, between her and her mother.

'Just thinking about dinner,' she said, glancing around.

'Well, it seems you've done a lot already,' said her father.

She brought him his tea, and he touched her arm when he thanked her for it, and somehow there was something – an air of detente, a thaw – that struck them both.

Fintan came in next, looking around crossly.

'Oh right, the cleaning fairy's been in,' he said. 'Showing us the error of our ways, are you, sis?'

'Why are you being so aggressive?' said Flora.

'I don't know. Maybe because you're stomping around here with a face like a wet weekend because you hate everything about your background and family and heritage? Yeah, maybe that's it.'

Flora rolled her eyes.

'You smell. What have you been doing?'

'None of your business. Nothing intellectual enough for you, anyway.'

Eck looked up sharply.

'Have you been down in that dairy again?'

'I think it's going to be something special, Dad.'

'Well, it's wasting enough of our time, that's for sure. And our money.'

'It doesn't cost anything to do.'

'Well, it does, because I don't have you seeding the lower field.'

Flora wondered what the hell they were talking about and was about to ask when Fintan sniffed.

'I suppose there's no dinner again?'

'I'll get Innes to go to the chippy,' said Eck.

'No!' said Flora, fingering the notebook. 'I'm going to do it.'

They both looked at her and laughed, and Flora's fragile good mood dissipated almost immediately.

Chapter Sixteen

If Flora had had a fantasy about coming home, it might have gone a little like this: everyone would be thrilled to see her, and desperate to hear her stories of life in the glamorous big city. Okay, maybe not the Tinder dating stories, but definitely the others. And her handsome boss would turn up and extol her virtues and she would be incredibly busy and important taking meetings with Colton Rogers and effortlessly doing his business all round town, instead of hanging about trying to look inconspicuous and fill time.

Then, over meals the boys all pitched in to make, they would open a local ale and trade anecdotes about their mother, and her near-white hair, and how funny she could be over a sherry at Christmas, and all the stories she used to tell about life on the island – bogles and witches and selkies and pixies – which she thought were comforting and charming and they found bed-wettingly terrifying, and they would laugh and bond and celebrate her life and Flora would basically have put the family back together and they would all thank her sincerely and be very impressed by her amazing work, and then she would go back to London and pick up where she'd left off. Except better and more successfully, and she'd look healthy and well from the open air and good food.

She looked around resentfully. Her father was already snoozing by the fire, first whisky well on the way. Fintan had disappeared again, God knows where. Oh well.

She opened the book at pies and took out the mince, gently heating the pan and chopping the onion. Unlike yesterday, when she'd panicked and gone too fast and turned up the heat and felt watched and judged and had an absolute disaster, she tried to calm down. Remember what her mother had done. Mix the pastry carefully with cool hands, nothing rushed, as if she'd done it hundreds of times before.

While the pie was cooking, she heated up carrots and peas for the side, and mashed the locally grown potatoes with a great wodge of butter from the dairy – she added more and more, it was so good – and plenty of salt, until she had the most gorgeous golden mound of fluffy goodness and every single bad carb and fat and salt sin under the sun in a single earthenware bowl, and it was all she could do not to scoff the lot, and she didn't even have to call everyone in; they all appeared automatically at 4.55 p.m., summoned by the wonderful smells.

'I like it, Flora,' said Hamish, and for once the others didn't disagree with him, simply traded glances.

'Did you get this out of a packet?' said Innes.

'Shut up,' said Flora. 'And say thank you.'

Eck looked up in surprise. 'This is—'

Everyone knew he was going to say, 'just like your mother used to make', but nobody wanted him to get to the end of that sentence. Flora cleared her throat and changed the subject.

'So, anyway, I know I'm repeating myself, but … how's the farm doing?' she said, trying to sound cheery.

Innes blinked.

'Why? Are you going to sell us out to Colton Rogers?'

'Of course not! I was just asking.'

Eck sniffed.

Hamish smiled.

'I like Chloe.'

'She's a terrible goat,' said Innes.

'I like her.'

Innes sighed.

'What?' said Flora.

'Nothing. Just … transporting livestock … I don't want to get into it. It's just. I mean, you must have heard what's happened to the price of milk.'

Flora nodded. 'Not up here, though?'

'Oh yes. There's no escape for us. And trying to sell the cattle on the mainland … I mean, the cost of transportation … '

'What about keeping it local?'

'Where? There aren't enough shops, there isn't enough trade, there isn't enough for us to do here. Haven't you noticed? Talk to your friend Lorna; ask her how many people are raising their families here these days.'

He sat back bitterly. Hamish had simply taken the bowl

of mashed potatoes and was eating straight out of it with a spoon. Flora would have told him off for it if she hadn't wanted to do exactly the same thing herself. God, she had forgotten how good real food could taste.

'How bad is it?' she asked, glancing at their father, who either hadn't heard or was pretending not to.

'Really, really bad,' said Innes. He shot Fintan a foul look. 'And someone isn't helping.'

Fintan stared straight ahead, chewing and not taking part either. Innes sighed, just as his phone rang. It was Eilidh, his ex. He stood up and wandered over to the big window at the back, where the white sky was fading to a high late blue, but it didn't hide the fact that they were clearly bickering.

'Fine, I'll take her!' shouted Innes finally, ending the call.

'Agot? Don't you want to see her?' said Flora before she could stop herself.

'Of course I do,' said Innes. 'But we're ploughing tomorrow. It's no place for a kid.'

'She loves the tractor,' said Hamish.

'I know,' said Innes. 'Loves it enough to run in front of it.'

Innes paced up and down, then glanced at Flora.

Flora had never looked after her niece before. Agot had been a baby at the funeral. Quickly she banished all thoughts of the funeral from her head. She didn't really get children per se; they seemed nice enough, if a bit demanding, if her friends who'd sprogged were to be believed. Unfortunately, once they had sprogged it was a bit hard to keep up, as they immediately moved out of London, and if you made it out there for a pint, they tended to fall asleep after half an hour or so.

Eck looked up from his scraped-clean plate.

'Our Flora could look after her, couldn't you?' he said, pushing his glasses up. 'You're not doing much else.'

'Oh Dad, you know she has a Terribly Important High-Profile Job as a Lawyer,' snarked Fintan, and Flora flashed him a cross look. It wasn't her fault that she had to wait on a billionaire. But it was aggravating that they obviously thought she basically did nothing, just as they'd always expected, particularly when she knew that back in London there was a huge load of paperwork piling up for her.

And actually, slightly encouraged by her success in cleaning up the kitchen, Flora had considered tackling the biggest, most horrible job of all: her mother's wardrobe. She had hoped against hope that her dad might have taken it on himself to do it, but he hadn't. She wasn't going to get rid of anything if he didn't want her to, but it needed sorting out a little.

'I've got plenty to do,' she sniffed.

'Yeah, injuring the dogs,' said Fintan.

'SHUT UP, FINTAN!' she yelled.

He stuck his tongue out at her.

All eyes were on her. They were, Flora reflected, the only two girls left in the family.

'Is she toilet-trained?'

'Yes,' lied Innes.

Flora sighed.

'All right then.'

Chapter Seventeen

'Once upon a time there was a ship. And a girl was stolen away.'

'Where?'

'Oh, from far up north where the castles are, to be taken a long way away across the sea. And she did not want to go.'

'Why not? Why not?'

But the rustling skirts had gone and the love and the comfort had vanished and she was cold and alone and . . .

Flora woke crossly in the little single bed, the sun already high across the counterpane although it was only 6.30, her hair rumpled and her eyes sticky. It took her a while to remember where she was. And there was still no word from London.

Agot turned up at 8.30, deposited by an unsmiling Eilidh, who nodded briefly at Flora and said she'd heard she was 'popping in', as if 'popping in' was the worst insult she could devise.

Little Agot was three, and surprisingly formidable for such a small person.

'It's your Auntie Flora,' Eilidh said, and if Flora detected some sarcasm in it, well, she was in a sensitive mood.

'HEYO, AUNTIE FLOWA,' came an unusually loud and deep voice, even muffled by the thumb stuck firmly in her mouth.

'You two are going to play and have a wonderful time.'

Nobody in the kitchen looked particularly confident at this analysis. Eilidh handed Flora a huge backpack containing nine Tupperware boxes full of food, various packets of wipes, and, ominously, two spare pairs of knickers.

'Can you feed her?' said Eilidh.

'Of course!' said Flora, bristling.

'Sorry, it's just . . . I heard you were working.'

'I can multitask,' said Flora through gritted teeth.

'Great, great,' said Eilidh vaguely, kissing her daughter – without, Flora noticed, telling her she had to be good or anything – and heading out.

It was a bright, brisk, breezy morning – rather lovely, in fact, as long as you were wearing a jumper – and normally Flora would have suggested walking Bramble, but he was still a little wobbly on his paw. Instead, she and Agot regarded each other carefully.

'THIS GRANMA'S HOUSE,' said Agot eventually. Her hair was white blonde, just like her grandmother's had been. According to Eck, they were the spit of one another. It hung long and made her look somewhat other-worldly; like a sprite, swept in on the northern waves from who knew where. Innes kept grumbling that it got in the way and was going to get caught in the farm machinery, and Agot herself complained that raccoons didn't have long hair, no way, but her mother – whose own hair was a light mouse – was far too proud of her daughter's crowning glory to have it cut; it never had been in fact, and the ends were tiny white baby ringlets. Flora expected it to be subject to a few covetous looks from other parents; there were a lot of fair babies up here, but most deepened to red eventually. It looked like Agot would be a sprite all her life.

'What do you want to do this morning?' she said. Agot looked at her askance, and Flora felt, obscurely, that this was something she ought to know; that she needed some kind of plan.

'BUT!' said Agot.

'Yes?'

'THIS GRANMA'S HOUSE!'

'I know,' said Flora. She led Agot outside, and they sat down on one of the rocky outcrops at the front of the farmhouse. Out of the wind, the sun suddenly felt hot on her face, and she made a note to put suncream on the little girl, whose skin was white as milk.

'But your grandma, she was my mummy.'

Agot pondered that.

'SHE DADDY'S MUMMY.'

'She was. And she was my mummy too. Daddy and I are brother and sister.'

'YIKE GEORGE AND PEPPA?'

Flora blinked and decided it was best to agree with this statement.

'Yes,' she said. 'Just like them.'

Agot swung her legs against the warm rock.

'SHE NOT HERE?'

Flora shook her head.

'AUN' FLOWA SAD NO MUMMY?' She asked it entirely conversationally.

Flora watched the tide beating against the rocks below the lower field.

'Oh yes,' she said. 'Very sad.'

Agot's face started to crumple.

'WAN' MUMMY,' she said in a low voice. You didn't have to be a child expert to realise that trouble was brewing.

'It's okay,' said Flora quickly. '*Your* mummy is fine. I'm just old.'

'I'S THREE,' said Agot.

'That's right. But it's okay. I'm a grown-up. I'm . . . much older than three. So. You see. It's okay.'

Agot's thumb was finding her mouth again. Flora cast around quickly for something to distract her.

'Um . . . do you want to go throw stones?'

Agot shook her head dismissively.

'Look at the cows?'

'I YIKE PIGS.'

'We don't have any pigs.'

Agot's lip started to tremble once more.

'Ah. Well . . . '

'DADDY SAID GRANMA MAKE CAKES,' announced Agot, as if the thought had just suddenly struck her. She looked at Flora craftily. 'I YIKE CAKES.'

'Have you been hanging out with your Uncle Hamish?' said Flora.

And then she thought of her mother's light lemon cakes, her tiny little fairy cakes, and the heavy fruit cake always sitting on the shelf in the larder.

She wondered, suddenly, if there was a recipe in her mother's book.

'We could go and have a look,' she said, and beaming, Agot jumped up and grabbed her hand in a way Flora found unexpectedly gratifying.

There were, of course, several cake recipes at the end of the book. Birthdays and Christmas and many happy things. Thinking of Eilidh's fairly strict boxes of raisins and dried fruit that she'd provided in the rucksack, Flora decided that filling Agot up with sugar might be mildly taking the piss. But here was something she hadn't made for a long time. And she already had the ingredients. She smiled to see it. Scones. That was it.

Her mother had circled a note at the top of the page: *HOT OVEN COLD BUTTER*.

'WHA'S THAT SAY?' said Agot, who had pulled over a chair from the kitchen table, dragging it noisily across the flagstones. Bramble huffed as if aggrieved.

'It says "hot oven cold butter",' said Flora. 'Because that is what you need when you're making scones.'

Agot's face brightened. 'I YIKE SCONES. MAKE SCONES!'

Everything Agot said, Flora noticed, was short, emphatic and announced at high volume. Flora looked at the little girl's contented face and wondered why she herself wasn't clearer like that. Clearer in her job, with her family; with what she wanted.

'Hmm, okay.'

She turned up the oven, cleaned Agot's sticky hands, then set her to work mixing the flour, milk and chilly butter.

A thought struck her. She didn't know why it hadn't occurred to her before. She wondered if the boys had got to it first.

She went into the larder, the cold store off the main kitchen. The boys didn't seem to use it much. There were endless tins of beans and fruit – when her mother was young, it was difficult and expensive to get fresh fruit on the island. Annie had loved tinned mandarins, and peaches and pears. When fresh fruit finally did turn up on a regular basis, she always professed herself disappointed with it compared to the syrupy contents of the cans she absolutely adored – and here they still were.

And up on the higher shelves – yes! Treasure, glowing in the light coming through the tiny dormer window. Pink, deepest purple, bright red. Damson. Strawberry. Blackberry. Cloudberry. It was like discovering an entire seam of her mother.

Looking at the jars, Flora realised that that was it. The very last of the jam; the very last of her mother in those little misshapen bottles, touched by her hands. Much of it had been given away to friends and neighbours, but some had been kept to get them through the winter. A winter she hadn't seen.

Flora sat down suddenly and started to weep.

'WHA'S WRONG?' Tiny sticky hands were grabbing

at her, concernedly lifting her hair from her face. 'YOU CRYING?'

'No,' said Flora.

'ISS,' said Agot, in the manner of one who was very experienced at spotting crying. 'YOU CRYING.'

She paused for two seconds.

'BETTER NOW?'

Flora found herself half smiling and rubbed her face fiercely.

'Yes,' she said. 'Yes, I am.' She blinked.

'I YIKE JAM,' announced Agot cheerfully. And Flora thought about it, and looked up at the field of wild raspberry, and thought, well, there was no point in leaving it, after all, and removed a jar, wiping the dust off the top lightly with her finger.

The scones in Agot's paws were rather lumpy. Flora, on the other hand, had forgotten the simple pleasure of shaping things and the feel of the dough in her hands, and she cut them out with the little shaped cutter and lined them up neatly on the buttered tray.

'SCONES!' shouted Agot loudly as Innes came in from the fields for lunch.

'Oh great!' he said instinctively, then recoiled slightly as she insisted that he try one of her slightly charred offerings. Flora's, in contrast, were absolutely perfect, and she felt ridiculously proud of herself. Innes even looked at her with a bit of respect in his eye.

'Can I have one of each?' he asked tactfully.

The scones were still warm, and the butter melted on them beautifully, and then came the glistening jam.

It was, Flora knew, just jam. But with its deep sweetness, the slightly tart edge of the raspberries, came memories of her mother, standing right there, stirring frantically, her face pink with the heat, warning them off if they got too close to the boiling sugar. Jam day was always an exciting rush; a prolonged wait for them to be allowed to try the very first batch, spread on freshly baked bread, with melting butter from the dairy. A jeely piece, her father had called it, and Flora had eaten it every day, coming home from school up the dark track, the evenings getting shorter and shorter until it felt like they were living in the night all the time; but always, when she came in, there it was: that fresh bread smell and the sweetly spreading jam.

Without speaking, Flora watched Innes go through exactly the same process. He lifted the scone to his lips, but before he took a bite, he breathed in the scent of it and, briefly, closed his eyes. Flora flicked her gaze away, embarrassed that she'd caught him in a moment so personal, one that he clearly hadn't expected to be witnessed. There was a pause. Then he bit into the scone.

'Oi, sis,' he said. 'I think you could probably sell some of these down at the caff.'

'Shut up,' said Flora, but she was smiling.

Agot, meanwhile had taken full advantage of their distracted attention to wolf down three of the scones – not, Flora noticed, her own. Then she pulled her father down to her level, with a look of something very important to impart.

'DADDY!' she whispered loudly.

'What is it, small fry?' he said, crouching down on his hefty haunches.

'I YIKE FLORA!'

Flora found herself grinning.

'AND!' she went on, sticky fingers grabbing at her father's arm. 'AND JAM!'

'Well, yes,' said Innes. 'So you should. Your grandma made this jam.'

'GRANDJAM!' said Agot, and they both smiled at that.

'Where's Fintan?' said Flora.

Innes shrugged.

'Dairy, probably. Hides out there all the time these days. Don't know what he's doing in there. Nothing good.'

'Do you think I should take him a scone?'

Innes smiled ruefully.

'Peace offering?'

'Is it that obvious?' said Flora. 'Why is he so down on me all the time?'

Innes shrugged.

'It's not just you. He's down on all of us, haven't you noticed?'

He looked at the cooling tray of scones.

'Better leave nine for Hamish.'

She made up another couple, and some fresh tea, and headed out, leaving Agot chattering into Innes' patient ear. Bramble, she noticed, got up too, and followed her slowly. She scratched his head and resisted the urge to stick her tongue out at Innes. This dog was fond of her, and that was that.

She crossed the open courtyard, through which chickens and ducks roamed. Flora wasn't fond of the chickens, even though everyone loved their eggs. There was something about their beady eyes; the way they ganged up on the ducks and stole their corn, and triumphantly – and, Flora thought, on purpose – pooed on the farmhouse steps. Occasionally she'd come in the house and find one unexpectedly on the sofa, which caused quite a lot of kerfuffle. Bramble, as useless at guard-dogging as at basically everything, kept very quiet when the chickens arrived, otherwise they attempted to peck at him and chivvy him about. They were very bossy chickens.

'Move,' she said to them as they eyed her suspiciously. 'Come on, out the way.'

'DON'T KICK CHOOKS!' came a voice behind her.

She turned round. Agot was standing there, looking at her severely.

'YOU DON'T GET NICE EGGS IF YOU KICK CHOOKS,' she said, in a voice that indicated that she had personal experience of this.

'You're right,' said Flora. 'You shouldn't kick chooks.'

Agot beamed, happy to have been correct in her analysis, and Flora continued on her way.

The dairy was on the right coming out of the house, slightly raised to make it easier to sluice and for the truck to get in and park. Compared to the flat grey elegance of the farmhouse, it was a rather more basic building, with corrugated-iron sides and long lines of machines.

To the side of the dairy was the wet room, where her mother used to spin butter; they had also occasionally hired a dairymaid to supplement their income in the winter months. Flora hadn't been in it since she'd got back. It had a heavy smell, and chill winds blew in through the gap between the shed and the ground. She hadn't liked it as a child either; it was so cold and odd, even though she loved the butter as much as anyone else.

She knocked at the door, feeling as she did so how strange that was; it was barely a door at all, just a bit of iron knocked up on hinges.

'Fintan?'

Her voice echoed around the dairy. It was empty of cows, of course, done for the morning, then a lad from town sorted them out in the evening. Their essence remained, but Flora, after wrinkling her nose constantly for the first day or so, had finally ceased to notice it, or if she did, she found the warm scent oddly comforting.

There was a pause. Then a suspicious 'Aye?'

Flora rolled her eyes.

'Fintan, it's obviously me,' she said. 'I brought you something. If you like.'

The wet-room door was pulled open a tiny crack. Fintan was wearing a large old sweater covered in holes. His hair was getting seriously long now; it was a bit ridiculous. And his beard was equally unkempt.

'What?'

Cold air came out through the gap.

'It's freezing in here,' said Flora. The contrast to the suntrap courtyard was absolutely noticeable.

'Yeah, it has to be,' said Fintan. 'Don't worry, it's a farm thing, you wouldn't understand.'

He went to shut the door.

'Fintan. Please,' said Flora.

He glanced down at the tray she was carrying. She'd put the jam pot next to the plate.

'Is that . . . ?'

'I didn't think she'd mind.'

'It hasn't gone off?'

'No,' said Flora. 'She was brilliant at making jam.'

'She was brilliant at lots of things,' said Fintan.

There was a pause.

Then he sighed and relented, opening the door.

'Well then,' he said, trying to sound casual. 'Want to come in?' He looked at the jam again.

'I'm amazed you didn't all guzzle it before,' said Flora.

'I know. It . . . it felt wrong, somehow. To eat the only things we had left of her.'

Flora paused.

'I think she'd have wanted us to eat it.'

Fintan nodded.

'Yes. I suppose she probably would.'

'Agot definitely thinks we should eat it.'

'Well if *Agot* thinks so . . . '

He smiled, took a scone and ate a large mouthful. Then he paused.

'That's exactly how she used to make them.'

'Well, I used her recipe.'

He snapped up another scone in one bite. His face contorted for a moment.

'Amazing. Weird. Amazing.'

Flora handed over the plate and the cup of tea. She glanced around.

'What are you doing in here anyway?'

There was a pause.

'Oh, well . . . '

'You don't have to tell me,' said Flora.

'No, I want to but . . . don't tell Dad and Hamish and Innes.'

'Why not?'

'I don't know. They'd laugh at me.'

'That would make a change from everyone just laughing at me the entire time.'

'That's true. So maybe I won't tell you.'

'No! Tell me! What is it?'

Fintan beckoned her in, then closed the door behind them as if expecting to be overheard.

'I was just experimenting,' he said.

'What with?'

'Well, with . . . Sit down.'

Confused, Flora did as she was told.

'Right,' he said. 'You're to try this and tell me what you think.'

The room had a huge deep sink, metal surfaces and a hose; it had to be kept spotlessly clean at all times due to the possibility of bacteria entering the milk. Fintan disappeared into a corner and returned with a huge cloth-covered circle; as Flora focused, she saw that there were several of these sitting on the shelves.

He unwrapped it very carefully, as if undressing a baby. Inside was a huge, soft-looking cheese. Flora looked at him, her eyebrows raised, but he wasn't paying any attention to her whatsoever. He took a tiny sharp knife and nicked a sliver off the wheel, proffering it to her.

'Seriously?' said Flora. 'You made this?'

'Just try it.'

'Just try it? You get cheese wrong, you could kill me.'

'I'm not going to kill you.'

'I'm not saying you'd do it on purpose.'

'Look,' he said. 'I've eaten loads. I've been working on this stuff for years.'

'Years?'

'Yes. It's been . . . kind of a hobby.'

'*Years?*'

'Just try it, will you?'

Flora took the knife, then, not entirely trusting herself, picked up the cheese with her fingers and popped it into her mouth.

It was one of the most exquisite things she had ever tasted. It had the sharp bite of an aged Cheddar, but a softer creaminess, more like blue cheese, with a huge depth of flavour behind it.

It was astonishing.

She blinked.

'Oh my God,' she said. Then she handed back the knife. 'Give me some more.'

Slowly, a huge grin crossed Fintan's face.

'Seriously? You like it.'

'*Seriously!* It's amazing.'

Fintan shot a worried look at the door.

'Don't tell them,' he said. 'I mean it. Please. Don't.'

'Why not?' She looked around. 'There's loads of it. How long exactly have you been doing this?'

He shrugged.

'Oh, you know. I just ... I just needed to get away when ... you know.'

Flora did know. When their mother had gone into hospital and, really, never come home again.

'Well, are you going to do something with it?'

'I don't ... All Innes cares about is money.'

'Well, it's his job to.'

'And Dad complains that I'm work-shy.'

'Do they really not know what you're doing?'

'They don't care, do they? It's just Funny Fintan, doing his thing.'

He sighed. Flora looked at him.

'Families aren't easy,' she said.

'No,' said Fintan. 'They fricking aren't.'

'You can swear in front of me,' said Flora, almost laughing.

'Oh, is swearing cool in London, then?'

Flora looked longingly at the cheese.

'Let me have a little more?'

Fintan half smiled.

'Really?'

'Yeah! I want Agot to try it. Does it melt?'

'Should do, it's a hard cheese that tastes soft.'

Flora picked up a hunk.

'I'll say I bought it in London.'

'Then they'll never try it.'

Flora turned on the grill and heated the cheese up on top of the bread until its edges had turned a delicious aromatic brown with a slight crust, and the pale yellow middle was bubbling. The bread was fresh and just a little scorched round the edges, and Flora ground some black pepper on the top and passed it to Agot, who wolfed the whole thing as soon as it was cool enough to eat.

'YUM!' she said, rubbing her tummy approvingly. 'THA'S GOOD.'

Flora smiled, pleased. It was fun, feeding other people. Everyone ate their fill, and she exchanged smiles with Fintan at how appreciative they all were, even for something as simple as toasted cheese, and for once, the evening was calm.

Chapter Eighteen

'This is total and utter BS.' Joel was grouching around the office and Margo was trying to placate him again, without much success. 'Why hasn't he seen her already?'

Margo shrugged. 'Busy. Or just thinks she's too junior.'

'She's not too junior to be kicking about there on holiday at his expense. This could be a big client for us and she's listening to local gossip . . . doing God knows what.' He grimaced. 'Oh God. I'm going to have to go. How the hell do I get to this godforsaken place anyway?'

'You can take the train overnight, then a ferry . . . '

'Screw that. Seriously. You can't fly?'

Which is how, furiously, Joel found himself on the tiny prop plane taking off from Inverness with a handful of birdwatchers and oil men, staring out of the window at a white sky and feeling entirely frustrated at the whole ridiculous business.

He disliked the sucking-up-to-clients part of his job, especially for something so trivial. He liked the cut and thrust of the courtroom; he thrived on the tense all-nighters that made his staff miserable; the tough negotiating and, above all, winning.

He looked down. Whoever knew this tiny country could go on so long? They were flying over endless sea. It had been vastly colder than London as he'd walked across the tarmac and boarded the little twelve-seater Loganair plane. He was going to turn this around, do the charming thing, which he didn't enjoy, set the girl in the right direction then get back to London as soon as he could. She'd sounded absolutely startled to hear from him that morning. Had probably forgotten how to work already.

The sun broke through the clouds as they started to circle down towards Mure, the fishing trawlers plashing out across the wide blue waters; but Joel was deeply engrossed in briefs for other jobs, and saw nothing until they landed in front of the unprepossessing shed that passed for an airport, bumping and jolting along the ground.

After the calm evening, Flora had been unutterably panicked by the phone call. She'd expected to hear from Colton's office; she'd expected to hear from Margo, snootily asking her why the hell she wasn't getting more work done. Kai had suggested it might happen, but when she'd seen the unfamiliar number come up on her handset, she hadn't been thinking much at all.

Stuttering good morning, she'd caught sight of herself in

the mirror above the old dressing table in her little room. Surrounding it were the rosettes from her Highland dancing. Her mother had carefully kept them all; them and the cups. She'd shaken her head, half embarrassed, half pleased.

Her hair was sticking out at all angles. It was 8 a.m.; she couldn't remember the last time she'd slept this late. It was all this fresh air; it was knocking her out. It was only since she'd got back that she'd realised how sleep-deprived she actually was. It felt like she was catching up on years of light London sleep, always half awake, waiting to hear burglars, or returning flatmates, or police helicopters, car chases, neighbourhood parties.

Here, apart from the occasional barking seal and scuttling wildlife, there was nothing, nothing at all; just fresh air and the distant lulling of the waves if you really listened hard, and she had been completely and utterly knocked out every night.

'Did I wake you?' said the dry, laconic voice, and Flora had leapt up as if he could see her.

'Um, hi, Mr Binder.'

'Joel is fine.'

'Um, I'm just . . . I'm waiting. I've been making calls but I keep getting put off and I'm not sure whether I should stay here or . . . I mean, I've been keeping on top of my paperwork.'

This was a stone-cold lie, and Flora wondered if he could tell over the phone line that she was blushing. She cursed herself. Bramble woofed encouragingly from next door and she could hear Hamish hollering and looking for his shoes. This place was a madhouse.

'I'm arriving today.'

At first Flora didn't understand what he was saying. It was noisy and confused and seemed so very unlikely.

'You're what?'

Joel sighed with frustration. 'I'll get Margo to send you the details. You haven't seen him at all? I thought it was small where you are.'

'No,' she said. 'Nobody sees him, as far as I can tell.'

'What else do you know about him? Have you spoken to everyone? Don't tell them what you're doing.'

'I don't know what I'm doing.'

There was a pause, and Flora swore to herself for saying something so stupid. He let out a weary sigh.

'I'll get Margo to send you the flight details.'

There was only one flight a day, but Flora didn't bother pointing that out. Nervously, she headed to the kitchen. Maybe she could dig out another recipe . . . make something to calm herself down.

Flora made the five-minute drive to the airport in the farm Land Rover. She hadn't driven in so long, she had to refamiliarise herself with the heavy gears. Also, policing was light on Mure, always had been. Nobody was ever terribly concerned about kids driving without a licence at fourteen or so; they were needed to help out on the farms and that was that. As a result, Flora had more or less bumped through her driving test with a very distracted examiner in Fort William, and then proceeded not to drive at all for ten years. It was a challenge, to say the least.

'Where's he staying, this posh boss of yours?' Fintan had asked as she left, genuinely interested. 'You're not bringing him here, are you?'

Flora spluttered.

'Ha! No.'

The idea of Joel walking through the door in his hand-made suit and leather shoes was completely mad. She couldn't even imagine it; it would be like two worlds colliding, then instantly vaporising in a cloud of dust.

'Is the Rock not finished?' she asked.

Fintan frowned.

'No. It's been a disgrace. He's used no local workers at all, everything flown in. It's going to be an eyesore.'

The Rock was the fabled Colton Rogers hotel that was meant to be bringing investment to the island and providing jobs, and so far had done neither of those things.

'But he's still building it? He says it's nearly finished.'

'Well, it's been finished without us.'

Fintan looked at her.

'Are you defending a baddie, Flora?'

'You don't know much about the law,' said Flora.

Fintan tutted.

'Right, sorry, I forgot you London types know everything. Fuds.'

'Excuse me?'

Fintan shrugged.

'I said we need more suds. Soap powder.'

'FINTAN!'

And their temporary truce was broken.

Chapter Nineteen

At least it was a day that showed Mure at its very best. Clouds raced across the sky as if in a speeded-up film, and the wind blew fresh, but if you could find a calm corner, the sun popped in and out every two minutes so you could enjoy the changing light on the water and the streaks of gold across the hills. It was absolutely lovely, and still early enough in the season that they weren't overrun by Lycra-clad climbers, or concerned naturalists, or lost tourists.

Flora had put on one of her work suits, and the boys had teased and laughed at her. Sure enough, within ten seconds her tights were totally spattered with mud. She frowned.

'This place is ridiculous.'

'Dress properly,' said Fintan, who was wearing trousers that appeared to be tied with string.

Flora looked at him.

'It's the middle of the day. Shouldn't you be at work?'

He sighed and sagged a little.

'Yeah, yeah, all right.'

He headed off.

'AND STOP SAYING "FUDS"!' Flora yelled after him, but he didn't turn around.

Flora had noticed, once she'd done her hair in her old mirror – she'd tried to plug in her straighteners but had blown all the fuses and had lots of people shouting at her – that her skin, normally a little sallow from late nights and long days under fluorescent lighting, was looking pink and healthy; she had some colour in her cheeks where she was normally so pale. She added the mascara she used religiously, otherwise her eyelashes had no colour in them at all, and rubbed some lip gloss on, her heart beating anxiously. Kai had called earlier that morning.

'The big man's flying in!'

'I know!'

'The two of you. By yourselves.'

'Shut up.'

Flora was already quite nervous enough. Kai paused and lowered his voice.

'Look,' he said, even though he knew it was completely futile. 'Don't lose your head, okay? He's still your boss. He's not allowed to sleep with you. And if he did, it would only be because he was waiting for room service or something, okay?'

'*Kai!*'

'What? Come on, I'm just saying. He only dates really really hungry-looking women with spiky heels and yellow hair. They could all be the same woman, except he gets older and they stay twenty-two. I'm just saying, because you're away together ... don't do anything daft you'll hate yourself for. And if Human Resources get to hear about it ... I mean, you know what pricks they are.'

'That's because you slept with two people in HR.'

'And they were pricks about it!'

Flora sighed.

'Maybe,' she said. 'Maybe that would be okay, and if we had a one-night stand I'd get him out of my system and that would be fine.'

'*Flors!* How is that you? You don't do one-night stands! You don't do anything spontaneously! You've been considering dyeing your hair since I knew you. And I've known you for three years! Just dye your hair!'

'It could work!'

'The silver, probably not. Some marine blue, maybe ... '

'No, I mean me and Joel.'

'Listen to yourself!'

'What's stupid about it? I really fancy him, we sleep together, then I never think about it again.'

'That's not you.'

'Well, maybe you're very wrong about me.'

Kai paused, then sighed.

'Yeah. Maybe. How's everything else? Still awful?'

Flora was about to agree vociferously. Then she glanced up.

'Actually,' she said, looking out of the window as the sun caught on the fells. Bramble had limped over to the sunniest patch on the floor and was following it around the room.

She smiled.

'Ah, you know. What's it like down there?'

'Scorching. Everything smells of barbecues and bins.'

'That sounds great,' said Flora, glancing around. There was a windsurfer in the harbour, whipping across the waves, bouncing up and down, racing with the wind.

'Also,' said Kai triumphantly, 'how would you buy condoms? If Mure is as teeny-tiny as they say, it'd be all round the village in five seconds.'

'I think Joel probably carries them,' said Flora, feeling herself blush bright pink at the very idea.

Kai sighed.

'He probably does too. He probably gets a massive discount for bulk-buying them. To hold in all his skanky diseases!'

They both laughed.

'Honestly, nothing is going to happen,' said Flora. 'He has no idea who I am. He'll probably only stay half a day. And now I have to go and fetch him.'

'Good,' said Kai. 'Good. Flora, I know we joke about it, but ... It's not just that he's your boss. He's a wonderful lawyer. But I think he's cruel. I've seen him with clients. And you don't deserve that.'

But Flora was temporarily lost in a vision of his cruel lips crushed up against hers, and could only nod as she hung up.

She'd set off from the farm when she saw the little prop plane begin its descent, knowing that that would take exactly the right amount of time. It was making a bumpy landing as she jolted over the potholes on the old road. She imagined him walking off the plane; stopping short, realising he'd never really noticed the admin girl in the acquisitions department before; coming to a whole new conclusion about her as the scales fell from his eyes . . .

'Right, there you are.'

He was staring at his phone rather than her, trying to connect to something.

Even in a ridiculous tin shed at the end of the world, he looked like he'd just stepped off a private jet. It was hard to imagine him out of a suit, really; she'd never seen him dressed casually, not at the firm's Christmas party (which she hated; she'd spend hours getting ready, then hover near him as he socialised with the partners and flashed brief smiles at the crowd of support staff also all done up to the nines and also all trying to hover close to him, before he left after an hour or so to go somewhere more glamorous), not on Friday afternoons in the summer; never. She couldn't even imagine what he looked like with his tie loosened, although she wanted to, very much.

'The car's just there,' she said, hoping that she hadn't gone too pink.

Joel strode towards the Land Rover, the wind catching him slightly off guard as they left the airport building.

'Is it always this cold?' he said.

Flora hadn't thought it was the least bit cold. She must be adjusting, she realised. She shook her head.

'Oh no. It gets much much worse than this.'

Joel half nodded, then opened the door of the Land Rover and got in.

They both paused for a second. He'd got in on the driver's side.

Flora decided that the best thing under the circumstances, the circumstances being that he was her boss, was simply to go along with it, so she got in the other side.

It was very rare to see Joel flustered about anything.

'Um . . . I got in the wrong side,' he said.

'Yes,' said Flora.

'In the States . . . this is the passenger side.'

'Yes, but you live in the UK, don't you?'

There was a pause as Flora realised what they both already knew: he never sat in the front seat of a car. It was only because the Land Rover didn't have a back seat.

'You can drive if you like,' she said, smiling. Joel didn't smile; he clearly felt on the back foot.

'No, no,' he said.

'You can if you like,' said Flora, wondering how on earth they'd got themselves into this awkward situation.

Joel looked down, obviously feeling the same.

'I . . . This is a stick,' he said.

'A what?'

'A stick shift. I can't drive a stick shift.'

Flora suddenly wanted to giggle, but had a hideous feeling this wouldn't go down well at all. Some men were not very good at being laughed at, and Joel was definitely one of them. Instead she simply hopped out of the car, and they crossed round the boot without catching one another's eyes.

'So, you're going to the Harbour's Rest?' she said, once they were both ensconced and she'd jolted the car into reverse out of nerves.

'What?'

'Where you're staying.'

'Right. Yes. What's it like?'

Flora didn't answer straightaway.

'That good. Great! Perfect.'

They turned into the harbour. Joel made no comment on the pretty little houses, or the way the narrow street gave way to the huge wide sweep of white sand. Most people did. He was stabbing at his phone crossly, searching fruitlessly for a signal.

'Christ, how do you stand it?' he said.

Suddenly Flora felt incensed. It was an utterly glorious day. If you couldn't see that this place was amazing, then you were an idiot. It felt odd to be so defensive when, as everyone kept on pointing out, she hadn't been able to get away from it fast enough.

She couldn't help it; she glanced over towards him. His long legs were stretched out in the footwell, the expensive suit covering rock-hard thighs. This was ridiculous; she felt like a dirty old man.

She parked in front of the pale pink building next to the peeling black and white paint of the Harbour's Rest. It had once been a chemist, but the owner, who'd been an English incomer, had moved back down south to help her daughter with her new baby. Nobody had taken it over, and it sat there like a missing tooth in the harbour parade. It made Flora sad to see it.

Outside the Harbour's Rest, two old fishermen with big beards were pulling on pipes. They looked like east London hipsters. Flora hoped this was what Joel would think they were. Whether he'd think the sticky curly-patterned carpet was ironic was a different matter, though.

Inge-Britt, the lazy Icelandic manager, came to the door. She was wearing some kind of slip – it couldn't be her dressing gown, could it? Flora wouldn't put it past her. She got out of the car and Joel emerged with his expensive luggage. Inge-Britt smiled, showing her perfect teeth, when she saw him.

'Well, hello,' she said, raising her eyebrows.

'This is my boss checking in,' said Flora meaningfully. 'Joel Binder? Have you got his booking?'

Inge-Britt shrugged and looked at him with unveiled interest.

'I'm sure I'll squeeze him in somewhere.'

Joel, who wasn't paying attention, went to follow her in, before glancing round at Flora.

'Pick me up at two,' he said.

Flora shrugged and turned round to see Lorna on the other side of the road.

'I was just passing,' lied Lorna hopelessly. Flora rolled her eyes. Lorna watched Joel striding into the breakfast-scented interior of the Harbour's Rest.

'Well?'

'He's a very handsome man,' said Lorna. 'You'll have to keep him out of Inge-Britt's clutches.'

'She smells of bacon,' said Flora petulantly.

'Oh yeah, men hate that,' said Lorna.

Lorna came back to the farm for lunch. Flora sat her down, made tea and, to cheer herself up, decided to whip up a quick batch of oatcakes; heavy on the salt, with a perfect nutty crunch to them. They didn't take long to bake, and before they'd cooled, she topped them off with wedges of Fintan's cheese.

'*Jesus*,' said Lorna, as she took her first mouthful.

'I know,' said Flora.

'These oatcakes are sensational.'

'Thank you! And that's Fintan's cheese.'

But it was the combination with the perfect crunch of the immaculate little biscuits that made it something else.

'This almost makes up for not having had sex in ... humphy humph, a while,' said Lorna.

'Don't say that,' said Flora. 'You'll jinx us ever having it again.'

'I won't care if I can just eat this stuff all day,' said Lorna. 'Seriously. More. More. Yes. Yes. Yes.'

'Let's be clear, this isn't actually sex,' said Flora.

'Well, I'm putting nice things in my mouth, so it's definitely close,' said Lorna defensively, grabbing another two oatcakes with a combative look.

She stared down at the cheese.

'Fintan? Really?'

'He's been making cheese in his spare time. And other stuff, I think.'

'That boy just hates working on the farm.'

Flora blinked.

'Does he really? I thought he was just a bit of a lazy arse.'

'Totally.' Lorna looked at her. 'You can't say you hadn't noticed?'

Flora felt silent.

'Seriously?'

Flora shrugged.

'I thought he was fine.'

Lorna looked at her strangely.

'Flors, he's never had a girlfriend, he's patently depressed, he drinks too much . . . '

'That sounds like half the island,' said Flora nervously.

'Well it's amazing he's managed to make something like this,' said Lorna tactfully. 'So anyway, what are you all dolled up for?'

'I am actually at work,' said Flora. 'I do actually have a job.'

Lorna raised her eyebrows.

'Making oatcakes. Because I will say, you're good at it.'

Flora shook her head.

'We're . . . we're heading out to meet Mr Rogers after lunch.'

Lorna sniffed.

'Oh, *we* are, are *we*? By the way, Charlie was asking after you.'

'The gigantic Outward Adventures guy?'

'He's nice,' said Lorna. 'Have sex with him.'

'Is Jan his wife or what?' said Flora.

'What do you care? You're so in lurve with Joel . . . '

'Shut up!' said Flora. 'You are *so* not meeting him.'

Lorna blinked, and put her hand over Flora's suddenly.

'You do have it bad, don't you?'

'Yup.'

'Does it help?' she said in a softer voice. 'Thinking about him all the time rather than your mum?'

There was a pause.

'Can't I think about both?' said Flora. Then: 'Yes. It does.'

Lorna nodded.

'Good. But don't take it too far, okay?'

'You haven't even met him!'

'A sharky lawyer who only dates supermodels and hasn't noticed you for years and is up to defend some dodgy golf course owner?'

'Well, when you put it like that . . . '

'What do your friends say – the ones who actually have met him?'

'Yeah. More or less the same.'

'He sounds like a prince.' Lorna grinned. 'I'll see you later. Give me some of the oatcakes and cheese to take away. And while you're at it, some butter. Actually, can I just take all of it?'

Flora looked at her as she decanted the remains of lunch into her bag.

'How do I look?'

'More mascara. You have the selkie's curse.'

'There is a world out there where white eyelashes are considered to be the loveliest thing on God's earth,' sighed Flora. 'And people will sign up for really expensive white mascara.'

'Why would they have to?' said Lorna. 'They still make Tippex, don't they?'

Flora flicked the wand at her.

'Stop it! Stop it, you weird albino freak!'

'*Ginga!*'

Giggling slightly, Flora left the house and got back in the Land Rover. Bramble, now fully restored to walking duties, was lying in the front seat, basking in a patch of sunshine.

'Out,' said Flora, wondering if Joel liked dogs. Maybe she should take Bramble along. On the other hand, the prospect of him *not* liking dogs was just too dreadful to think about. She could fancy a tough guy; a bad guy even; someone who wasn't necessarily very nice.

But nobody could conceivably fancy someone who didn't like dogs. Best not to risk it. Plus: unprofessional, even though nobody from Mure ever went anywhere without their dog. She shooed Bramble out of the car.

Chapter Twenty

Ollie the vet passed her with a brief nod of the head as she parked up at the little harbour. Honestly. Why did everyone still treat her like a snooty southern mainlander who'd abandoned her homeland?

Joel was waiting for her outside the hotel. Flora had wondered if there was any chance he might have changed out of his suit – you could sometimes get a real shock when you saw someone in their civvies, she knew. A bloke could look fantastic in his work clothes, then you'd see him at something casually and he'd be wearing some gruesome three-quarter-length trousers that were meant for overgrown toddlers, and something nuts like a hoody or an earring or sandals over hairy toes, and suddenly everything that had previously been appealing about him would vanish completely. She'd hoped this would happen with Joel.

He was, however, still wearing his beautifully cut suit, although Flora noticed – she couldn't not; she felt like she was exquisitely attuned to everything he did – that he'd changed his shirt. He nodded to her brusquely then went back to his phone. He was very careful to get in the right side of the Land Rover. Flora wondered if she should have been more careful to brush the dog hairs off the seat.

'Sorry about the dog hairs,' she said, thinking she might be able to get to the bottom of the dog thing sooner rather than later, but he simply shrugged.

'Okay,' he said, leafing through the paperwork she'd prepared. 'Now to find out what the hell I've come four thousand miles for.'

Flora turned along the narrow track that led up to the north side of the island. At the top was the vast estate that belonged to Colton Rogers. People did wonder, as the winds swept down from the Arctic, why on earth, if you were an American multibillionaire, you would choose to come to this tiny outpost at the end of the world for your holidays rather than the Bahamas, the Canaries, Barbados, Miami or literally, some days, absolutely anywhere else. Of course, they said this to one another; if anyone not from Mure had said it, they'd have been shouted down in a chorus of nationalistic pride in five seconds flat.

'I mean,' Joel said. 'Nobody here really cares what people do on the islands, right? It's not like you don't have enough sea to look out on.'

Flora shrugged.

'Are you kidding? *And* they don't like change. And they're a bit suspicious of outsiders.'

Joel gave her a look.

'You make it sound like the Wicker Man.'

‘Wouldn’t say things like that around here.’

He sniffed and lapsed into silence.

‘It’s a nice place to grow up, though.’ Flora realised she was babbling to fill the silence. ‘Where did *you* grow up?’

He looked at her crossly, as if she’d stepped over a line.

‘Here and there,’ he said shortly, going back to his papers.

A lone strand of sunlight pierced the cloud at the top of the glen, and Flora looked up at Macbeth’s sheep, shorn for the summer, who were starting to wander down the hill, towards the shed. She could see young Macbeth now: Paul, who’d been in her class at school, a funny, lazy boy who was going to become a shepherd simply because he couldn’t think of anything better in life than looking after sheep, going to the pub in the evening with his da and all their mates, and marrying the prettiest girl he could meet at the monthly ceilidh, all of which he’d done in short order. Flora watched him striding from rock to rock, on the same earth his family had farmed for generations, his stride long and relaxed; doing something he was born to do, that he understood instinctively.

Her eyes were still on the hillside as she pulled the car to a halt at the large metal gates, then got out and pressed the intercom. A camera buzzed and whirred and looked down on her, and Flora realised, having never really thought about it, that she was quite excited to see inside Colton’s place. Nobody was ever invited there; there was a ghillie who looked after the land, but he was a taciturn type who didn’t mix, so there was no gossip to be had there either. There were rumours of celebrities and sports stars, but again, nothing had ever been confirmed.

The huge iron gates gradually began to pull apart. There was a long gravel driveway ahead that wound up through perfectly manicured trees. It didn't really look like Mure at all; immaculate flower beds lined the road, and the grass looked like it was trimmed with nail scissors.

The house had once been a great grey manse; a huge, forbidding place that had been built originally for the local vicar, who came from money. But the vicar hadn't been able to hack the long, dark winters, and his successor had been a bachelor who had much preferred the original lodgings next to the church, dark and chilly as they were; and now the vicar lived on the mainland and commuted, and the local doctor had the church quarters. And Colton Rogers had bought the manse, and was restoring the Rock on its land.

The house looked nothing like Flora remembered it from her childhood, when they'd peered at it through the gates and some of the braver boys had scampered up to explore it, or at least implied that they had. Then, it had been dark and forbidding. Now it looked like it had been peeled back to the bones. The windows, while still traditional, were brand new, no longer rotting in their sills, but gleaming. The stone had been sand-blasted and was a light, soft grey that fitted in beautifully with the soft environs of the garden. The gravel was pink and immaculately tidy; the huge front door a glossy black, while miniature topiary hedges lined the windowsills. It was one of the most beautiful houses Flora had ever seen.

'Wow,' she said. Joel looked unimpressed. Maybe it wasn't all that great to him.

Behind the house were outbuildings, including a huge, incredibly tempting swimming pool complex with a roof that could be pulled back on sunny days (Flora wondered if it was ever pulled back), and a vast number of fancy cars, including several Range Rovers, all polished to a shine. There didn't appear to be any dogs; probably dogs would make the perfect gardens untidy.

It was the strangest thing: everything looked like a large traditional house, but so much tidier and nicer. There were artfully displayed baskets of lavender, and an old stone well with a gleaming bucket. It felt like a Disney version of Mure – but here they were, on the island all right, with faintly ominous clouds swirling above them to back this up.

A little maid, who sounded foreign, and was actually wearing a black-and-white costume, answered the door. Flora was astounded – she'd never seen a maid on the island – but once again Joel didn't react. This must be, she figured, how rich people lived in America, never noticing this kind of thing happening, and completely okay with it. Well, perhaps it was okay, she thought, breathing in the warm, expensive, candle-scented air as they stepped into the spotless boot room, which had rows of green Hunter wellies in every conceivable size, right down to a baby's. Flora squinted at them, fascinated.

'Hi, hi!'

Out of the confines of the London office, Colton Rogers was still tall and rangy; he looked a little intimidating. He still had the air of the professional sportsman he'd once been, before taking his sports earnings and investing them in a bunch of start-ups in Silicon Valley, at least two of which had become wildly successful.

'Hey, Binder, good to see you again. I'd say thanks for

coming all this way, but I don't think visiting Mure is ever a hardship, is it?'

Joel made a non-committal noise. Flora wondered what his room at the Harbour's Rest was like. The nicest one was directly above the bar, which got increasingly noisy as the night drew on. She hoped he liked fiddle music. And very, very long songs about people who came from the sea.

'Flora, isn't it?'

'Hello, Mr Rogers.'

'Wanna take a look around?'

Flora almost said, 'Sure,' then remembered just in time that it wasn't up to her.

'We've got business to get to,' said Joel.

'Yeah, yeah, but I'm paying for this, right? I'm always paying for you fancy-schmancy lawyers. So I might as well enjoy myself while you bill me up the yazoo, am I right? Come on, I'll give you the tour,' said Colton.

He strode out past them into his yard full of shining vehicles, then chose, of all things, a quad bike.

'This is the way to get around,' he said. 'Right? Beats that awful London traffic.'

Flora perched on the back, holding her skirt down against the wind, and they set off around the property. Again, everywhere she found herself amazed by the amount of energy and work that had gone into – that was going into – taming the beautiful nature of Mure, and turning it into a neater, more precise version of itself. There was a hand-built trout stream, where they had widened the original burn, made it wend round the prettiest trees, added artificial waterfalls to help the salmon spawn, and stocked it with trout and salmon for fly fishermen to come and pick out of the glittering waters. It was beautfiul, but it felt a little to Flora like cheating.

'I get more business done over a bit of fishing than I do in three days of stuffy meetings in air-conditioned offices,' said Colton. 'I hate New York, don't you?'

This question was asked of both of them. Joel shrugged non-committally. Flora didn't know what to say; she'd never been there.

'Those scorching summers! Unbelievable. You can't breathe out there. Nobody can. I don't know why on earth you'd stay. And those winters! Freeze the breath out of you. Face it: the weather in New York is always terrible. Always.'

'And here's better?' said Joel mildly.

'Here! It's perfect! Never too hot! Breathe that air. Just breathe it.'

Obediently they breathed, Joel thinking crossly about money, Flora enjoying the fresh air but wondering why Colton appeared to think it all belonged to him.

'Where do you live?' he asked suddenly.

'Shoreditch,' said Joel. Flora tried not to roll her eyes.

'I was talking to her,' said Colton.

'MacKenzie Farm,' said Flora.

'Which one is that?'

'The one that goes down to the beach.'

'Oh yes. I know it. It's a beautiful spot.'

'Are you opening the Rock?'

'Trying.' Colton wrinkled his nose. 'I can't . . . My people don't want to work here. And getting stuff brought in . . . I'm not sure it's worth it.'

'Why can't local people work here?'

'Because you all move away,' said Colton, eyeing her coldly. 'You don't really live on Mackenzie Farm, do you?'

Flora flushed, and shook her head.

'How's it doing? Making a living?'

Flora thought uncomfortably back to what Innes had said about the books.

'But there's great produce here,' she offered.

'I don't see much of it. Most of your fish goes straight out the door. Turnips, if you like that kind of thing.'

'People do, done right,' said Flora. 'And there's seaweed. And cheese . . . '

'Cheese? Where?'

Flora bit her lip.

'And there are some great bakers on the island.'

Colton shrugged. 'Huh. Well, we were meant to be ready . . . I'll maybe give them a push.'

The quad bike bumped over several large open areas of wilderness, broken up by new forests. The young trees were host to hordes of deer, more than Flora had ever seen in one place. There were family groups, the little bobbing tails of the fawns, newly born in the spring, dancing up and down; and larger stags crashing through the undergrowth behind.

It was an awe-inspiring sight.

'You can hunt stag here?' said Joel, sounding genuinely interested for once.

'Stag. Grouse. Pheasant. Just keep away from the golden eagles.'

'You have eagles?'

'Yeah, and if I shoot one I get ceremonially burned to death, then arrested, then put in prison for a hundred years, then hung, drawn and quartered,' said Colton. He saw Flora's face. 'I don't *want* to catch an eagle, Jeez. Just joking. Have to be careful, that's all.'

'So you'll bring your clients over here?'

Flora could swear she saw dollar signs in Joel's eyes. He'd probably learn Gaelic if it would get him access to Colton's colleagues.

'I'll bring anyone over here,' said Colton. 'Anyone I like. No one who's going to ask me where the nearest Gucci store is.' He rolled his eyes.

'Where is it?' said Flora, interested. She hadn't expected to like Colton but was finding out that she did. And she'd hoped to like Joel but was finding out that she wasn't sure about that.

'Reykjavik,' said Colton. 'See, no distance at all if you take the jet, don't know what people moan about.'

They turned down a perfect sandy path – seriously, was someone up here raking it every morning? Flora supposed that when you were as rich as Colton, it was no hassle to have someone doing that. Where did all his staff come from, though? Did he keep them hermetically sealed in his basement? It was very odd.

And there it was.

Colton raised his arm.

'Look at this,' he said. 'Look at this. Nothing. Not a thing. Not a telegraph pole. Not a television aerial. Not a house or a skyscraper or a metro system or a bus stop or a power station or an advertising billboard. Not a sidewalk, not a rubbish bin. Nothing man-made at all. In every single direction.'

Except for the Rock.

It was undeniably beautiful. Flora knew it wasn't finished, and wasn't expecting much of an improvement on the little ruined croft that used to sit here. But as she stepped off the quad bike, she realised immediately that this was a long distance on from that.

She was genuinely amazed. She'd got used, she realised, to that swanky metropolitan outlook that there was really no point in going outside of London for anything, and that anyone north of the Watford Gap probably couldn't make you a cappuccino that wasn't out of a packet.

But this . . .

There was a little jetty at the front, lined with lanterns that would be lit up when the dark months came. An actual red carpet led up a rocky path. They moved round to the front of the building, and walked up a flight of stone steps so clean they appeared to have been hoovered.

The hotel itself was low, built of grey stone, the same colour as the landscape, as if designed to look like part of the earth. There were pale grey wooden doors and window frames, and gentle lighting at each window, even during the day, that made it look like the most welcoming place ever.

There were circling coos from birds, but apart from that the only sound was the light tinkling of gentle music. Flora raised her eyebrows.

'We can pick guests up from the harbour, see?' said Colton. 'Then nobody has to come past my house to get here. Plus you get to arrive by boat, which is, like, awesome and cool.'

To the side was a beautiful Japanese knot garden, with succulent plants that could survive the winter onslaughts while still giving off a heady scent. Next to it was a large herb garden with rows of lavender and mint. Flora found herself wishing she'd brought along a pair of nail scissors for clipping. And along the back was a walled vegetable garden, where she could just glimpse rows of cabbages and potatoes – she guessed everything grown there would be used in the hotel restaurant. Colton certainly had high ambitions.

The entire edifice was on the edge of a perfectly white beach, the sand bleached startlingly pale, like bone. It went on for what seemed like miles. Behind them were low gorse bushes leading back into the dunes. Ahead of them was nothing but sea, all the way to the North Pole. It seemed to Flora there was complete emptiness ahead of them; complete tranquility all around. She thought briefly how much Bramble would like it.

'Apart from the Rock itself, there is nothing man-made here at all,' continued Colton gravely, as if he was narrating a film trailer. 'Nothing at all. Do you have any idea how rare this is? How unlikely it is? Especially in this itty-bitty little country. But anywhere now. There are mobile phone masts in the desert. There are plastic bags strewn over the endless jungles of Africa. There are ads everywhere. All over the world. And this little piece of it – with the freshest air and the best water – this is mine, and I'm paying a lot to keep it this way. Perfect. Pristine. I'm not developing the Rock to get rich – I *am* rich. I'm developing it to be wonderful, and beautiful, and after I'm dead, I want to leave it to the people of Scotland ... and this is why you had to see it.'

Flora blinked.

'Why?'

'Because, just as we're ready to open it, they want to stick a big wind farm right out there. Whirring away. Right across the eyeline of anyone who comes here. Spoiling my view, but most importantly, spoiling everything that makes this place special.'

As if on cue, two sandpipers marched past, chittering to each other with their long pointed orange beaks, as if making an arrangement to have lunch, which perhaps they were.

'The uniqueness of this place, what makes it special – what will make it special to anyone who comes here – all gone, to fulfil some stupid targets on renewables. Which, by the way, don't even work; by the time you've used the fuel to make them and, Jesus Christ, to transport them out into the sea and put them down, that's like half an oil field right there. But if they must – if they absolutely must do it, to line some guy's pockets in Brussels or whatever – then they can take them a little further. Or round the headland. Or, hell, opposite your damn farm; it's hardly a beauty spot.'

'Thanks so much,' said Flora.

'I just want it off of here. Away. And that's what I need you guys for.'

'Normally we handle business mergers and acquisitions,' said Joel thoughtfully. He was looking at the landscape, Flora noticed, but not like he really got it. Not like he saw what it meant; more like he was measuring it up, in pounds and pence. 'I mean, Scottish planning ... it's different.'

'Yeah, but can you do it? I know you guys. I don't want to have to start talking to some self-satisfied prig in Edinburgh who spends a lot of money on stationery.'

Joel nodded.

'Who approves these things?'

'Town council,' said Flora automatically. 'They handle planning. Unless it's a massive problem, then I suppose Mure Council would decide.'

'Why won't they move it?'

Colton shrugged.

'I don't know. I don't know what they think of me round here, but I haven't had much support so far.'

Both men were suddenly looking at Flora.

'What?' said Flora, who didn't want to answer the question and had been looking out to sea because she thought she'd suddenly seen a seal's head pop up. She looked again; yes, there it was, its whiskers glinting in the sun. She wanted to nudge Joel to show him, but obviously it would be completely inappropriate.

'What do they think of Colton on the island?' prompted Joel, looking annoyed that she hadn't been paying attention.

'Oh . . . ' Flora wasn't sure what to do here: tell the truth or flatter the client. 'Well . . . they don't see you around that much,' she said, adding diplomatically, 'You know, you're not here that often.'

Colton frowned.

'But I bring a lot of money to this island.'

There was a pause.

'With respect,' began Flora. Joel shot her a warning glance, but she figured there wasn't a lot of point in beating around the bush. The locals weren't going to come out and support him, and that was that. 'You don't . . . I mean, you bring your own people in, and you don't shop in the village.'

'That's because the produce is—'

'I'm just saying,' said Flora. 'You don't drink in the pub.'

'Why would I do that?'

'I don't know,' said Flora. 'It's just something people do.'

'Why?'

'Why do pubs exist?'

Colton smiled.

'Okay, go on. How else am I failing Mure, apart from investing in it, building on it, protecting its flora and fauna . . . '

'You'll be shooting quite a lot of that.'

'Law firms are definitely getting quite bracing these days,' said Colton to Joel, who was watching without saying anything. Flora felt nervous, like she'd gone too far.

'Sorry,' she said.

'No, no,' said Joel. 'Actually, Colton, it's useful. To know where you stand when we're putting our strategy together.'

'What, that everybody hates me?'

'No!' said Flora. 'But nobody knows you.'

There was a pause, as the waves lapped quietly against the perfect sand.

'So I should go and make nice? So people will support me?'

'You could just make nice anyway,' said Flora, smiling slightly.

Colton smiled back.

'Yeah, yeah, all right . . . so speaks a lawyer.'

'I'm not—' began Flora, but Joel stopped her.

'What about an animal protection measure?' he said.

Flora shook her head.

'What?' said Joel.

'Island's too small,' she said. 'If you couldn't have a wind farm because of the wildlife, the protection zone would go all the way round. You couldn't put it anywhere.'

'Well, let's *not* put it anywhere,' said Colton.

'Then they'll build a nuclear power plant,' said Joel. 'Then you'll be sorry.'

'There he is,' said Flora, pointing.

'What?'

Colton and Joel followed her outstretched arm but couldn't work out what she meant at first.

'Look!' she said, surprised. 'Can't you see?'

The seal popped up with a surprised look on his smiling face, his whiskers trailing water.

'Well, look at that,' said Colton.

'Don't shoot it,' said Flora.

He rolled his eyes.

'No, ma'am. Well now, isn't he lovely?'

'He is,' said Flora.

Joel squinted.

'What is that, a sea lion?'

They both looked at him.

'You've spent too long with sharks in suits,' said Colton. He looked at Flora. 'I notice it was you who spotted it.'

Flora blinked impatiently.

'I can see why there's that old legend.'

'What old legend?' said Joel.

'Seal people,' said Colton. 'They believe that stuff up here. Seals that turn into humans. They get married sometimes, but they always go back to the sea in the end. Are you one? Is that your cousin?'

Flora desperately tried to smile, but couldn't.

'Don't they have your colouring?' said Colton.

She suddenly flashbacked to the funeral, that awful, awful day, and was filled with a terrifying sense that she might cry.

'Hmm,' she said.

Joel looked at her. Her pale face was distraught. On the white beach, with the green sea behind her that exactly matched the colour of her eyes, he saw, suddenly, that what looked colourless in the city was right at home here. He changed the subject.

'So, what's the answer?'

'Further out,' said Flora promptly, grabbing her way back to the conversation. 'Somewhere you can't see it. They could put it behind Benbecula; that's uninhabited apart from the birds. You have to tow the turbines out anyway; that's your cost. Moving them a bit further ... I can't see how that can matter. And the birds won't mind.'

'They'll probably like it,' said Colton. 'Something new to shit on.'

'So there's a solution,' said Flora. 'It's basically a PR job now.'

Joel shot her a sharp look.

'That we could also totally handle for you,' she continued smoothly.

'Okay, where would you start?' said Colton.

Flora smiled at him. 'Councillors.'

Something struck her.

'Oh,' she said.

'What?'

'I might have a … a bit of a conflict. My dad's on the council.'

'This is excellent news.'

Flora shrugged.

'I'm not sure he's your biggest fan.'

'Seriously? Am I going to have to charm-offensive everyone?'

'Couldn't hurt.'

'It can hurt me!' said Colton. 'This is meant to be my haven of peace and tranquillity! I don't want to have to spend every minute of the day chatting up old drunks I can't understand. No offence to your father.'

'Ahem,' said Flora.

'Who else is on the council?' Joel said. And they wrote down the list: Maggie Buchanan, old Mrs Kennedy, Fraser Mathieson. Not a group naturally in favour of radical change. Which might work, Colton pointed out, if you didn't want a wind farm on your doorstep. And might not if it would bring cheaper electricity to the residents.

'Well,' said Joel as they headed back. 'You guys know what you're doing. I'll get back to London and you can keep me abreast of any developments.'

'Hang on,' said Colton. 'I want you here to help me draw up the new proposals. People will want to see a real lawyer, and that I'm serious about this.'

'Won't she do?' said Joel. Flora glanced at him, alarmed, and he had the grace to look slightly shamefaced about it.

‘We’re going to make an impression,’ said Colton. ‘Get on the ground tomorrow, ask around, then we’ll meet and have dinner. You can bring someone local if you like,’ he said to Flora. ‘We might as well get started.’

Chapter Twenty-one

Flora backed the Land Rover out carefully, anxious not to touch any of Colton's priceless cars. Joel sat beside her, making notes.

'Well done,' he said, and she glanced at him, surprised. 'He took to you. Now you have to get the rest of the place on your side. God knows why I have to be here.'

'So he's got a real lawyer?'

'A real lawyer with a lot of work to get on with.' He turned to her. 'But if this works out … he could bring the most tremendous amount of business our way. So.'

'So don't mess it up!'

He looked at her, his lips twitching slightly.

'Is that what I sound like?'

'What? No!' said Flora, panicked.

'You sounded like you were finishing my sentence for me.'

'So I remember not to mess it up,' said Flora quickly.

'Hmm,' said Joel, looking at her. 'Uh, good, I guess.'

Flora tackled Maggie Buchanan first. She lived alone in one of the big houses along by the vicarage, and had always seemed rather grand to Flora.

'Ah, the wanderer returns,' she said as she answered the door, dressed neatly in a jumper, scarf and waxed jacket. Two or three dogs pottered around her heels.

'Hello, Mrs Buchanan.'

Flora felt as if she was about to ask the woman to sponsor her for a charity fun run, and didn't feel massively better when Maggie didn't invite her in.

'So. You're a city girl now.' There was disapproval in every word.

'Hmm.'

Awkwardly, Flora explained the situation.

'Oh, right, you're working for the American.' She said 'the American' as if referring to Donald Trump.

'He wants to do things right up here,' said Flora. 'Make things nice.'

'Well he can start by filling in that awful gap along the harbour.'

'What do you mean?'

'The pink shop. The empty one. He bought it and hasn't done anything with it. He's just going to buy up everything on this island and turn it into his personal theme park, and I'm not having it.'

'Okay,' said Flora, making a note. 'I'm sure I can talk to him about that.'

'Are you?' Maggie regarded her over her spectacles. 'Well,

good luck with that. But that wind farm could bring a lot of money to Mure. And we don't see much of his.'

Mrs Kennedy wasn't much better, and she also had a lot to say about Flora's dancing, or lack thereof. Flora listened to her to be polite and ended up half promising to look out her old dance outfit again, though if it fitted her, it would be an absolute miracle.

Disheartened, she headed to the shop to pick up something for dinner – she found, to her surprise, that she was looking forward to cooking – and practically ran headlong into a large figure who was counting out sausages into his basket.

'Hello!' he said cheerfully when he saw her. It was Charlie, the genial Outward Adventures host. Flora found herself thinking how few men in London looked like him. Outdoorsy. Healthy. Not as if they spent too long under strip lighting, and inside windowless bars.

'Where's your dog?' he said, frowning. 'How's he doing?'

'He's doing fine, thanks,' said Flora. 'Where are all your little shadows?'

'Oh, that lot are done,' he said. 'They've had their time. Back home again. It's businessmen next week. That's why I'm buying the posh sausages.' His voice sounded glum.

'You don't like them so much?'

'The team-builders? Neh. They moan all the time and are weirdly competitive with each other, then they get drunk and get off with each other and treat it like a party.'

'Can't it be a party? Or is wet and miserable the point?'

'They don't take it seriously, so they don't learn anything. They complain about the midges and never see the beauty of it. If I can get them to lift their heads out of their screens for ten minutes, I consider that a triumph.'

Flora thought of Joel, buried in his phone or his files.

'So why do you do it?'

'Because they're idiots who pay a fortune for it. And that pays for the lads.'

'Oh come on, you must teach them something.'

'I try,' said Charlie, his face softening a little. 'Sorry. It's just we sent the lads home this morning and I've been worrying about them. Some of them come from really tough backgrounds. I wish . . . sometimes I wish they didn't have to go home. One of them said that to me. How bad does your home have to be when you're twelve years old and you don't want your mother?'

They stood in silence for a minute.

'So. Probably why I'm not so cheered by the prospect of a dozen management accountants from Leicester who are turning up to form better inter-team disciplinary practices.'

He glanced into her basket.

'Sorry, ignore me, I'm banging on. What are you getting?'

'I'm not quite sure,' said Flora, looking down. She'd popped into the butcher's for some good stewing steak, and had added some flour, and was now reading from her mum's recipe book for whatever else she needed to make Yorkshire puddings. She wasn't sure, though, that mere ingredients would be enough to replicate the light, golden, puffy joy of her mother's Yorkshires.

‘It’s nice you’ve come back to look after your family,’ observed Charlie.

‘I haven’t!’ said Flora. ‘Honestly! I’m working. But doing a bit of cooking. They’re big boys. They should be looking after themselves. I just want to show them how.’

‘Well, whatever it is you’re here for . . . ’ he began, then pinkened a little, as if he’d said too much.

‘Actually, I’m trying to stop the wind farm.’

Charlie squinted.

‘Why?’

‘Because it’s ugly.’

‘Do you think? Have you not seen them all whirring around on a windy day? Harnessing all that lovely free energy? I think they’re beautiful.’

Flora glanced in his basket. There were oatcakes and Weetabix along with the sausages.

‘There’s a lot of brown in your shopping,’ she observed.

Charlie followed her gaze.

‘Next thing you’ll be telling me that oatcakes and Weetabix don’t go together.’

Flora smiled.

‘I mean . . . you could make a really good pie out of what *you* have,’ said Charlie.

She looked up at him.

‘Are you hoping I’ll ask you to dinner?’

‘Maybe I’ll just put the Weetabix between two oatcakes and bite in . . . ’

‘Can I change your mind about wind farms?’

‘No.’

Flora took a bottle of the deep-brewed local ale off the shelf.

'I could make a steak and ale pie,' she mused.

'I hate wind farms, and always have,' said Charlie.

Flora smiled.

'All right,' she said. 'I'm already cooking for a bunch of ingrates. I might as well get some compliments while I'm at it.'

Flora finished her shopping and Charlie carried it up the track to the farm for her.

'Do you live in a tent all the time?' wondered Flora as they walked along.

Charlie shook his head. There was an office on the other side of the island, he said, and he had a croft around there.

'So when it's raining, aren't you tempted to just go home?' she said in surprise. 'Seeing as you're nearly there?'

'For rain?' said Charlie. 'It's just a bit of rain – why would I?'

'Because it's yucky and disgusting?'

'Not as yucky and disgusting as a hot, sticky tent,' said Charlie. 'Neh, give me a bit of wind and fresh air any day.'

As he strode along, Flora admired his broad shoulders and the way he carried all the shopping as if it weighed nothing at all.

'I don't know how anybody can take the heat, I really don't.'

Flora thought again of sweltering London days when the air con wasn't really working and everyone was a bit begrimed and couldn't sleep and moaned about it; and the stink rose from the pavements.

'So where do you go on holiday?'

Charlie smiled.

'Och, anywhere with a few mountains. There's not enough to climb around here. Sometimes I'll go bag a few Monroes. I went to the Alps last year. Oh, Flora, it's beautiful up there.'

'You climbed the Alps?' said Flora, undeniably impressed.

'Um, one or two of them.'

'With Jan?'

'She's an excellent climber.'

She would be, thought Flora, looking at him to elaborate, which he did not do.

They arrived at the farmhouse.

'Hi, Innes!' Charlie waved.

'*Ciamar a tha-thu*, Teàrlach,' said Innes, who was bent over the books and pushed them away with relief when he saw them.

'No,' said Flora. 'Don't switch. It's boring and I can't remember any of it.'

'But he's from the Western Isles!'

'Exactly! He's a plum foreigner anyway. So.'

Charlie shrugged. 'I don't mind,' he said. 'Although I do prefer Teàrlach to Charlie. Just sounds more like me.'

Flora rolled her eyes.

'Well, you should have said that when we met!'

'I'm bored of spelling it.'

'What are you up to anyway?' said Innes. 'Where's your little line of waifs and strays?'

'Boatload of wankers turning up tomorrow,' said Charlie. 'So tonight I'm grabbing at straws.'

'Oh yeah, thank you so very much,' said Flora.

Innes leapt up.

'Beer?'

They all piled through into the kitchen, which, amazingly enough, the boys had cleared up from lunch. Flora blinked. Maybe it being tidy to begin with was going to make a difference. Or possibly it would last for twenty-four hours, then all fall apart again.

'I heard your boss is here,' said Innes. 'Why? To check up on you?'

Flora briefly coloured as she imagined what that might be like.

'Of course not,' she said. 'He's here to help Colton. We're fighting the wind farm.'

'The wind farm?' said Innes after a pause.

Flora nodded.

'He's called up expensive lawyers and got everyone scuttling about . . . for a *wind farm*?' Innes was shaking his head.

'What do you mean?'

'The problems . . . the things he could be doing. Improving local employment. Putting money back into the island instead of importing everything. Looking after his properties – that pink house has been empty—'

'Yeah, I know.'

'But instead he wants to bring businessmen up here to shoot pretty animals . . . Fuck's sake, Flora, he doesn't even get his milk from us.'

Flora blinked.

'Is that true?'

'Good luck finding anyone willing to go along with what

he wants. This island is under siege, for God's sake. Wind farms . . .'

Flora was starting to realise the size of the task ahead.

'Okay then.'

She propped up the recipe book and put Charlie on onion-chopping duty. Soon the aromatic smell of caramelising beef and garlic and onions filled the kitchen, steaming up the windows. She popped round to the back of the house and, to her absolute amazement, found, with the spring, a few of her mother's herbs still growing in their pots. She'd have thought the winter storms would have taken them long ago. She snipped some thyme happily into the pot.

Charlie made up a spinach salad to go with it. Oddly, she liked having someone else in the kitchen with her. They didn't get in each other's way, but instead moved around each other neatly as she passed him a knife or the grater, and by the time Fintan, Hamish and Eck came in from the fields, groaning and removing their boots, everything was ready, the top of the pie had puffed up into a great delicious golden bowl in the oven, and there was plenty of gravy. Hamish wore a broad grin as they all tucked in. Even her father ate, Flora noticed, rather than sitting staring into the fire as he usually did.

'That was great,' said Charlie eventually, as everyone scraped the very last bits of gravy off their plates.

'What's for pudding, Flora?' said Hamish, who'd had three helpings. Flora looked at Fintan. Then she grinned.

'Oh, okay,' she said.

She went into the larder and, with a flourish, brought out what she had put together that morning when she should have been working on her files but was too restless waiting for Joel.

Sitting there on the ancient cake plate was a beautiful, shining fruit cake.

'It hasn't steeped,' she warned. But the effect on the room was instantaneous. Everyone brightened up. Hamish grinned broadly. Flora caught Charlie's eye and realised he was staring straight at her, and she couldn't stop blushing.

'Are you sure you didn't know I was coming?' he said, grinning at her. Then, as she searched unsuccessfully for a knife, he took out a large Swiss army knife from his pocket and flicked open the biggest blade, handing it over with a flourishing bow. She smiled and started to cut huge slices.

'I like having Flora home,' said Hamish quietly as Innes went over to make the tea.

'You know what we need?' said Flora, looking straight at Fintan.

He shook his head.

'Naw.'

'You can't have fruit cake without a slice of—'

'Leave me out of it, Flora.'

'Leave you out of what?' said Innes.

Fintan glanced nervously at their father. Flora folded her arms and looked as if she was about to withhold cake. Fintan got up and went outside.

When he slipped back in, they cut slices of the cheese and served them up with the cake. The idea was that you took a bite of cake quickly followed by a bite of cheese and washed it all down with red wine. They didn't have any red wine, but tea was working equally well.

Charlie looked up appreciatively.

'Well,' he said, shaking his head. 'That is something else.'

Fintan smiled.

'Thanks.'

'Did you make it?'

Eck turned his head.

'Did you?'

Fintan shrugged.

'Ah, just something I've been looking at.'

'But it's . . . it's . . . '

'I just matured it next to some old whisky vats.'

Eck shook his head in consternation.

'Is that what you've been doing all this time? Instead of helping out in the fields?'

'Well, I wasn't at the cinema, if that's what you're getting at.'

There was silence, and Eck put the rest of his cheese down without tasting it.

Picking up on the tension, Charlie told a funny story about one of his awful Outward Adventures teams getting into a fight with a sheep, and Bramble came up and put her head on Flora's lap, and everyone had a glass of Eck's home-made wine, which was perilous stuff at the best of times, and Flora sat back near the Aga, listening to the happy voices, and felt, for the first time, almost content; even more so because Charlie was clearly enjoying himself too (she figured it had something to do with being indoors and not under canvas in a storm, whatever he said).

At eight o'clock he took his leave, even as the big old kettle was being boiled up once again.

'That was amazing,' he said. 'Are you that good at being a lawyer too?'

'What, rather than just chef and chief bottle-washer to an overgrown bunch of lads?' she said as she walked out with him to take Bramble down the hill. 'I hope so.'

'Don't talk like that,' said Charlie, rubbing Bramble on top of his head. 'There you go, lad. It's important what you're doing. Food. Bringing your family together. I almost saw your dad smile.'

Flora rolled her eyes.

'Not at me.'

'It's a skill. A gift. You should be proud of yourself. Anyone would want to do something as well as you can.'

'It's all from my mother really,' said Flora, feeling she didn't deserve this. 'She taught me.'

'She taught you very well. Hang on. Fintan!'

Fintan was crossing the courtyard, heading back to his beloved dairy.

'Yeah?' he said.

'I need a kilo of that cheese. For the catering. Can you sell me some? It's tremendous.'

Fintan coloured.

'Well, I don't know . . . I mean, it hasn't been passed by the cheese council or anything . . . '

'The cheese council?'

'To sell it. You need to make sure it won't poison anyone.'

'You just fed it to us.'

'Yeah, well, that's just us. I mean, if you've got clients and stuff . . . '

'You could leave yourself wide open,' said Flora

self-importantly. 'To a civil case. Maybe even criminal, seeing as we're just discussing that it could poison people.'

Charlie sniffed.

'I let them drink out of mountain streams filled with nineteen different types of cow piss,' he said. 'I reckon they can take a little unpasteurisation.'

In the end, Fintan agreed to sell it to him on the understanding that he'd make everyone eating it sign a waiver that Flora promised to draw up. Charlie nodded with an amused look on his face.

'Or,' he said, 'you could just get the cheese people round to okay it.'

Fintan looked confused, but Flora nodded.

'You should, Fintan.'

Flora and Bramble accompanied Charlie back to the gate.

They stood either side of it, and looked at each other. The wind had dropped, but the familiar pattern of dark clouds and bright sunshine lit up the side of the hill like an alien landscape. The heather pressed down quietly; the air tasted of spring. Charlie leaned down to scratch Bramble on the neck, which Bramble liked very much.

'So,' he said.

Flora looked up at him. He was so solid. Joel was tall, but he was fine-built; lithe. She groaned mentally. When would she stop comparing every other man in the universe to one annoying one? When she would get over her crush and start living in the real world?

Charlie's handsome, broad face was completely open,

but also calm. She could see how safe he must make his charges feel. When she was with him, she just … she felt like she was in the moment. Not worrying about the island or what people thought of her; not thinking about work, or missing her mum, or anything other than standing with this slow-talking, solid, comforting man. She smiled at him. He smiled back shyly.

'Well, it was good to run into you,' he said, just at the very second her phone, which could just about get a bar of connection out here, rang. She jumped and turned away.

'Flora.' There was no greeting. 'I'll need to see your notes and who you spoke to today. How the land lies. Can you get them over to me? First thing in the morning? I don't know how much longer I can stay here.'

'Of course,' said Flora. She looked up at Charlie, but the spell was broken. 'That was my boss. I have to—'

'I know, I know,' said Charlie. He smiled. 'Your real job.'

He turned to go.

'I'll see you in a week.'

'Unless it rains!' said Flora, grinning.

'Especially not if it rains.'

And she watched him walk, nimbly for such a big man, all the way down the track, raising his hand briefly in farewell, before she turned back to the farmhouse to shout at the boys to do the dishes.

Chapter Twenty-two

Dr Philippoussis was the closest Joel got to ... Well. Whatever. Joel often called him at antisocial hours; and he didn't bother to ring when he didn't have something on his mind. Dr Philippoussis was also, fortunately, about the only person on earth who could put up with this behaviour. He just wanted to know that the grave little boy he'd got to know as he'd bounced in and out of child services – and who had now become a serious, hugely successful high-flyer – was okay, or as more or less okay as anyone could be.

In his years as a professional child psychiatrist, Dr Philippoussis had seen many difficult things, and done his best not to think too much about his clients, beyond how he could help them professionally. But when it came to Joel, who had escaped – in such spectacular fashion – he found it hard not to think about him. Because, as he and his wife often reflected, they were the only people who did.

'Where are you?'

'God knows,' said Joel. 'Seriously, it's the end of the earth.'

He peered out of the window.

'It's ten o'clock at night, and it's broad daylight.'

'Yeah? That sounds awesome.'

'Well, it isn't. I can't sleep.'

'What are you doing instead? Work?'

'Sure,' said Joel, looking at the files on the rickety desk in his room.

'Can't you take a walk? Have a look round?'

'It's an island. There's nowhere to go, and it's a bullshit case, and . . . I dunno. I think I might be ready for another move.'

'You haven't . . . you haven't met anyone?'

'I've told you. I'm not . . . that's not what I'm about. Work helps me. Work is what I want to do.'

'There's a whole world out there, Joel.'

'Good. Well, I'll move to Singapore then. Sydney maybe. See some more of it.'

'Did you try any of those mindfulness exercises?'

Joel snorted.

'I'm not your worried well, Phil.'

Dr Philippoussis knew better than to try and fix Joel. He just needed to be there to pick up the phone.

'Okay, Joel. Marsha says hi.'

Joel nodded, then hung up and pulled his laptop towards him. He considered drawing the curtains, but there was nothing outside except the waves beating gently against the beach, patiently, for ever.

Chapter Twenty-three

Flora had now seen all six members of the island council except for her dad, who she was going to leave to Joel and Colton to tackle. None of it was particularly encouraging, although at least the heavy-set vicar had been kind to her and interested in what she was up to. Although that may also have been because she'd taken him a box of jam tarts she'd made that morning.

It was the oddest thing: it felt like now she'd begun, she couldn't stop. It was as if she'd shut that side of herself down when she'd moved, as surely as she'd suppressed every other bit of her old life. But the simple act of sifting flour; of chopping in butter and one-handedly cracking eggs actually made her feel closer to her mother, rather than giving her sad memories, and she wished she'd thought of it before.

Even with the vicar (possibly) won over, though, there was still some pretty bad news for Colton. And, she remembered, tonight they were having dinner. With Joel.

'What are you so cheerful about?' said Fintan, sitting in front of the fire back at the house, listening to her sing little island songs as she put together a seed cake. He didn't think she realised she was doing it. He remembered his mum doing it too.

'Come here, Fintan,' she said. 'You're going to have to step up when I go. You're obviously massively talented. Let me show you how to make a shepherd's pie.'

Fintan frowned.

'Oh, now it's my turn to get Mummy's tuition, is it?'

Flora turned round, surprised and cross.

'What do you mean?'

Fintan, who'd already had a bitter row that day with his father about wasting his time on this cheese nonsense, was in no mood to be conciliatory.

'It was always you, wasn't it? Always you that Mum had up at the stove. Sending us outside so you could have peace and quiet for your precious exams. Always special little Flora with her mum.'

The words stung, and tears sprang into Flora's eyes.

'What do you mean?'

'You hardly have to come back here, rubbing it in how much time she spent with you.'

'That is so unfair,' said Flora, utterly riled. '*So* unfair. For years everyone has been on at me to come back and do my "duty". And when I do, I get abuse for it.'

Fintan shrugged.

'Well, good for you. I don't need you to impart your

amazing secrets of fricking shepherd's pie.' He scowled. 'I can cook fine. I just didn't get to learn at Mum's knee, did I? Out you go, boys.'

He was mimicking their mother, and Flora wanted to hit him.

'What are you saying?'

'What do you think I'm saying? You were always her favourite. You're the one who got to go away and do whatever you liked. Oh no, Flora's school work is so important. Oh no, Flora needs new dancing shoes. Oh, Flora's off to university!'

The pain on his face was clear. Flora put down the knife she'd taken out for the carrots.

'You can't think that. She adored you.'

'She never saw past Innes and you.'

'Of course she did.'

There was a pause.

'Well, if she did, she never saw me.'

Flora moved forward.

'Oh, Fintan. I think she was just . . . She saw the life she had. And she didn't want it for me; she wanted me to get away, that's all.'

There was a horrible silence then, and Flora turned, knowing somehow without knowing that it was her father; that he had come home at exactly the wrong time and had heard what she'd said.

Her face went a deep pink.

'Dad! Dad. Hi! I was just . . . I was thinking about making a shepherd's pie with Fintan.'

Eck looked at both of them. His face was so tired.

'Neh, no need, lass,' he said quietly. 'Chippy will do us. Don't want to put you to the trouble.'

'It's no trouble!'

'Is that what you reckon?' he said. Then, with the entire kitchen still in silence, he picked up his newspaper and went and sat by the fire.

'Right,' said Flora, wiping her hands on a dishcloth and slamming the seed cake in the Aga. She couldn't make things any better; she was getting out before she made them much worse. 'I'm off.'

'Off where?' said Fintan sulkily.

'I'm going to the Rock. I'm having dinner with Colton Rogers.'

Fintan blinked.

'It's open?'

'Nearly. I think they're having a test run on us.'

'They've got a chef and everything? I've heard . . . I've heard it's amazing up there.'

'It's beautiful,' said Flora truthfully.

Fintan stood up.

'Take me,' he said.

'You're not invited,' said Flora.

'Oh yes, with your posh proper London people, isn't it? And Americans, of course. You'll all sit round and quaff champagne and giggle at the rubes who live here. The idiots, as you think of them.'

'Fintan! Stop it!'

He threw himself sulkily back into the chair.

'Don't worry about me! I'll just stay here by myself.'

Flora snapped.

‘Oh for Christ’s sake. Where are all your friends, Fintan? I mean, you’re young, you’re apparently not bad-looking. But you just sit in all the time looking at cheese and blaming me. What’s the matter with you?’

‘In case you hadn’t noticed,’ said Fintan, ‘my mum died?’

Eck was ignoring them both.

Flora moved towards her brother.

‘I know,’ she said quietly. ‘And that’s when I needed my friends more than ever.’

‘Well, mine all moved to the mainland,’ said Fintan. ‘But I couldn’t. Could I?’

There was a long pause.

‘If you like,’ Flora said eventually; Colton *had* said she could bring someone, ‘you could come tonight.’

It hardly made things all right. But she couldn’t leave him here, with their miserable father, the two of them staring at each other.

Fintan blinked.

‘What do you mean?’

‘You could come to dinner, if you like.’

‘Seriously? With Colton Rogers?’

‘With Colton Rogers. And my boss.’

Fintan didn’t care too much about her boss, but he perked up immediately.

‘You know he invented BlueFare?’

‘I do know that. Techie stuff. Blah blah blah. He invented everything.’

‘Wow,’ said Fintan.

He looked down at his clothes.

‘I’ve got nothing to wear.’

'You must have something.'

Fintan sighed.

'I've got my funeral suit.'

'Don't call it that,' said Flora. 'Call it your wedding suit. You bought it for Innes' wedding, didn't you?'

'Oh *God*, that travesty,' said Innes, banging through the door with Hamish, both completely oblivious to the atmosphere in the room. 'God, no. Call it a funeral suit, please.'

He looked at the stove.

'Ooh, fantastic, what is it tonight?'

'Actually, nothing,' said Flora. 'Me and Fintan are going out. Sorry.'

'Can we come?'

'Nope. But you can take the seed cake out in twenty-seven minutes.'

Chapter Twenty-four

Flora had changed into a sober black dress, which she'd looked at in the mirror and decided made her look utterly washed out, like a Victorian child ghost. She had nothing else, though; she'd have to find something to liven it up a bit.

In the back of the wardrobe was her mother's jewellery box. Her mother had never worn any jewellery apart from her wedding ring and one pair of tiny diamond stud earrings she put on at Christmas time, but Flora knew there were a couple of things in there she'd inherited – they were Flora's now, she supposed, although she'd probably rather they go to Agot. Mostly she didn't feel quite strong enough for her mother's things. She'd have to one day, she knew. Face up to the fact that once a person was gone, they didn't need the things that had surrounded and defined them.

Not yet, though. Surely not yet. Well. She'd start small and see how she got on.

It was just as she remembered from playing with it as a child. A bright peacock-feather brooch; blue and green feathers set in a dulling silver filigree, woven in and out. There was no such thing as a peacock on Mure, so heaven knows where it had come from originally: perhaps some wealthy distant relative in Edinburgh; or one of the cousins who had moved away to Newfoundland or Tennessee, wanting to show off their success.

Wherever it was from, it was beautiful. Her mother never wore it – she would have seen the colours as too flashy, and she thought it fragile too, and possibly valuable, although Flora didn't know about that. But what a shame, she thought now, gently lifting it out. What a shame to own something so very beautiful, and to have spent an entire lifetime keeping it for best; a best that never came.

Her mother and father would go to the town ceilidhs; everyone did, it was part of your job if you lived in Mure. Her father would line up with all the other farmers at the bar and drink local ale and talk about feed prices, while her mother, unusual-looking in lipstick, would stand with the other women. Flora couldn't remember her parents ever going out to dinner, doing anything just to spend time together. She had absolutely no memories of that ever happening at all. So there was never a reason, never an occasion quite good enough for the brooch.

She picked it up, looking in the mirror, and placed it on the top right-hand side of her dress.

At first she was worried it would look a little Highland chieftain, but as she inspected herself more closely, she saw that the green of the feathers made her eyes look greener;

the blue was just such a pretty colour that it drew the eye anyway, and the entire thing lifted the plain dress and made all the difference.

Smiling cheerfully, she headed into the sitting room. Her father hadn't moved.

'Dad, do you . . . do you mind if I borrow Mum's brooch?'

He barely glanced around, just waved his hand. Innes and Hamish were standing at the stove, looking confused.

'Come on, you two,' she said. 'Shepherd's pie. Here. I'll leave the recipe. Mince. Potatoes. Fintan's cheese. Nothing too tough.'

'Oh God, look at the pair of you,' said Innes. 'You look like the town parade. La-di-dah.'

'Shut up,' Fintan said.

'Don't listen to Innes,' said Flora. 'Why are you even listening to him? He's being a divot.'

'I'm not a divot!'

'You're being a divot, stop it.'

'You stop it!'

'Dad!' shouted Fintan. 'Everyone's having a go.'

'Tell Innes to stop being a divot,' said Flora sulkily.

'Everyone stop being a divot,' said Eck from behind his paper.

Innes stuck his tongue out at Flora.

'Right, we're out of here,' said Flora. 'Good luck with the shepherd's pie.'

Hamish turned round as she got to the door.

'You look nice, Flora,' he said.

'THANK YOU, HAMISH,' she replied loudly, to make the point.

Colton had said he'd send the boat to bring them round to the Rock. Flora was excited.

She and Fintan walked down to the harbour, enjoying the soft light on their backs, past the lush fields where the cows were lying, post-milking. Fintan looked smart in his suit, but nervous, which made Flora slightly irritated, because she didn't want to appear to be nervous too, even though she was; she felt the need to be playing the grown-up, in-control London employee.

The evening air was clear and fresh and tasted as clean as a cold glass of water. The sea was like a mill pond, reflecting a little stream of white cloud above it across the flat horizon. It was truly very beautiful. Flora felt smugly glad that Joel was visiting now and not in the depths of winter, when the rain swept in and out, to be caught up in a quick, dashing rainbow and a crack in the clouds before descending again. Not that he appeared to have noticed his surroundings at all. The weather could be so changeable, but tonight everything felt quiet and still, and there was a sense of absolute timelessness about the place as they turned into the high street and the same old coloured buildings sloped down towards the harbour wall. Flora counted them off as she used to as a child – purple for the baker's, yellow for the butcher's, orange for the doctor's, blue for fish and chips. Nothing in the pink house, not any more.

Bertie Cooper, who was running the boat, was standing by the dockside, his cap off, waiting politely. He thought Flora was absolutely tops, but felt too shy to ask her for a drink, especially if she was cavorting about with posh blokes from out of town, and Colton Rogers of all people. He sighed. Probably for the best.

'Hello,' he said shyly. 'You look nice.'

Flora smiled, which did make her look prettier. She realised as she did so how long it had been since she'd smiled properly; not business grins or consoling brave smiles when people asked how she was getting on, and not nights-out-with-Kai smiles, when she finally had enough wine to forget about everything that was going on. A proper, happy smile and the unusual sensation of having something to look forward to.

She had Snapchatted a selfie to her friends, just to make them horrified and amused on her behalf. Kai had got back saying that if she slept with Joel he would never speak to her again, ever. Lorna had asked, quite reasonably, if her boss had turned any nicer since he'd arrived, and by the way, if he looked like a moose nobody would ever let him get away with his behaviour. Flora smiled to herself yet again. There was, she'd come to realise, absolutely no chance that anything was going to happen between her and her taciturn, self-obsessed boss.

But that didn't take anything away from the fact that it was a beautiful evening. They were going to a proper grown-up restaurant. She was accompanied by a handsome man – okay, he was her brother, but who cared about that? – and it was going to be lovely. She stepped lightly into the boat with an unusual air of confidence about her. Perhaps it was the brooch.

Chapter Twenty-five

Flora enjoyed watching Fintan's reaction as they approached the Rock. It was even more impressive arriving by sea than by road. The idea of spoiling its idyllic outlook with vast metal structures did seem terribly wrong.

Although it was still light, the lanterns on the jetty were all lit, and Bertie helped her off the boat with a wide smile.

Joel and Colton were already in the bar, which was on the right as you entered the grand hall, a roaring fire in the grate although it was scarcely needed that evening, or so Flora and Fintan thought. Both of them were to go through their entire lives with no tolerance for heat at all; anything over twenty degrees tended to bring them out in a nervous rash. Blowy and fresh was their default setting.

Flora tried her best not to stutter, but she felt a telltale redness rise in her face. Joel had changed his shirt to a soft pale green cotton that contrasted perfectly with his large dark eyes. He smiled, looking at Fintan with interest, which made Flora feel even more wobbly. She knew Fintan was good-looking; the girls at school had always liked both her tall brothers. Innes had the smiling eyes and cheeky ways; Fintan the curly hair and melancholic air.

Colton was wearing his standard polo neck, jeans and trainers, with wire-rimmed glasses. It was such an aggressively ugly outfit, Flora wondered if he was doing it on purpose; like, if you saw someone so horribly dressed, the only possible solution was that they were so rich, they never had to worry about impressing anybody.

'Hi,' said Flora, trying to sound normal and in fact sounding squeaky. Fintan was staring at Colton Rogers like he was a celebrity, which she supposed he was around here; so little seen, yet so much speculated about. 'Um, this is my brother, Fintan. You did say bring someone.'

'Hi!' said Colton, smiling widely.

Joel merely gave a little nod, as if he'd expected something like this, and Flora felt a flash of annoyance that of course she couldn't have a good-looking boyfriend, apparently. She sat down and Colton offered her a glass of champagne. She snuck a quick glance at Joel to check if this would be okay, but he couldn't appear to be less bothered.

'Yes, please,' she said.

'Just half a lager,' muttered Fintan, visibly rummaging in his pockets. Flora cursed herself for not having warned him beforehand that he wouldn't be expected to pay. Colton waved his money away.

'Shall we move through?' said Colton, and they picked up their drinks and followed him into the restaurant. 'You are my very first guests.'

'We're honoured,' both Joel and Flora said at the same time, then glanced at one another.

Here, after the cosy, gleaming bar, things were quite different. It was formal and very quiet and it felt extremely odd to be just the four of them in the restaurant. Flora picked up the brand-new, very stiff and fancy menu.

Here at the Rock we want to give you a very special dining experience ... a dimension of sensory explosions; the primary tastes of extraordinary love and creativity, said the introduction, which Flora correctly interpreted as evidence that it would all be very, very expensive.

Everything was 'curated': there were 'orchards' of fruit and 'symphonies' of vegetables, and 'intensities' of oysters and sardines. Fintan looked in total agony. Flora smiled widely to help him out.

'Colton, maybe you should order for us?'

'What d'ya think, though?' he kept saying, looking around. There were stags' heads lining the walls and the carpet was tartan.

'I'm sure it's going to be lovely,' said Flora. 'It is fancy, though. Is this what you like to eat?'

'No,' he said. 'I prefer steak.'

He ordered the chef's tasting menu, and a couple of bottles of wine Flora couldn't pronounce, but she found she was quite happy to go along with someone else's choices. Plus, there was always the possibility that Joel's tongue would loosen after a few glasses. Might she get to know him a little better? Maybe that exterior was all for show, and he was one of those people who was lovely underneath. She imagined saying that to Kai – oh, once you get to know him, he's really nice. Works at an animal shelter in his spare time, but doesn't like anybody knowing about it.

The first thing to go wrong was the bread. It professed to be freshly baked, but patently wasn't. And the butter came in a little floral pattern, hard from the fridge. Fintan blinked twice.

'They've bought in this butter,' he whispered to Flora.

'Stop whispering,' said Flora. 'It's a restaurant. Of course it's got to buy in stuff.'

'Well, outside it looks like it pretends it's making it. And read this guff in the menu: "All our ingredients are sourced as close to the very heart of our island as possible." There's ten dairy farmers on Mure,' said Fintan crossly, 'and I tell you what, none of them put their butter in airy-fairy little baby flowers like this.'

'What's that, guys?' said Colton, leaning across the oversized table. The lighting was so subtle she could barely make him out. They were basically eating in the dark.

'Nothing,' said Flora quickly.

'Well—' said Fintan.

'No! Shush!' said Flora.

'So how did it go today?' asked Colton.

'Ah,' said Flora, glancing at Joel.

'You can put in a new schedule and a new proposal,' said Joel, opening his briefcase. 'I've got the paperwork all done and ready for you to sign before I leave. Scots law isn't much more complicated. It's a solid proposal, just to move the wind farm behind the next island. It has some cost implications for maintenance, but ought to save on keeping the island's unique heritage for visitors and future generations, yada yada yada.'

'Okay, good work,' said Colton, scanning it. 'So I just need to get this past the council, right? And how did that go?'

Flora took another gulp of wine. It was absolutely delicious.

'Well,' she said. 'There are a few issues.'

'Such as?'

'Everyone's bothered about the pink house.'

'What's that?'

'The pink building. On the main street. You've left it empty.'

Colton looked confused.

'Here?'

'Yes, here!'

'That's mine?'

Flora looked at him, aghast that someone could buy a building and not realise they'd done so.

'Apparently so,' said Joel.

'Damn,' said Colton. 'What else?'

'Staff?' said Flora. 'There's lots of island teenagers who might come home if there was more work here that wasn't milking.'

Fintan made a sarcastic noise but Flora ignored him.

'But really,' she said, 'what it boils down to is this. People don't know you. They don't know who you are. They think you might be Donald Trump or something, and that if they let you get away with this, the next step will be something really terrible.'

'But I'm trying to protect the place.'

'Then protect everyone here,' said Flora simply.

'Huh,' said Colton.

He turned to Fintan.

'I mean, you live here full time, right? What do you do, then?'

'I'm a farmer,' said Fintan resignedly, knocking back more wine.

'Yeah? You don't look like a farmer.'

'What, because I'm not chewing a stem of hay at the dinner table?'

He sounded prickly and defensive and Flora knew it was because he felt out of his depth.

'No,' said Colton. 'Are you always this aggressive?'

'Seen *Braveheart* too many times?' said Fintan. 'Scared of the violent locals?'

'Fintan! Shut up!' hissed Flora.

She turned to Colton.

'Sorry, sir. That thing they say about not being able to choose your family . . . '

'Yes, well, you certainly didn't,' muttered Fintan, whom Flora belatedly realised had drunk quite a lot of wine already.

There was a pause.

'That's enough,' said Flora, and Fintan, she could see, realised immediately he'd gone too far.

'Sorry, sis,' he said. Then he looked round the table, rubbing the back of his sunburned neck with his hand. 'Sorry, everyone.'

The waiter brought them something he called an 'amusing bouche'; with an odd kind of strangled laugh, he uncovered a large tray with four tiny little ramekins of oysters swimming in some kind of congealing jelly.

'What's this?' said Colton, a little crossly.

'It's oyster *surprise de la mer*,' said the waiter proudly. It certainly did look surprising.

They all prodded at it. Flora had grown up eating wild oysters, either straight from the shoreline, or sometimes her mother would stick them by the fire until they smoked themselves and their shells popped open, and she and her brothers scorched their fingers, but they didn't care, as the smoky, salty deliciousness inside was too good to wait for.

This was just a lump of horrible fish jelly, surrounding another fish jelly. Fintan didn't even pick up his fork.

'What is this?' he said. 'I didn't understand that wee guy the first time.'

'Well . . . ' began Colton, then shook his head. 'I'm sure I don't know.'

After the ramekins were removed, they all took an unenthusiastic shot at the asparagus and anchovy mousse. Conversation was definitely slowing. Fintan was blinking in disbelief.

'But why?' he kept saying, his face going pink. 'Why?'

'Well,' said Colton, who looked aggrieved and not unlike a man who was not happy to have been denied a steak. 'I just said I wanted to recruit the best and my people got on to it and—'

'That's what happens when you want something done?' said Fintan. 'You have to get people on to it?'

'Well, yeah. I'm quite busy,' smirked Colton.

'Telling people to get on to things,' said Fintan.

There was a pause.

'Yeah, and . . . '

'What?'

'And now some prawn marmalade,' said the waiter. Fintan waved him away irritatedly.

'So you came here into our community and decided that someone else who wasn't ever here should make decisions about us?'

'He's meant to be one of the top experimental chefs in the world,' said Colton.

'Yes. Experiments in horrible things,' said Fintan. 'And why does it say "locally sourced"? Excuse me, waiter. Why does everything here say "locally sourced"?'

Joel, Flora noticed, was watching all this with a wry smile of amusement. He seemed to be almost enjoying himself, for once; or engaged, at least. Why, oh why, did she find horn-rimmed glasses so incredibly attractive? Had she always thought this or was it just because he wore them? His eye-lashes were so long they were brushing against the glass. She wondered briefly, taking a sip of wine, what would happen if, while Fintan and the waiter appeared to be having an argument, she simply slid her foot . . .

No. No no. No. She was at work.

She took another swig of wine.

'Um . . . ' The waiter looked hot and embarrassed. It was bad enough having the boss in. 'Well,' he said. 'We use local salt.'

'Which salt?'

'Hebridean rock salt.'

'The Hebrides are two hundred nautical miles from here.'

The waiter coughed.

'I believe that counts, sir.'

Fintan blinked.

‘So you’re telling me you just sprinkle salt on everything.’

‘Uh-huh.’

‘And that magically turns it into “locally sourced”.’

‘It’s a key ingredient, sir.’

‘I don’t believe “locally sourced” is a legal term,’ observed Joel drily.

‘Hang on,’ said Colton. ‘So I’m telling my friends and clients and customers that what we’re getting here is the very best of Scottish produce . . . ’

Fintan pushed his plate away and took another swig of his wine, which he had been drinking like beer because he normally only drank beer.

‘Sorry, can I have a look at the cheese board?’

The waiter’s blink rate was now through the roof.

‘Um, I’ll see . . . ’

‘You won’t see,’ said Colton. ‘You’ll bring it.’

The waiter disappeared, and the maître d’ replaced him, looking pink and sweating in a way that had absolutely nothing to do with the temperature.

‘Is there a problem, Mr Rogers, sir?’

‘We don’t know,’ said Colton. ‘That’s why we need the cheese board.’

A trolley was rolled in with what was clearly a selection of chilly, recently unwrapped bought-in cheeses, including a suspiciously industrial-looking white Cheddar. Fintan sniffed them in turn.

‘Know your cheese?’ said Colton, amused. He’d watched Fintan necking the wildly expensive Bordeaux he’d ordered.

‘Yes,’ said Fintan. He cut himself a slice of each, and chewed them slowly.

'How much does your cheese plate go for?'

'Twenty-one pounds,' said the waiter. 'You get four for that.'

'You're ripping people off,' said Fintan flatly. 'This isn't . . . this isn't the real deal.'

'Well, there's a lot of pasteurised cheese . . . '

'Yeah. It's crap.'

'In the States, it's illegal to eat unpasteurised cheese,' said Colton. 'Filthy European habit.'

'How many people does cheese kill every year?' said Fintan. 'I'll tell you how many: none.'

'What about listeria?'

'Yup, that's why we have nonety-none people hospitalised every year with listeria,' said Fintan.

'I was wrong about you,' smiled Colton. 'You do know your cheese.'

Colton, Flora noticed, had angled his entire body towards Fintan, and was watching him with an air of sly amusement.

She realised suddenly that she hadn't speculated at all on Colton's sexuality; had assumed he'd be one of those men who trailed a flock of expensive ex-wives. She had absolutely no idea if he was married, had a girlfriend, what. She wondered if Fintan had noticed, and glanced at Joel.

To her total surprise, he caught her eye and gave her the tiniest of grins. She instantly tugged her head around and stared straight ahead.

'So you can suggest better?' Colton was saying to Fintan.

'I make better,' said Fintan. 'We have better butter, better fishing, far better oysters . . . I mean, you name it. Mrs Laird in the village, her bread is a million times better than this. Flora can outcook anything here. And we have much, much better cheese.'

Colton eyed him for a second.

'You make better?'

'Christ, yeah.'

'Show me.'

Fintan shrugged.

'I'll send some over.'

'No. Show me now. Have you got some on your farm?' He clicked his fingers at the maître d'.

'You'll need to send someone.'

Fintan got up to go.

'No, no, you sit down. Someone else will do it.'

A member of the catering staff hurried out of the kitchen, and Fintan told him where to find the various types of cheese, and to take the butter out of the fridge – but the stuff in the cow dish, not the paper, he explained, as if he didn't believe the waiter would know the difference between real and bought butter. The man practically scurried out of there as if his job depended on it, which it did. The maître d' explained that the chef wouldn't come out to speak to them: he was too scared. Colton sighed, ordered gigantic whiskies all round and they headed back into the bar to wait.

Joel hung back and walked with Flora. She couldn't help her heart leaping. She could smell a tinge of something expensive – lime cologne – and even though he had obviously shaved that day, a distinct hint of stubble was already noticeable along his tight jawline. Her senses felt so finely attuned to him, to every tingly iota, to the very aura that surrounded his body, that she forgot about everything else: the restaurant, the island, the job, the fact that he was her boss. How could he not notice how she felt? Or was he so used to it from every woman? Or perhaps he simply didn't care.

'Unusual strategy,' he observed as they moved through.

'I know,' said Flora. 'Sorry, do you want me to take him home?'

He turned to her.

'Is he gay?'

'No,' said Flora.

She paused.

'I've been away for a while.'

Joel blinked.

'You don't know if your own brother is gay?'

'It's not the kind of thing I'd . . . Do you have siblings?'

Joel had drunk too much of the good wine, and eaten too little of the bad food; he didn't mean to blurt out what he said next, and he cursed himself as soon as he did.

'I don't know,' he said.

Flora stopped abruptly. Joel froze.

'What do you mean, you don't know?' she said.

'I mean, no,' said Joel. 'I mean, even if I did, it wouldn't matter.'

'I didn't say it mattered,' said Flora. 'I said that I . . . I'm not a hundred per cent sure.'

Joel nodded and walked on ahead of her, moving towards the large picture window as she stared, confused, at his back and towards the landscape beyond.

Outside there was a gentle fog rising, rendering everything softer and more mysterious. The water was still absolutely perfectly flat as a pond; it looked less like the sea and more like a gentle pool of smoke. The long, flat, familiar outline of Mure rose up behind them in pastel shades of green and brown, the little lights of the harbour just visible around to the right.

Joel glanced at his watch.

'This place is nuts,' he said. 'It's ten p.m. and it looks like eleven o'clock in the morning. I can't sleep at all. When does it get dark?'

'It doesn't,' shrugged Flora.

'What are you guys, like Finland?'

'Oh no,' she said. 'We're far further north than that.'

He turned round to look at her, bathed in the strange white light from the window. Once again, he noticed, her eyes were the colour of the sea, even though the sea he was looking at now was grey from the mist, not green as it had been the other day. It was as if her eyes changed with the water. It was so strange.

Flora was feeling strange, but not for that reason. She was watching Colton, who'd headed out the front door and lit a large cigar out on the wooden deck, and was now offering one to Fintan. Fintan paused for a couple of seconds – Flora was reasonably sure he'd never had a cigar in his life, but what did she know? – then accepted, and they moved to sit on one of the expensively hand-hewn wooden benches, with the expensive cashmere blankets strewn over them. Little candles in jam jars fluttered everywhere, even though their lights weren't needed; and the air was heavily scented with something that smelled amazing but was in fact designed to keep the midges away.

'It's like Avalon,' Joel was saying, turning back towards

the sea view. 'Like a mirage; like the entire thing will fade away at any minute.'

'I think you're confusing us with the mobile phone signal,' said Flora, and was rewarded with a hint of an extremely rare smile. But he didn't take his eyes off the floating horizon.

Chapter Twenty-six

Bertie dashed back with the boat as fast as he could; the waiter was utterly terrified that he'd upset Mr Rogers. To Innes and Eck's bemusement, the young man had crashed into the dairy and basically grabbed everything he could find. Glancing around, Innes had added Flora's leftover fruit cake and oatcakes to his haul, along with various jars from the larder.

When they saw him rushing back up the lit path, Joel and Flora left the house and joined Colton and Fintan on the terrace. It was chillier now, but braziers had been lit, so it felt cosy instead. The music had been turned off, and there was nothing to be heard except the low cooings of birds, which seemed to know it was night-time even if nobody else did, and a barking noise from the water.

'Are there dogs here?' said Joel, glancing around. The others laughed.

'Seals bark too,' said Flora.

'You're telling me I'm listening to a pack of barking seals?' said Joel. 'Seriously, man, this place is completely made up.'

They all watched as, marching like a slightly tiddly toddler, a grouse processed slowly along the red carpet behind the waiter. Then, suddenly, they all burst out laughing.

'*Completely* fucking made up.'

'There you go,' said Colton. He raised his glass to Joel. 'Everyone falls under its spell sooner or later. The entire damn place is woven out of clouds.'

'Whatever you say,' said Joel.

The waiter, looking terrified and slightly breathless, handed over a huge basket.

'Here you are, sir!'

Plates, knives and more whisky arrived without anyone appearing to do anything. Colton drew out the oatcakes together with two rounds of dark yellow butter – one studded with crystals of salt that caught the light, the other plainer and darker – and three cheeses: the hard, the soft and the mix.

Flora took a breath; there too was some of her mother's chutney, and her chilli jam. She couldn't work out how it had got in there. Quick-thinking Innes, it had to have been. Fintan was desperately searching for somewhere to put out his cigar. He looked nervous and proud.

Colton frowned.

'Seriously, if your plan here is to poison me with bacteria . . . I mean, this stuff is full of bacteria . . .'

'All cheese is bacteria,' said Fintan. 'Your body currently has about a hundred and thirty billion different strands of bacteria in it.'

'Yes, that's why I drink probiotics.'

'Really? I thought it's because they taste like strawberry milkshakes.'

'That too.'

Fintan got up and picked up a small knife. Leaning over the heavy oak table, he carved thick wedges of all the cheeses. He settled back down and gave everyone a challenging look.

Oddly, Joel went first, ignoring the oatcakes and simply scooping up a large piece of the blue cheese and popping it in his mouth. Everyone watched him closely – Flora making the most of the opportunity to look at his lips – as he blinked, quickly, as if slightly surprised by something, then brought his hand down from his mouth.

'Well,' he said.

'What are the first symptoms?' said Colton. 'I mean, do you just start puking or what?'

Deliberately Fintan took a piece of the soft cheese and spread it on a slice of bread. Flora grinned and dolloped chutney on a piece of the rye before adding a chunk of cheese on top. God, she had forgotten how good it was. She didn't want to appear greedy, but they'd had no dinner, and it was all she could do not to grab the entire lot and stuff it in her mouth. Washing it down with twenty-five-year-old Laphroaig, she realised, was also an absolutely perfect combination.

Joel couldn't remember the last time he'd seen a woman eat with such genuine pleasure. He found his mind wandering briefly to whether she had other appetites she couldn't control. Then he put the image out of his mind and focused on his client.

'Okay, okay, what is this?' said Colton. 'Last one to eat the deadly cheese is a coward? I should warn you, my nutritionist told me I'm probably lactose intolerant.'

'What are the symptoms?' asked Flora curiously.

'Mood swings, tiredness . . . '

'Maybe you're just a grumpy bastard,' said Fintan, and there was a slight pause – nobody, but *nobody* ever took the piss out of Colton Rogers, mostly because he spent a ridiculous amount of time with people whose lives depended on him paying their salary. Then Colton laughed and made to cuff him.

'Uh-uh,' said Fintan, feinting out of the way. '*Try it.*'

Colton's face was comical to watch. If Flora, as a massive cheese fanatic, had adored Fintan's creation, it was nothing to how a man raised on American cheese and finally tasting something so full and bursting with flavour and richness and full-bodied depth and nuttiness was going to react.

'Good God in heaven,' he said eventually. 'Jesus. Joel, you tasted this?'

'Yes, sir.'

'Have you ever had anything like it?'

'I have spent some time in France.'

'*I have spent some time in France*,' mimicked Colton. 'You pussy. I bet you didn't get anything as good as this there.'

'No,' said Joel, sounding surprised at himself. 'I don't think I did.'

Colton cut himself another thick wedge, then another. Suddenly Flora realised that Innes had put the fruit cake in the basket, and she immediately instructed the Americans how to take a bite of the cake, a mouthful of the hard cheese and a sip of the smoky, peaty whisky, washing them all down together.

For a time there was no sound except for some slightly orgasmic noises that could easily be misinterpreted.

'My God,' said Colton eventually. 'I mean, my God. I mean.'

'Taste the butter,' said Flora evilly.

'You're trying to kill me.'

'Not before you've had some butter. Try the salty stuff on the rye. Nothing else.'

Colton tasted a corner and waved his hands about.

'Christ. Right, *now* you've ruined me for butter.'

Fintan smirked.

'You haven't touched the blue.'

Colton looked at it regretfully.

'Oh Christ, man, I don't think even I can go that far. I'm just a Texas boy, you know! Mozzarella on pizza and American Jack on everything else. That's all I know.'

'You have to try it,' said Fintan. 'You want to be accepted . . . '

'You want me to eat cheese that actually has veins in it? Blue varicose veins?'

'Buk buk baaaaaaaak.'

Colton smiled.

'Can't do it, my friend. There's a line.'

In answer, Fintan jumped up and cut a slice off. He came round the table and started advancing. Flora was absolutely startled. Colton blinked several times. It was apparent that nobody had treated him like this for a long time. Possibly ever. How strange it must be, thought Flora, to be so rich that everyone tiptoed round you. Was it nice? Was it strange? Did anybody ever know?

But the two of them had taken off onto the beach, Colton laughing, holding his hands up over his face, and an expression in Fintan's eyes Flora had never seen before. The sullen, guarded look was gone, as he pretended to wrestle Colton to the ground to make him try the cheese. In the end, he rugby-tackled him down onto the sand. Flora's hand flew to her mouth.

How could she have been so blind? So caught up with her own life, her own dramas and feelings? Fintan had been a quiet teenager, but there had never really been any debate in the house, had there? He would go into farming like all the other lads, make a good living, keep the circle of the seasons turning, go to Inverness a couple of times a year, bet on some horses, maybe. Watch the shinty. Find a good strong local lass. That was just what boys on Mure did, and she hadn't questioned it any more than her ancestors had.

She watched as a giggling Colton sat in the sand, finally acquiescing to try a bit of the cheese, then screwing up his face in mock horror.

'You never knew,' said Joel quietly, gazing steadfastly at his whisky glass. She was so shocked she barely heard him, but when she realised he'd spoken, she was struck by something: she'd never heard him speak gently before. To anyone.

'Half my friends are gay,' she stuttered.

'And it never even crossed your mind?'

'Things have been . . . complicated with my family,' said Flora. Joel raised an eyebrow.

Colton and Fintan came back up from the beach, still giggling slightly.

'This is,' said Colton, arriving back at the wooden table, 'possibly the strangest business dinner I've ever had.'

'We haven't really discussed any business,' said Flora, looking at Fintan's flushed face.

'What are you talking about? It's obvious,' said Colton. 'This was a pitch, right?'

'What?' said Flora.

'Local suppliers,' said Colton patiently, as if she was an idiot. 'You guys are going to do it? Reopen the pink house? Hire as many folk as you want. I'm in. It's a good plan. I like it. Can you get moving before the council meeting?'

'*What?*' said Flora.

Fintan put out his hand to stop her.

'Sure,' he said.

'I suppose I'd better have an opening party,' said Colton, looking around. 'Ugh. I hate parties. But I can knock off meeting everyone at once too. Great.'

Fintan glanced at his watch and his face fell.

'I've got to go,' he said. 'I've got milking.'

Colton blinked.

'But it's early,' he complained, glancing at the light horizon. He looked at his watch. 'Oh yeah,' he added. 'Huh. Will you look at that. Normally I'm bored by now.'

Fintan smiled awkwardly.

'Right, shall we go, sis?'

'But . . . ' said Flora, feeling slightly fuddled in the head. What was happening?

'Okay,' said Colton. 'Sort out the pink house. Organise the party. Lobby it up. Then we'll be good to go.'

'But ... ' said Flora again. She felt pressure on her left shoulder. It was Joel, manoeuvring her towards Bertie and his little boat.

'This has been great,' said Colton. And he stuck out his hand to shake Fintan's, and held on to it for rather too long.

Chapter Twenty-seven

There was white all around. The sky was white; the sea was the palest grey, reflecting the strange light straight back until it felt as if she was sailing across a blank page, the ripples in the waves sentences stretching out behind her. She was on a ship, an old creaking sailing ship, its bare masts high – where were its sails? Someone was missing. Who was it? Stop! she found herself shouting. Stop the boat! Stop it. But nobody was listening, and they powered on. Someone had gone over the side, and she wanted to reach them, but the ship was going further and further away, and she was shouting, but nobody could hear her and nobody would stop . . .

It was probably – no, certainly – the whisky, but Flora woke bolt upright at 3 a.m., her mouth dry, from a strange white dream of ships and ice and cold. Her thin duvet was half thrown off; the house freezing.

She'd protested all the way home in the boat, and Joel and Fintan had, absurdly, ganged up on her and told her they'd discuss it the next day.

The first thing she noticed was her phone blinking. She rubbed her eyes, pulled a blanket round her trembling shoulders and picked it up.

It was work: memos, plans, a flurry of ideas, from Joel. But it was the middle of the night.

Aren't you asleep? she texted.

He replied immediately.

> It's BROAD DAYLIGHT. How can anybody sleep in this?

Flora thought nothing of it. She'd been accustomed to going to bed in bright sunlight since she was a child; and conversely, of course, going to school in the pitch dark in the winter months.

> Draw the curtains? she suggested.

> They're dirty.

Flora felt for him. The Harbour's Rest was pretty grim, after all.

> Why couldn't you stay at the Rock?

> Apparently they're still finishing the bedrooms.

Seriously, could they have been worse?

That's a very good point. I should have pushed it. Three walls would have been better than this.

Flora smiled at her phone.

A bit of salt spray aids a restful night.

That's an island saying, is it? I might suggest to the landlady that a bit of cleaning spray aids a restful night.

Oh come on. Admit it. It's not so bad here.

I never said it was.

Joel was enjoying their conversation. It felt strange just to be chatting like this, especially late at night. Not after anything. Not a booty call. He frowned. She wouldn't think . . . No. She couldn't. She was the office junior, right? It was clearly professional. It was just she was easy to talk to. And Christ, he really couldn't sleep.

He jumped up and paced the room. The peeling wallpaper was making him depressed, but outside it looked unearthly and rather beautiful.

Is it safe to take a walk here?

Be careful of the wild haggis. They can be tricky. But you can run away from them; they have one leg shorter than the other from stomping round and round hills.

Hahaha.

Flora looked at the message, feeling suddenly excited.

Where are you going for a walk?

I thought I'd start at Broadway, then head up to the shopping district, then maybe stop off to eat in Chinatown . . .

Hahaha.

Joel pulled on his overcoat. He felt restless.

Dunno. Harbour? Everything's shut.

It's 3.30 a.m.

There was a long pause. Finally Flora typed:

Would you like me to come down?

He squinted at his phone. He normally . . . Well. He did well without company. The lone wolf, Dr

Philippoussis called him. He looked out again at the pale water.

If you like.

She scrubbed her face, grimaced at her hair and plaited it back so it fell over her shoulder, then stuck a bunnet on it. She hauled on her jeans, a striped T-shirt, a fisherman's jumper and some big boots. She absolutely did not look like someone out to seduce anyone, she told herself sternly. Well, maybe another fisherman. Certainly not her slick hot London boss who she was meeting in the middle of the night. No.

And actually that was quite far from her mind as she headed for the stairs. What she really wanted to discuss was Colton's mad idea that she and Fintan were going to somehow take over his catering. This needed to be nipped in the bud sharpish.

She drank a large glass of freezing water to flush the whisky out of her system, then made up a flask of strong coffee. Bramble had perked up as she walked into the kitchen, and Flora nodded to him that he could come along. She stepped out of the farmhouse into the bracing freshness of the morning air, even though morning, technically, was several hours away.

Never busy at the best of times, at this hour Mure felt like the moon; it felt like everyone else on earth had simply disappeared, that it was the very end of everything. A light haar was still lying on the land, giving a dreamy quality to every shape looming out of it: the hilltops swathed in bottomed-out clouds; the telegraph poles vanished; the freshness of the air changing to dankness as you walked through great banks of mist.

Flora saw him before he saw her, standing by the harbour wall, staring out to sea. He looked utterly out of place in his well-cut coat and smart shoes; like an astronaut washed up on a strange shore he didn't understand, who had found everything he had been sure of in his life completely alien to him.

Bramble whined enquiringly, and Flora bent down. 'He's all right,' she whispered, rubbing the dog's soft ears. 'It's okay.' Please like dogs, she thought, crossing her fingers.

Bramble, soothed, shot off across the cobbles of the harbour.

Just at that moment, Joel turned round, to be greeted by a huge, slightly muddy, overenthusiastic dog leaping up on his expensive clothes. He nearly toppled over, trying to both push and welcome the dog at the same time, then turned to see Flora laughing a few feet away, the fog settling around her like a living thing.

'Yes, all right, very funny. Thanks for having me attacked by a carthorse,' he said as she approached.

'BRAMBLE!' she shouted. 'Come here, you bad dog.'

Bramble totally ignored her, as usual, and bounded off to have an early-morning dip. Joel looked down at his muddied trousers.

'I wonder if Colton will cover my dry-cleaning costs.'

'We'll get Fintan to ask him.'

He looked at her and smiled. She looked so different

from the girl he'd hardly noticed in the office. In the big old jumper, no make-up, just the pink of her cheeks, her hair tumbling out from underneath the cap, and those strange watery eyes.

He looked at what she was carrying.

'Is that . . . is that a flask?'

'It might be.'

'Are we going fishing?'

'Do you want coffee or not?'

Joel smiled.

'I want coffee more than anything in the entire universe.'

'I thought you'd have been calling room service to get it for you.'

'They have room service?'

'Not normally,' said Flora, thinking privately that Inge-Britt might prove amenable in this case. 'Maybe if you asked nicely.'

'I always ask nicely!'

She gave him a look and he was taken aback.

'Well, for New York,' he admitted grudgingly.

Flora poured him a cup, sweet and hot. He took it appreciatively, and even said thank you, and they sat on the harbour wall and looked at the low rising sun.

'I can nearly see it, you know,' Joel said, gazing at the horizon. 'I can see what Colton sees in this place. It's like . . . it's not like anywhere else.'

The haar had lifted now, and the colours of the dawn were fading in and out of the clouds, giving a striped effect to the water, stippled pink and gold and yellow beneath the eerie white sky.

'It's not,' agreed Flora.

'You look at home here.'

Flora shrugged.

'Well. I'm not. Look. The project . . .'

'I know it's irregular,' said Joel.

'That's one way of putting it.'

'I was thinking . . . Did you read my notes?'

'No,' said Flora. 'I was asleep. Do you never sleep? Are you Batman?'

A thought struck her.

'That would explain *a lot*.'

Joel smiled.

'Really?'

'I didn't read your notes.'

'Well,' said Joel. 'Basically, this is a PR job. If you could organise something like – say – a pop-up shop in that pink building. Get local people on his side. Plus the party. Plus selling your cheese or whatever the hell it is that Fintan wants to do. I mean, that would swing it, wouldn't it? Convince people that he's got the best interests of the island at heart. Then it goes our way. Then we take millions of dollars from his future business. I'm being frank with you here.'

'I see that,' said Flora. She sighed. 'But I have a job! A proper one, not running a shop.'

'That is a proper job,' said Joel. 'And also, I have a load of paralegals. Most of whom could handle your briefs.'

He looked out to sea.

'But I don't know anyone else who can help out our potentially biggest client.'

'Seriously?'

‘It’s only for a few weeks – when will the council decide? You can leave after that; that’s what a pop-up means. I just think it would mean a lot to the firm.’

Bramble came bounding back up, covered in salt and water.

‘Come on,’ said Flora. ‘Let’s walk the Endless.’

‘The what?’

‘The Endless. The beach.’ She jumped off the wall. ‘It’s not really endless.’

Joel followed her up and over the headland at the bottom of the harbour wall, where the houses petered out. At the crest of the headland, as Bramble hopped about sniffing for rabbits, he stopped.

The beach ahead went on for miles. The sand was purest white, the pale sea gently lapping at its edge. In the light remnants of the sea fog, you couldn’t see where it ended; it faded into infinity. The world was nothing but this glorious beach, completely and utterly empty, as if nobody else had ever stood there. Bramble made pawprints in the virgin sand.

It was a combination of absolutely no sleep and a lack of contact with London, but for some reason, it took Joel’s breath away. As if this was the first time he’d looked up. The air felt burstingly fresh in his lungs; the smell of coffee on the salted wind; the breeze ruffling the dog’s hair. He felt . . . he didn’t know what he felt. A kind of strange freedom. Something new.

He took a step forward.

‘Wow,’ he said. ‘Jesus. It’s like . . . it’s like we’ve discovered it.’

'You have,' said Flora simply.

'It's . . . it's just . . . '

He was lost for words. Bramble was cavorting about, leaping high in the air and desperately snuffling around for sticks. Flora went to help him, then turned to look back at Joel, who was still transfixed. She felt strange all of a sudden; she'd been so desperate for this moment – the two of them alone; him talking to her, looking at her, for once. And yet now here he was, and she felt . . . Well. He looked suddenly small, standing on the Endless – almost humbled. She was curious about him: what kept him so locked up, so very tight? Had he lost someone too?

But those thoughts led her, once more, and always on Mure, to somewhere she didn't want to be; to the hand to which she'd entrusted her own, the first time she'd walked the Endless and heard the stories: of Vikings, wreckers, fairies . . . all the old, old tales of the isles.

She screwed her face up. She was so tired of it, running through her head over and over again. So weary.

Bending over, she found a stick on the ground, the perfect size for throwing. Kicking off her boots and rolling up her jeans, she hurled it as far as she could, then, in the bright clear air of the everlasting morning, ran as fast as she could, side by side with the dog, splashing through the gentle waves. It was the best way she knew to get rid of her thoughts, to chase away the dreams of the night; to escape the clutches of this island and the ridiculous thing that had happened to her. Just run, and never look back.

The beach unfurled in front of her until she was far out of reach, until she could no longer hear Joel calling after her, and she and Bramble collapsed on the sand, and the dog licked her face anxiously, and she buried her face in his fur until she felt more herself again, and began to wander back along the beach, slowly, out of breath, but somehow fuller, more alive than she'd felt for some time.

'Sorry about that,' she said as she reached Joel. 'Sorry. I just felt a bit of an urge . . . '

Oddly, Joel had very nearly followed her. Cast off his shoes, run as if he could outrun wolves. He'd come extremely close to trying to catching her up . . . and then grabbing her, pulling her down on to the sand; both breathless, hot, sweating . . .

He had buried the thought at once. She was a junior employee, and as far as he had a personal life at all, it was never getting remotely near work.

They looked at each other for a moment. Then Flora caught her breath and straightened up, and they set off again, more sedately now.

'It's different in the summer. Mobbed. As teenagers we'd light fires here and get up to all sorts of mischief.'

'I bet you did.'

'What was it like where you grew up?'

There was a pause. Joel looked out over the clear water and sighed. He even considered, for a moment, telling her.

'It was . . . '

The treacherous thoughts meandered back into his head. He wondered what that cool, clear skin would feel like. The porcelain whiteness of it; the delicate freckles here and there. He wondered what look she would get in those ocean eyes.

Then he looked around at the alien landscape. And he thought, why not? He thought: Dr Philippoussis would approve.

Because he was tired. Tired of bars and late nights working and stupid office politics and hot girls who wanted to be taken to the best restaurants but refused to eat anything when they got there. Tired of who had the best office, the newest client, the most expensive road bike, the most ridiculous holidays, the hottest table in a nightclub, the coolest apartment, the best-looking girlfriend. It went on and on and he didn't know how it ended, he never had; he didn't even know, now that he was here, what it was for. There was a friendly dog, and a windswept girl, and nothing else as far as the eye could see. And he wasn't just tired from staying up all night. Three a.m. was nothing to him. He had never slept. Never.

He almost told her.

Then the damn dog jumped up at him again.

'BRAMBLE!' shouted Flora. 'Oh God, I am so sorry. So sorry. There must be a way of getting the mud off.'

Bramble was going nuts. Flora eventually got him back under control. She looked sideways at Joel. She had felt . . . what? Something. As if he was on the brink of saying something. But she hadn't been able to tell what it was. And now, it seemed, the moment had gone.

They walked on, both of them, talking through the case, and by the time they'd reached the end of the beach and turned round (Joel feeling ridiculously disappointed that it did eventually have an end, a lighthouse manning the headland), the white sky was turning the faintest of blues, promising the most beautiful day ahead.

And by the time they'd got back to where Flora's boots were, where they'd started, she had, reluctantly, agreed to marshal the troops while Joel went back to London, and stick to Colton like glue until the council meeting.

'Breakfast?' she said.

Joel glanced at his watch. 'It's five a.m. We were still eating four hours ago, and also, by the way, it's technically the middle of the night.'

'Okay,' said Flora. 'Just a thought.'

'Would it have to be cheese?'

'No.'

Oddly, Joel found he was actually hungry again. Something about the air, he suspected. Normally he controlled his diet the way he controlled every other aspect of his life.

'Where's open for breakfast?'

'Oh, the boys will be up soon. You can come to the farm.'

Chapter Twenty-eight

By the time they'd picked their way up the track to the farm, the boys were indeed up and the place was buzzing. The warmth of the kitchen was delicious after the fresh morning air, the Aga and the fire turning the room cosy and fuggy.

'Hey,' said Innes, stomping across the floor in worn pyjamas and holey socks. He filled the kettle at the sink and stuck it on the stove; only then did he turn round and notice Joel standing there.

'Who the hell are you?' he said.

Joel's coat was slightly damp, as were his expensive shoes and the bottoms of his trousers. His glasses were starting to steam up. For the first time, Flora thought he looked vulnerable.

'I'm Flora's boss, Joel Binder,' he said quietly, sticking out his hand.

'It's five o'clock in the fricking morning,' said Innes. 'What kind of hours do you lawyers work?'

'Not as hard as farmers,' noted Joel.

'DADDY?' came a small but definite voice. 'MUCH MOST NOISE, DADDY.'

Everyone stopped as a pair of tiny feet pattered into the kitchen. Her pure white hair all mussed up, one hand rubbing her eye, the other clutching her beloved raccoon, Agot stood barefoot on the flagstone floor, squinting at everyone.

'WHY NOISE, EV'BODY?' she said fiercely.

Joel blinked.

'Why don't I make everyone a cup of tea?' said Flora quickly. 'Good morning, Agot darling.'

Agot grinned to see her, and ran into her arms.

'WHO MAN, AUNT FLOWA?'

'This is Joel,' said Flora awkwardly.

Joel gave a half-smile.

'Hi,' he said.

'HI,' said Agot. 'ME AGOT.' She turned back to Flora. 'BEKFAST?'

Eck loomed into the kitchen.

'Dad!' said Flora. 'You shouldn't be getting up for milking!'

'And how am I supposed to sleep with all of you havering about in here?'

Eck seemed to take Joel's presence for granted, and tea was handed around.

'GRAMPA!' shouted Agot.

'What is it, bairn?'

'BEKFAST? SAMWIDGE?'

Flora smiled. Agot's favourite thing.

'Oh, I don't know about that,' frowned Eck. 'You wouldn't rather have a nice bowl of porridge?'

'SAMWIDGE!'

'Okay, okay,' said Flora. 'Seeing as I woke everyone up, apparently, Innes, you make coffee – not everyone drinks that horrible tea slop – and I'll make bacon sandwiches.'

'YAY!' said Agot. 'AN' MUSIC.'

Innes turned the radio on to BBC Radio Gael, and Agot started swirling around the floor, her nightie streaming out behind her.

'You spoil that bairn,' said Eck as Flora went over to pull out the huge old blackened frying pan.

'I bloody will,' said Innes. 'After what she's been through with me and Eilidh, I'll spoil her every day.'

Flora fetched the bacon, simply wrapped in paper, from the cold store, while Innes brewed up coffee: good dark stuff that Flora had found, along with a cafetière, and that most of the farm boys turned their noses up at; they preferred the powdered stuff still. Agot was still dancing, and the big kitchen windows were steaming up with noise and chat and happy music.

'Oh God,' said Flora suddenly, turning to Joel. 'Do you eat bacon?'

Eck noticed him for the first time.

'You're not one of the hands?'

'Dad, fix your glasses, for God's sake! Before you try and milk Bramble!'

'Aooo!' agreed Bramble, lifting his head at the sound of his name.

'I'm … I'm with Flora's firm,' said Joel. Flora looked

closely at him. Was he … was he *smirking*? 'And yes, don't worry, bacon's fine.'

'Why wouldn't it be fine?' said Eck, and Innes told him to shut up.

Fintan wandered in whistling, with his head up, which was extremely unusual. Innes narrowed his eyes.

'What are you so cheerful about?'

'Nothing,' smiled Fintan, filling his cup. 'Oh wow, that smells awesome. Make one for me, sis.'

He grabbed Agot and whirled her round and she screamed and giggled.

'Good morning, my gorgeous girl.'

As he turned, he saw Joel.

'Oh my goodness, did you stay the night?'

The entire kitchen fell silent.

'What?' said Eck.

'YOU HAVE SLEEPOVER?' said Agot.

Flora went bright red.

'Of course not!' she said.

'You know this guy?' said Innes to Fintan. 'I thought he was working with Flora.'

'He is, and shut up,' said Flora.

'You're very red, sis,' observed Fintan.

'SHUT UP, EVERYONE! Just get out and milk the damn cows,' said Flora. 'Or you won't get a sandwich.'

They all sat down eventually round the huge table. Joel didn't say very much. Flora thought he was horrified by their rough ways.

In fact, although he had spent time with plenty of families as a child, he hadn't got to know any of them well. He'd been always passed on – the smart little closed-up boy who wasn't cute or smiley or friendly or appealing enough ever to be adopted; who was so difficult to reach; who said curious things; who beat the older children in every exam they ever sat and every book they ever read.

By the time Dr Philippoussis had spotted his obvious fierce intelligence and found him a place in a good school with a sympathetic teacher who provided him with all the books he could read and fed his hunger for study and learning, he was a teenager, and nobody wants a teenage boy around the place, not really. He had won a scholarship to boarding school, and with a sigh of relief social services had washed its hands of him.

He found his current situation unnerving. Flora's family talked so much; yabbering away as they grabbed sandwiches and drank endless cups of tea. Joel kept his diet very tightly controlled; he never ate bacon sandwiches, though it had nothing to do with any religion – he'd been brought up by a ragtag of different sects: Evangelicals, Baptists, atheists, and had taken nothing from any of it. No, it was because they were made up of carbs and fat, two things he had attempted to banish from his diet for ever, to keep himself fit and healthy and one step ahead of the baying pack he somehow always felt right on his heels. He couldn't have told you who the baying pack was. He just always knew it was there.

He took a tentative bite of his sandwich. That was another thing he was wary of: don't leave your food for a second. Someone would take it. Eat when you could.

He blinked. This kept happening. He didn't know anything about catering or running a business. But he knew quite a lot about high-quality food: expensive client dinners; vast amounts of money spent at hot new restaurants. And he could tell one thing: this stuff was miles ahead. Absolutely miles. The bread might have been yesterday's, toasted, but its astonishing qualities showed through. The crispy, salty bacon; the chipped enamel mugs of strong tea: you could sell this absolutely anywhere. Flora was going to be fine. He looked at her, effortlessly dishing up seconds to a huge, quiet boy who must be yet another brother – how many were there? This, he thought, was where she could absolutely shine.

And as he watched the laughing, noisy, teasing clan and concentrated on his sandwich while a plethora of incomprehensible conversations about cattle feed and yields and bloody cheese went on over his head, he realised, to his surprise, looking down, that there was a small shape scrambling up onto his lap; Agot had wandered over to him completely unselfconsciously and was crawling up his leg.

'Agot, get down,' said Flora when she saw her.

Agot pouted.

'I YIKE MAN,' she said defiantly, scattering crumbs from her sandwich all over his trousers and the floor.

'Sorry,' said Innes. 'Agot, get down.'

Joel had frozen. He wasn't used to children; didn't have the faintest clue what to do.

'I'S NOT GET DOWN,' said Agot, offering Joel a piece of her toast.

'It's fine,' said Joel, taking the toast and putting it on the table. Everyone else visibly relaxed. Be normal, he told himself. This is completely normal. Families are totally normal. It's you that's weird.

And although it was an unfamiliar sensation, it was not, he realised, at all unpleasant. The child's chubby little legs kicked out in front of her as she made herself comfortable; she smelled nice too, of toast, and a faintly familiar shampoo, and sleep.

'AHHH, SAMWIDGE,' she said happily, taking a large bite and causing a spot of grease to land on his now basically ruined trousers. Flora winced, but when she caught Joel's eye, she realised he was smiling.

'This is,' he said, 'a pretty amazing sandwich.'

He looked at Fintan.

'You're going to do this, you know. I really think you are.'

Fintan blinked.

'Thanks!'

Joel glanced at his watch.

'I have a flight to catch,' he said.

Flora nodded.

'I know. And I'd better get to it too. Come on, Agot, let's go put you back to bed.'

'I'S NOT TIRED!'

Joel made to stand up, and Agot immediately flung her arms around his neck.

'MAN NOT GO!'

'Sorry,' said Flora. 'Agot! Stop that!'

'NOT GO BED!'

Joel carefully disentangled Agot's arms from round his neck and put her down on the floor. Flora watched him, feeling ludicrous at how much she wanted to do exactly what Agot had just done: throw her arms around him and see that gentle look in his eyes.

No. She didn't want a gentle look in his eyes. Not at all. She breathed in and out. She had to get a grip. She had to.

'NO GOING TO BED!'

No, thought Flora. None of them were.

Chapter Twenty-nine

After that, things moved with extraordinary speed. Flora had briefly wondered, with a bittersweet pang, whether Joel would come back up to deal with the paperwork, but of course it was far beneath him.

Within weeks, everything was organised. New equipment arrived every day, along with very stern people from the Food Health and Safety Executive, who inspected everything, demanded changes and then came back again to check them. Fintan worked day and night to get everything in the dairy regulation and utterly gleaming.

All of Colton's old staff were sent over to help, even as he went on a huge recruitment drive in the village, offering decent wages and flexible working at the Rock just to get everything moving. Lorna held a competition for the schoolchildren to design a logo; an extremely happy cow standing in a field with the pale sea behind it won the day. Agot scowled furiously when the triumphant child had their photo taken for the *Island Times*, and refused to appear alongside them, instead hurling herself on the ground and kicking her little boots against the cobblestones.

Flora got in touch with some of the girls she'd been at school with and asked them if they wanted a bit of work, of if they knew anyone who did. Which was how they got a couple of bonnie girls, Isla and Iona, back from the mainland for the summer, all cheery and ready to work.

She also recruited Mrs Laird, who 'did' for the doctor and the vicar, but who was also, Fintan happened to know, the best breadmaker on the island.

'There were a lot of ladies popping by for Dad,' he told a horrified Flora. 'She was by far the best baker, though.'

'You didn't let them do that!'

'We did! They brought over a lot of frozen stews. Although we mostly just stuck to sausages.'

'I wondered how we'd managed to acquire nineteen new casserole dishes.'

'Hmph,' said Fintan.

'I hope you didn't string Mrs Laird along.'

But it was true, she did make wonderful bread, bannocks and bridies.

Flora had them all up to the farmhouse, and together they pored over the increasingly battered recipe book.

'Everything is to come from here,' she told them. 'Scones. Cakes. Pancakes. We'll do two soups every day. Toasted sandwiches. Nothing too complicated. But you HAVE to follow these recipes.'

Mrs Laird nodded.

'Those are Annie's recipes,' she said seriously. 'And she was the best cook I ever knew here.'

'Which is high praise coming from you,' said Flora.

They divided up the work. Flora took pastry, as she had such a knack for it, and found it comforting to do, although she wasn't above kneading a loaf once in a while. She and Mrs Laird took the new recruits step by step through the cakes. Iona and Isla, both fair-haired, pink-cheeked, healthy-looking girls, smiled happily. They were being paid rather better than the other island jobs were offering for the summer season.

Everyone pitched in to clean out the shop, and the boys came down to give it a lick of paint on the inside, Innes flirting up a storm with the girls home for the summer. Fintan didn't give them a second glance. I've been such an idiot, thought Flora, reminding herself that she must talk to him about it sometime. When they'd stopped teasing the great big fancy-pants London legal hotshot for being down on her hands and knees scrubbing behind a radiator.

POP-UP they wrote on the sign outside.

'Just so people know,' Flora said. Once the council had had their vote, she was going back to London. If they wanted to carry it on afterwards, that was fine, but she wouldn't be here.

'Pop-up?' said Mrs Laird. 'What does that even mean?'

'It means it's temporary. That it's only here for the summer.'

'Well, just call it "summer", then.'

Flora shrugged. 'All right.'

'You could call it Annie's Café,' said Mrs Laird.

Flora looked at her, but didn't say anything.

'I don't think so,' she managed finally. Mrs Laird nodded kindly.

'The Summer Seaside Café,' said Isla.

'It's Mure. Everything's seaside,' pointed out Iona, and Isla rolled her eyes.

'It's not really a café, though,' said Flora. 'It's just odds and ends from our kitchen.'

'Well, call it a kitchen then,' said Mrs Laird. 'Then people will know they can't order stupid things. Just normal stuff you can make at home.'

'That will do,' said Flora. And 'The Summer Seaside Kitchen' was stencilled on a nice white wooden sign that went well on the pink wall, and Innes and Hamish shinned up and hammered it in.

They'd been thoroughly checked over and the shop was full to the brim with scones and cakes; Mrs Laird's bread and Fintan's cheese; warm pasties, and pies glistening with fruit. Looking at it, Flora couldn't suppress an incredible feeling of pride as to what they'd accomplished in a few short weeks. She quelled the thought immediately. But this wasn't just pushing paper about or running to help the lawyers, or filing or sitting in front of the computer. This felt, for the first time, as though she'd actually built something. Made something that was useful, and beautiful. It was a very unfamiliar feeling.

'Wish me luck, Dad,' Flora said as she headed out to open up on the first morning. The pink had long gone from the sky; it was a clear, beautiful day and you could see for miles. They were now well into June, when the days never ended, and the tourists had descended, exclaiming over the beauty of the landscape and the deep tranquillity of the island.

Eck only grunted.

'Seems like a will-o'-the-wisp thing to me,' he said. 'And I lose the boys again.'

Innes bit his lip.

'Is it still that bad?' Flora said. 'Surely selling the cheese will help?'

'You're going to have to sell a hell of a lot of it. We got the bill in for the calf transportation.' The farm was taking its yearlings to Wick to sell at the market. 'We'll be lucky to cover our costs.'

Flora rubbed her hands over her eyes. She didn't know what to say.

'And now you're taking Fintan away for good.'

They both looked at him. He was wearing a dapper new blue and white striped apron over a white T-shirt and tight jeans.

'I think Fintan checked out a long time ago,' said Flora.

'Maybe you're right,' said Innes. 'Well, good luck. Save us a pie.'

Chapter Thirty

In fact there was to be no pie saving. From the second the Seaside Kitchen opened, it was massively popular – at first through rampant curiosity and a few people down to see what Flora was up to. But after they'd tried the produce – the bread, the cakes, the cheeses of course – it became simply an obvious thing to return. Flora could barely look Inge-Britt in the eye, even though the Icelandic woman was manifestly unbothered and in fact they were hardly in competition with a bar that would reluctantly hand you a watery cup of coffee.

The very first customer Flora had, at 8 a.m. on that bright morning, was Charlie.

'Teàrlach,' she said with pleasure. He looked so cheerful and handsome coming in, taller than the door frame. She caught sight of a bunch of waifs behind him in a motley selection of red and yellow wet-weather gear that had obviously seen a lot of use.

'I see you're back with the wee boys again.'

'Thank God,' said Charlie. 'Last week it was lawyers – no offence.'

'Look at me!' said Flora, who was also wearing a stripy apron.

'Are they all so competitive and joyless?' said Charlie, shaking his head. 'So status-obsessed and uptight?'

Flora thought about Joel.

'Pretty much,' she said glumly.

'Anyway,' said Charlie, rubbing his hands, 'they pay the bills. Right! I want a dozen sausage rolls, two loaves of bread and that entire fruit cake.'

Flora looked at him.

'Seriously?'

'I'm planning on making them very hungry.'

'You'll empty out half the shop.'

'Make more! I'll come back and have a scone this afternoon.'

Flora grinned.

'Well, you can have that one on the house.'

'Thank you, ma'am.'

She bundled the whole lot up, threw in a couple of extra sausage rolls and waved heartily at the faces outside the window, some of whom waved tentatively back. She smiled to herself, knowing what a wonderful day they had in store, especially if it stayed as light and bright as this. As Charlie turned to go, she was struck by something – excitement and happiness at the lovely day, and the weird amazingness of being surrounded by things she'd made herself; even though this wasn't, she told herself, her real job, her real life. Which meant she didn't have to behave the way she did in London.

‘Teàrlach,’ she called as he dipped his head through the doorway. ‘Can we … would you like to have a drink sometime?’

He looked at her in mock-horror as all the kids gathered round, laughing and shouting at him. He held up his hands.

‘Oh, don’t do this to me.’

‘Och, sir, she loves you! Is she your girlfriend, sir? What’s Jan going to say, sir?’

‘Pipe down at once, all of you … Come on, come on, get moving, keep it up.’ And he started to herd them up the little harbour road, but just before he vanished out of sight, he turned round, nodded comically and gave Flora a huge wink.

She was still smiling as she went to check on Iona and Isla in the back, taking things out of the oven, and even when Lorna popped in on her way to school.

‘OMG, look at you, you run a shop!’

Flora went pink.

‘Shut up!’

‘This is going to sound mad,’ said Lorna. ‘But you’re looking well. Like, happier.’

‘That’s because people have stopped spitting at me in the street,’ said Flora.

‘They didn’t do that. People forget. And you’re here.’

‘Temporarily,’ said Flora stoutly. ‘Anyway, what would you like?’

‘What’s the spiciest thing you have?’

‘Is this for you?’

Now it was Lorna’s turn to go pink.

'Sometimes Saif and I have lunch when he's got a quiet surgery.'

'Do you now?'

Flora started bagging up a haggis pasty.

'Just as friends,' said Lorna.

'Obviously,' said Flora.

Lorna sighed.

'What happened to your hot lawyer bloke?'

'He went back to London,' said Flora. 'And I haven't heard from him since.'

She handed over the bag.

'Christ, we are *shit* at this,' said Lorna.

'We are seriously the pits,' agreed Flora, rubbing her eyes. 'Seriously. Isla and Iona both have boyfriends.'

'There's three times as many men as women on Mure,' said Lorna. 'How can we suck so badly at this? Especially you, you're a seal.'

'Shut up, colleen of the glens.'

'We are *such failures*!'

Flora sighed.

'At least we're failures together. Oh, I meant to ask you. Charlie . . . '

'Mr Outward Adventures?'

'What's his deal?'

'I don't know him,' said Lorna. 'Honestly. He's not from here.'

'He's from, like, three islands away!'

'I know,' said Lorna. 'Total stranger.'

'Oh my God, you are so useless.'

'Why, do you like him?'

Flora shrugged.

'I think . . . I think he's cute. Which means I am instantly doomed. That is how it must always be for me.'

Lorna laughed and turned to go.

'Well, have a very successful unsuccessful day.'

'And to you,' said Flora. 'Can we meet up soon and drink lots and lots and lots of wine? And then feel sick but not care and drink some more?'

'Yes, please,' said Lorna fervently, ringing the bell on her way out and startling Colton, who was heading in.

'Well well well,' he said, sounding pleased. 'You did it. Not bad for a bunch of money-grubbing sharks!'

'Thank you,' said Flora.

'Have you told them about the party?'

'You're going to feed people till they give in, aren't you?'

'Are you kidding? Look at the day out there. It's so beautiful. And yes, I'm going to stop a marauding horde of great big metal monsters from storming across my landscape. Yes, I am. Now give me some cheese.'

He scratched his beard casually.

'So. Um. Your brother.'

Flora looked up expectantly. There was definitely something in the water today.

'Mmm.'

'Is he . . . ?' Colton took his glasses off and then put them back on again.

'Yes?'

'Well, I mostly wondered . . . '

Even billionaires, thought Flora. Even billionaires turn

into teenagers once again when they like someone. This felt like school.

Colton looked a bit pink as Iona bustled in with a fresh tray of Annie's iced buns. It was amazing, Flora thought, to see everything her mother had done for them rising again. Being enjoyed again. Because it had felt, when she'd died, that she'd left a big empty hole. And yet here it was. And she had thought it would be sad, but she felt, strangely, anything but.

She turned her attention back to Colton.

'Yes?' she said, smiling.

Colton looked around, as if realising where he was, and blinked. Whatever it was he'd been meaning to say, the moment had gone.

'Um. Right. Well. Whatever. I mean, you'll ask him ... you'll ask him to cater, right? Over at the Rock? He can give it a shot, can't he? The two of you. Well, all of you.' He gestured to the shop.

'Oh!' said Flora, who hadn't been expecting this. 'What about your expensive chef?'

'He's ... Yes. He's still with us. But he'd work under Fintan. For Fintan. *For* him.'

Flora smiled.

'Wow. I'm sure Fintan will be amazed. If my dad can spare him.'

Colton looked as if he had something to say about that, but just then Maggie Buchanan came in, with her usual distracted smile and perfect clothes.

'Hello, Mrs ... '

'Buchanan,' hissed Flora.

'Mrs Buchanan! Great to see you! Like what we've done here?'

Maggie looked around. She sniffed loudly.

'Not before time. It was a disgrace leaving this place empty. I hope you're going to paint the outside.'

'Um, yes, ma'am,' said Colton. 'I'm Colton Rogers.'

She looked at him blankly, which was pretty ballsy, Flora thought, given that she knew exactly who he was.

'Yes,' she said. 'Nice to meet you.'

'I'm having a party at my new place, the Rock,' Colton went on, undeterred. 'And I'd very much like for you to come.'

'Would you now?' said Maggie. 'Four scones, please, Flora. No raisins.'

Flora got to it, fumbling with the till rather, and Maggie turned round with a good day and left the shop without another word.

'She hates me,' said Colton.

'You'd better make it a great party,' said Flora.

The painters had arrived before close of business.

And so it went on. Right from the start, the Summer Seaside Kitchen was incredibly busy; from the first lattes at 8 a.m. until the final slice of cake was taken away at four, every day was a blur.

The oddest thing was, given everything that was going on both there and on the farm, as well as in London, if you were to ask Flora what her worries were at that point, she would have looked at you confused. Because she was too busy worrying about what fish were coming in that morning to make fishcakes with, or whether they were going to run out of cream, or whether the bramble jam was going to be too sour.

On top of that, there was the party to plan.

They met up at the Rock on a cool, clear July day, with fragments of cloud banked against the bottom of the sky as if waiting until they were needed. Fintan was playing hookey from the farm for the day, and looked as ever overjoyed to have thrown off the yoke. His entire gait was looser.

'So the cheese is going out on, like, taster plates,' he was saying. 'You've make those oatcakes again, but you know, if you're making some more, what about adding, maybe, a little chilli to the mix? And some cheese, just to make them incredible? And we'll use the farm butter, and we can just brand it; then if we've already got, like, the fruit pies . . . '

'You've planned it very well,' said Flora encouragingly. 'It's going to be great.' They walked up the path together, touring the little cottage garden.

'Because look! They have raspberries here, and fresh mint and everything. My God, what you could do with this place. Look at it all!'

He looked so happy, standing among the rows of fresh herbs and vegetables, completely in his element. Flora smiled at him.

'And you're going to like working with Colton,' she said, not really considering her words.

He stiffened suddenly.

'What do you mean?'

Flora had hoped this wouldn't be so difficult. Yes, of course Mure was a small island, but this was the twenty-first century. There was gay marriage, the Church seemed to have more or less given up pontificating about it . . . just because the island was traditional. It had never been cruel.

Fintan wouldn't catch her eye.

'Nothing. I mean . . . Just, you guys seemed to get on well.'

'So?'

'So, nothing.'

There was a very uncomfortable pause.

'I get on well with lots of people,' said Fintan.

'Of course you do,' said Flora. 'I know that.'

'I'm not the one sleeping with my boss.'

'I'm not sleeping with him!'

'But you've thought about it.'

'Ugh, person I am related to, *shut up*, bleargh, yuck, not listening.'

'You have! You have! So. Don't lecture me.'

'Shut up! I'm not listening to you!'

'You so fancy him! I'm not surprised. He's hot.'

They both stopped. Fintan looked as if he'd been caught out in something.

'He is,' said Flora quietly.

'Who is?' came a cheerful American voice. Today Colton was wearing jeans and large boots and a massive hoody sweatshirt that made him look like an overgrown teenager, presumably the effect he'd intended all along.

Fintan turned away, but Colton took his arm.

'Hey,' he said. 'Great to see you kids. It's going to be an

awesome party and everyone is going to love me and vote for my proposal, right?'

'We'll give it a shot,' said Fintan gruffly.

'Come on then, we'd better have an early lunch, given I have six million pies to oversee this afternoon.'

They sat out in the sun and ate cold-water oysters with rye bread. It was funny: as children they'd never liked it, the dark, solid bread, and had always moaned and whinged at their mother and longed for the squishy white pan that you got at Wullie's and that lasted for weeks. Now, as an adult, Flora could appreciate it for the lovely, deep-flavoured, evocative thing that it was. Agot, on the other hand, had declared it 'ASGUSTING'.

She added some of Fintan's butter, of course, and for the oysters some vinegar and freshly squeezed lemon juice, and they ate sitting on the extensively carved bench outside the Rock, gazing out at the great northern void, as well as peering round towards the little harbour going about its business, the boats moving slowly in and out.

'God, I love it here,' Colton said suddenly. He was sitting very close to Fintan. 'No phone calls, no stupid meetings, no lawyers . . . present company excepted, of course.'

'Of course,' said Flora.

Colton blinked.

'Why did you ever leave?' he said, looking out across the bay.

'Why do you?' said Flora.

'Because I didn't even discover it until I was forty, by which time I was a multinational conglomerate with offices and employees on four continents. Also, I asked first.'

Flora shrugged, and threw her oyster shells into the sea. They made a satisfying *plouf* noise.

'Because I wanted to work,' she said. 'I wanted a job that wasn't just tourism.'

'There's plenty of jobs,' said Fintan.

'Yes, if you want to work in the Harbour's Rest.'

'Your teacher friend Lorna does all right.'

'My teacher friend Lorna lies awake at night because there aren't enough babies being born to make up the roll and the school might get shut down.'

'Because people like you go away and don't have any babies.'

'You want to talk about not having babies?'

'All right, stop squabbling,' said Colton. 'But don't you want to come back now? Now that you're here?'

Flora smiled.

'I like working for you. But my home is elsewhere.'

She glanced behind her. A clutch of men – and boys; the students back from the mainland once more – were working on the hotel, getting it ready for the night's festivities. It was, hopefully, going to be a big hit.

'Hmm,' she said. Then she stood up. 'I have to get back. Make sure everyone's coming tonight. Get the girls on the ovens. Is the bar ready?'

'Sure is,' said Colton. 'Even for Scottish people. And we have a band, pipers, dancers . . . '

'Kitchen sink,' said Flora.

'Covering all the bases,' said Colton. 'Just like your boss said.'

'Is he coming?' Flora asked, too quickly.

'Oh. Wouldn't have thought so,' said Colton. 'The vote isn't for another month.'

'No. No, I realise that.'

Flora tried not to betray how deflated she felt. She'd been sending Joel reports, but hadn't heard from his office at all. Kai said that if she didn't hear, that meant everything was fine, but it wasn't exactly reassuring.

'Fintan, can you stay here and oversee?' she said.

Colton looked at him, a smile playing on his lips.

'Sure,' said Fintan.

Flora watched the Rock retreat in the rear-view mirror, smiling to herself as she saw Fintan and Colton's heads together. Well well well. She wondered if Innes had suspected. He must have done. Should she mention it, or not under any circumstances? It was a tricky one.

Stepping off the boat, she nearly stumbled into a small elderly form, standing straight and completely ignoring her own walking stick.

'Mrs Kennedy!' gasped Flora. 'Sorry, I didn't see you there.'

'You didn't pay me much mind at the time, either,' said Mrs Kennedy, without smiling. Flora attempted to smile for her, but it went unheeded.

'Well,' said Flora, straightening up.

'So off you went,' carried on Mrs Kennedy, 'leaving us completely wide open, with nobody there for cover.'

'Mrs Kennedy! I'd told you I was moving.'

'Right at the start of the Highland Games season!'

‘I had to do my internship and find a flat.’

It was ridiculous, Flora reflected, how everyone on this entire island conspired to make her feel fourteen years old.

‘Well, I’m back now,’ she said, remembering that Mrs Kennedy was on the council. ‘If there’s any way I can make it up to you . . . ’

Mrs Kennedy looked up at her with those beady, shrewd eyes.

‘There might be, actually,’ she said.

Chapter Thirty-one

Margo blinked.

'But there's the Yousoff case that needs your attention … I mean, you don't really have to go back there, do you? I thought it was all in hand.'

'Colton Rogers could be a massive part of our business. I want to make sure he's happy.'

'Up in that godforsaken place? Amazing. And you should be prepping New York.'

Joel glanced at his calendar.

'I can do that on the plane. I just feel I should be there. He called today.'

Rogers had been very keen for him to be there, it was true. But there was something else that he couldn't put his finger on. Something about the island … He didn't know what it was, but since he'd got back, the rush and frenzy of work hadn't appealed to him quite so much. Another massive heatwave had hit London and everything felt soggy and damp and slow, and he had put it down to lethargy. But when he thought back to that big white beach which went on for ever, and the freshness of the air, and the sheer lack of people, the great emptiness, it felt almost like a dream. But an energising one.

'Rogers was very insistent.'

Margo blinked once more.

'I'll get it booked.'

'Also, I need an outdoor shop.'

'What do you mean?'

'Somewhere you buy outdoor stuff. I don't know.'

The only personal thing Margo usually spent time on for her boss was rudely deflecting calls from breathy-sounding girls. This was new.

'What kind of outdoor stuff?'

'I don't know! That's fine! Off you go! Close the door!'

Margo always knew when to beat a hasty retreat, which was why she'd lasted so long with Joel, who got through staff at the speed of light, generally unable to avoid sleeping with the pretty ones, who then got upset, and taking no interest in the older ones, who then got upset. Margo was both gay and unflappable, which made her more or less perfect for the job, and every time he was rude to her, she put in for another pay rise, which he would always approve without comment. She picked up the phone to the airline.

'Well, it's settled then,' Mrs Kennedy was saying.

'Oh, Mrs Kennedy. Honestly. Anything but that. I haven't danced in years.'

'What's settled?'

Charlie had seen her from the other end of the street, and hurried up to say hello.

'Would you still fit the costume?' said Mrs Kennedy.

Flora rolled her eyes.

'Yes!' she said crossly.

'Well then, it's settled,' repeated Mrs Kennedy.

'I don't think it's settled!' said Flora.

'What's settled?' said Charlie again. 'Flora, I need your leftovers.'

'There are none today. Everything's going to the party.'

'Oh yes.'

'Flora's going to dance at the party,' said Mrs Kennedy.

'*Are* you?' said Charlie.

'No,' said Flora. 'I'm out of practice.'

'Can you still get a bun out of that hair?' said Mrs Kennedy.

'No,' said Flora, who had bad memories of the tightly scraped-back hair she'd always had to have to show off her neck. 'So you'll have to disqualify me.'

'We'll be doing Ghillie Callum and Seann Triubhas.'

'To a band?' said Charlie.

'Aye.'

'This will be great.'

'Teàrlach, you're not helping.'

Charlie smiled to himself.

'What?' said Flora.

'Ach, you won't remember . . . I think I've seen you dance before.'

Flora narrowed her eyes at him.

'I don't think so.'

'We came over from Bute. While back. There was an inter-islands mod.'

Flora blinked. The mod was the Highlands and Islands celebration of traditional music. And also a great opportunity for teenagers to get away from their parents and misbehave.

'I knew I recognised you from somewhere,' he said, his smile crinkling his blue eyes.

'What? Which one were you?' said Flora.

'Oh, just one of the pipers.'

'That doesn't really narrow it down.'

'No, I know.'

'I don't want to see the pictures,' said Flora suddenly. 'I had a bit of a rough hand with the blusher.'

'I had quite a lot more hair then,' said Charlie.

He fell quiet for a moment.

'You were a good dancer,' he said.

'She wasn't that good,' said Mrs Kennedy.

'I do remember you,' said Charlie. 'Your hair came loose.'

'It always did.'

'It was the palest colour I'd ever seen.'

'Imagine you remembering that.'

'I'll see you at six,' said Mrs Kennedy.

Flora glanced anxiously at her watch.

'What? But I've got to instruct the girls!'

'They're dancing too,' said Mrs Kennedy smugly. 'Just make sure they know what they're doing . . . '

'Oh for God's sake!'

'. . . if you want me to come to Mr Rogers' party. And think well of him.'

‘I’ll be there,’ said Charlie, smiling.

‘This is blackmail,’ said Flora, looking at Mrs Kennedy’s stooped back walking away.

Charlie glanced around. Jan was striding purposefully up the street towards them.

‘Okay. Duty calls,’ he said, and lifted his hand and walked away. Jan immediately started bending his ear about something.

‘See you later,’ said Flora.

Chapter Thirty-two

The rest of the day was a crazed frenzy. Everyone baked and baked until the windows of the Summer Seaside Kitchen were completely fogged up. The entire village dropped by because they knew Flora was somehow behind all this and they wanted to know what to wear and who else was going and whether they'd feel strange. There was barely a household that hadn't received an invitation.

Fintan kept calling, beside himself with nerves as professional caterers and drinks suppliers turned up, but as far as Flora could tell, he seemed to be dealing with it admirably.

Meanwhile, the Summer Seaside Kitchen carried on, pie after pie, great piles of oatcakes; Innes driving vanloads of food over to the Rock. They were all pink in the face and quite sweaty, but it looked like they'd be done in time. Raspberries, piles of them; frozen batches of last summer's brambles; plus, mostly, the glorious cloudberries that grew at the very tip of Mure, their sharp, burstingly fresh flavour scenting the kitchen and making Agot, whom Innes had dropped off after she kept being a pain in the neck in the van, and who was now being an utter menace in the kitchen, run round and round in circles and point-blank refuse to take her afternoon nap, which boded very badly indeed for the evening ahead. Even the offer of a hunk of grilled cheese didn't settle her; she eyed it and declared that she actually needed pie instead.

Flora decorated the top of each pie as carefully as possible, with cut-out berries, and leaves, and even a little Mure flag. The radio started playing a Karine Polwart song – 'Harder to Walk These Days Than Run' – which they all knew. Flora and Agot sang along very loudly to the fast bits and even did a bit of dancing, and they were both giggling and covered in flour when suddenly, completely out of the blue, Joel walked in carrying an overnight bag.

Flora dropped the sieve right away.

'Ah,' she said, as he stood there framed in the doorway.

With him there, all the excitement of the last few weeks seemed somehow inappropriate; she wasn't sure if this was the kind of thing he really wanted her to be doing, whatever Colton said.

And God, with the light behind him, he looked . . . he looked so handsome. She'd thought she'd started to forget about him. She was wrong. Out of place, of course, in his smart City suit and his phone clutched in his hand, as if it would magically conjure up a signal on its own.

She realised she had flour on her nose, and moved to brush it off. Joel still didn't say anything. Was he angry? Should she be doing more paperwork? But her brief was to get the island onside, wasn't it? And that was what she was trying to do.

Joel was taken aback, suddenly, by the startling nature of seeing them there. It was the oddest thing. He'd never known anything quite like this; he had never thought about families, not in this way. But if he had . . . It was so strange. The laughing girl with the pale hair; the tiny child who looked like a miniature witch, who even now was running up to him, that strange white hair cascading out behind her, shouting 'YOEL!' with a huge grin on her face; the music; the turning, laughing women; the soft scent in the air; the warmth of the lights.

It was like walking into something he was already nostalgic for, without it ever being his; without it even having passed him by. It was a very strange feeling. From when he was very young, Joel had learned that if ever he wanted something, he should just take it, because so few people seemed to care what he did or how he did it. But this; this didn't belong to him. He couldn't even see how it ever could. You couldn't buy what they had.

He blinked.

'Sorry,' said Flora, moving forward, concerned at his stern face. Agot meanwhile had grabbed onto his leg and didn't seem to be in the mood to let go. There was flour everywhere, as well as the salt spray from the harbour. 'I'm not sure you're dressed for Mure.'

Joel didn't mention the bag full of brand-new outdoor clothes Margo had picked up for him. He'd looked at them and felt it would be unutterably ridiculous to put them on; to pose as something he so obviously was not.

'No,' he said. 'I'm not sure I know any other way to dress.'

Suits, Flora thought, were his armour. Why, she didn't know.

He stepped into the room. They'd kept it feeling like somebody's house, and the little tables had cloths on them. Every surface was taken over with baking for that night.

'It smells good.'

'Is there something else I should be doing?' Flora asked, a little shakily.

Joel smiled.

'No. I'm not sure these aren't some of the more useful billable hours we've ever done. Can I have a slice?'

'HAVE PIE!' said Agot loudly, offering him a grubby piece of pastry from her little paw.

'Oh,' said Joel. 'Actually, you know I've changed my mind.'

Both Agot and Flora looked at him with a comically similar expression.

'Ah. Thank you.'

Bramble got up sleepily to examine him, and added some dog hairs to the mix on his trousers.

'So are you dressing for tonight?' said Flora cheerily, wishing she wasn't quite so red in the face and sweaty and had washed her hair.

'I've got a suit,' said Joel.

Flora looked at him, raising her eyebrows.

'Not a kilt?'

'Oh no,' he said. 'No. Definitely not.'

'Well, it's kind of a tradition.'

'Yes, well, so's taking heroin and I'm not doing that either.'

'Joel!' said Flora crossly.

'WHA'S HERON?' said Agot.

'Sorry,' said Joel. 'Honestly, I'd . . . I'd feel strange.'

'The first time,' said Flora.

Joel shook his head.

'It's just not me. Is Colton dressing up?'

'It's not dressing up!' said Flora. 'It's just what you wear. And yes, of course he is. In fact he's going a bit too far.'

'What do you mean?'

'It doesn't matter.'

'No, seriously. I want to please the client.'

'Well, you'd better find yourself a kilt, then.'

Joel sighed.

'And how will I do that?'

'One of the boys will have one.'

'Really? A spare?'

'Well, Fintan will be in the kitchen all night. I don't think he's wearing his.'

'So he gets to wear trousers like a normal person.'

'Oh no, he'll have his kilt on. Just his regular one, not his formals.'

'Oh God,' said Joel. 'I don't think so, Flora.'

'Okay.'

'So, is everything . . . ? What's our strategy for tonight?'

Flora looked down at the pies.

'Well, this is mine, more or less.'

'Yes, but apart from that?'

'Just be charming, and mention moving the wind farm further out if the subject comes up. I'll point out the councillors to you. Go charm Mrs Buchanan if you can – she's tough as old boots. You could talk to my dad. Oh. And Reverend Anderssen. He's from a proper old Viking family; don't let the chubby hail-fellow-well-met routine put you off.'

'And being related to the invading power is a good thing, is it?'

'Seemed to work in America,' observed Flora, taking out a batch from the oven and putting another one in.

Joel smiled.

'So if he's Scandinavian, he won't mind if I don't wear a kilt?'

Flora gave him a look.

'Yes, well, try it and see how you get on.'

'Oh God,' sighed Joel, starting to regret his impetuous decision to come.

'It could be worse,' said Flora. 'Wait till you see what I have to wear.'

'Well, I'll think about it.'

He looked as if he were about to tarry a little, but instead he turned back towards the door.

'Right, I'd better check in with Colton.'

'Don't say I mentioned his outfit,' said Flora. He'd shown her what he was about to wear, and she'd attempted to be complimentary. But Joel just nodded briskly, and was gone.

'HE SAD,' said Agot sagely.

Flora looked at her curiously.

'What does sad mean?' she asked.

'DOAN NO,' said Agot, losing interest. 'MORE PIE!'

Chapter Thirty-three

'Well, it just about fits,' said Mrs Kennedy doubtfully.

Flora wasn't so sure. But everything else was ready. Great jugs of the evening-churned cream, foamy and yellow in the plain earthenware pottery, had been delivered to go with the pies, which would be cut up and served later by the giggling local girls the hotel had recruited to help out. She hadn't seen Fintan, assumed he was loitering outside the kitchen with the big-boy caterers. Obviously no expense had been spared; she'd seen Kelvin the fisherman and his boys deliver huge amounts of locally sourced langoustines and raised her eyebrows.

'I know,' said Kelvin. 'I wish he'd asked us before. How much money does he have, anyway?'

'All of it, I think,' said Flora.

She'd had a quick shower back at the farmhouse, then headed out for the Rock, which was a hive of people setting things up and rushing about busily. She went to the room that had been set aside for performers and looked at her old costume. She'd already brushed the kilt and washed the shirt, bodice and socks. The shoes she'd had to borrow; her own were so soft and used they were falling apart. Dancers' shoes weren't designed to last.

She had always loved this pale green tartan. Most of the girls liked the big brash colours that made you stand out: the vibrant blues and reds and purples that drew the eye as you all flew together. But this subtle pale colour with the forest-green bodice was one of the few things she'd ever worn that emphasised her pale eyes, rather than making them disappear.

'Have you practised?' said Mrs Kennedy.

In fact, she had run through the dances a few times – in private, in case the boys teased her. She didn't have the height she'd once had on the jumps, but as soon as the music had started up again, her muscle memory had kicked in and she'd remembered the steps immediately.

Iona and Isla arrived, giggling when they saw Flora – whom they thought of as grown-up, and very glamorous for living in London – fully dressed in the regalia.

'What's London like?' asked Isla timidly as they laced up their shoes. 'Is it busy and full of robbers and that?'

'Yes,' said Flora. 'But it's still . . . it's good.'

In fact, she found it difficult to remember, at this distance, exactly what it was like, in the same way you can't remember what it's like to be cold when you're hot, and vice versa. Her brain just seemed to eradicate anything that wasn't the simple experience of being back on the island.

'There's loads of bars and places to go and things going

on, and the buildings just go on for ever, and people come from all over the world, not just like summer here, but really from everywhere. Albania and West Africa and Portugal and everywhere you've ever heard of.'

'Have you ever seen anybody famous?'

Flora smiled.

'I saw Graham Norton on the street. Does that count?'

They thought about it and decided that it did.

'So are you all leaving again after the summer?' said Flora. They shrugged. What else was there to do? Most of them would be going, to Inverness, or Oban, or Aberdeen, or Glasgow, or further. Even though some people did move to the islands, they were different: English eccentrics who thought they'd find a purer way of life up here (this provoked many an eye-roll); Canadians in search of their roots; retired people. Not really the lifeblood of a community. Not these young girls with their fresh blooming skin and flashing eyes, warming up and stretching their long pale limbs.

They were in a back room at the Rock, a place that was meant, Flora assumed, to house functions or weddings one day. It was a beautiful room, filled with oil paintings and pale tartan wallpaper; a massive fire was lit, and comfortable sofas were dotted around. Everything gave off an air of luxury and ease and comfort, but once again those huge picture windows opened on to extraordinary empty views; in this case towards the rocks behind the resort, where pining gulls and eagles dipped and soared in the beams of the endless light.

The girls were clustered around the doors, though, watching everyone arrive as seven o'clock came round.

Mure done up for a night out was quite an amusing sight;

women accustomed to spending the entire year in wellingtons or thick fur-lined boots for the unforgiving winter trying out pastel dresses and high-heeled shoes in exotic colours. Thankfully the rain had stayed away. There was no sun, but the sky was palest blue and white and grey; one of those evenings where the sky shaded into the sea, which shaded into the land, with no difference between them.

The braziers at the doorway had been lit again, and Bertie had been given reinforcements; the much larger boat was out tonight, ferrying people back and forth, dropping off excited pink-faced groups, some already clearly refreshed in anticipation. A piper greeted them, playing a classic lament rather than anything too rousing. The younger dancing girls peered out as the local boys disembarked.

'Ooh look, there's Ruaridh MacLeod,' whispered Iona, and they all laughed rather desperately as a handsome blonde boy marched up the steps, laughing with his fellows and pretending that his mother hadn't arrived on the same boat, and then checked their hair. Yet again Flora's wouldn't behave, and she was sad to see that the rest of the girls had immaculate huge lustrous buns – which they'd clearly bought.

She enjoyed the laughter, but it also made her wince, rather. Oh, the depths of a teenage girl's crush. And having something so very similar … Well. It was not edifying at her age.

She looked around for Joel, but he hadn't arrived yet. She would have to change after the dancing. She'd brought her prettiest dress; she could put it on later, take off her ridiculous kilt. She tried to picture him wearing his. If he did. Well. That would be a sign.

Lorna dashed up. She looked fabulous in a dark green dress that showed off her lovely auburn hair.

'Damn,' said Flora. 'This is very annoying. Couldn't you also have dressed as a teenager?'

'Are you wearing socks?!'

'Shut up!'

Lorna grabbed a glass of champagne and raised her eyebrows meaningfully.

'I can't,' said Flora. 'I might fall off the stage and tell everyone not to vote for Colton.'

'Do you get paid really, really well?' said Lorna.

'I'm beginning to think not nearly enough.'

'Your hair's falling out.'

'I know, I know, shut up.'

Suddenly there was Colton, glad-handing every new arrival, introducing himself, bidding them all welcome. He caught Flora's eye and grinned broadly, coming over.

'Look at you!' he said in delight. 'Now this is what I call going above and beyond in a law firm.'

'Don't you start,' she said This was so far away from the sophisticated London person she liked to project. And closer, she knew, to who she really was.

'No, I mean it! You look wonderful!'

'You do,' said Lorna, kissing her cheek and vanishing into the throng.

Flora stretched her leg behind her.

'I hope I'm not too rusty.'

'Have a dram before you start. You're on pretty early; you can have plenty more afterwards.'

She smiled.

'Mrs Kennedy would actually kill me. Actually kill me dead.'

Colton smiled.

'Well, this is my house. I'd hate to not offer traditional hospitality.'

Flora drew back enough to get a proper look at his outfit. She almost burst out laughing but managed to hide her mouth just in time.

'What?'

'Nothing,' she said.

His eyes narrowed and Flora tried to remind herself that he was still a very, very mega-rich client.

'You don't like it?'

Colton was wearing the entire regalia of a clan chief – and then some: a full Highland dress kilt in bright red and green tartan, with a long frock coat, a huge hairy sporran, a massive dagger stuck in his cream sock, an embroidered tartan waistcoat, a bow tie, a sash in the same tartan across his broad chest and, perched on top of his cropped hair, a massive tartan bunnet with three grouse feathers sticking out of the top.

'Is there a Rogers clan?'

'My mother was as Scottish as you,' said Colton. 'A Frink, she was.'

Flora blinked rapidly.

'Well,' she said. 'You look very nice.'

Colton beamed.

'Thank you.'

The piper began to slow down as a fiddler joined him and the music weaved itself among the gloaming evening. Mrs Kennedy appeared and coughed loudly.

'Is that your cue?' said Colton.

'Looks like it,' said Flora.

'Where's your brother?'

'He's out back helping set up. He's very nervous.'

Colton smiled.

'I think he'll . . . I think he'll do well, don't you?'

Flora nodded.

'I don't think he's cut out to be a farmer.'

'I agree,' said Colton.

'AHEM!'

Outside the building, on the lawn leading down to the sea, a small stage had been erected, surrounded by more braziers. It could be better, Flora thought, but it could be worse. She could see it being used for weddings when the weather was nice enough.

Gathered around it, she thought, was all of Mure. Old teachers; old friends who'd stayed; old friends who'd left and were visiting. The butcher, the postwoman, the milkman, the boys from the farmers' club and the old men from the bowling. The Norse festival committee and the Fair Isle knitters, who took work on when that island was too busy: she recognised them all, and even the ones she didn't know personally she saw the faces repeated; saw pale green eyes like hers. All of them looking at her; judging her for going away.

And the face that wasn't there. Suddenly Flora thought she was going to cry. To collapse, to not be able to dance at all. Her mother had never missed one of her performances – even if, she realised now, it meant leaving the boys alone; leaving Fintan stuck behind doing something – who even knew what? Playing shinty when he didn't want to? Forced to sink or swim with the bigger boys?

She felt a pang of guilt, followed by an even bigger flash of sadness for the gap in the crowd. Oh God, she missed her mum so much. Even though she'd thought that dancing was embarrassing and stupid and pointless when she was a teenager, she'd known, always, how much it had pleased her mother that she did it; that she was good at it, won competitions and rosettes and cups, none of which she'd even glanced at; simply left behind to gather dust in the bedroom she had never thought of.

She blinked back the tears.

'You okay?' came a voice. She turned round to see Charlie at her elbow. He was wearing a simple outfit – a loose shirt with leather lacing; a muted hunting tartan rather than a formal one. He looked like a man who was born to wear it, which of course he was.

'Oh yes, I'm fine,' she said. 'Hi.'

'You look worried.'

She frowned.

'Do you go around telling people to cheer up, it'll never happen?'

'Oh,' said Charlie, his normal laid-back composure disturbed. 'No. Not usually.'

'Sorry,' said Flora, wiping her eyes quickly. 'I was just . . . lost in thought.'

'Okay,' said Charlie. He paused. 'Are you missing your mum?'

She glanced up at him, struck by the gentle kindness of his words, just as the pipes skirled up into 'The Bonnie Wife of Fairlie', and she was borne along on the tide with the other girls, streaming out past the smoke and the crowds, and completely caught up.

Flora realised she'd forgotten, over the last years of being a comfortable student, then a commuting office drone, how much she'd lost. She'd forgotten how much she loved to dance, especially to live music, which moved in and out of her every pore. She fell completely into it, lost herself to the intricate trails of the sword dance as they jumped and kicked in perfect synchronisation, her head whipping past long after the rest of her body had moved; her hair, as ever, starting to fall out of its bun, the pale colour reflected in the firelight as the crowd clapped and whistled, and the girls moved, faster and faster, in and out of each other, never stopping, as the music sped up and the flames leapt higher; and Joel, who had arrived late, feeling unusually out of place, mounted the steps from the soft grey lapping water, herons taking off on his approach, and stood at the lit-up entrance of the garden just in time to see her.

She turned her head then, although she wasn't looking at him, her pale skin reflecting in the firelight, in the happy faces of the onlookers; deep in concentration in the middle of a step, and then she was gone, twirled back into the dance, leaving just an impression of herself behind, her now loose hair darting behind her, and Joel caught himself. And realised. And cursed profoundly.

Because he couldn't understand how he had never noticed this bewitching girl before, this strange foreign creature; and he was utterly annoyed at recognising something he now realised he'd known for a while, and his fist curled slightly in irritation.

He didn't want to ... Well. For starters, she wasn't remotely his type. His type very rarely wore kilts and danced through a night that wasn't dark, on an island that wasn't anything like or anywhere near any place he'd ever been before: a place moreover that felt itself practically like a dream, with its crags, and birds, and endless seas and ageless people who looked at you from the depths of knowing where they were rooted and where they belonged and always had.

This wasn't for him. This wasn't what he wanted. He couldn't risk everything. Everything he'd fought so hard for; every piece of armour he'd built around himself.

The music skirled faster and faster; the clapping louder and louder.

Joel was not a man given to introspection. He had never found it remotely helpful in his circumstances. And he didn't want to do it now. It was self-preservation. And it was important. He couldn't ... He'd managed for over three decades on his own. He thought about what Dr Philippoussis would say. 'There's more to life than work.'

And Joel would counter with all the men he knew – and they were mostly men – who did nothing else; who did get married but left their families miserable and lonely to dedicate themselves to the constant distraction work bestowed.

He needed that. It had saved him. Families and personal relationships could not save him. Not in his experience.

He blinked and vowed to find some cute barmaid, someone, something to distract him.

He looked up again, just as she twirled round and saw him, suddenly, for the first time, and her colour peaked as she caught his eye and, completely involuntarily, a huge smile spread across his face, and for once in his life, he found he had lost his cool completely.

Joel couldn't remember the last time he hadn't been on his phone making a deal, or chasing up a client, or taking a meeting, or chatting up a hot girl in a bar just to prove to himself that he could, or pushing himself beyond his limit at a triathlon . . .

And now here he was, doing none of those things: just standing, watching a girl dance, on the northernmost tip of the world. He felt as if he were moving in a dream; in a different world to anything he had ever known, as the past that he never dwelled on came to him in fragments: gliding effortlessly from bullied junior to superior senior at his fancy boarding school, scooping up awards and scholarships as he went; channelling his loneliness and frustration into grasping for everything, in a way that his profession and adopted cities absolutely encouraged.

And as he'd grown older, filled out, the fierce sports training that honed his body into something women couldn't resist; his ever-growing wealth – he hired someone to find him an apartment and furnish it; the moves to New York, Hong Kong and now London, but never staying long enough to do more than make more money, hang out with the other associates, let the women come and, ideally quite quickly, go.

And they would shout and scream and cry and tell him he was heartless and soulless and empty, everything people already thought about lawyers, making it an easy profession for him to fall into. As if he didn't know.

And yet now here he was, out in the middle of ... God knows where. And there was a girl twirling and flickering in the firelight, and he couldn't take his eyes off her, and he was still smiling, he realised – not a lawyer's smile, not a give-me-your-money smile, not a shit-eating grin, not a flirtatious come-on to a wannabe model.

This was a smile that he absolutely, simply couldn't help; and she held his gaze even as she twined through the web of other dancers, each of them moving so fleetly it seemed impossible they wouldn't bump into each other as the music came faster and faster, so strange-sounding to him, and they were practically a jumping, laughing blur; and he closed his eyes briefly and rubbed the bridge of his nose, because something strange was happening to him and he didn't know what it was, and it scared him worse than anything ever had, and he wished he hadn't come.

Chapter Thirty-four

Flora was genuinely surprised at the huge gale of applause that greeted the Mrs Kennedy Highland Dancers as they ended the dance and with hands on their hips made a low bow. It rolled over them like a wave; and she glanced around those faces that she had found so judging, so hostile before.

Well, now they just looked like faces. Like home. Like people she knew; had always known. She felt a little teary but didn't want to go over the top, as the girls held hands and bowed once more. Then the full band came on to clear the way for a ceilidh, and she ran back inside to change. She had smiled at seeing Joel, realising that he hadn't given in to her teasing and capitulated into wearing a kilt. He was wearing a slightly darker suit; she guessed that was about his limit. It was a message. A sign to her; a reminder that he was slightly apart.

He had, though – and she realised she'd just seen it for the first time – a beautiful smile.

Charlie came up to her on the way in.

'That was … that was lovely,' he said, looking rather pink.

'Thank you, Teàrlach,' she said, feeling funny and giggly, as if she had already been drinking Colton's whisky.

'Will you dance with me later?'

'I might.'

She felt bubbly and fleet and happy … and even more so when she caught sight of her father. She hadn't thought he would come; had told the boys to mention it, but whether or not they would, of course, who could say? And he never went out, not really; she couldn't remember the last time she'd seen him off the farm.

Of course she'd asked him to visit her in London, but when she prodded her heart, she knew how secretly relieved she'd been every time he'd said oh no, oh no, he couldn't leave the farm.

But when had he got so small? She remembered him striding the fields, huge, with a clutch of dogs by his side, visible from miles off as she sat doing her homework, occasionally glancing up, watching as the shadows passed across the hills, the clouds rushing, chasing one another, bouncing like the April lambs in the stone-covered fields below.

Now she towered over him, it felt like; could see he needed a haircut. He still had some hair, white, over his ears, which were hairy too. He was wearing the old kilt that was all he'd ever needed: a Lindsay, the dark reds faded now, from his own mother's side; a mainlander, she'd moved up from Argyll to marry his father after he returned from the war and the troop ships of the North Atlantic. He'd never seen the need to buy a new one; it had seen him through every wedding, every Hogmanay, every Viking festival and every Samhain, and it seemed unlikely to change now. His cheeks were red, the veins broken from years of walking through the wind until he'd become, as the old Mure saying went, a man who couldn't stand upright; but he was, for the first time since she'd got back, looking happy to see her.

'Och yon, dhu,' he said, overcome, and Flora embraced him, the old tweed tickling her nostrils.

'Well, I can't say ... I can't say I like everything that's been going on, all this fuss and folderol.' He indicated the brilliant room. 'But aye, love, she would have been ... She would have ... '

But neither of them had to say any more, and they both knew it.

'Come on,' said Flora, rubbing her eyes. 'Let's go eat.'

She'd change later.

In the restaurant, the tables had been cleared to the side, and there was a huge array of food laid out on them, heavy silver plates gleaming on white tablecloths.

There was lobster and Kelvin's langoustines; herring done the Norwegian way, bristling with little red onions and cloudberries and capers; loaves of crusty rye bread; thick slabs of fresh butter gleaming slickly, great crystals of local salt shining through like jewels. There was locally cured salmon, including the whisky-cured, which was always incredibly popular; as well as huge trays of kedgeree.

Nothing fancy, nothing complicated. No posh cooking

with frills on top. Just everything that was good and fresh and native to the islands; the type of food that had been cooked and eaten there for centuries, overseen by Fintan, who couldn't stop grinning.

Whisky, of course, was plentiful, but also gin, which had become a huge export – made in side vats where the whisky was matured, but a lot quicker to produce, with nothing like the twenty-five-year requirement of the single malts – and Colton stood near the refreshments table making sure everyone's glass was topped up.

And then there were the puddings. Flora couldn't help a quiet internal smile of satisfaction. The pies, almost all of them perfect, took up a full tabletop. There were cakes, too, brought by other people, but the pies were the real sensation, the fruit shining like jewels, the heavy cream pitchers beside them. It seemed almost a shame to cut into them, more than one person commented.

Next to them, on a separate table, with a large MACKENZIE'S FARM banner over the top of it, were the cheeses, cut already into neat triangles, a little taster of each on every plate, with the large wheels at the back, and endless freshly baked oatcakes lined up next to them. It was a feast.

'No, no,' Colton murmured to her, seeing her gazing at the sight. 'You go back to a horrible desk in a horrible city.'

He handed her a dram of Mure single malt, and she drank it, rather too quickly, feeling it going straight to her head, mixing with the adrenalin.

'A desk at a firm that will be working on all your requirements,' she pointed out.

Colton, who was, Flora noticed, quite drunk, flung out his arm.

'This kind of thing is hard to find, kiddo. Harder than you'd think.'

Flora smiled as he refilled her glass.

'Come on, you're working. Let's get you round the entire council.'

Colton sighed.

'This is worst than pitching my first start-up.'

'Yes, it is,' said Flora, smiling. 'Because now you know what you have to lose.'

She didn't mention that she was a little nervous too. People had long memories. But she had a job to do. She squared her shoulders.

'Flora.'

'Maggie!'

Maggie Buchanan sniffed.

'That was not bad. Not bad at all.'

'I realise that. You've met Colton.'

'Thank you for the party,' said Maggie drily. 'With such noble and selfless aims.'

Colton smiled.

'Please,' he said, through gritted teeth.

A Dashing White Sergeant had just started up in the next room. Maggie, who although nearly seventy was still incredibly light on her feet, thanks to her habit of cycling everywhere on rocky terrain through terrible weather, actually took Colton's hand.

Well, thought Flora. That was a step forward.

Also, she realised, looking on and laughing, Colton had

learned all the dances. He wasn't a natural ceilidh dancer, as the boys and girls of the island were, keeping up this side of their Scottish heritage: everyone danced at weddings and parties and celebrations from as soon as they could walk, and it was as natural as breathing, or singing if singing were required.

Colton, Flora soon twigged, was quite different. He kept referring to something in his pocket – at first she thought it was a hip flask, but then she realised it was a tiny book of ceilidh dancing. He was checking up the figures and the moves, all of which he executed with exaggerated care, unlike the general flinging that was going on in other directions, smiling at everyone as he did so.

He was a much more interesting, thoughtful man than she'd assumed, that first morning she'd seen him, brashly making noise about how crap London was in the conference room.

She looked around for Fintan, and saw him tinkering with the cheese plates, looking full of pride, while actually following Colton's progression round the dance floor with more than passing attention.

She turned and went into the main crush of the room, away from the tables.

'That baking,' said an ancient woman Flora dimly remembered from the post office. 'That baking . . . oh, it was like having Annie back.'

Flora blinked.

'Thank you,' she said.

'You're like her – she was a proper selkie girl.'

Sometimes there was no point in fighting it.

'I know,' said Flora.

'There's a lot of her in you.'

'I'm glad,' said Flora. 'I'm so glad.'

'Welcome home,' said the woman quietly, and many of the older people sitting there echoed the sentiment. 'Velcom, velcom,' echoed around the table in the local accent, and her glass was refilled yet again.

Charlie appeared at her shoulder.

'Come and dance with me; you promised,' he said, even though he was still forking large pieces of pie into his mouth.

'You're eating!' she said.

'Yes.' He smiled. 'I thought I'd better book you up before you got too popular. And it's utterly tremendous. Try it!'

Flora had been too wound up to eat, but she tried a mouthful. It was the cherry, and it was indeed pretty good. She smiled.

'Yes, it's true, I am fabulous,' she said, teasing.

'It's your night, Ms MacKenzie,' he said, putting down his empty plate and proffering his arm.

'Where's Jan?' she asked suddenly. This was absurd: he was definitely flirting with her, and if he was in a relationship, it wasn't fair. Because, undeniably, she liked him. He didn't make her heart leap and her pulse race like Joel did. But that was stupid, because Joel was unattainable. Charlie was right here. His large, broad solidity; his bright blue eyes and open face. The opposite of Joel. But if she was going to get to know him better, she had to know.

Charlie blinked.

'Oh, she's around,' he said vaguely.

Flora caught sight of her then, going at the pudding display with great gusto.

'Are you two . . . ?'

'Separated,' said Charlie quickly. 'We're separated. I'm amazed you didn't know. I thought everybody did.'

'Well, I'm not everybody,' said Flora brightly.

'You're not,' agreed Charlie.

She wished she'd had a chance to get changed. Although in fact, what she was wearing suited her far better than the slightly too small Karen Millen dress she'd bought the previous year for a wedding and that wasn't repaying its investment at all.

'But you still work together?' she went on.

'Oh yes. We run the firm together. She's a decent sort, Jan.'

'So why—?'

'Are you dancing?' said Charlie. 'Or do we have to stand around here discussing every element of our lives like we're on some mainland reality show?'

Flora smiled.

'I wouldn't have thought you'd have had much time to be watching that kind of thing,' she said.

'Oh yes, because you know everything about me.'

He took her hand and led her into the dance. Colton was now dancing with two old ladies from the curling society, in a move that involved two girls for every boy and vice versa, and very pleased they looked to have got him. Charlie happily whirled her in and round with Bertie on her other side, and they joined the throng.

Flora gave herself over to the music, dipping and spinning at high speed without pause, the men's kilts whirling and her twirling herself in and out of them. She felt so free suddenly.

Behind one of the heavy curtains, deep in shadow, Joel watched her laughing with that big man who followed her around everywhere as far as he could tell; watched her with a hungry look he recognised in himself, and despised.

He cursed and left the room.

Giggling at the end of the dance, Flora realised she hadn't checked how Joel was doing, which was utterly remiss of her considering he knew hardly anybody there. She had to introduce him to people and look after him, seeing as Colton was busy. Also, she realised, while she'd been dancing with Charlie, she hadn't thought of him at all.

'Excuse me,' she said, looking around the room, but there was no sign of him. 'I have to go. Can you ask Mrs Kennedy to dance?'

'No,' said Charlie. 'She's terrifying.'

'Yeah . . . but she's on the council.'

Charlie rolled his eyes as Flora slipped away from the dance floor.

Flora wandered through into the little nooks and crannies of the downstairs of the hotel, all beautiful cosy sofas and soft lighting; large open fires everywhere. She felt very warm from the room and the noise and the dancing and the smooth whisky now coursing through her veins.

Suddenly, over the back of a sofa, she spotted his glossy nut-brown hair, and round the side, the shiny dark outline of his shoe and the long line of his trouser leg, his expensive suit, immaculate as always, so different from the rest of the men in kilts. Just himself. Just Joel.

And it flashed across her mind once more the way he had looked at her when she was dancing – it was just a split second, but she hadn't been imagining it, had she? Had she? God, what the hell was she doing?

Slightly drunk, she forgot everything else. Forgot the rest of Mure beyond the doorway; forgot Charlie, waiting to dance with her again; forgot that she was meant to be sticking by Colton's side, loyally listening to him and introducing him to everyone and getting people onside. She forgot everything except her proximity to Joel; to this man she had wanted so much for so long. And now they were a thousand miles away from everything else in their normal lives; everything that mattered to him – whatever that was.

She had come here to please the firm. She had left Mure to please her mother. She had stayed away because … because she hadn't known what else to do. Flora felt like a boat sometimes, tossed about on the tide, not sure where she was going to end up or why. Suspecting that she would look back on her life one day and not really remember making the choices that she had made.

The fire crackled enticingly; the noise of the party faded behind her. He hadn't seen her; his head wasn't moving.

Flora breathed in. This wasn't like her at all. She didn't feel in the least like herself. But even if it was just for tonight … when she wasn't feeling guilty, or down, or a bad daughter, or out of place. When she was feeling good; feeling that she deserved something; that her hard work was paying off. When people were getting what they wanted. Couldn't she?

She bit her lip nervously one last time, then stepped forward.

'Joel?'

'Flora! Hi! Great to see you!'

Chapter Thirty-five

Inge-Britt Magnusdottir rose to greet Flora, assuming she was looking for her boss, although Joel hadn't mentioned that she might want to speak to him. Not that Inge-Britt had been listening particularly; she'd been nestling suggestively in the huge sofa, concentrating on his flat stomach and long thighs and wondering how soon would be too soon to suggest they leave and go back to the Harbour's Rest. Inge-Britt had a very straightforward approach to what she felt like doing, something that Joel, in his turmoil, had been appreciating. This was territory he understood.

'Inge-Britt!' said Flora, completely wrong-footed and going instantly brick red. She felt like she wanted to cry. She did want to cry, very much. 'It's great to see you!'

'Well, everybody's here, so I wasn't going to be doing too much business tonight,' said Inge-Britt, smiling. 'You never mentioned that your boss was so . . . interesting.'

'Didn't I?' muttered Flora.

Joel couldn't look at her. Couldn't. Was she annoyed with him? Disappointed? Did she want him? He wanted . . . more than anything he wanted, suddenly, to take that pale hair in his hands, to pull her into his arms. He wanted to sleep with her; of course he did. Joel wanted to sleep with most people. But it was more than that. He wanted to talk to her. He wanted to comfort her; he wanted his sadness to touch hers; he wanted to share.

Joel had never wanted to share. When you have no toys, you cannot learn to share.

He shut it down. He didn't lift his head.

'You need me?'

Yes, she wanted to say. I need you. I need something pure. I need good sex and the sensation of choosing something for myself, of not waiting to be chosen. I need to be myself; to sleep with someone people wouldn't think was right for me; I need to be, for once, wild and dangerous, and not do what everyone expects a hard-working, quiet, colourless girl like me to do. Not in a million years.

She swallowed.

'No,' she said. 'It's fine. I just came to check you were all right. I don't know if your ceilidh dancing's up to much.'

'I'll teach you,' said Inge-Britt cheerily.

'I don't dance,' said Joel shortly.

'Well, why did you come?' said Flora before she could stop herself.

'Thank fuck,' said Inge-Britt, carelessly splashing more of a bottle of vodka she'd commandeered into both their glasses. 'Scandis think it's hilarious, I should tell you. A-diddly-diddly-diddly-diddly.' She was quite drunk.

Flora was suddenly very aware of the ridiculous tightly laced velvet bodice she was wearing; the childish soft tartan hanging to her knees; her tumbling hair. She must look unutterably silly to them, a local hick.

'I'll get back to it then,' she said, trying to smile and failing miserably. 'Colton will probably want a word later.'

'Great,' said Joel, although it hurt him tremendously to do so. He took a sip of his drink in the hope that it would numb him. 'Let me know if you need anything.'

She went back to the dance, where Charlie was bravely trying to accompany Mrs Kennedy. Without even caring about being rude, she walked up to him as the music stopped, took his hand and pulled him away before he had a chance to bow.

Outside, the sky was white, a tiny hint of blue at the edges indicating it was close to midnight. On the lawn where the stage had been, fairy lights were still hanging, and the rustles and whispers of other couples came from among the trees. She held his huge hand and looked up at him, and he returned her gaze with those clear blue eyes; then, as the music started again, he put his hand on her face, and emboldened, she reached up and kissed him, hard, all her passion in it.

When the shock came, it was like being drenched with cold water. Which, Flora had absolutely no doubt, would also have happened if there had been any available.

There was a hand on the back of her waistcoat, hauling her off. She turned round in shock. She had been lost, entirely, in the sheer pleasure of kissing a handsome man under a clear night sky.

Jan was standing there, her face brick red.

'What the hell do you think you're doing?'

Flora staggered back, then glanced at Charlie, who looked defiant, cross and incredibly sexy.

'You told me—' she began.

'We're taking a rest, you said!' shouted Jan. 'Not broken up!'

Charlie looked at her, then back at Flora.

'It's been months,' he said. 'Look, Jan, be reasonable . . . '

'No,' she said, her mouth a tight line. '*You* be reasonable. You know what Daddy said.'

Flora had absolutely no wish to hear what Daddy had to say. She tugged down her ridiculous kilt for the last bloody time, her own face bright red, conscious that people would be wondering where she was and what she was up to, then backed away. She was going to find the Land Rover and get out of there; she wanted nothing more to do with Charlie, Jan, Joel, Inge-Britt, Murians, Londoners, Americans or basically anyone else on earth.

She caught sight of the ongoing party as she left. Colton was still grandstanding in the middle of it, but the music now sounded grating to her ears, the happy sounds of people having a good time were like the silly twitterings of birds in a zoo, and the beautiful warm, happy rooms were ruined, as if someone had turned on a nasty fluorescent light and shown every line on people's faces, every mark on their clothes; and soon everything would turn dark and dingy and fade away.

Chapter Thirty-six

Flora had sobered up enough to give Lorna a lift home from the Rock. On the way she'd told her what had happened with Charlie and Jan.

'And what's her bloody dad got to do with it?' she had finished, furious. 'She's a grown woman. She should act like one.'

'Yeah, about that,' Lorna had said, genuinely hating to be the bearer of bad news. 'He's Fraser Mathieson. That's Jan Mathieson.'

'Fraser Mathieson, member of the town council?' said Flora quietly.

'Um, yup,' said Lorna.

'Fraser Mathieson, the island's richest man? Apart from Colton? Oh *crap*,' said Flora. 'God, men are nobbers.'

'I liked Charlie.'

'I wasn't even talking about him,' said Flora glumly, and went on to tell Lorna about Joel and Inge-Britt. 'Everything sucks ass.'

They carried on online when they reached their respective homes. Kai and Lorna had never met, but they were getting aquainted on WhatsApp and were absolutely united, and it was helping, it really was. Flora sat by the light of the dying fire, drinking tea to try and make herself feel better, though it wasn't working. Thank God for Bramble, who had his big head in her lap, occasionally gently licking her hand, as if bestowing tiny kisses.

Nobber, typed Lorna.

Awful, awful man, said Kai. Would you like us to have him killed for you?

That would be nice.

I'll get some poison from Saif's medicine cabinet! added Lorna. 💉💊

I'll put fish in his desk drawer.

Flora smiled and sighed and tucked into some cookies she'd left behind in the kitchen, thinking they'd probably need sustenance later. That was the thing about dancing and heartache: it made you hungrier than you'd think. She had heard there were girls who just faded away when they were sad. Flora was not one of those girls.

She was almost smiling when she heard a car pull up at the door. She frowned. Her father had returned with Innes and Hamish a while ago and they were now all tucked up in bed; she could make out her father's snoring from here. Agot had had to be dragged away from the party, loudly protesting; she had danced every dance, often simply appearing in front of the first available man and demanding they partner her. Heaven knows what she was going to be like at fourteen.

So who was this then?

For a tiny second, a bit of her thought it might be Joel, come to beg or say sorry; that he'd much prefer a mousy legal aide to some six-foot blonde Icelandic Amazon. But of course he didn't have a car here. She'd been driving him about. She shook her head, furious with herself again for being such an idiot. Oh God! It suddenly struck her: when he had seen her dancing, had he been laughing? Was that what she'd seen on his face? Amusement? Ridicule at her funny little rural ways? She felt her face burn red. This evening had started so well, had gone so amazingly; she couldn't have counted up the compliments about the food. And now here she was back in the stupid old kitchen, staring at her tea. Again.

Or could it be Charlie? His kiss had been strong and heartfelt and had awakened something in her, something she hadn't felt for so long ... she didn't even want to think how long. All this time, with work and confusion and grief and a silly unobtainable crush that kept her from looking around, she'd been ignoring herself, what she needed, what she wanted. She touched her mouth experimentally. It felt puffy. Just to feel wanted again, to feel desired ... to know it was still there ...

Whoever was outside didn't seem to be coming in. She crept to the kitchen window, but the lights were off. She could just make out two heads moving in the windscreen – it was a large Range Rover – then suddenly realised that she could be seen with the light from the fire behind her and scuttled away.

Seconds later, Fintan pushed through the kitchen door and the car drove away, bumping down the rocky path.

Flora looked up and went to pour another cup of tea.

'What time do you call this?' she said in a teasing tone, trying to cover up her own heartache.

Fintan looked at her and smiled a slow smile, then blinked, equally slowly. He looked a little dazed.

'Sorry. Sorry, I . . . Yeah. Colton offered me a lift home.'

'Colton offered you a lift home?'

'Uh, yeah.'

'Are you sure he hadn't drunk too much whisky?'

'Oh yeah,' said Fintan, taking the tea gratefully. 'He totally had. I thought it was bumpy coming home.'

'FINN!'

'No, it's okay, Officer Clark was passed out under the cake table when I left. It was stripped clean, by the way. People were licking plates. You really aren't half bad.'

Flora frowned and ignored the compliment as she poured some milk into his cup.

'So . . . '

Fintan bit his lip and tried to hide his smirk.

'Mm?'

'Well . . . '

'Flora, if you want to ask, just ask.'

'I do want to ask. Does Dad know?'

'Why? Do you think the shock would kill him?'

Flora shook her head.

'I don't know why it never occurred to me,' she said.

'Because you never gave us a second thought.'

'That's not true.'

'You know it is, Flora. You know it. You left and you never thought of us again, up here, shovelling cowshit.'

'Stop it,' said Flora. 'Please. I'm exhausted. Please can we not fight any more? Tonight should have been good. It was good.'

'Oh no, it's fine, we don't have to fight. Fintan's gay now, wow, isn't that amazing, your family's almost cool enough for a mainland girl.'

'Fintan!' Flora was properly crying now, furious that she could barely get the words out.

'Yeah, now you've got something acceptable for your smart metropolitan friends, eh?'

She took a deep breath, stood up and looked him straight in the eye.

'What, so you had a boyfriend before I came back? Before you met Colton?'

Fintan didn't answer.

'So you were already breaking out of your old life and trying to make a go of catering and setting things up and making your own way . . . before I came back?'

There was a long pause. Fintan shrugged.

'I was all right.'

'Or you could say, thank you, sis, for introducing me to Colton.'

He looked at her, and they were both up to the brim with pain. Eventually Fintan shrugged.

'I'm sorry.'

Flora swallowed.

'I'm sorry too.'

They sat down together at the old table, Fintan fiddling with his spoon.

'The funeral . . . '

'I said some stuff I didn't mean.'

Fintan nodded.

'So you never came back at all.'

'I was ashamed.'

'And did staying away make you happy?'

Flora shook her head.

'I'm not sure I even know what happy is. It made me busy. Isn't that enough?'

'I don't think so.'

He reached his hand over to her.

'Sorry I yelled. It's been brewing a long time.'

'I know,' said Flora. 'I realised that.'

'And I have . . . It has been good since you got back, Flora. I mean it. You've just . . . I shouldn't have got stuck in that stupid rut. I was so bitter.'

'Thanks,' said Flora.

'Still, don't tell Dad just yet,' said Fintan.

'I won't. He's barely talking to me anyway.'

He smiled.

'He's pretty awesome, though, don't you think?'

'Colton?'

Fintan nodded.

'Yes. Did he keep the hat on?'

'None of your business.'

'His great big gigantic feathery headdress.'

'Shut up, you!'

Flora smiled.

'So, you're not seeing your boss tonight?' He narrowed his eyes at her. 'You do like him, don't you? I'm not imagining things?'

Flora shook her head.

'You can forget about that. Anyway, it doesn't matter. He met Inge-Britt.'

'Oh, the Spicelander.'

Flora nodded.

'So. It's okay. I'm fine.'

She debated whether to tell him about Charlie and decided against it. Presumably it would be round the island by the morning anyway.

'He didn't seem like your type.'

'I wish everyone would stop saying that.'

'I mean . . . well, I don't know. I think I just saw you with somebody nice. Like Charlie MacArthur.'

'Joel is nice!' flared Flora.

'Is he?'

'Oh God, I don't know. You know what it's like when you're just so mad for someone and they're all you think about and you can't get them out of your head and you just want to—'

She stopped herself.

'Oh yes,' said Fintan. 'God, the crush I had on Officer Clark.'

'*Really?*' said Flora, remembering a certain Viking festival a long time ago.

'Oh yes. Years.'

'But I . . . I got off with him!'

'Yeah, I remember. Thanks for that.'

'Christ, no wonder we used to fight so much.'

Fintan smiled.

'Don't worry. I got my revenge at the Christmas party.'

'Who with?'

Fintan named Flora's boyfriend from when she was fifteen; he had worked down the garage and she had thought he was terribly risqué because he rode a motorbike. Her mother had been incensed.

'NO WAY!'

'Och aye the noo, up here on Mure there's nothing much going on, you know.'

Flora narrowed her eyes at him.

'I'm going to bed before you tell me anything else utterly horrifying.'

'Oh yes, nothing to see here; just us and the pixies and the selkies and the—'

'Shut up!'

'Yeah, yeah. Anyway, I'm off to bed. It's the bloody yearlings' transportation tomorrow. Off to the mainland with a bunch of coos. What could be more fun?'

They embraced, warmly, and Flora switched off her phone and felt better. Just about.

Chapter Thirty-seven

Joel stood staring at the white waves outside his window. Behind him on the bed, Inge-Britt lay fast asleep, magnificently long and tousled, looking to Joel like so many other girls. She'd already told him she had to get up first thing to make breakfast.

He turned back to the streaked window. It was broad daylight again, even though it was only 5 a.m. How could anyone stand it? When did anyone here ever sleep? How could they? Did you just get used to living your entire life in the light? He supposed you did. It wasn't dawn; it was morning.

But a rough, squally, frenzied morning it looked to be. The waves were pounding, and although there weren't any trees to gauge the wind speed, he could see the heather bowed low in the gusts. A heron took off down by the edge of the surf, and he saw it struggle for a moment, stretching out its wings and heading determinedly into what looked like a proper storm.

He looked up. There was just so much sky here. The clouds were moving across it so fast it looked like they'd been sped up, as if he was watching a film in fast motion. He found himself slightly hypnotised by them.

Even though he was tired, so tired – he never slept these days, even by his standards – there was the dim and distant fact that work would be piling up on his desk; things he shouldn't be missing or losing out on; that the world was rushing on without him; that he should probably sit down and get a few hours in right now if he wasn't going back to bed.

But he didn't. Instead he grabbed a glass of water, pulled on a large navy jumper from the pile Margo had packed for him and sat in a chair next to the window, his feet up on the ledge.

He found himself just watching the clouds, losing himself slightly drowsily in the whirling patterns and shapes they made fleeing across the sky, and he realised that in some strange way, despite everything, he hadn't felt so calm for months, for a long time. He thought about Flora. He had dodged a bullet; he had seen her face. That should make him feel better. But somehow it didn't.

On the other hand, he would see her that day. And that made him feel oddly comforted.

He watched the clouds tumble here and there, and as he did so, he felt his heartbeat gradually slow, and before he knew it, it was eight o'clock, and although he hadn't realised he'd dozed off, there was no sign of Inge-Britt, and the storm was still blowing, and it was time to go to work.

Chapter Thirty-eight

'Can I have it to go?' Flora was saying to Iona and Isla, who were both nursing the truly gigantic hangovers only achievable by students who haven't met a free bar before. Also Isla had pulled young Ruaridh, which was not pleasing Iona. Unless it was vice versa.

'You shouldn't have a paper cup. You should bring a flask,' said a bossy voice.

Flora turned around. There was Jan, wearing a bright pink fleece that would have looked unflattering on Mila Kunis. Her heart skipped.

'Jan!' she said. 'Look. You have to believe me. I had absolutely no idea . . . Charlie told me you'd split up. I would never have—'

Jan passed over her flask without acknowledging her.

'Hello, Isla.'

'Morning,' said Isla. 'Did you have a good time at the party?'

'No. Apart from everything else, such terrible showing off,' said Jan. 'I can't stand that kind of over-the-top display, can you?'

Flora thought about how much food she'd seen Jan stuff down her gullet last night at Colton's expense, and clenched her fists.

'Och, I thought it was nice,' said Isla. 'You looked bonnie, Flora.'

'Thanks,' said Flora. 'I thought I looked a bit daft.'

'Yes, there's a time for squeezing yourself into a dancing kilt, isn't there?' said Jan, as if she weren't, Flora thought crossly, wearing a bright pink fleece. 'And a time when you're just a bit past it.'

She swept out, leaving Flora staring behind her.

'Can I bar her?' she wondered aloud.

'You're going to start barring locals?' said Iona in surprise.

'You're right,' said Flora. 'It's not wise, is it?'

'What did you do?' said Iona.

'Ooh!' began Isla, a cheeky look on her face.

'All right, all right, you can gossip when I've gone,' said Flora. 'But you should know, I thought they'd broken up.' She rolled her eyes. 'It's almost like *Friends* has finally made it to Mure, only twenty years after everywhere else.'

She glanced around.

'Right. I'm taking all the bannocks.'

Joel might not fancy me, she thought, and I don't know I can face mentioning the potential bad news about Fraser Mathieson. But they can't not welcome a warm, crusty bannock on a chilly morning.

Colton had sent the boat for her, as the boys had taken the Land Rover to tow the protesting yearlings to the airport. It was a nasty, messy business and none of them ever enjoyed it, especially on such a horrible morning.

In the dining room at the Rock, though, everything was spotlessly cleared away, the fire was lit and all was warm and cosy. It looked lovely.

Colton glanced up as Flora entered, bearing a tray.

'I've forgotten,' he said. 'Are we mounting a legal challenge or launching the MacKenzie Catering Company?'

'Legal challenge,' said Flora, just as Joel said, 'Can't it be both?'

But she didn't look at him, didn't raise her head, and he felt a little tawdry and embarrassed.

Flora concentrated on spreading local honey on the bannock from the Seaside Kitchen. It was delicious, and with coffee from Colton's expensive machine, utterly perfect. Outside, it was now blowing an absolute hooley. The sea was almost completely white and grey, the sky still filled with infinite clouds. Flora frowned. It had been bumpy getting round the northern point of the island; she didn't want to think about getting back.

Joel was on the other side of the table. They'd barely glanced at each other. He looked different; Flora couldn't quite work out what it was. Then she realised: he wasn't wearing a tie, just a simple blue shirt, with a jumper of all things. Probably lost it tying up Inge-Britt during lots of athletic and hearty Icelandic sex, Flora thought bitterly.

The image flashed across her mind and she shook her head to clear it.

'Well,' said Colton. 'I think last night went rather well.'

He looked delighted, like a tall cheeky gnome, and was obviously expecting an enthusiastic response. Both Joel and Flora were extremely muted, however, and Colton's face fell.

'No, it was great,' said Flora, trying to rally. 'Everyone came, everyone had a great time. They were all grateful, you know. Did you really dance with everyone?'

'Everyone,' said Colton, 'who wanted to. I think some of the church elders were a little stuffy.'

Flora smiled.

'That's okay. They're allowed to be stuffy, it's their job.'

'Well, jobs I get.'

'I think it's all going well,' said Flora. 'I would propose carrying on with the pop-up – I mean the Summer Kitchen. I think the girls can handle things there pretty well. Fintan can help out too.'

'Can he?' said Colton, smirking a little.

'You have to spend the rest of the summer just being visible, out and about, reasonable. Talk to the locals. Use local facilities. Enjoy the island. I think you'll find everyone *much* more amenable by September. This is really working out well.'

Colton nodded.

'Actually,' he said, 'I've already asked Fintan to come work with me full time. Didn't he mention it?'

Flora blinked. What?

'No,' she said. 'He didn't say anything to me.'

'Makes sense,' said Colton. 'He could run the Rock's

catering for me. He's got the skills; he's got the feel. You saw what he did last night. He knows all the local suppliers.'

Flora shook her head.

'You don't understand,' she said. 'He can't. He can't leave the farm. He's needed.'

Colton shrugged.

'That's not really . . . I mean, I've already asked him.'

'Oh my God,' she said. 'But my dad. If he doesn't have anyone to work the upper field, he'll have to sell it. We can't afford to hire anyone new. Everything will go to pieces . . . '

She fell silent, thinking about how happy Fintan had been last night. How much he wanted – needed – to do this. And she knew, too, that she had absolutely no right to ask him to stay. Not after everything she'd done to the family. There would be no point talking about loyalty now.

'What'll happen to your farm?'

Flora frowned.

'Well. These things . . . I mean, there have been MacKenzies farming there for God knows how long. But times change, I suppose. Dad's getting too old for it now. Innes is distracted half the time with Agot, and Hamish, well. Not so hot on the management side of things. Might eat all the stock.'

Colton looked out across the water. You could see the farmhouse quite clearly, its pale grey walls glinting in the early-morning sunlight.

He leaned forward.

'How much cheese does Fintan make again?'

'Not enough for mass production,' gabbled Flora. 'Apart

from the cheese, there's seaweed if you wanted it . . . dairy, obviously, some sheep . . . I mean, it's just a farm.'

Colton nodded thoughtfully.

'It could,' he said. 'I mean, it would solve a lot of my import problems and get me in with the community even more . . . '

Flora looked at him, not sure what he was saying.

Joel understood, though.

'You're not going to turn this into a conveyancing case.'

Colton smiled.

'Is that beneath my fancy London lawyer?'

'Yes!' said Joel.

Colton smiled even more.

'Well, that makes it totally worth my while to do it.'

'What do you mean?' said Flora.

'Isn't it obvious? I buy the farm. Your father can live there, no problem. Fintan works with me, those other boys help him with the cheese and butter and so on, and everything I need that can come from you comes from you. And this place . . . ' He indicated the room they were sitting in with an expansive wave of his arm, 'will become world famous!'

Flora sat back.

'Are you going to employ everyone on the island just to get the wind farm scheme abandoned?'

'No, Flora,' said Colton crossly. 'I want to employ you lot because you're good.'

Flora let out a long breath.

'What? It's clearly a win/win.'

'Yes, well, you're not the one who'd have to convince my father to sell his farm.'

'He doesn't have to move! He doesn't have to go anywhere!'

'It's not about that.'

Colton blinked.

'I'll offer a good price.'

'It's not about that either.' Flora strove to keep the annoyance out of her voice.

'It's certainly one solution, Colton,' said Joel. 'Let's talk it over. Right. I need to get back to London. Flora, you have to stay here until it's settled.'

Flora wanted to argue but didn't dare. Instead she glanced out of the window.

'Um, Joel . . . I don't think you'll be going back today.'

'What do you mean?'

Outside, the waves were up to the sea wall, and the clouds were scudding ever faster.

'They don't land planes in this.'

'What do you mean?'

'No ferries, nothing. The weather's on.'

'Don't be ridiculous,' said Joel. 'In Chicago they land in nine feet of snow.'

'Yes,' said Flora. 'Nice, fallen, calm snow. This isn't like that. And they're small planes too. I don't think you're getting home today.'

'Of course I am,' said Joel.

Just as he said this, there was a ripple and a short crackle, and the power went out.

'What the hell?' said Joel.

'It's just a power cut,' said Flora carefully. 'Happens all the time.'

Joel glanced at his phone.

'Which means the Wi-Fi has gone.'

'Yup, the Wi-Fi's gone.'

Joel swore at some considerable length.

'But there's the Foulkes deposition. The case is coming up. I was literally meant to be here for one night. And the Arnold convention. I absolutely don't have time for this.'

'I was surprised you came,' said Colton.

Joel grimaced. Not as surprised as he'd been.

'Yes, but now I have to go.'

Flora and Colton looked at each other.

'Well, I don't know what to do about that,' Colton said.

'Oh God,' said Flora. 'And the boys have gone. They've got cattle on a plane, they've headed to the mainland. They'll be having a terrible time of it.'

There was another huge crack of thunder.

'I'm stuck here?' said Joel.

'Can we take one of your cars?' said Flora to Colton. 'Drive back to the village?'

'Ah,' said Colton. 'Actually, they've all been put in the underground storage unit for safekeeping.'

'The what?'

Colton looked embarrassed.

'Well, salt spray is bad for the paintwork.'

'You must have kept out a Range Rover ... something, surely?'

'The thing is, it's Overfinch?'

Flora didn't know what that was but she recognised the tone of voice that indicated he wasn't remotely interested in putting a vehicle at their service.

'COLTON!' said Flora. 'Seriously, have you ever lived here in the winter?'

Colton looked embarrassed.

'If you want to be one of us, if you want to truly belong . . .' Flora stood up, her eyes flashing. 'If you want us to give up our livelihoods, work for you, cook for you, stand with you, you have to commit. You have to be with us. You can't just cherry-pick the pretty days. We have to be together, or we have nothing.'

She realised belatedly that she was trembling, and that both men were staring at her. She swallowed. This was not the kind of thing she'd ever done in her professional life before.

'Uh,' she said. 'I'm sorry.'

Colton shook his head.

'No,' he said. 'I see. I think I do.'

Joel was still just looking at her.

There came a shout from outside. It was Bertie Cooper, warning them that if they wanted to get back over, they had to do it now. He was having enormous trouble keeping the boat steady, even just in the narrow channel they had to cross.

'We'd better go,' said Flora. 'I know it doesn't look far, but we lose boats out here all the time. You can wreck-dive to your heart's content down there. Every one in full view of the shore, and no way to save them. Never has been.'

'COME ON!' came Bertie's voice. 'I'm leaving! I'm leaving now!'

The triple-glazed windows of the Rock had kept out the howl of the crashing summer storm, but once they were outside, they felt it. You couldn't speak, couldn't hear anything at all: the pounding of the waves and the huge shriek of the wind was all-encompassing. Colton marched on ahead – he refused to let them go alone – and Flora followed in his slipstream. On the jetty, she slipped suddenly, losing her footing. Before she knew it, Joel was there, grabbing her, holding her up, and she lost her breath and tried to thank him. He kept hold of her, kept hold of her elbow as he steered her towards the boat, and she felt his strong grip on her arm and was comforted.

The short crossing was filthy. The boat pushed up and down, fighting them every step of the way. The motor kept giving out and Bertie nodded at them to bale in the back. Joel's clothes were completely soaked. Their eyes were stinging, and Flora's hair was flying round her head like a wild thing. Joel turned his head to her mid-crossing, as she stopped baling for a moment and craned her neck to see how far they had to go to reach the land, and suddenly, with the water pouring in and the spray hanging in the air all around them, she looked like something from the depths: a nymph or a naiad.

She caught him looking at her and guessed he was worried.

'It's okay,' she lied. 'I've been in worse than this,' and he shook his head and took off his glasses, which he could no longer see through, and Flora looked at his beautiful dark brown eyes, then forced herself to turn back to watch the shore, as Bertie cursed, and flushed the water out once more from the drenched engine. Finally, as the boat started to list alarmingly, and even Colton was looking concerned, and several people had come to their doorways to watch them; finally, soaked through and teeth chattering, they struggled to shore.

They were very relieved when Andy the barman came out of the Harbour's Rest with blankets for them all. Flora took one gratefully, as well as the hot toddies he appeared with next. He ushered them into the bar.

There was a huge commotion suddenly and an enormous woofing was heard. Flora glanced around in consternation as a wet, hairy Bramble threw himself up against her, desperately pleased to see her, panting and wuffing with excitement. Flora was happy to kneel down and bury her head in the dog's damp shoulder. She'd been much more frightened out on the sea than she'd let on. Joel and Colton, she suspected, hadn't realised how much danger they were in – after all, it didn't look terribly far. But every Mure child knew. She glanced at Bertie, who had necked his hot toddy and was lifting up his second with trembling fingers, and he nodded back at her.

'Nobody else is out there today, are they?' she said.

Bertie shook his head.

'Nope, that's it. No ferries, nothing.'

Joel looked down.

'Christ,' he said. 'I've no more dry clothes.'

He had stared at the bag of outdoor gear Margo had bought him for the longest time before concluding, regretfully, that it wasn't for him, that he wasn't going to pretend he belonged up here when he knew, deep down, that he didn't belong anywhere.

He'd been about to throw it out, then had wondered what Flora would have thought about that and instead asked Inge-Britt if she knew of anywhere to donate it. Inge-Britt had promptly handed it over to Charlie and Jan.

He regretted this now.

'I thought I was going home this afternoon.'

'Nae ferries nor planes noo,' said Bertie, and Joel got enough of his drift to nod. He glanced down. His expensive trousers were wringing wet.

'Ah,' he said.

'I've got clothes you can borrow,' said Colton. 'But we'd have to get back there. Also, if the power's off, my electronic wardrobe isn't going to work.'

'Colton!' said Flora, shaking her head and starting to giggle, mostly from relief.

As if in answer, the rain battered hard against the window panes of the pub. Some of it was rain, right enough, and some of it was seawater from the waves coming clear across the harbour wall and hitting the glass.

'Maybe in a little while,' Colton said.

'I've got something,' said the barman, going into the back of the building and bringing out a huge boiler suit. Colton and Joel looked at one another.

'Of course you must take it,' said Joel. 'You're the client.'

'What are you going to do?' said Colton.

'I have to head back,' said Flora, who didn't really like the idea of leaving the cosy bar – it was growing more and more crowded, with folk caught in the storm looking for shelter and deciding they might as well have a snifter if they were passing, and the windows were starting to steam up. 'I'll bring you back something of the boys' if you like. Though not a kilt,' she added.

Joel glanced around the bar, torn. Then he looked into her face. Her hair was coiled around her neck, her eyes like passing clouds.

'Okay,' he said.

Bramble headed cheerfully for the door. Flora opened it and the gale howled in at what felt like a hundred miles an hour. Bramble cowered back.

'No, come on, pup,' she said, bowing her face against the wind. 'We can do it.'

'Are you sure?' said Colton. 'You'll catch your death.'

She turned round and shook her head.

'It's fine,' she said. 'This is my home.'

And she vanished with the wind, out into the whiteness of the churning sky and spray, as if she were a part of it.

Chapter Thirty-nine

Joel stood there looking at the closed door. Colton stared at him.

'I'd follow her,' he said simply. 'That's not a professional opinion, by the way. Those damn MacKenzies.'

Joel didn't even hear him.

Every instinct told him to stay put; to fold himself up; to do things as he'd always done them. The wind banged the door. Outside was a white maelstrom; a mystery; a pure and perfect storm.

He hesitated. Colton had turned away. Nobody else was looking at him. The bar was crowded with villagers, but no one was paying him any attention.

He was thirty-five years old. He thought about his instinct to run after her on the beach; to pull her out of the crowd at the dance. He thought of everything he had to lose; the complications of life.

Even though, up here, things felt so much more simple.

He wanted . . . What did he want?

He wanted to go home. He didn't know where that was. He glanced once more around the bar. Then he crashed out of the door.

'Wait!' he shouted. 'Wait, Flora, I'm coming. Wait for me!'

The shock of the air took his breath away. It was almost impossible to believe he was in temperate, damp, muggy Britain. It was like being slapped in the face.

'FLORA!'

The wind whipped his words away. He glanced around through the rain and could just about see Bramble's tail, still wagging, as it disappeared up the track at the far end of the harbour.

'Wait!'

He tore after her, cold and weather forgotten as his expensive shoes splashed through deep muddy puddles; as his glasses became completely useless once more and he had to take them off and stick them in his pocket, rendering the world even fuzzier and less defined than before, a world where sea and sky had completely merged – had possibly always been merged – with nothing but the thinnest line on the horizon to separate them or tell them apart. In this great white watery world, he finally made himself heard, finally saw her turn around, that light hair, that startled look on her face as he caught up with her; and as she saw him looking such a mess, so unlike his normal composed, organised, in-control self, his hair plastered down on his head, and water pouring down his neck, and his shirt completely see-through, Flora couldn't help it: she burst out laughing.

And Joel looked at the sky and thought of all the work he had to do and everything that was late and how many billable hours he wasn't putting in and what kind of ridiculous set of circumstances had led him to this, and wondered whether he had the faintest idea about what he was getting into, and whether he gave a rat's ass about that anyway, and decided that he didn't. And he found he was laughing too; and he couldn't remember the last time he'd done that, and thought maybe he never had.

And Flora ran on, through the rain and the wind, the laughter punching the breath from her lungs as he pursued her, and Bramble barked joyously and jumped in and out of puddles on purpose, and they finally scrambled up and through the gate, Flora more soaking than she'd ever been in her entire life, and the farmyard was empty; there was nobody there but them, and the cows and the chickens, with everyone else on the mainland.

Flora collapsed against the heavy old wooden farmhouse door, underneath the ancient lintel, panting and utterly out of breath from the exertion, the storm and the laughter, closely followed by Joel, running up behind her, and she knew, immediately, instinctively, what was going to happen; regardless of Inge-Britt – and all the other Inge-Britts; despite Charlie; despite everything her friends had said. Even as she was still giggling helplessly about how sodden and ridiculous they were, how absurd everything was; even as she was still laughing, he had fallen on her lips and was kissing her furiously, frenziedly hard, and she was kissing him back the same, and neither of them could breathe, until there was no breath left in them, and the tiny door Charlie had unlocked unleashed a torrent.

Chapter Forty

Joel felt like he was kissing a mermaid; something from the sea. Her long, damp body pressed up against him felt absolutely astonishing, but they were both starting to shiver, from cold, and from excitement, too. Flora opened the latch on the door behind her and they fell into the cosy, scented kitchen, the Aga warm, the fire still glowing in the range. Bramble shot in behind them and dumped himself in the prime spot right in front of the stove, shaking himself out madly, but Flora and Joel were oblivious.

Flora immediately started undoing the buttons on Joel's shirt, pulling him over to the warmth of the fire. She thought about stopping herself, in her crazed hysteria, but then he drew her closer to him, his own fingers fumbling, and she knew that he wanted her just as much as she wanted him, and was overwhelmed.

She ignored the fact that she was in her childhood kitchen; was completely blind to anything that wasn't him:

his cold, clear skin against hers as he cupped her face and kissed her hard, his lightly haired olive chest glinting in the firelight as they sank to the floor – there was no other light; the power had gone off in Mure after all.

He broke away.

'Undress,' he said breathlessly. 'Undress. Please. I have to see you. I can't . . . I have to.'

Flora sat back a little, blinking.

'Ha,' she said.

She peeled off her damp top, realising as she did so that this was an unusually tricky manoeuvre to pull off in broad daylight without having spent the preceeding hours in a bar. Particularly when her brain was shrieking, 'It's HIM! It's HIM!' at her in a panicky high-pitched voice, and another voice was going, 'You're in your mum's kitchen! It's your mum's kitchen,' and trying not to look at her school photo hanging on the wall above the mantelpiece.

Then he simply leaned forward and kissed her again, and for a moment she couldn't think of anything else at all.

Her skin was exactly as he had imagined it: pale as milk, white as the sky outside. It was flawless; unutterably lovely. He wanted every inch of it; wanted to see the clouds reflected in those pale dreamy eyes; to let her hair tumble down her back. His eyes searched her face hungrily, drinking it in.

She pulled back then. All she wanted to see was him, but suddenly the room around her was full of ghosts. No, that wasn't it. In this strange half-light of the encroaching storm, it felt like she and Joel were the ghosts. That all around them real, normal family life was going on: people shouting and arguing, and playing the fiddle, and looking for homework, and drying muddy boots by the range; she could almost feel them walking through her. She blinked, overwhelmed by the sensations, both past and present.

'Oh God,' she said. 'Oh God, I am so sorry.'

Joel sat back immediately as Flora felt around for her damp shirt. He held up his hands.

'It's okay,' he said. 'Sorry, I'm sorry.'

'No, no, it's not that. It's not you.'

'What's up?' said Joel, resting his forehead on his hand as he leaned on the coffee table. 'Fuck, I want you. I want you so much.' He gently traced the shape of her face. 'I shouldn't have . . . Sorry. I stepped over a line.'

'Oh God, no,' she said, bright pink – how he would have loved to bring that blush to her another way. She stared at the floor. 'Sorry.'

He shook himself, and leaned forward.

'It's okay, Flora.' He tucked her hair behind her ears. 'It's okay.'

He smiled at her, slightly wolfishly.

'Although I will say it's a shame. It's one of the very few things I'm any good at.'

Flora's heart lurched. She couldn't believe that something she'd dreamed of for so long, lain awake thinking about, was here. And she couldn't do it. She wanted to cry.

He held out his hands to her.

'Do you want me to go?'

She shook her head fiercely.

'Do you want me to stay and not do anything? Not move?'

She shook her head again. He smiled.

'Do you want me to stay and do other things?'

She nodded, feeling shamed.

'But I can't,' she said regretfully. 'It's not right. Not here. And you're my boss.'

He smiled again.

'You know,' he said, reaching out for her, 'you know it's all right to ask for what you want?'

'I do want that,' she whispered, and a tear slid gently down her cheek. 'Oh Joel,' she said. 'I'm sorry. I think ... Oh God. It's like there's a hole in me. Since my mum died. I thought I was fine. And now I come back and I'm not remotely fine. And I can't even ... It's like there's something missing. Even with you.'

'What do you mean, "even with me"?' said Joel. 'Am I that awful?'

'No,' said Flora, desperate not to give away how long she'd wanted him; completely twisted up inside because she was making such a mess of it.

He sat up on the old kitchen rocking chair and pulled her into his lap. There were two faded tartan blankets on the back of the sofa, and he tugged them over and wrapped them round the pair of them. He just needed to hold her close, not think of anything else.

'What is it?' he whispered.

The tears Flora knew were waiting, so close to the surface, started to pour down her face.

'Oh God,' she said. 'It's ... coming back here. It's been so hard.'

Joel frowned.

'I thought you were having a good time.'

'I know, but . . .'

He thought back.

'You didn't look pleased. That first day.'

'I didn't think you noticed me.'

'I didn't,' he said, with some of the clipped Joel she knew so well. 'But I caught a sense of . . . reluctance.'

Flora sighed.

'When my mum died,' she said, 'there was a big funeral. Everybody came.'

It hurt her to think of it, even now. It had been a beautiful day. The chapel was small, on a little raised hillock, next to the ruined abbey overlooking the bay. It was more ancient than anyone could conceive; one of the first signs of Christianity on an island that had older allegiances: to Thor and Odin, and before them, to green men and fertility goddesses and the Lughnasa gods of the equinox, and before them, even, who knew?

It was a plain building, with a cross in the churchyard to honour the war dead, the carved names repeated – Macbeths and Fergussons and MacLeods predominated; inside were unadorned pews and hymnals, and little decoration, for the church of the northern islands was austere and preached hard work and no showiness.

As ever, you could see the weather coming in for miles across the long, flat beach, with the mainland just a line in the distance; and the black clouds that pounded up in the lower reaches of the sky were soon overtaken by a line of blue poking through here and there, until finally the entire sky cleared, and a cool white light shone brightly through the plain glass windows of the little chapel.

It had been full to the brim, of course. Everyone was there. Fields had been left to look after themselves, shops untended for an hour or so as people came to say farewell to Annie MacKenzie, née Sigursdottir, who was born and lived on Mure her entire life, her grandparents had spoken Norn; who had brought up three sons, none of whom, unusually, had left the island – and a flibertigibbet daughter, of course, who raised a few whispers as she went past: not married, you know, not settled, down there in that London, goodness knows what she was getting up to, probably thought herself too good for Mure these days.

Flora was inured to it, truly, and didn't really listen, instead accepting the kind wishes expressed about her mum, nodding gratefully and thanking people for coming.

But she felt increasingly wound up. Afterwards, at the reception, cakes and tea were passed around by friends and neighbours, sandwiches from the bakery, and whisky was poured into teacups as they ran out of their meagre stock of glasses. Someone had brought a fiddle and started to play a mournful air, even as the chatter grew louder, and there was a sense that a proper wake for Annie was coming on.

And all Flora could think of was the way people were looking at her, and her memories of her mother: the endless patience, the work, the kindness; the frustration that had surely made itself felt in the way she'd pushed Flora, out to dancing, out to tutoring and extra lessons, out into the big wide world. But nobody saw it. They saw someone who had done everything right; and she, Flora, was letting the side down.

The house was filled to the brim with people who had

known Annie all her life – many, she couldn't help notice with sadness, much older than her mother had managed – talking about her many kindnesses and hard work. Hamish was simply sitting staring into space, not even crying, which was far more worrying than him crying would have been. Eilidh, Innes' wife, was breastfeeding Agot and Flora caught sight of them having an argument about when to leave. Fintan was nowhere to be seen.

People were talking to her father but he wasn't listening – he could barely see them by the looks of things – and suddenly they were all talking to Flora too, and holding on to her, and Mrs Laird was asking if she was going to come home to look after the boys – the fourth time she'd been asked precisely that question in the last half an hour – and she took another long draught of whisky, furious with them all, and went and stood next to her father, glowering.

She hadn't realised quite how much she'd had to drink. Her father, too. He got up and wandered out of the house, down across the courtyard towards the sea, followed by his friends. Flora stumbled after them.

'She came from the sea,' he was saying too loudly. 'She came from the sea; it sent her here and it has taken her back again. She was never ours really.'

And the other men were nodding and smiling and agreeing, and Flora, suddenly, felt a rage as powerful as she'd ever felt, and turned on him, shouting:

'That's CRAP! Stop it! She never went anywhere and she never did anything and it was YOUR FAULT. You kept her CHAINED to the kitchen. She wasn't a selkie! She wasn't some kind of creature sent from the sea to be your slave! And don't say it to make yourself feel better, because all the life she had was spent in this . . . this shithole . . .'

And she had stormed down to the harbour wall and sat there staring out to sea, feeling utterly numb, not just because of the cold wind, but because of all the things she was meant to feel, or felt, or didn't know how to feel, and her fury at people saying it was natural, it was normal; grief for all the things her mother would never see if they even happened to her, all the grandchildren she wouldn't know, all the things they couldn't tell one another. All of it. Gone. For ever. It wasn't right and it wasn't real, and Flora vowed to herself that she would not return, even as she heard the sounds of the wake trailing down on the wind, and finally let Lorna take her to her house for the night, and caught the first ferry in the morning, back to London, back to work, thinking nothing but 'I have to get away. I have to get away. I have to get away.'

Joel looked at her.

'You actually said "shithole"?' he said mildly.

She half smiled.

'Yeah.'

'And you haven't come back since?'

'Too embarrassed,' said Flora. 'It was an awful thing to do.'

'No,' said Joel. 'I'm sure it was great. Gave them something to talk about for weeks.'

'Maybe,' said Flora. Somehow, telling him about it had

taken the weight of it off her. That and the gradual thawing she'd felt from the island. And she felt so comfortable and safe and warm in his arms. 'What's your mum like?' she asked suddenly.

There was a long pause, and she felt him stiffen slightly. She hadn't thought it was too personal a question. But maybe it was.

'Sorry,' she said. 'It's okay.'

But Joel was shifting, looking uncomfortable.

Overhead the storm still raged. He looked into the fire.

'Christ,' he said. 'I'm exhausted.'

Flora looked at him.

'Do you want me to put you to bed?'

He looked at her.

'I don't think I could bear it.'

Flora smiled. But neither of them wanted to break the spell. She put the wet clothes to dry by the fire, and led him to her bedroom.

'Seriously?' he said, looking at all the dance rosettes hanging from the walls.

'Oh, everyone gets those,' she said, colouring.

He shook his head.

'No,' he said. 'You were beautiful.'

Nobody had ever called her that before.

He lay down on the soft bed and smiled sleepily. Seeing him lying there was so odd; her childhood bed, home of all her young fantasies and dreams, and here he was, come to life.

'Tell me a story,' he said, half asleep; he meant it as a joke, but it didn't come out that way at all.

Flora pulled the covers over him and sat down by his side.

'Once upon a time,' she began. Joel thought the sing-song lilt of her voice was the most beautiful thing he'd ever heard. 'Once upon a time, a girl was stolen away. From far up north where the castles are, to be taken a long way away across the sea. And she did not want to go . . .'

Flora paused. Her mother used to tell her this story, she was sure of it. But what came next? The next instant, though, she realised that it didn't matter. Joel had closed his eyes and was completely and utterly fast asleep. She stared at his face for a long time, mesmerised by his beauty – the curve of his mouth and the slope of his cheek – and for the hundredth time she cursed herself for not being able to go through with what she so wanted to do.

Unutterably disappointed, she pulled off the blanket, and eased herself, practically naked, under the covers with him, as the howling gale deposited great handfuls of rain against the window. She felt his sleeping body against her, breathed in the wonderful warm scent of him; her pale hand tangled in the dark hair on his chest. It wasn't enough; it wasn't nearly enough, but it would have to do.

At one point they both woke, and what time of day or night it was, neither could say. Flora fetched them cold draughts of water from the old sink tap and they made a tent under the covers, very close to one another, and Joel put his arm round her.

'I'm sorry,' he said, and he sounded like he was stuttering and nervous, which was so unlike him she had to look at him to reassure herself.

'I . . . You asked me about my mother.'

Flora nodded.

'I don't . . . I don't normally . . . '

'You don't have to tell me,' she said gently.

'No!' he said, and it came out harshly. 'No. I do. I want . . . I do.'

He took a long breath.

'I . . . I grew up in the care system. I didn't have parents. I never knew them. I had . . . foster families. Different families. Lots.'

Flora turned her clear eyes towards him, trying not to show the pity she knew he must be so very terrified of.

'And was it awful?' she asked him directly.

'I don't have much to compare it to,' he said, swallowing. 'But I think perhaps it was.'

'And is it over?' she said more softly.

'I don't know,' he replied, as honestly as he was able.

And then it was her turn to trace the angles of his face, as she pulled him down to her, and kissed him.

Suddenly there was a fierce banging at the door, and they both leapt up, sharing guilty looks, the spell broken, glancing around for clothes and shoes. Joel still had nothing to wear.

'Oh God, it's Colton telling us this isn't billable,' said Flora, with a terrible nervous giggle. Joel shook his head.

'Is it your father?'

'Knocking? Wouldn't have thought so.'

Flora pulled on a loose jumper and trousers and ran downstairs. The bright post-storm sun dazzled her eyes as she strained to see who was there and what time it was. Who on earth would knock round these parts? The banging came again as Bramble woofed, but not in an alarmed way, which meant it must be someone they knew.

'Hello?' she shouted tentatively.

'Hey!' came the voice. 'Fintan? Innes?'

Flora opened up.

'Sorry,' she said. 'Just me.'

The person standing there nodded, even as his gaze went over her shoulder to the clothes Flora had carefully hung out to dry in front of the fire – the suit jacket; the striped shirt. She blinked rapidly.

'Teàrlach! What is it! Have you got boys out in this?'

'No, thank God, we got them into a bothy in time.' Bothies were small stone buildings in remote places that provided shelter from bad weather.

Flora glanced at her watch. Oh my God, it was after five o'clock. They'd been asleep all day.

'How long have they been there?'

'They're heading back down now.'

'Oh. Is this about . . . ?' Flora flushed bright red. Oh God. And with another man in the house.

'No, it's not that. It's . . . '

Charlie seemed disinclined to finish that sentence.

'Um . . . I have to borrow Eck's tractor.'

'Why?'

Charlie winced.

'Och, it's a bad business.'

'What?' said Flora, suddenly alarmed. 'Is everything all right? Is someone hurt?'

'Don't worry,' said Charlie. 'It's not a person. But . . . can you drive a tractor?'

Joel was standing by the fire now, watching them deep in conversation with each other; he couldn't hear what was being said. Then she turned, and he saw from her face that she was leaving, and leaving with this man, and he wasn't sure he could stand it.

'I have to go. There's a whale beached.'

'There's a what?' said Joel, looking around for his glasses. He was feeling alarmingly shaky and vulnerable, not himself at all. And Flora was walking out the door.

'A whale. It happens sometimes. They get lost in the storm.'

Joel shook his head, completely bamboozled. He absent-mindedly pulled his phone out of his pocket. All the connections were back up, and it was filling up with messages. He couldn't make head or tail of those either.

'Flora! The keys!' Charlie was agitated.

'I'm coming, I'm coming.'

She moved towards Joel.

'You can stay.'

'But you're going.'

'Not for long. I have to do this.'

He looked at her. He didn't want her to go.

His phone beeped.

'I have work to do,' he said shortly, and shut up like a clam.

'No,' said Flora. 'No. Don't you dare. Don't you dare do that. Don't.'

'FLORA!' said Charlie. 'Please, for the love of God, can you have an argument with your boss later?'

Chapter Forty-one

They could hear the poor creature before they saw it. With the passing of the storm, the day had turned ridiculously beautiful, the last few dark clouds in the distance pierced by strong shafts of biblical-looking sunlight that bounced across the water, now flat as a millpond.

The whale was singing; calling loudly to its friends.

Flora was familiar with the sound from her childhood; as she grew up, it had happened less and less often. But fishing policy over the last few years, however much the local fisherman had decried it, had helped, and now the whales could be heard once more at the high latitudes.

This poor beast was a cow orca, about fifteen feet long, greasy and heavy of head, its back curved and its dorsal fin flexing up and down on the shore. Thankfully they'd already got Wallace the fireman jetting water on her to keep her wet, and her head was up, so her blowhole wasn't blocked. But they would need to get her back into the waves, which was a tricky job; towing her out far enough to refloat her and stop her simply getting beached again; doing so without injuring her.

The RNLI was already out in force, and the expert team was flying in from Shetland, so until then they needed to get her as close to the shoreline as they could manage, and as comfortably as possible: stress could kill her just as surely as being beached could. The police had already pegged out privacy notices all across the beach to stop people approaching and taking selfies, or children coming down to pat her. The crowd stood at a respectful distance.

It was usually Flora's brothers who drove the tractor, but it didn't mean she wasn't capable. Her father had taken her into the fields as soon as she could reach the pedals, as he had with the boys, and although she hadn't been quite as enthusiastic, she'd figured it out pretty fast. She swung up into the cab – of course the keys were there; they always were – then ran into the barn to grab tow ropes, a vast tarp, and anything else she thought they might need.

Joel grabbed his clothes and dressed at top speed, stopping at the door to be greeted by the sight of her, hair flying behind her, chugging down the hill in a bright yellow tractor. He had not, he thought, met many girls who could do that. He watched her go, but did not follow, and she did not stop or look round.

Charlie was directing things at the bottom of the hill. They were going to get the whale onto rollers, once everyone was there, and tow her out as far as they could manage. It was a delicate and tricky operation, particularly as the large creature was distressed and thrashing her tail. It was difficult to watch. There was a lot of shouting and disagreement about what was best; some people thought they should wait for the coastguard vet, while others thought that would take too long and they'd lose her. Flora sat in the cab of the tractor for a while, then, feeling like an idiot, slipped down, pointing it out to Charlie, who thanked her. The fishermen were knotting their nets together. Flora watched them, incredibly touched. It would take them a very long time to sort them out again, if they even could. Horribly badly paid, they were sacrificing even this.

Flora looked up as she saw a small plane begin to circle around the island. Now that the storm had lifted, the experts could come in. And, she supposed, her father and the boys would be back too.

And Joel would leave, she thought, biting the inside of her mouth to stop herself from crying. She needed to be here, at least until the vote. He most certainly did not. He worked on huge mergers and acquisitions; big, technical court cases that required incredibly specialised expert knowledge . . .

'Penny for them,' said Charlie. She blinked, and went redder than ever.

'Um, just worried about the poor creature.'

'Aye. I know.'

He looked at her.

'It'll be all right. Thanks for the tractor.'

'What can I do now?'

'Wait, I suppose,' said Charlie, as the men started to

tentatively approach the creature. She was the size of about three adult males; impossible to lift and making heart-rending noises. Flora was beyond the barrier now and didn't feel able to walk back.

As the men heaved and slipped in the sand, trying to manoeuvre the whale onto the nets, Flora meandered round to the creature's head. It smelled very intensely of the sea. Its eye was the size of a tea plate; its huge mouth had a great lolling tongue, and strands of seaweed covered its teeth.

She never knew what inspired her to do what she did next (although her father and half the island never had the faintest doubt). While everyone else was occupied with moving the creature, Flora crouched down at its head, very softly and slowly, not making any sudden movements.

'Shh,' she crooned lightly, looking straight into its huge eye. 'It's okay. It's okay.'

The whale continued to thrash and twist in the sand, its tail carving out a great trench. If they weren't very careful, it would hurt itself. The men jumped back, not wanting to be hit by the great animal.

Flora ignored all of this.

'It's okay,' she said again, gently and soothingly. 'Oh, it's okay.'

Carefully, slowly, she extended her hand, and laid it on what she supposed was the whale's cheek, next to its mouth. And as she did so, almost unbidden, an old song of her mother's came to her; the old mouth music, from a time before instruments, a time at the very birth of music itself.

Flora, in a bar in London, wouldn't have performed karaoke at gunpoint. But here, it felt absolutely normal.

O, whit says du da bunshka baer?
O, whit says du da bunshka baer?
Litra mae vee drengie

she sang, not even noticing the waves crashing or the men shouting, or the lashing of the whale's tail.

Starka virna vestilie
Obadeea, obadeea
Starka, virna, vestilie
Obadeea, monye

And slowly, astonishingly, as the clear evening light broke through the clouds once more, the whale stopped thrashing and lay still long enough for the lads to slip a knot of fishing nets around its belly and, using the tractor, pull the creature carefully out to sea.

Flora moved with them as Charlie drove, keeping her eyes on the whale all the time, singing as the creature made noises too, but quieter ones, as if it realised Flora was trying to help it; and Flora found herself splashing into the shallow water with it, heedless of getting her second drenching in as many days, and stayed with it until the tractor returned and the lifeboat took up the rope, and it was only then, with regret, that she leaned forward and – without even thinking about it – kissed the animal on the nose.

Then the boat took up the slack and the whale started to move again, and Flora stayed and watched as they towed it out to sea, and long beyond, when the boat was only a dot on the horizon, disappearing towards the mainland. And as she watched, she thought of the greatness of the animal, and the dancing silver sea, and everything that had happened.

As Joel stood on the dockside, waiting for Bertie Cooper to drive him to the airport for the delayed evening flight, he watched this amazing girl, this strange foreign girl, in this place where she belonged and he didn't, and he cursed himself for allowing her to get so close; for making him do what he had sworn never to do, what he had protected himself from all his life. It had been a reckless day; a reckless time. He would leave; return to where he belonged, to a world of tall buildings and important, complicated work. He would seriously consider Colton's offer of a job in his New York office . . . get back into triathlon training.

And yet all the way back down south, all he could think about was skin so pale that each time he kissed it, however gently, it left the shadow of a mark.

Chapter Forty-two

Everyone involved in the whale rescue ended up back at the farmhouse for some reason. Flora hadn't noticed Joel down on the beach, and was bereft that he had gone without a word. She tried to explain it to herself, but couldn't. Was he back at the Harbour's Rest? Or maybe he'd moved into the Rock. It must be ready. That would . . . She liked that idea. Him waiting for her in one of those beautiful rooms . . . She smiled ruefully. That would be a step up. And it wouldn't remind her of Inge-Britt either.

Colton showed up, an arm casually thrown round Fintan's shoulders. Fintan was weary and dirty after the cattle transport.

'Is Joel back at the Rock?' she asked as lightly as she could.

'Oh. No,' said Colton. 'He's gone. It's not him I need, sweetie, it's you.'

Flora told herself she wasn't going to cry. They'd been

interrupted, that was all. She'd talk to him in London and they'd get to know each other properly, and . . .

Actually, she had no idea what that would be like. None at all. She imagined telling Kai what had passed between them, and it was horrifying. But how could she . . . seriously? They were going to have a relationship? In London? That was actually going to happen? They'd turn up to work together, the senior lawyer and the unremarkable little paralegal. That would totally happen.

She pushed away the painful thought of how unlikely that was.

'I'm thinking of recruiting him for my New York office anyway. Or LA. Can't decide,' said Colton conversationally.

Flora froze. She picked up a hot toddy from the stove and sipped on it for a long time.

'And what did he say about that?' she said tightly, her throat constricted.

'Oh, you know lawyers,' said Colton. 'Can't get a straight answer out of any of them.'

This relieved her anxiety a little, but not entirely.

'You know I can't stay for ever,' she said.

'Ah, you'll change your mind,' said Colton.

'Only for the summer,' she warned. 'Until the nights draw in.'

'That's what selkies always say,' said Mrs Laird in passing.

'Shut up!'

In the parlour, someone had taken out a fiddle, which was a good sign if you wanted a party, but a bad sign if you hoped that anyone was leaving any time soon.

'I can't ... That cattle transport?' said Fintan. 'I got kicked nine times. Got shit all over me. I'm thirty-two years old and I can't do this the rest of my life.'

Flora nodded.

'It can't carry on anyway,' she said. 'Not like this.'

'It's like ... I've found something satisfying. Something that really and truly makes me happy. Finally.'

'What are you two chittering about?' said Innes. 'Also, you're a total freak, Flora.'

'Shut up,' said Flora. 'You're just jealous.'

'That you kissed a fish? Yeah, right.'

'It's a mammal, actually, Captain Ignorant.'

'*It's a mammal, actually, Captain Ignorant*,' repeated Innes annoyingly.

'I thought having a child would make you grow up.'

'Did you?'

He grabbed a few bottles of the local ale from the fridge and headed back to his farmer mates.

'And Innes,' said Flora. 'What's he going to do? After Dad, it was always going to be Innes' farm. And God, what will we do with Hamish?'

'Hamish,' said Fintan, 'will always be fine.'

They looked over to the corner where he was sitting, bursting almost comically out of his shirt. He looked too large for the room and was glumly watching the women, some of whom had started to dance.

'Nobody has to go anywhere. Nobody has to move,' said Fintan. 'And our future ... It could be anything with Colton. There's no future here, you know it.'

'Hmm,' said Flora.

'I mean, with new things ... It could be amazing. But the farming – we can't compete, we really can't. With cheap milk from super farms. And transporting those animals; you know what that does to our profits.'

Flora nodded.

'It's just a long, slow decline ... you know it, Innes knows it. Unless we reinvent ourselves.'

'But this is MacKenzie land,' she said. 'And it has been for such a long time. Such a very long time.'

'I know,' he said. 'We need to pick our moment. Let's feed up Dad.'

Flora smiled.

'On it,' she said.

She was dishing up some vol-au-vents that Isla and Iona had made after studying the recipe book and deciding on balance not just to gather wild mushrooms from the hedgerows and hope for the best when a tall figure marched into the kitchen. Flora looked up. It was Jan, and she looked utterly furious.

'Oh good, you,' said Flora. 'Um, this is my house, so if you've wandered up to be insulting, can I ask that you don't? Or perhaps leave?'

She was slightly beyond trying to be nice and reasonable. It hadn't really got her anywhere in the past.

'I've got a bone to pick with you,' said Jan.

'No, you have a bone to pick with *Charlie*,' explained Flora, too irritated to care about her tone of voice.

'Apparently you've been touching wildlife,' spat Jan.

Her colour was high and Flora wondered if she'd been drinking.

'Um, sorry?' said Flora. 'Vol-au-vent?'

'You touched that whale.'

'Yes, I did,' said Flora. 'It seemed scared and I wanted to make it less scared. So I just kind of patted it a bit.'

Jan shook her head.

'Unbelievable.'

'I wouldn't pat a whale in a zoo,' protested Flora. 'I just wanted to help.'

'You don't interfere with the animal kingdom.'

'What do you mean?'

'Exactly that. You start messing about with animal populations, all hell will break loose. You don't think we interfere enough in the food chain? That we haven't already done terrible, terrible damage to almost every species on this earth, particularly whales?'

'I wasn't harpooning it. I was soothing it.'

Jan rolled her eyes.

'Do you think so?'

'What would you have done? Left it on the beach to die?'

'That's what you're meant to do! Whales beach themselves for reasons we don't understand. Maybe she was old! Maybe she was sick! How would you know?'

Flora felt her skin starting to prickle.

'Well, I don't. But it seemed like the right thing to do at the time.'

'Oh, people always think they know what the right thing is. They think they know. You sitting here in your posh farmhouse with your posh friends.'

The idea that MacKenzie Farm could be called posh by anybody who'd grown up in a First World country – and in the richest family on the island at that – riled Flora beyond belief, but she tried to keep calm.

'Well, I'm sorry,' she said. 'But I couldn't have watched it die.'

'No. Too busy showing off,' said Jan, which truly stung. Flora folded her arms.

Charlie wandered into the kitchen, his face breaking into a smile when he saw Flora.

'Hey,' he said.

Jan whipped around; he hadn't previously noticed her.

'Jan,' he said.

Flora looked at them carefully. What the hell was going on?

'Um, I'll just grab a couple of beers.' Charlie moved hastily to the fridge. 'Good work today, Flora.'

Jan practically hissed in annoyance. Once Charlie had left again, she turned to Flora once more.

'And we're back together,' she said. 'So you can stop eyeing him up.'

Flora threw her hands up.

'Oh for God's sake. I don't care! There's . . . there's someone else.'

She couldn't believe that of everyone she could have mentioned this to, it was Jan.

Jan looked at her.

'That American guy who thinks he's it?' she almost spat. 'Good luck with that. I heard he was halfway up that Icelandic barmaid.'

'Thank you,' said Flora pertly, resisting the urge to tell Jan to get the fuck out of her kitchen, and her house, and in fact her life for ever.

Then she checked her phone again; but still nothing.

Chapter Forty-three

Joel had squash buddies, drinking colleagues, work acquaintances and college frat-boy chums who held regular get-togethers all over the world.

He never spoke to a single one of them. Not about anything real.

'Where are the newspapers?' he said brusquely.

Margo looked up. He was being belligerent even by his standards, had been in the week or so since he'd got back from Scotland. On the other hand, he'd caught up on his work in record time, which meant a vast amount of overtime for her.

'*Times*, *FT*, *Telegraph* and *Economist*,' she recited, looking at the lobby table. 'What's missing?'

Joel frowned.

'I made an addition to the periodicals list,' he said.

Margo checked her post.

'Oh yes, here it is,' she said. 'Obviously comes out a day or two late.'

She stared at it.

'*Island Times*?'

'Just covers all our bases,' said Joel.

'Shall I put it out here?'

'No, uh, give it to me,' and Joel stalked off to his office with it tucked under his arm, Margo staring after him in astonishment.

How, thought Joel, how could he not have noticed Flora before? Because all he noticed in his office now was a huge Flora-sized hole. He thought he saw her everywhere he went, her pale hair blowing in the wind. Except he was in a hermetically sealed office fifteen floors up, and the windows didn't open and the breeze never reached him.

But he couldn't. He couldn't. He'd picked up the phone to Dr Philippoussis more than once, but he knew what he'd say. Go to her. Tell her.

But she didn't fit in his life. She couldn't. She didn't know it yet, but she belonged on the island. Communing joyously with that whale, or baking up something marvellous, or bantering with her brothers. Her face, so pale and pinched in London, was something else at home. And even if she thought she'd be happy back in the city, he could see deep down that she wouldn't be.

And there certainly wasn't room for him up there. That huge chap, Charlie, though that wasn't what she called him. Always there. Biding his time. He'd be more suitable. Not someone like Joel, who carried around more baggage than Newark. What if she tried to fix him? She wouldn't be the first. And then they'd really be in trouble.

It wasn't in his nature to be unselfish. He'd never been able to take care of more than himself. But when it came to her . . .

He picked up the paper. There it was, as soon as he turned the page, the story about the whale. What was it about her? She wasn't a supermodel. But somehow, that face, with its clear, direct gaze; the milky, creamy skin that must cover every inch of her . . . it made everyone else look overdone, too made up; those ridiculous eyebrows that looked like they'd been drawn on with a Sharpie. All the other girls he knew looked like bizarre overpriced cocktails, while she was a cool, clear glass of water on a boiling hot day.

Margo came in with a box full of files and he started as if he'd been caught looking at pornography; thrust the paper underneath the box.

Normally he could attack his work like a machine. Get through it. Get to the nub of things, the nitty-gritty of contracts and points of law, and see clearly to something that was always to his clients' advantage. Always.

Now he was staring out of the window, wondering what kind of bird he was looking at.

He should call her. But what was he going to say? It felt like stepping out into mid-air.

He sighed and picked up the phone.

The voice on the other end was gruff, and belatedly Joel remembered that it was very early in New York. This in itself was utterly uncharacteristic; normally he held all the time zones in his head in a tight line, accustomed as he was to doing business everywhere.

'Sorry,' he said.

'Who is that?' said the voice. 'No, of course, it's Joel, isn't it?'

There was a pause, and the noise of a coffee machine grumbling. Then the voice immediately turned softer.

'I seem to be hearing from you a lot recently.'

There was such kindness in it. Such a gentle tone.

It struck Joel that he had never known how to return the kindness, and thus never had. But now, when he had a real problem, he realised he didn't really have anywhere else to turn. Flora ... yes, it was bad what she'd been through. But she had that huge noisy kickabout family of hers. And all her friends on the island, and all those people walking past who just seemed to know her anyway.

'So,' said Dr Philippoussis. 'You must have met someone.'

Joel pulled the newspaper out from under the box.

'Um,' he said.

It was a beautiful shot; someone had caught her kneeling down, nose to nose with the beautiful animal, the sun lighting through her hair. There was no one else in the frame at all; they'd cropped out the RNLI and the tractor so that it was just Flora, alone with the whale, singing it back to sea.

'She? He? It?'

Joel blinked.

'She.'

'Interesting.' Dr Philippoussis hummed.

'Don't make humming noises,' said Joel. 'I don't need a therapist.'

'You don't?'

'No,' said Joel firmly.

He paused.

'I need a friend. For proper advice. Not just for me. Real advice.'

Dr Philippoussis looked out of the window of his downtown apartment. He never got tired of watching the sun rise through the skyscrapers, even on days that were guaranteed, like this one, to be hot and sticky and difficult to get through. The humidity made him want to shave off his beard. In the bedroom, his wife was still asleep. She'd be delighted to hear Joel had called. She'd have adopted him if it had been remotely possible; if they hadn't run the risk of making things far worse than they already were. Joel hadn't been neglected, exactly. He'd been clothed and fed, more or less, all his physical needs seen to.

But there was something about the boy; something so closed. Abandoned by his mother, then passed around, he had not, as so many children in his situation did, become overaffectionate; clingy and desperate to please in a way adults could find appealing. Instead, he had shut himself off to such an extent it was thought he had a diagnosable illness, like autism.

Dr Philippoussis had not tried to prise him open; he had simply let the young boy be himself, pointing him towards things he might like – books, order, comprehensibility. Studying the law had been perfect for him – things were black and white, right or wrong. They could be categorised and put into boxes in the way human emotions and messy human lives could not.

'I'm that too,' said Dr Philippoussis, watching the tall buildings of Manhattan gradually sparkle pink and shiny gold, and the city bristle into life, the streets full of joggers and dog walkers and hurrying professionals whose faces looked every bit as closed off as Joel's always did.

'She lives on an island ... sometimes ... and it's so strange up there. And she's a part of it. And I don't think ... I don't think I should drag her into all my stuff.'

'Why not? Is she cruel?'

'No.'

'Would she make you feel small about what you've been through?'

'I don't think so.'

'What's the worst that could happen?'

Joel couldn't say it. A long silence fell between them.

'Well, call her,' said Dr Philippoussis.

'But I'm not ... I'm not sure I'm ready.'

There was a long pause.

'What? I asked you to give me advice!'

'I can't,' said the good doctor. 'I know we're friends. But I have a professional responsibility towards you too.'

'You don't!'

'I do.'

'Well, if it was you ... '

'Nobody can ever stand in for anyone else,' said Dr Philippoussis.

'Oh, great, thanks.'

'I could also say that nobody ever thinks they're ready.'

'Is that your professional opinion?'

'No. You'll have to choose for yourself.'

'How?'

'Use your imagination.'

'I don't have an imagination! I'm a lawyer!'

Joel stared at the paper. His own life, below the surface, was empty. A gaping hole, he sometimes thought. And hers was not. It could not be a little step. It would be everything. And he knew what the worst thing that could happen was, because it had happened every single time he'd been moved on to a new family. Until he'd learned to seal himself off.

Chapter Forty-four

Several weeks had passed, and Flora had never known what it was like to be so busy, even after the ridiculous fuss of her being in the paper had passed. The Summer Seaside Kitchen was absolutely inundated. They started doing picnic hampers with homemade Scotch eggs and ploughman's lunches, and these were even more crazily popular, with locals and visitors alike. The visitors liked to take them up the fells, or through the ancient abbey, whose grey stone walls cast a sombre shadow on gloomy days but in high summer proved an irresistible playground for young children, who ran up and down the ruined spiral staircases, jumping in and out of the low glassless windows, as their parents sat in the long grass, sharing a bottle of Eck's bramble wine, which they shouldn't technically exactly be selling, at an utterly shameless mark-up.

The oddest thing was, Flora couldn't be heartbroken. She couldn't. She was sad not to hear from Joel – and she had to occasionally file reports, to which Margo would respond.

But she didn't blame him, or wonder whether what had happened had meant anything to him. It was all on her side. She had to get over it. Her crush had extended slightly, one strange afternoon, that was all, and now she had to . . . well. She had to get over it. Get on with things. Get on with the job. Even the less pleasant parts.

Which was why, finally, one glorious August day, as the breeze rippled across the sea – meaning everyone needed a cardie, but otherwise it was so very pleasant to sit out on the stone wall and watch the insects buzz lazily over the headland – Fintan summoned Innes and Hamish down from the fields, had a quick telephone call with Colton and whispered urgently to Flora. She nodded.

Eck was snoozing outside the farmhouse with Bracken at his feet.

'Dad,' she whispered. 'Dad, can we talk to you?'

'Family meeting!' said Fintan.

Agot was dancing in circles and swinging on Innes and Hamish's hands.

'I'S THE ONLY GIRL! I'S THE PRINCESS!'

'Hi, Agot,' said Flora, bringing warm shortbread from the oven and a fresh pot of tea. Innes eyed it warily.

'Are you trying to bribe us?'

'I don't know what you mean.'

'YOU NOT PRINCESS, AUNTIE FLOWA,' came the insistent voice.

'Yes, I know that, my darling,' said Flora.

'YOU SELKIE.'

'Could you stop with this, please?'

'YOU IN PAPER.'

She didn't like to think of that day. Not any more. She was here till the Lughnasa – the late harvest. Then Joel would be gone to the States and she could simply go back to work and all would be fine. And she would never see him again. And everything would be beyond awful.

No, she wouldn't believe that. She would get on with the job in hand. And she was making a difference; they all were. They absolutely were. But they'd hit crunch point now, if Fintan was going to go and work at the Rock.

'Dad,' she said.

Innes looked concerned. Hamish as usual sat silent in the corner of the yard, his face still smeared with muck from doing the lion's share of the heavy work.

'Well, everyone really,' she added. The farm was in their father's name, but there was no doubting the way of things. The boys would inherit, and that was how it had always been and always would be, as long as the sun set in the west and the tide reached the wild sea grass.

'Fintan and I . . . ' She turned to him. 'Do you want to do it?'

He looked straight at her and shook his head.

'Can you do it, Flora?' he said.

'No,' said Flora. 'Well. Both of us.'

She took a deep breath.

'There's been an offer,' she said. 'A good offer. A really, really good offer. To buy the farm.'

It was as if Eck didn't quite understand. Flora found herself repeating it in the old tongue, just to make sure he knew what they were saying. Fintan was on his phone, obviously repeating everything to Colton.

'But,' her dad kept saying. 'But I'm fine, Flora.'

'This is Agot's birthright,' Innes was saying.

'NO FARM! ME PRINCESS!' Agot yelled.

'I'm not sure we need a three-year-old at the negotiating table right now,' said Flora, slightly peevishly.

'But Flora ... I mean, it's fine.' Eck was completely bewildered.

Flora looked at the sagging lintel over the door; the rusting farm machinery out in the field. He couldn't see it, she knew. In his head he still lived in a long golden summer where she and the boys ran about the outhouses half naked, utterly filthy and laughing their heads off; or lined up in front of the television, furiously pushing and shoving for space to watch *Countdown*; or begged him to tell them stories of the olden days, when they'd had to make their own clothes and were regularly cut off from the mainland for months at a time and there'd been no television, they'd just had to make their own music; at which point she and the boys would giggle and sigh in utter disbelief, and their mother would tell them to hush, it was exactly like that, though it was nice too, and she'd smile, and suggest a round of cheese on toast and homemade soup for everyone, and they'd all cuddle up in front of the fire, until Flora and Fintan fell out about who was taking up too much space, then everyone would collapse laughing and the dogs would bark madly.

That was what he saw. Flora knew it.

'Dad,' she said. 'I've seen the books. You know I have. Innes knows it. You know we can't go on like this.'

Suddenly she wanted to sit in his lap, like she had as a very little girl. But he had shut himself off from her a long time ago, and she knew why.

'There's nothing left.'

'And Da,' said Fintan, his face as pale as Flora's suddenly. 'Da, I don't want to farm any more. I want to work with Colton Rogers.'

Her father blinked. Flora looked at Fintan intently.

'And also. Colton's my boyfriend.'

Even Agot was silent at that.

The blood rushed to Fintan's face.

'Well. He's someone . . . someone important to me. I don't know if I'd call him . . . I mean, it's very early days.'

Innes and Hamish just sat there, unmoving. Flora wasn't entirely sure Hamish had even understood; or Eck for that matter. Fintan's stance was sullen, as if daring them to challenge him. He looked more like sixteen than thirty-two.

Agot went up to him.

'YOU GOT BOYFRIEND?'

Fintan smiled shyly, and shrugged. 'Well, kind of. Not sure. He is nice, though.'

'I'S GOT BOYFRIEND.'

He crouched down.

'Who's your boyfriend?'

'PEPPA,' said Agot.

'Pepper?'

'PEPP-A! HE PIG.'

Fintan smiled.

'Well it's nice to know I haven't got the actual weirdest relationship in the place right now.'

Innes stood up and stepped forward, bright red too. They weren't used to talking like this, the MacKenzies. His hand went to the back of his neck. Flora flashed back to all the teasing – at school, yes, but at home too. Pansy. Girlie. Wimp. All of it. On and on.

Innes stuck his hand out.

'Congrats, bro,' he said, with some difficulty. 'Glad you've met someone.'

Fintan started shaking his hand, but they ended up in an uncomfortable hug.

'Mum would have liked him,' he said.

'Mum knew?'

'Of course she knew. She didn't tell you?'

'No, she just skited us round the ears if we ever wound you up.'

'You deserved it.'

'I suppose we did. But yeah, she would have liked him – he's got money.'

'Oi!' said Flora.

'What! Excuse me, fancy-pants posh girl, what was that exactly?'

'She might have liked him because he's nice.'

Hamish raised a hand.

'Well done, mate.'

'No problem.'

They all turned to Eck. He was still sitting there, shell-shocked.

'Dad?' said Flora. She wondered if it was too early for whisky, and decided it was not.

'Oh weel,' said Eck. 'Weel weel weel weel.'

Flora put a hand on his shoulder. Fintan was trying to look unconcerned, but Agot was in his arms and he was holding her very tightly in a way that betrayed his nerves.

'I DOES LOVE PEPPA,' she said again, hoping to repeat the positive effect this had had the first time.

'Weel . . . '

Eck seemed almost untethered with confusion.

'Are you all right, Dad?' Flora knelt down at his elbow. 'It's okay, you know,' she said. 'It's okay.'

Eck shook his head.

'I know,' he said in a bewildered tone. 'I know youse all think I'm an ancient fuddy-duddy from the dawn of time.'

'Why would we think that, Dad?' said Innes. 'Just because you *are* an ancient fuddy-duddy from the dawn of time.'

'You know, in those days,' said Eck, ignoring him. 'I mean, what the minister said at the kirk . . . that was all we needed, you know. That was how we lived and what we all believed. And everything was normal.'

'No, that's what people pretended to believe,' said Fintan. 'Think back. You must know that's true. What about old Mr MacIlvaney, who ran the sweetshop? He never married, he lived with his mother. Why do you think he got so fat?'

'Because he ran a sweetie shop,' said their father.

'NO!' said Fintan. 'Because he was repressed. Because he had to hide what he was. You can't look at the past and think that life wasn't like that just because it wasn't talked about. Because it absolutely certainly was.'

'But the kirk—'

'Och, the kirk was as bad as the rest. Worse.'

Eck sighed.

'Nothing changed, you know. My life was much the same as my grandfather's, which was the same as his grandfather's, and so on, and so on. And then suddenly, BANG. Everyone wants everything and it all changes.'

Flora shook her head.

'I promise, Dad, it hasn't changed. Not that much. Not compared to the world outside.'

'That's why I never bother with the mainland,' said Eck.

'Quite right too,' said Flora. 'But you can handle this, can't you?'

Eck looked up.

'Do I have to like it?'

'Naw,' said Fintan.

'Is this why you hate working on the farm?'

'No,' said Fintan. 'I hate working on the farm because it's shit hard and freezing half the year.'

'The other boys dinnae mind.'

'I don't like it either,' said Innes.

Eck's face really fell then.

'Hamish?'

Hamish shrugged.

'I'd rather be inside sometimes,' he said quietly. This was a very long speech for Hamish.

Eck got up. The sunshine was glowing over the fields, even as a stiff wind blew through the tall, spiky grass of the dunes.

'Bramble! Bracken!' he growled. 'Get in noo. Dhu going fur a walk.'

The dogs leapt up, looking round warily, as if they could

sense the atmosphere. Eck grabbed his old stick from the doorway and strode away, Bramble and Bracken at his heels.

The siblings looked at each other.

'Well,' said Flora, cautiously. 'That went—'

Innes had already turned round.

'You're dating a *millionaire*?' he said to Fintan.

'Ah. No,' said Fintan.

'What?'

'Kind of a billionaire,' said Fintan, and Innes swore mightily.

'What do you want to work for, then?'

'Because I do.'

'Can he give us a million pounds for the farm?'

'No,' said Fintan. 'That's not how you get rich.'

'Oh, like you'd know.'

Flora dished up steak pie, and she and Fintan set out their plan around the table: a restaurant farm, belonging to the Rock and growing everything the Rock needed and wanted for its menus – seaweed; dairy, including the cheeses; meat, obviously.

'It'll mean going all organic,' said Flora. 'And getting specialists in to advise on the best crops, not just what will grow.'

'That will cost a fortune,' said Innes.

'That's where the investment comes in. Seriously, Innes. Flying cattle to the mainland. How's that going to work as a long-term strategy? You're getting killed by the mega farms and you know it. It's a downward spiral. And people are going to come here who aren't going to mind paying a proper price for milk and butter, and the best meat and wonderful fresh ingredients. We'd be mad not to.'

'But to lose the farm . . . '

'The farm isn't going anywhere,' said Flora sternly.

'They'll be happy to brand everything with the MacKenzie name,' said Fintan. 'Gives it proper authenticity to be a family farm.'

'But it won't be ours.'

'Technically, no.'

'So it won't be Agot's one day,' said Innes. Agot had, in the commotion, quietly stolen into Flora's handbag and was now smearing lipstick all over her face.

'Yeah, that's a loss,' said Flora.

They sat there, looking at each other.

'I don't know if we have a choice,' said Fintan.

'Well, no, you wouldn't,' said Innes. 'What if you two break up? Do you have to give all the money back?'

'Actually,' said Fintan, 'I have a very good lawyer who's going to take care of all that for me.' He looked at Flora.

'Hamish,' she said. 'What do you think?'

'Will I get more money,' said Hamish, 'if I work for the restaurant?'

'Yes,' said Flora.

'Enough to buy a car?'

'Yup.'

Hamish nodded. Everyone waited, but this appeared to be all he had to say on the topic.

'Well . . . ' said Flora.

Just then there was a knock at the door. Most Mure people just rapped and walked in – that is, if the door was even shut in the first place. Eventually Innes got up and answered it.

Charlie was standing there, twisting his hat.

'Hello,' he said.

'Tractor's outside,' said Innes.

'No, no. I don't need that.'

He looked around the room, saw all the brothers and Agot there, and went very pink about the ears; not his normal, stolidly calm self at all.

'Um,' he said. 'Flora.'

The boys, delighted that the pressure of all the serious conversation was suddenly off, leaned back cheerfully in their chairs.

'Flora!' said Fintan. 'Someone's here to see you!'

'Looks like Fintan's not the only one courting!' said Innes. 'I bet Charlie hasn't got millions of dollars, though.'

'Shut up, everyone,' said Flora, although it wasn't entirely awful to have things back to normal. They'd done quite enough hugging and talking about feelings for one day, and it was nice to be bickering again.

'Um, do you want to walk Bramble?'

'He's . . . he's out,' said Flora stiffly. She still hadn't forgotten her conversation with Jan.

'Oh. Right,' said Charlie, and turned to go. 'Sorry,' he said.

Flora bit her lip. She still hadn't got to the truth. And for now, she had had enough of the farmhouse and their worries, and more than enough of the sleeples nights and bitter disappointment and horrendous self-doubt she'd been through ever since Joel had left. Absolutely more than enough.

'I mean. I'll come for a walk with you. If that's what you were asking.'

It was funny to think what a confident, bluff character she had thought Charlie was when she had first met him. He didn't look very confident now as he ran his huge hand through his hair.

'Um. Yeah. Yes. All right. Yeah.'

'I'll find Dad,' said Flora, grabbing her cardigan and ignoring the knowing looks and eye-rolls the boys were giving her. 'Also, shut up, all of you. And wash up.'

Agot came marching up to them, totally covered in a random collection of Flora's make-up.

'HE BOYFRIEND?' she asked seriously of Flora. Then she turned to Charlie. 'I'S BOYFRIEND.'

'That's very nice to know, Agot,' said Charlie seriously. 'And a very good evening to you.'

Chapter Forty-five

It was a glorious evening. The sun hung steady and unmoving in the sky, its trajectory slowed right down for the very height of the summer months. Flora had taken the lipstick from Agot's sticky fingers – she'd leave it to Innes to sort out the rest – and quickly added some to her own lips. The sun had just about allowed some freckles to pop out on her face, and she'd realised that the near-constant activity since she'd arrived had helped to burn off some of the London office flab she'd acquired.

Charlie was walking next to her in silence. He didn't seem to be the type of person who needed to fill every space with conversation, or daft jokes and observations. Apart from being momentarily flustered on the doorstep, he seemed ... comfortable. Happy in his skin. The exact opposite of Joel, she supposed. No. She wasn't thinking about Joel. She wasn't. That was done. And this ... She took a sideways glance at Charlie, his powerful shoulders; his strong, calm profile.

'Teàrlach,' she said quietly. 'I don't want to assume anything. And I might have picked up the wrong impression . . .'

He turned to her, still not saying anything, quite content just to walk and listen.

'But Jan,' she said. 'What happened at the party. I mean, seriously, what the fuck are you doing?'

'They do say selkies get straight to the point,' said Charlie.

'Don't change the subject. You said you were separated.'

'We are.'

'She . . . she says you're not. That you're on a break but you're still together.'

'Well. We're not. I spoke to her about it.'

It struck Flora that Jan hadn't been in the shop in over a week. Maybe that was it.

'And? Tell me what happened, because this has been really gruesome for me.'

'All right, all right,' said Charlie.

They walked on in silence, and Flora suddenly missed Bramble terribly. It was nice, during awkward moments, to have a dog to cuddle and pet.

Charlie sighed.

'I'm sorry. It's complicated. It's been complicated. We run a business together. We were together for eight years. I didn't want to . . . I mean, too much upset and it could have just ruined everything. In fact it would have done; it would have wrecked the business. Her father put up the money for it to begin with, and . . . I mean, her family, both families really, they expected us to get married.'

'That must have got tricky round about year five,' said

Flora, but it came out wrong and didn't sound funny at all, and she regretted saying it.

'It's not that I don't think she's magnificent, because she's a wonderful woman in many ways,' said Charlie stoutly. 'She's helped more underprivileged children than anyone I know, and she cares for everyone and everything.'

'So why did you decide to break up? What caused it? Did you meet someone else?' said Flora curiously. Most of the men she knew only got out of one relationship when they spotted another one.

Charlie gave her a sideways glance.

'Well,' he said.

'Well, I don't want anything to do with it,' said Flora fiercely.

'No,' said Charlie. 'No, I hadn't met you. It was at Hogmanay. Everyone had had a few, you know?'

'I do know,' said Flora, remembering with some fondness the crazy parties in the square that went on throughout the night; the bonfires and first-footing and everyone out together. Her mother had never wanted her to go, but the boys had promised to look after her – which was absolute nonsense. Hamish would stand and grunt with his cronies; Innes would be after winching some young girl somewhere, and Fintan would generally sulk and refuse to go and declare it all bogus ruffian behaviour; and Flora had felt so wild and dizzy and free, staying out all night in the freezing cold, passing around the cider and laughing until she thought she'd burst.

'Well, I was up at Fraser's hoose, with Jan, and everyone was badgering me to make an honest woman of her, you know, as they do, and I thought, if I was to make an honest woman of her, I'd be making a dishonest man of myself. So.'

'But you didn't say you were finishing it.'

'I'd like to present myself as a brave man, Flora. But I will say I am not.'

They both smiled.

'She went a bit mad.'

'But that was in December! It's August now!'

'We still have to work together.'

'You have to tell her it's over. She doesn't think it is.'

'I know,' said Charlie. 'I know.'

He turned to face her. Completely without realising where they were going, just following the pathway their feet had taken together, they'd reached the headland. He looked at her shyly.

'You're the person ... the person who's really made me feel ... Well. That I have to change, that I have to move on in my life ... the way you've moved on in yours.'

'I haven't. I'm only here until the Lughnasa. I'm just doing a job.'

He shook his head.

'I think you're doing more than that.'

She looked at him. His thick curly hair blew off his strong forehead. He stood on the point, the crags and the bright sky behind him, as blue as his eyes. He looked as if he grew out of the land. He was such an islander, such a north Briton. She couldn't imagine him in London; could barely imagine him in a town at all. He was grown from the soil he stood in.

She thought about Joel. A movie star, that was what he had been to her. She had to see it. Like that year she'd spent at fourteen watching the *Lord of the Rings* films over and over again and slowing down the bits with Orlando Bloom in them, thinking that maybe there was a possibility that they might come and film in Mure if they got sick of New Zealand.

That hadn't happened. Or at least not yet.

That was where Joel belonged. In a little box of fantasy, of something to make your commute pleasanter on a dull day. He had a lovely smile, sometimes – and hey, at least she'd slept with him, kind of, in a funny way. She supposed. But it had been, she told herself firmly, nothing to him. Nothing. There hadn't been a phone call, not a text, not an email. He'd left and gone back to his old life and forgotten all about her, and the island, and everything. He might be moving to the US and he hadn't even told her. What was she going to do: waste years on him? Years of her life without him ever giving her more of a thought than Orlando Bloom did?

But looking at Charlie, she felt her stomach flutter. This was real. This was something solid.

'I live in London,' she said.

Charlie shrugged.

'Yes, but you're Mure. You're an islander. Or more, if that lot of superstitious maniacs are to be believed.'

'They aren't,' said Flora.

'Well, all I mean is. Islanders understand one another.'

He swung his arm around her. From their position, at the very end of the point, they could see such a long way around the island. The harbour; the beginning of the endless white beach beyond; the crags behind them; the farm. Bertie down there on his boat, next to the ever-scurrying fishermen; the shops, now closing up for the day, to the surprise of holidaymakers, who never quite got the hang of the fact that just because it looked like noon didn't mean that it was. And round to the Rock, the beautiful building there, all ready and waiting for them.

Before her father's time, most people born on Mure simply never left it. The horizon defined the limits of their entire world. They had visitors, sometimes invaders, but for most, this little village, this stretch of fertile sea and windswept soil, was all they'd ever known. And it was beautiful.

'This is the blood in your veins,' said Charlie in a low voice, and Flora realised suddenly that they were very close together now, as her hair whipped out in the wind and her skirt danced behind her. She turned towards him, blinking as he loomed above her, as solid as the ground beneath her feet.

He reached out his large hand and she took it, gazing out to sea, watching the seals' heads bob up and down.

'They can't put a bunch of windmills here,' she said.

'That's the spirit,' said Charlie. He squeezed her hand and they both looked at it. Then she looked back up at him. Everything – the scudding white clouds, the darting birds, the whispering grass – seemed to slow down. She moved closer to him; just a little.

Suddenly a massive WOAUF! burst out at them from the undergrowth. They jumped back guiltily, both of them.

Bramble was there, woofing at them frantically.

'Hey,' said Flora, kneeling down. 'What are you doing?'

He kept on woofing, tugging at her arm.

'He's like Skippy the kangaroo,' said Charlie, laughing

as the tension broke. 'Look, Flora, he's trying to tell you something. Has little Timmy fallen down the well again?'

Flora shook her head.

'Don't be daft; dogs know stuff.'

'Either that or you left a sausage in your pocket.'

'Why would I leave a sausage in my pocket?'

'You're very committed to your new career in catering?'

Flora smiled, but felt worried.

'Where's Dad?' she asked Bramble. 'Have you run away from Dad?'

She thought of Eck's serious, weary face as he'd left. She hadn't seen him on the way down – although she'd hardly been looking, she thought. She'd been walking next to this large, broad man, trying to make her feet match his long strides, thinking of how capable his hands were, how strong he seemed. She shook her head.

'He wants us to follow him,' she said.

Charlie laughed.

'You're not serious?'

'I need to find Dad anyway.'

'Can you understand all animals, or is it just whales and dogs?'

'You can make smart-alec remarks,' said Flora. 'Or you can come with me.'

Charlie grinned.

'Can I do both?'

She looked at him, squinting in the sun, and they smiled at each other.

'Plus,' she said, turning serious as they headed down off the point, 'don't you have someone you need to talk to?'

People were watching them as they descended into the town together. She wondered if there would be gossip. She had also thought Charlie might reach for her hand again, but he didn't. Of course he didn't. She felt herself blush. But she liked having him there.

'Have you seen my dad?' she asked shopkeepers. Andy at the Harbour's Rest hadn't seen him; neither had Inge-Britt, who had, Flora had noticed, taken up with a strapping Norwegian lobster man and seemed as cheerfully and oppressively healthy as ever.

Bramble didn't seem to be leading her anywhere, just content to know that they were together and that she was on the move. Flora started to get worried. She'd assumed that the pub would be the obvious spot for her father to go and chew the fat and complain about the uselessness of his ungrateful offspring – and, she had hoped, wobble back after a few hours, mind slightly clearer on the issue. But no, there was no sign of him at all.

She didn't want to call the farmhouse, but she did, quickly.

'No, he's not back,' said Fintan. 'Isn't he with you?'

'No, but Bramble is.'

'Bramble left his side?'

'I know.'

'And for you, when only terrible things happen to that dog when you're about.'

'Okay, okay, shut up.'

Fintan paused.

'And you're one hundred per cent sure he's not in the pub?'

It slightly astonished them both for a moment, realising how few places there were for him to be; how little he did that wasn't endless work on the farm. They both fell silent.

'Is the Land Rover still there?'

Fintan paused.

'Yup.'

'Should we just be leaving him to have his walk? I mean, it's a lot to take in. A lot of new things. And the weather isn't bad.'

'Probably,' said Fintan. 'That is weird about Bramble, though.'

They paused.

'I hate being a grown-up,' said Flora.

'No, it's awesome,' said Fintan. 'Ooh, and how's that strapping lad of yours?'

'Call me when Dad gets in,' said Flora, hanging up.

A crowd had gathered now; the girls from the bakery were out looking concerned, and Flora could hear mutterings about Eck's age and general condition. But he wasn't that old, was he? He was fine, her dad. Wasn't he?

Clark the polis came up, frowning.

'Can't you alert the authorities?' said a passing backpacker, who'd stopped to see if he could help. Everyone turned to look at him.

'Um, he's it,' said Andy from the pub.

The backpacker blinked.

'Well, have you got a pic?'

Everyone looked at Flora, who flushed bright red.

'Um,' she said, looking at her phone and realising to her horror that while she appeared to have about seventy pictures of Bramble and Bracken, lots of the views over to the Rock, and two of the party with Joel in the background (she had desperately wanted to take one of him while he was sleeping but hadn't dared for fear of being super-creepy), she didn't have a single one of her father.

'We all know what he looks like,' said Andy, to her unending gratitude. Lorna and Saif came down the high street to join the posse.

'Come on then,' said Clark. 'Let's split up. Westers search wester, easters search easter. I'll knock up hooses.'

Flora nodded, her heart racing, amazed that it had turned so serious so quickly. He'd only been gone a couple of hours.

Charlie came forward.

'Do you want to start searching the mountains?'

'No,' said Flora. 'He won't . . . he wouldn't do that.'

'That might explain why Bramble wouldn't go with him.'

Bramble was lapping noisily at a water dish Andy had put out for him. He wasn't used to the heat.

'No, his sciatica's too bad for that, I would say . . . '

They scanned the horizon. It was so clear, they could see all the way to the top of the fell, which was usually shrouded in cloud or low-lying mist.

'I'll radio Jan,' said Charlie, then stalled suddenly as he realised what he'd said.

Flora looked at him.

'Please do.'

She pretended to busy herself with her phone as he took out the walkie-talkie. Evidently Jan had started pitching camp for the night. Flora felt slightly concerned that this was the only time Charlie had felt it safe to see her. She heard him mutter into the walkie-talkie, quite shortly, and it quickly became evident that there had been no sign of her father, but Jan would keep an eye out. Then Charlie paused, and glanced over at her briefly. Her heart skipped a little.

'Also, Jan,' he said. 'When you get down . . . can we talk?'

Flora wandered off so as not to eavesdrop. Where had her father gone? Did he want people looking for him? Was he just fed up of the lot of them?

Although the sun was still high in the sky, it was getting on for nine o'clock. If only he'd got a mobile phone, but he couldn't be persuaded, not ever. It simply didn't cross his mind that he might need one. Everyone he wanted to speak to either lived five feet away from him or he could wander down to the village to find them. Anything more than that just wasn't for him.

Oh God, Dad. Where the hell are you? Where have you gone? It gripped her, cold around the heart. She couldn't. She couldn't lose another parent. The silly old fool. But what if he'd got lost? Tripped and fallen down a cliff? Those paths could be hazardous, even in clear weather. And the wind was up again now. Oh God. No. She couldn't bear it.

She thought about Joel, but for once in a different way: as someone without a family. Without parents. That was what it was about him. Not that he was arrogant or felt above everyone. But because he was so alone in a cold universe. No wonder he was such a brilliant lawyer, such a great negotiator. He had absolutely nothing to lose. Everyone had got him wrong.

She couldn't imagine it. Even when she'd been far away, she realised now, as she watched the street thronged with people, passing on the word, going up and down to talk to each other, the news spreading quickly, more and more people coming out of their homes to look for her father; wherever she'd been, those skeins from her home had invisibly surrounded her, protected her, kept her safe. Showing her that she always had a way to come home, even if she'd never known it.

She blinked at the tears in her eyes.

'Dad!' she called. 'Dad!'

She looked at her phone again. Nothing. Bramble moved closer to her, and she dug her fingers into his thick fur, calmed by the dog's heavy warmth and slow heart rate.

'DAD!'

Charlie was behind her, she knew. And on all sides stretched a line of people, protecting, helping, caring.

A tear ran down her cheek.

'DAD!'

Who? thought Flora fiercely. Who would he want to talk to? Who would he want to be with?

And then, all at once, in a flash, she knew.

Chapter Forty-six

The churchyard was set behind the ruined abbey; they shared the grounds. Most people were surprised when they came to explore the weather-worn ruins to see that there were recent graves among the ancient fallen stones; but there they were.

Flora's mother's grave was plainly marked. Her father hadn't seen the need to make a big fuss – he'd never made a fuss about anything in his life and he wasn't going to start with some fancy ornate dedication to his wife, particularly since – as Flora knew, and had fallen out with him so badly about – he thought she'd gone back where she came from.

Telling Charlie she was going to quickly check something, she had rushed down the high street, Bramble bounding joyously, delighted she'd finally cracked what he meant. At the little gate that led to the churchyard, she paused. Behind her, the ancient stones of the abbey loomed up, ageless and sombre, even in the bright summer sunshine. The tourists had gone back to the pub to eat scampi and remark on the never-setting sun; the place was empty.

Almost empty. Bramble frolicked on ahead, but Flora didn't need to follow him to know where he was going.

Her mother's headstone was set at the very furthest end of the cemetery; right up against the sea wall, facing due north. She found her father sitting in a heap behind the stone, tears silently dripping off his chin – it looked like the end of a very long crying jag – and Bracken lying with his head in his lap.

'Dad,' she said quietly. At first he didn't hear her. He was just leaning against the stone, an old man, crying.

'Dad,' she said again, and sat down.

'Och,' he said crossly when he saw her, and rubbed his hands across his face impatiently. 'Och no, away with you. No, Flora, no.'

'Dad, it's all right.'

He shook his head.

'Ach, no. Please.'

'I understand. But I didn't know where you'd gone.'

'I've no been missed.'

Flora tactfully decided not to mention that about eighty per cent of the village was currently searching the island's every nook and cranny, and was going to make it to the churchyard eventually.

'Oh, Dad. I'm so sorry. Nobody wanted to upset you. Fintan . . . '

He shook his head.

'Och no, I'm no worried about the lad.'

He turned his face away, still ashamed of letting Flora see his tears.

'But the farm ... that's hard. That's a hard one on a man. Generations of MacKenzies have worked that land.'

'But they still will, Dad, that's the point! If you don't change, that's what will end it. This way your name will reach out, will carry on ... way beyond the island. Way beyond you even having to work! I mean ... It's the best thing. You see that, don't you?'

The old man stared out to sea.

'And think of the money. Wouldn't it be nice to have a little bit of money?'

'What would I do with money?'

'You could travel! Go places. Buy ... '

Flora realised he was absolutely right. Her father had never seemed to want for a thing. Changed his Land Rover once every twenty years; wore the same clothes, then stitched them up himself when they grew threadbare. The idea of him going to a fancy restaurant or staying in a hotel, sitting by a pool ... Her mother had once insisted on taking him away to Spain on a package tour when the children were all grown up, and he had hated every single second of it.

'Oh, it wasn't so much that he hated it,' her mother had said later. 'It was that he simply didn't comprehend what he was doing there. It just made absolutely no sense to him at all.'

'It will still be our farm,' Flora said. 'People will call it the MacKenzie Farm long, long after all of us have gone.'

Her father patted her mother's grave.

'Och, and does that even matter?' he said.

'Of course it does!' said Flora, horrified.

He nodded, and gave one great sigh. Then he turned to her.

'She loved you so much, you know.'

'I know,' said Flora. 'I miss her too. Every day.'

'She missed you. She missed you.'

'She told me to go.'

'Of course she did. She thought it was the right thing to do. She thought there was a grand life out there waiting for you.'

Flora blinked back tears.

'She couldn't bear to make you stay. She didn't mind so much for the boys. And I think yon Fintan felt the thin edge of that.'

Flora nodded, the lump in her throat making it impossible for her to speak.

'But she always hoped . . .'

'Please, Dad,' Flora managed, with some trouble, staring hard at the ground. 'Please don't say she always hoped I'd come back. I couldn't bear it.'

He looked up, startled.

'Oh no, love. Oh no. Not at all. She always hoped you'd make a life for yourself that you loved, wherever you were.'

He hung his head.

'After the funeral . . .'

'I didn't mean it, Dad. I was so upset. I was out of my mind. I'm so sorry. I wish I hadn't . . .'

'No. No. I thought on it. These last years, I've thought about it a lot. And I think maybe you were right. That I should have let her spread her wings. Not that I actually thought she had wings, before you go accusing me of anything else.'

This was a long speech for her father, and Flora listened intently.

'That's why I never chased you down. Never fussed you. I didn't . . . I hated the thought that she felt chained here. Chained to us, to the farm.'

Flora shook her head. A thought struck her, and she rummaged in her bag.

'I thought that for years, Dad. I did. But now that I've come back, I realise I was wrong.'

'What do you mean?'

She pulled out the tattered old recipe book, spattered and worn.

'Look,' she said.

'Your mother's recipes.' Eck, confused, put on his glasses. 'Aye, right enough.'

'No,' said Flora. 'Look inside.'

She turned to a chocolate cake entitled 'Best Birthday Cake in the World Ever for My Best Big Boys'. Another, for soup, had an asterisk with 'Good for Hamish when he's crushed the other kids again and feels bad'. There was a recipe for tablet with a picture of all their happy faces, crudely drawn, and 'WILL FIX MONOPOLY FIGHTS!!!!' written next to it. All the little phrases she'd used, ingredients she'd liked – 'More white pepper than Eck can stand' was scribbled on one page – tumbled down the years and out from the pages; the Christmas section was particularly delirious, with excited drawings of Santa, including some clearly done by the children, next to the Christmas cake.

Eck held the book like it was a sacred thing.

'That is not,' Flora said, never more sure of anything, pointing out Campers' Stew, and Happy Pie, and Goodnight Possets, illustrated by a crib in the light of the moon, 'that is not the work of a woman who was unhappy with her choices.'

Eck could barely speak. He looked up at her.

'Why are you carrying it around with you? It could get lost or stolen or anything.'

'Because I'm copying it,' said Flora. 'For the Seaside Kitchen. For posterity. For Agot. There will be lots of copies, I promise.'

'Good,' said Eck. 'Because I want this one.'

And he tucked it tenderly inside his old coat.

They sat there for a while, the two of them, Flora in her dad's arms, rocking gently in time with the waves behind the churchyard wall.

And when she was all cried out, he said, 'Give me a hand up, dearie,' and she did, of course, and as they stood up, arm in arm, they saw the first of the searchers entering the churchyard, shouting, 'Eck! Eck!' and then yelling with happiness and relief to one another. The old man blinked, entirely surprised, leaning his hand on Bracken's broad back to steady himself.

'Och no,' he said. 'You didn't send out a search party.'

'They sent themselves out,' said Flora. 'They were worried about you.'

He shook his head one last time. Then he looked at her.

'Oh, I will miss you when you go, Flora MacKenzie.'

'I'll be here till the Lughnasa,' murmured Flora. But her heart wasn't in it.

Chapter Forty-seven

'So, we're ready for the meeting,' Colton was saying. He was leaning back on one of the ramshackle chairs they'd pulled outside the farmhouse on a mild, clear night. Given the extraordinary luxury he lived in, Flora couldn't understand why he was always over here. Well, she could: he was in love with her brother; but if she lived somewhere as nice as the Rock, she'd never leave. Fintan was sitting on the arm of his chair, leaning against him from time to time, looking the picture of happiness. Everyone had a beer, and Flora, who had had a very long working day sorting out both dairy and shop issues, was perfectly happy for the evening, which stretched until the dawn, to meander on its own way.

Agot was sitting playing with Colton's incredibly expensive Gucci loafers. How on earth anyone could wear loafers to a farm and not get them filthy was beyond Flora. Maybe he just put on a brand-new pair every day. She had planted several twigs in one of the shoes and was attempting to make it sail down the sluice like a boat. Flora was going to draw his attention to it, but it was such a lovely evening, they all deserved to relax, and anyway, stopping Colton in full flow was harder than stopping Agot.

'Can you send all the council members a pie before the meeting? The blackberries are coming out, and they're sensational,' he said. 'And some of the cream.'

'You mean absolute and outright bribery,' said Flora.

'Not at all. A gift for the important dignitaries and respected elders of this island. Who sure hate wind farms. And love you and me.'

'Are you sure that won't just set them even more against you?' said Flora. 'Especially Reverend Anderssen. He'll want to make a point about not being corrupt.'

'A man who thinks so much about his belly, being sent a huge pie. Yeah, all right, whatever.'

'Everyone will see straight through it,' said Flora.

'Come on!' said Colton. 'I'm employing half the town here. I'm asking for an extra couple of hundred metres. Which by the way will easily be paid for with all the tax dollars I'm about to start handing over because I employ people. Did you know your country has maternity leave?'

'I know, we're psychos,' said Flora.

'Not that *you* need it,' said Colton.

'Shut up!' said Flora.

'No, I mean it. What happened to that nice chap who kept calling for you?'

Flora sighed. It had been awkward, to say the least, just as she thought she'd finally stopped being the focus of all gossip on Mure.

The day after her father had vanished, Charlie had turned up at the Seaside Kitchen for the last time.

His bulk had filled the doorway and she'd looked into his kind face and blue eyes, nervous and worried all at once.

Charlie was not a flame that burnt hot; that would scald her and go out as quickly as it had lit. He was a slow burn; an ember. Something she could keep close; that would smoulder for a long time. She moved closer to him.

'Teàrlach?'

Then she saw it in his face. And appearing behind him, the little crocodile – different children, she supposed, although the pale, haunted faces remained the same. They pressed sticky hands up against the windows of the pink house in awe.

'I'm sorry,' he said.

'What?' said Flora, shocked. 'You were going to talk to Jan.'

'I did.' He smiled weakly. 'She was going to get her father to withdraw . . . I mean. We'd have had to fold the business. Everything we've built and worked for.'

Flora nodded, aware of Isla and Iona pretending not to be eavesdropping from the kitchen.

'It would be a lot to give up,' she said softly. 'I understand. Of course.'

'You don't,' said Charlie sadly, raising his huge hand and gently touching her hair.

'No, I do,' said Flora, finding it difficult to swallow. Of

course. She wasn't worth it. She knew that. How many times did she need to be taught the same lesson? She wasn't needed. Never enough.

Charlie shook his head vehemently.

'No,' he said. 'You don't. I would have done it in a heartbeat. Started over straightaway.' His voice sounded strangulated.

'So why didn't . . . ?'

'Because none of that matters if you don't feel about me the way I feel about you. And you don't.'

Flora flushed, startled.

'What? But . . . but we could . . . '

Charlie smiled sadly.

'No, Flora. I tried . . . I hoped. That you might like me better than him. But there is always someone else behind your eyes. You're not hard to read.'

'That's bollocks!' said Flora crossly.

'And also Jan told me.'

'Oh, good. Right. I'm glad she knows,' said Flora bitterly.

'And I saw him in your house.'

'But he's gone! It was . . . '

She was going to say it was nothing, but she couldn't. She wouldn't say that. It might have been nothing to Joel. To her it had been everything.

'Oh, Flora,' said Charlie, looking into her face. 'Better a cold bed than no bed at all.'

Flora just stared at him.

'Good luck with everything,' he said. Then he rounded up his little gang and prepared to lead them away.

'Wait!' said Flora. 'Wait!'

She brought out the entire tray of little pastries they'd tried that morning, and put them in a large bag.

'Here,' she said to the children. 'Please. Have a wonderful visit to Mure.'

And the children, suspicious for a moment, gathered round the bag, chattering excitedly, and Charlie stood there watching as she retreated back into the shop.

Iona and Isla were standing at the back twisting their aprons, although Flora was too caught up in herself to pay them much attention until Isla stepped forward.

'Um, Flora?'

'Mmm,' said Flora, still trying to process what had just happened. Whatever spark there might have been between her and Charlie had been snuffed out, and she couldn't help but feel disappointed that he wasn't the man she'd hoped he was; that he wasn't brave enough, in the end, to give it a shot. To risk it. Damn it, damn it, damn it all.

'Iona and I were talking, and, well . . . '

'I mean, it's only health and beauty, my course,' said Iona. 'It's not like I'm learning anything that I couldn't learn here. I mean, about how to run a business and handle things and bake and cook and . . . Well.'

'We were thinking,' said Isla, the bolder of the two. 'If you wanted to stay. I mean. We would stay. If you wanted to run this place not just for the summer.'

'Also Ruaridh MacLeod's staying,' said Iona pertly.

'Shut up! That's got nothing to do with it!' said Isla crossly.

'It's got a bit to do with it.'

'He's got a job working for Colton Rogers. Running his gardens,' said Isla proudly. 'It keeps him in amazing shape.'

'Well … that's nice,' said Flora, flustered. 'But … I mean … I have to go back to London, but I could talk to Fintan for you. I mean, you might be able to run it by yourselves.'

The girls looked panicked, and Flora remembered they weren't out of their teens yet.

'I mean, with some help,' she said.

'Aye,' said Iona. 'From you.'

'I'll be up more often now … ' said Flora weakly.

'Town'll be sad if the pink house is empty again,' said Isla.

'Yes, they will be,' said Flora. 'But … '

The girls looked at her expectantly.

'I can't,' said Flora. 'I'm sleeping in a single bed in my dad's house. Come on. Can you get to it, please?'

And now it was nearly the meeting.

'IS GOOD BOAT, UNCLE COLT?'

'Uncle Colt?' mouthed Flora to Innes, who simply shrugged.

Colton looked down at the now mud-spattered shoe, which had taken off down the filthy rivulet.

'Oh good,' he said. 'At any point, if every single individual on Mure wishes to stop draining me of every cent I have, I'd be extremely grateful.'

'Well, it's still worth having,' said Flora. 'Give the kitchens a chance to show what they can do.'

Colton looked at her.

'You're so good at this, you know? I mean, who knew?'

'I'm not,' said Flora, blushing. 'I'm not half the cook my mother was.'

'It's not just about that,' said Colton. 'It's about organisation and management skills and being able to finish things. You're thorough, like a proper lawyer. I can depend on you. She raised you well.'

Everyone went quiet for a moment, and Flora thought she was going to cry. But fortunately Agot, chasing the shoe, went sprawling head over heels among the chickens, with a considerable amount of caterwauling from both her and the chickens, and she was able to distract herself.

'Who else is coming into town tonight?' said Colton, and Flora smiled and sighed.

'Everyone,' she said.

Then she corrected herself.

'Almost everyone.'

Chapter Forty-eight

Flora had been pleased to hear from Kai during the week. He had sounded nervous.

'What?'

'Well. Good news and bad news.'

'Um,' said Flora. 'Okay. Good. No, bad. No. Good. No. Bad.'

'Stop it,' said Kai. 'Okay, two bits of good news. One – I'm coming to visit.'

'You're coming up here?!'

'For some stupid meeting thing that's happening.'

'The town council. Of course. Oh my God, why are you . . . ?'

'That's the rest of the news,' said Kai.

Flora felt a deep weight in her stomach. She didn't want to hear what was coming.

'I've been promoted, Flors. Onto the account.'

'Of course you have.'

'Because Joel has . . .'

'He's taken Colton's job,' said Flora dully.

Kai didn't answer.

'LA or New York?'

As if it mattered.

'New York, I think,' said Kai. 'He's passed it on to me. Sorry. But still. Good chance to get over him, yes?'

Flora hadn't been able to tell anyone what had happened. Not even Lorna. Best if everyone could assist her in still thinking he was an arsehole and that she was better off without him. Which she was, absolutely.

'Of course,' she said. 'And it's brilliant that you're coming!'

It was, too; she'd missed Kai while she'd been up here.

'It's Lughnasa.'

'That sounds fattening.'

'It's not! It's a big pre-Christian festival, with lots of fire and dancing. Trust me, you'll like it.'

'Will it be a load of drunk Vikings carousing around the place?'

'Hmm, a bit.'

'That sounds *tremendous*! I shall pack something super-wenchy.'

They were all set for the meeting, then the party would start. The Summer Seaside Kitchen would be shut, but the Harbour's Rest would be doing a roaring trade. There was a firelight parade around the village, followed by music down on the Endless Beach, as they lit a hawthorn bower – meant to represent the green man of summer, and how his time was ending – and sent him off out to sea.

It was mild and clear for the time of year, with the scent of autumn everywhere. Flora went to collect Kai from the airport dressed in a tweed skirt and a Fair Isle jumper with green stitching that turned her eyes green again.

Kai stepped down onto the tiny windswept runway, waving madly. Flora was delighted to see him.

'Oh my *God*, this place!' he said. He looked like an exotic creature in his expensive tailored suit. He strode out and looked around at the towering crags, the sheltering town, the clattering harbour. 'Oh my God, look at it.'

Flora smiled. 'Um . . . '

Kai shook his head.

'Seriously,' he said, '*This* is the place you've done nothing but moan about since I met you?'

Flora ushered him into the Land Rover, where Bramble greeted him with massive licks and a batting of his tail against the seat.

'Shit, Flora,' said Kai. 'I grew up in Tottenham. And I can't even afford that now.'

It was, admittedly, the perfect time to show Mure at its very best. As the sun started to dip, the equinox tide made the waters recede so that the beautiful beaches were full of birds. Kai gasped and exclaimed to see a stork take off, its huge wings pink with the lowering sun. Then he became very overexcited at the sight of a seal grabbing some rays on a rock.

'I just want to take him home,' he said. 'That's all I ask.'

'He'll give you a nasty bite,' said Flora. 'Doesn't taste good either.'

'*Flora!*'

Next he exclaimed madly over the Summer Seaside Kitchen and how adorable it was. Though he never normally ate carbs, he tucked into an entire slice of Bakewell tart, then closed his eyes. 'I'm moving here,' he said. 'I think you're mad.'

More ecstasies followed as Flora took him to the Rock – finally ready for guests – to unpack, and showed him with a faint trace of sadness into a bedroom that was just as beautiful as she'd always suspected they would be, with deep sofas and driftwood furniture, and those extraordinary views. Innes was in the car park, dropping off a load of produce, and Flora brought him over. Kai perked up immediately.

'I don't think so,' said Flora. 'Just the one MacKenzie boy. I think.'

'Yeah, like you'd know,' said Kai pertly.

'This is Innes, director of MacKenzie Farms Ltd,' said Flora, introducing them. 'This is Kai, who's going to be my new boss.'

Kai waved her away. Innes smiled shyly. They'd only signed the papers a couple of weeks ago, and it still felt like a novelty.

'Are you coming to the Lughnasa later?' said Innes.

'I should think so.'

'Braw,' said Innes, and Flora grinned.

'Agot's going to like you,' she said to Kai.

'Who?' said Kai

They convened in the village hall at 6.30. Anyone was allowed to sit in on council meetings, but very few people did. Tonight, however, the hall was nearly full, as people came to see what would happen to Colton. Would he withdraw everything he'd brought to Mure if he didn't get his way? Or would everything be all right?

Flora sat nervously with all the paperwork between Kai and Colton, with Fintan on Colton's other side. The council filed in. Her father; Maggie Buchanan, face giving nothing away; Mr Mathieson, Jan's father, who scanned the crowd and, when he caught sight of Flora, frowned. Flora sighed. That didn't bode well. The reverend, who appeared to still have pie crumbs round his mouth. That was a better sign. Eck's old friend Gregor Connolly; Elspeth Grange; and, of course, Mrs Kennedy.

Flora touched Colton lightly on the shoulder. There was a lot of dull business to get through until it got to them.

Joel sat in his immaculate apartment. He couldn't settle. He knew the meeting was tonight. This was ridiculous. In his career he'd won great victories; triumphed for small companies over big ones, many times. This case had been absurd; about the concept of a place, rather than a point of planning.

It was still steaming hot and damp in London. He didn't want to walk. Too many people everywhere, shouting into their phones, making noise, blasting music, staring at screens, bumping into you, showing off. Everywhere. He didn't want to go out. Sit in some ridiculous bar, have the same conversation with the same type of woman, surreptitiously checking her own gorgeousness out in the bar mirror, grabbing at her phone for another selfie.

He checked his watch. Kai was going to phone him with the result. He thought about how hard Flora had worked; everything she'd wrought. She'd be fine. She was probably there with that big chap right now.

He ran his hands through his hair. Why was it so hot? He had the air con on, but he still felt so constrained; like he couldn't breathe. He paced about like a leopard in a zoo.

'And finally,' said Maggie Buchanan, who was chair, 'we come to the planning proposal for the North Mure offshore wind farm.'

Colton jumped up.

'I oppose this!' he said.

Maggie looked at him over her spectacles.

'All in good time, Mr Rogers.'

She glanced through the paperwork in front of her.

'This seems in order.'

Flora stood up.

'I have,' she began, her voice clear in the room, 'I have here a petition signed by ... many people in the village. Stressing their opposition.'

'Very good,' said Maggie, her voice chilly. 'However, they don't have to look at the turbines.'

'No, but my guests do,' said Colton. Everyone was watching him. 'Come on, ma'am. You must see that this here is a beautiful place. It's special, don't you think?'

'I don't think misty-eyed views of our island are

particularly useful, no. We're a real place that needs to be run well. And bringing in green jobs and cheaper electricity is a part of that.'

'There's no evidence that it will be cheaper, though,' said Flora. 'And you're going to disturb wildlife . . .'

'Yes, only terns,' said Maggie. 'I see no current shortage.'

Colton stood up again.

'Ma'am,' he said. 'I love this place. I've invested in this place.'

'Eventually,' said Fraser Mathieson.

'And I want to call it home. Am proud to call it home. I want to carry on investing. The people of Mure have been good to me and I want to return that. I want to keep things lovely. That's all. So I humbly suggest that we move the windmills further out.'

'That'll cost more to do,' muttered Eck, not looking at Flora.

'But for the views . . .' added the reverend.

'They're not everybody's views, though, are they?' said Mr Mathieson.

'It's everybody's island,' said Colton, 'and I want to make it feel that way. As much as I can. I've travelled all over the world and I think this is the most beautiful place on God's earth. I am so, so proud of it, and I want everyone else to feel proud of it too. I want everyone who comes here to feel the way I do, from the second they step on to the island.'

'Hear, hear,' said Kai.

Flora stared at Colton, amazed. This really was how he felt. And all round the room, people were nodding. People who she'd always thought, somehow, wanted to get away, dreaming of freedom. That wasn't true, she realised. This place: it *was* freedom. Home and freedom, all at once.

Colton was still standing, overcome with emotion.

'I love this place. I'm home. And that is all I have to say.'

There was a huge round of applause as he sat down. Fintan squeezed his thigh; Flora squeezed his shoulder.

'Well done,' she said, slightly choked.

Chapter Forty-nine

'Um, hi. Is Dr Philippoussis there?'

'Joel, darling. It's Marsha. He's got a client. Are you okay?'

'Um, yes. Sorry, I can call back . . . '

Marsha had always had a very soft spot for the serious, troubled boy; would have pushed for adoption if her own children hadn't been so small and needy at the time.

'Joel,' she said. 'I'm not a medical professional.'

'No,' said Joel, loosening the collar of his shirt. Why was he so hot?

'But we don't hear from you in years. And now it's every day, nearly.'

'I can stop,' said Joel, panicked.

'No. Joel. You're not hearing me. That's the opposite of what we want. In fact, when you come back to New York, we very much hope you'll spend some time with us.'

Joel swallowed.

'I'd like that,' he said. This was progress, he thought. Six months ago, he'd no more have admitted to needing someone than he would have walked in space.

'Good,' said Marsha. 'But that's not it, is it?'

'You're a much bossier therapist than the Doc,' said Joel.

'I'm not a therapist at all,' said Marsha. 'But I am a mother.'

Joel paused.

'Did you let her down gently, this girl?' asked Marsha softly.

'I don't think she minded,' said Joel.

'Do you think? Or maybe she minded very much.'

'No,' said Joel, thinking of the aggressive blondes who called and harassed Margo. 'No, she didn't make a fuss.'

'Maybe,' said Marsha. 'Maybe that's because she's different.'

There was a long pause.

'I'm not going to say what's the worst that can happen, Joel,' said Marsha. 'I know what's the worst that can happen. Women have vanished on you your entire life. Here's all I've got to say. If you're waiting for the Doc to give you permission . . . that's not going to happen. He can't. He's a therapist. He can't tell you what to do.'

She smiled.

'I can, though.'

Chapter Fifty

'All right,' said Maggie, looking stern. 'It's time to vote. All those in favour of continuing with the wind farm plans as they are, raise their hands.'

Mr Mathieson's hand shot up. Flora wondered vaguely if he had investments in offshore wind farms. She wouldn't put it past him. Elspeth Grange. The reverend.

'Reverend!' she couldn't help saying. At least he had the grace to look slightly embarrassed.

There was a long pause. One more hand, and they'd be defeated. Flora looked at her father, who had gone entirely pink. He had the chance to vote against the man who'd strode in, bought his farm, stolen his son away from him. He couldn't look at Colton. It must, Flora realised, be agony for him.

But he kept his hand down. Flora's heart wanted to burst with love for him.

'And those who reject?'

Eck's hand went up, slowly. So did Mrs Kennedy's, and Flora clenched her fists with glee. Gregor's, too, in solidarity with Eck, of course. She and Colton looked at each other. It was all down to Maggie. Had they done enough? They crowded together.

'Christ, this is better than Mergers and Aquisitions,' said Kai under his breath.

Maggie didn't speak for a long time. Then she leaned forward.

'Mr Rogers,' she said. 'I've been impressed by your … belated but nonetheless clear commitment to our community, and I hope very much that it continues … '

She looked pointedly at Flora then, who squirmed.

'Your obvious love for this island and what we have here is admirable. As are the efforts you've put in to back this up.'

Colton stood up, his face full of gratitude.

'Thank you so much, Mrs—'

She stilled him with a hand.

'That's why I'm sure you'll agree that bringing further investment – practical, near-at-hand investment, that will benefit every single resident, temporary and permanent – can only be a public good. However, in light of your impassioned defence, I am inclined not to place the wind farm in front of the Rock.'

She stopped. Colton and the MacKenzies, on the brink of a group hug, looked at her, beaming.

'To preserve the exquisite views for guests there, I propose moving it three kilometres to the west, which does not impact on costing and is an equally appropriate space for the work to proceed.'

There was a very long pause. Colton straightened up.

'You mean directly in front of the Manse? My home?'

'It's your choice, Mr Rogers. The Rock or the Manse. It's the second most appropriate location. Benbecula has huge cost implications for our tax base.'

Colton took a very deep breath and looked at everyone around him. He clutched his head.

'Seriously?'

Flora leaned over.

'It's up to you. It really is. You can say no.'

Kai nodded.

'Oh, well, great,' said Colton. He looked at Fintan. 'What do you think?'

'I don't mind,' Fintan said.

Colton blinked several times.

'What? If you were living there, you really wouldn't mind them?'

'If I was living there,' said Fintan, going bright pink, 'I don't think anything would bother me.'

There was a pause.

Colton swung around to the council table.

'Fine,' he said. 'That is absolutely fine.'

Maggie Buchanan made a small, neat note on her paperwork. 'Any other business?' she said.

Chapter Fifty-one

They left the chamber in silence.

'Well, that's great,' said Kai. 'I appear to have just lost my first case.'

'It's in a foreign jurisdiction,' said Flora. 'It totes doesn't count.'

Colton had disappeared on his phone. Fintan, on the other hand, was looking thrilled.

'Who says we lost?' he said, grinning with happiness.

As they emerged, they found themselves in the middle of a mob of people carrying flaming torches.

'It's the Lughnasa,' said Flora.

Lorna came running up.

'How did you do? How did it go?!'

'Well . . . we kind of lost,' said Flora glumly.

'No way!'

'Are you Lorna?' said Kai.

'Yes! Hello!' And Lorna embraced Kai so instinctively, Flora couldn't help perking up.

'I suppose it could be worse,' she said. 'The Rock will still be beautiful.'

'Come on!' said Lorna. 'Screw that. We've got mead!' She passed over a large bottle. 'Come to the Lughnasa!'

And they couldn't help themselves; the crowd was moving too fast, and they allowed themselves to go with the flow, down the road, towards the sunset and the oncoming darkness that Flora knew was about to settle on Mure and stay the entire winter long. The laughing faces of friends and neighbours were reflected now not in sunlight, but in the flickering flames of the torches.

Isla and Iona passed, their hair done up in leaves, symbolising the falling leaves of the end of summer and the harvest brought safely in. They were at the front of the procession carrying the great green man down to the harbour to be set alight.

'This place is INSANE!' shrieked Kai, swigging more mead.

Innes, without Agot, had somehow materialised at their side, and they paraded down to the sound of beating drums and high skirling pipes.

Ruaridh MacLeod was this year's king, as Isla's flushed and happy face attested, and he stood on the very tip of the harbour as the green man was lit and placed upon the ceremonial boat.

'Here we call you!' he intoned, as the first flames started to take hold of the great figure.

'*Domnall mac Taidc far vel!*'

'Far vel!' shouted the crowd, raising their cups and glasses.

'Donnchadh of Argyll far vel!'

'Far vel!'

The flames were licking up the structure now. It was the first properly dark night of the year, and the chill was coming down from the fells.

'Dubgall mac Somairle far vel!'

'Far vel!'

'Dughgall mac Ruaidhri far vel!'

'Far vel!'

The names went on and on. The figure was properly alight now, and was being cast off by the men closest. Flora glanced round. Lorna was standing close to Saif, although they weren't touching. She looked down at the road to the port. Parked there was a gleaming brand-new sports car with its top down. There were very few cars like that on Mure. She squinted. Who the hell was that?

To her total and utter surprise, Hamish heaved his enormous bulk out of it, alongside, of all people, Inge-Britt. Flora couldn't help it; she nudged Innes.

'Look!'

'Ah yes,' said Innes, smiling. 'I don't think he saw much point in saving his share of the farm money.'

'He wanted a *red sports car*?'

'All the time, apparently.'

Flora laughed.

'Oh for God's sake. I will never understand *anybody*.'

'Fingall macGofraid far vel!' bellowed Ruaridh.

'FAR VEL!'

The crowd was getting rowdier, the shouting and the music louder and louder. Andy would keep the bar open very late tonight.

'I'm sorry about your case!' Flora hollered to Kai. 'I'm sorry I didn't do a better job of persuading people.'

Kai glanced around to where Colton and Fintan were entwined and snogging madly up by the beer garden.

'Do you know, I don't think they're that fussed,' he said, smiling. 'Anyway, I don't understand the problem.'

'What do you mean?' said Flora.

'With the wind farms. I think they're beautiful, those turbines. They look like they grow out of the sea. I think they're absolutely lovely. I bet they'll love looking at them on windy days.'

Lorna and Flora looked at each other, shrugged and chinked their glasses together.

'*Harald Olafsson, far vel!*'

'*FAR VEL!*'

There were a lot of Haralds, Flora thought. And then she concentrated on enjoying the flames, and the night, and the mead, until suddenly Ruaridh stopped shouting and the drums fell quiet and they all stared as – what they often hoped would happen at Lughnasa but so rarely did – the Northern Lights began; gentle at first, then, soon, rippling across the sky, in skeins of dancing yellow and green. Fingers pointed, cameras were taken out; the Viking ship travelled on unnoticed into the dark of the night as awestruck people took in the greatest of all shows dancing the full width of the night sky.

Flora eventually broke away from the crowd. It wasn't

that she wasn't enjoying herself. She just needed to think. She decided to wander up the beach, knowing for sure that nobody else would be there. At the headland, she watched the incredible display above her, glancing back to the firelit group of happy people down by the harbour. Was she really going to leave this? For what? Dry paperwork all day? Cases that got lost? Sitting on a sweaty, overcrowded train every day, over and over? Heating up her dinner from a polystyrene tray; waiting for the ping of a dirty microwave?

She thought about what Colton had said. About the fresh faces of Iona and Isla, and their excitement about all the possibilities Mure presented them with.

She sighed and stared out to sea. Under the rippling lights, she caught sight suddenly – nobody across the harbour seemed to have seen it; they were still all staring up – of a pod of whales, orcas by their fins; tossing and turning in the moonlight and the aurora borealis. As if *they* knew where she belonged. Where she could be herself; could be valued, not just as a cog in a huge, impersonal machine.

Where it could be all right. Not perfect. But all right.

She stared at the lights for a little while longer. Oh, they were so beautiful. When she was wee, her mother had told her it was just the clouds dancing, and would wake her up at night to see them.

As she stared, one of the lights flashed and turned red. She looked at it again. What the hell was that? It wasn't part of the aurora display. It looked more like . . .

And then she started to run.

Chapter Fifty-two

Colton had said yes, without hesitation, even as Joel had apologised for the failure of the case. Colton waved it off; he would think about it later, he said. He had plenty to celebrate anyway. And he'd see him soon.

Joel had been on private planes before; even if he hadn't, he wouldn't have given a whit for the fine leather or the handsome smiling steward. He was staring out the window, heart racing, on the verge of panic at doing something so very, very out of his ordered life. At several points he felt like simply ordering the plane to turn round. But he didn't.

'Look, look!' the steward shouted as they descended. And there, outside his window, were great chains and rods of light, shimmering and dancing as the small plane prepared to land. He looked at them in consternation, confused by their beauty, then realised something: he'd never seen Mure in the dark before.

There was no one at the airport. He grabbed his bag; he was wearing a suit, because right up to the last minute, he hadn't been able to decide whether or not he was going. He could call Colton again, he supposed, see if he could send a car …

She was standing on the tarmac, the lights of the sky behind her; her skirt and hair blowing in the wind.

They looked at each other for a very long time. He put down his bag. They didn't run towards each other. It felt, strangely, too important for that. Flora felt like she was moving underwater as she stepped towards him. He took a step too, and gradually they drew closer. Then they both stopped, as though there was an invisible line between them. She looked at him, her jaw jutting slightly, as if she was struggling to control herself.

'If you take another step,' she said. 'If you take one more step. You have to mean it. You have to … I can't. I won't. Do you understand?'

He did. He blinked. He had fought so hard. He looked down at his shoes. Could he take this last step? Could he?

Suddenly there was an explosion of fur and barking. There was no way Bramble was going to let Flora go out on such an exciting night-time mission without him. No way. Flora had left him in the Land Rover, but he was having none of it and had simply leapt out of the back. Now he was jumping up at Joel to show his appreciation and happiness at seeing him again. Flora watched, still terrified.

Joel's face broke into a huge grin.

'Hey,' he said. 'Hey, Bramble. Hey.'

He got down on one knee, right there on the tarmac, and

proceeded to rub the dog's tummy, just as Bramble liked it, and scratch all the way up his neck under his ears.

Flora blinked.

'You like dogs,' she said.

Joel straightened up again, fiddling with his glasses.

'Who the fuck doesn't like dogs?' he said. 'But not half as much as I like you.'

And he took the final step forward.

Chapter Fifty-three

The Presidential Suite at the Rock, although not specifically designed for losers, Colton had pointed out, was just as beautiful as Flora could have wished. A fire burned high in the grate; there was a huge claw-footed bath in the middle of the room. Outside, it was pitch black now; the Northern Lights had faded; the green man was long gone, although if you opened the window, you could still just about make out the noise of the very late revellers. There was a vast four-poster bed. She glanced at it nervously.

Joel stood in the doorway.

'Are you . . . I mean, we don't have to,' he said, mindful of last time.

'No,' she said, fiercely. 'No. I want to. Very much.'

And very gently, he unbuttoned her dress; unleashed her white shoulders.

'No sealskin,' he said, smiling as he kissed along the top of her spine.

Flora blinked those pale eyes at him and slowly removed his clothes. And nothing, Joel realised, nothing he'd done before with women – no performance; no boundary-pushing act – had been as terrifying, as mutually vulnerable, as exposing to one another as this; this extraordinary unfolding of every inch of the very beginning of a story. They both had to apologise for crying. It did not matter.

When Joel woke the next morning, alone in the great bed, he had a sudden panic, until he read the note she'd left him.

He pulled on the blue jumper Margo had bought him so long ago, and a pair of jeans, of all things, and set off across to the harbour, remembering to thank Bertie as he stepped off the boat.

He was starving. Thank God, there she was, outside the Summer Seaside Kitchen, the delicious smells already playing on the fresh morning air. She turned and saw him, beamed; bounded up to him. Kissed him in front of the staff and anyone who cared to pass, and didn't give a jot; and neither, he found to his surprise, did he.

'Feed me,' he said.

'In a minute,' she said, smiling.

'What are you doing?'

Flora pointed upwards.

'Well,' she said. 'Two things. One – much as I'd like to stay at the Rock for ever, I think I'm going to have to rent a flat. And there's one going above the shop. So I'm thinking about that.'

She looked at him closely.

'And secondly ... '

Iona and Isla heaved, and the rope lowered gently, bringing down the 'Summer' part of the sign above the door.

'It's not just for summer any more,' she explained.

'So what are you putting up there instead?' said Joel.

'Annie's,' said Flora, after a pause. 'Annie's. Um. It was my mother's name.'

Joel nodded.

Flora loaded up a bag with pastries – she was definitely taking the day off – and they wandered back to the Rock, hand in hand. They didn't see Lorna, on her way to work, pause slightly, and sigh, and carry on; but everyone else they met, slightly the worse for wear, many of them, after the night before, waved cheerfully, and Joel felt the strangeness of it.

They went back to bed, getting crumbs everywhere, Flora giggling cheerfully, bubbling over with happiness and adoration. Afterwards, she lay tucked under his arm, listening to his regular breathing.

'Don't go,' she whispered.

He opened his eyes, not remotely asleep.

'How can any mortal man resist the siren call of an ocean sprite?' he said, stroking her lovely hair.

'But you're going to work for Colton, aren't you? Kai said you were going to New York.'

He nodded.

'Sure am.'

Her face looked distraught.

'Oh, you,' he said. 'Well. It's only ... it's only five hours from Reykjavik. Given that you live at the top of the world, I thought ... I thought maybe I could commute.'

'To New York?'

'Already halfway there,' said Joel. 'And Colton will be here most of the time anyway, if he needs me. He may not have got what he wanted with the wind farm. But nobody's going to turn down a fast broadband network if he puts one in.'

'They aren't,' said Flora. 'Gosh. Oh my God. Gosh.'

'And I have some . . . I have some friends in New York I'd really like you to meet.'

'Oh my God!'

'Stop saying that,' said Joel. 'Actually, I can think of a way to make you stop . . . '

He ran his hand up her back.

'Why can I not stop looking at you? Touching you? Everything about you? Oh yeah. Enchantment.'

'Enchantment,' said Flora, turning round to stare at him with those eyes, and he wanted to drown in them; to dive in; to live under the water; to call it home.

And she wondered, but only briefly: how long do spells last? When you've cast one, can you ever know?

Afterwards, she slept. And as she slept, it came back to her.

Once upon a time, as ice threw itself against the windows, there was a boat travelling north, far up beyond the isles and into the widest blue seas.

And they came to the ice and the snow, and the season being spring, the icebergs were calving down from the poles and making the water treacherous, even though they were very beautiful and contained all the colours of the sea and the sky as well as white, and bubbles of air, and rocks and pebbles frozen perfectly inside them from a world no one could ever know.

But the girl – 'Did she look like me?' Flora had asked, and her mother had smiled and said, 'Yes, she was busy and noisy and had eyes the colour of water, just like you,' and Flora had smiled, satisfied – *was not happy. She had been quiet on the voyage and determined not to complete the trip, which was taking her where she did not wish to be; she had had no choice. Had felt herself carried along.*

She watched the icebergs curiously as they passed, like tiny islands.

And the captain felt worried and strange as they went slower and slower so they would not get caught in the strange, beautiful glittering sea of ice.

One morning the sun dawned early and they found themselves drifting, next to the largest iceberg they had yet seen. It was a mountain; a glistening high cathedral of ice. The wooden hull of the boat was scraping up against it, with a screeching and a tortured creaking, but the strong oak did not break.

The captain cursed and stood at the helm, praying that the ship would not founder and the hull would not breach. With a terrible twisting and straining of the keel, it moved on, past the great ice mountain and on into the open sea, and the captain, sweat popping at his brow, let out a fervent exhalation of deliverance.

Then he turned back to the sunlit deck, as one of his sailors shouted; and saw, to his horror, that the girl had simply walked – stepped lightly – from the boat's side and on to the mountain of ice, and even now, as he turned his face in disbelief, she strode across the iceberg that would now be her home.

'TURN ABOUT! TURN ABOUT!' shouted the bosun; but

now the wind picked up, and the boat tossed on forwards, and when they managed to get her turned into the waves, the field of icebergs had glittered and merged, and search as they did until nightfall, they found no trace of the girl. And the captain said with bitterest regret when explaining his lost cargo, who could possibly live on such a place?

'*Could* you?' Flora had demanded, thinking how beautiful it would be to live in an island of snow and ice; and how very strange. 'Did she live there?'

'You can live in many different places,' said her mother, stroking her forehead once more. 'I would like to think you will step into many different worlds, many different places, and feel happy in all of them.'

'Even this one?'

'Even this one.'

And as Flora felt herself falling happily asleep, she asked one last question.

'What happened to the girl?'

'Oh, she's still there. She shines,' her mother said; or did she, for the voice was growing fainter and fainter and drifting away. 'She shines like the brightest moon, and she dives for fish, and she steers lost sailors home. Because we are selkies, my darling. And that is what we do.'

In memorium, Mary 'Moira' Colgan,
née McCann, 1945–2016

Acknowledgements

Thank you: Maddie West, David Shelley, Charlie King, Manpreet Grewal, Amanda Keats, Joanna Kramer, Jen Wilson and the sales team; Emma Williams, Stephie Melrose, Felice Howden, Jo Wickham and all at Little, Brown; Jo Unwin, Isabel Adamakoh Young. Thank you all.

Sincere thanks to the organisers of Faclan (the Hebridean Book Festival), Orkney Library and Worldplay (the book festival of the Shetland isles), both for inviting me and treating me with such wonderful hospitality when I visited your beautiful homes. Do have me back!

There are many versions of 'The Herring Song', quoted here (it has about 179 more verses too), but the one I like the best is Eliza Carthy's, from her wonderful album *Red*.

Special thanks to Dominic Colgan, Laraine Harper-King and Serena MacKesy.

Recipes

BANNOCKS

Bannocks are round, crusty, delicious flat rolls, best eaten warm and fresh. They're not a million miles away from what Americans call 'biscuits' (which aren't actually biscuits, obviously, friends. A jaffa cake: *that's* a biscuit).

You can either bake or fry them, and you can add fruit – blueberries are good, or raisins – or if you prefer a savoury taste, some grated cheese in place of the buttermilk or even some chilli and salt (skip the sugar for those ones obviously).

500g self-raising flour
50g butter
10ml milk
250ml buttermilk

1 egg
250ml natural yoghurt

Crumb the flour and the butter together. Add the sugar, egg, buttermilk and enough of the yoghurt to make the dough sticky.

Knead, adding extra flour, until the dough isn't sticky any more.

Roll out until it's about an inch thick, then cut into whatever shapes you like.

Bake at 160 degrees Celsius for 12 minutes *or* fry in a buttered pan until golden brown.

JAM

When I was growing up and would watch my mother making jam, it always looked like a kerfuffle with pots boiling and things bubbling over and a lot of steam in the kitchen. It isn't at all! Jam is really easy. The trick is not to try and make too much at one shot. A couple of jars is fine; it only takes half an hour. And it's lovely at the end of an afternoon bramble pick. If we didn't get enough brambles (blackberries), I just bulk it out with a couple of apples. Purists will balk, but I peel and chop the apples, add a touch of water and bung them in the microwave for five minutes to soften them up.

The big thing is, it gets so hot that kids want to help but they really can't. I make sure to buy stickers for the jars and send them off to decorate them while I'm doing the really boiling bit.

I use jam sugar, but I always add a touch of pectin powder at the last minute, for nerves. Also, running your jam jars through the dishwasher should sterilise them fine.

As much fruit as you've managed to collect plus apples if it isn't much/the five-year-old has a suspiciously sticky face
Exactly the same weight of jam sugar, or slightly less
Lemon juice
A knob of butter

Rinse the fruit. Some people like to sieve out the seeds. I don't – I like them, but I still have my own teeth, so maybe I'll think differently one day.

Cook the fruit and sugar over a low heat, stirring constantly. Add a squeeze of lemon juice. As the mix comes to the boil, add a knob of butter to keep it glossy and smooth and keep the scuzz down. Allow to simmer for ten minutes, stirring all the while. Skim off any fuzzy scuzzy stuff you get on top and wait for all the fruit to be completely soft.

Then bring the mixture to that most mellifluous of states: a rolling boil. You'll know what this is when you see it: great big glorious bubbles popping. Keep like that for five minutes if it's brambles, longer for strawbs. If you have a thermometer, it should be 105 degrees Celsius. If you don't, it doesn't matter – it'll be fine.

Take off the heat for five minutes – long enough to cool but not long enough to set! – then pour into jars. Very, very carefully.

STEAK AND ALE PIE

Yes, I buy the pastry.

500g stewing steak
1 can of ale of your choice. May I recommend the Swannay Orkney IPA?
250g mushrooms
2 carrots
1 onion
Butter for frying
500ml beef stock
Rosemary
Packet of puff pastry

Pre-heat the oven to 175 degrees Celsius.

Toss the steak in flour, salt and pepper, and sear quickly in butter. Set aside.

Gently sauté the onions until golden, along with the carrots. (You can either just add the mushrooms to this or use another pan and sauté the mushrooms separately in butter with two cloves of garlic and white pepper, which is also super-delicious.)

Add the steak, the ale and the stock, and let simmer for an hour or two with the rosemary on top. Don't let the steak boil hard.

Pour the mix into an ovenproof bowl and cover with the pastry, adding a hole in the middle for the steam and, if you like, some nice leaf designs. I think you should – this is a lovely meal.

Bake for 40 minutes or until golden brown on the top; serve on a cold night with mash and some nice dark green veg: cabbage or spinach or kale or something.

APPLE AND FRANGIPANE PIE

With huge and heartfelt thanks to my friend Sez, who is the best fruit pie-maker I know.

Pastry

1 ¼ cups of plain flour
1 (or less) tbsp sugar
½ cup (about 115g) of very cold butter, cubed. It's worth cutting it up, then sticking back in the freezer for 5 mins, as the colder it all is, the crisper the pastry comes out
A pinch of good salt
⅛–¼ cup of iced water
A spot of cream and a bit of sugar for scattering

Combine flour, salt, sugar and butter and process to a coarse meal. Best done in food processor as it's quicker so everything stays colder.

With the processor still running, very slowly add very small amounts of iced water till pastry holds together but is still on the dry side. The aim is to get it as close to shortbread as possible, but in pastry form.

Chill in the fridge for an hour before rolling out.

Roll out to fit your pastry tin. It's quite prone to breaking, so a) make sure there's a good, generous overlap round the edge of the tin and b) don't worry about any tearing – just fill in any holes with little wads of spare pastry.

Brush with cream and scatter with a wee bit of sugar.

Blind bake with beans in for 15 minutes at 180–200 degrees Celsius.

Blind bake without beans for another ten minutes or so, till it's golden.

Frangipane

½ cup ground of almonds
¼ cup of granulated sugar (vanilla sugar if you've got it)
3 tbsp of butter
1 tbsp plain flour
1 egg
½ tsp vanilla essence if using plain sugar
A pinch of salt

Process the dry ingredients, then add the egg and vanilla essence and process to a smooth paste. Chill in the fridge for an hour before using.

Apples/topping

Peeled, cored and thinly sliced 2–3 eating apples (not cooking apples) with the juice and rind of a lemon on them to give them some oomph (and stop them browning)

A jar of jelly of some sort: you can use pretty much any, but goosegage is my favourite for this. But plain old redcurrant from a shop works absolutely fine

When the pastry shell comes out of the oven, immediately spread the frangipane on top so a bit of it soaks into the hot pastry and makes it go ngggh.

Arrange the apple slices all over the top so they look pretty.

Sling it all back in the oven for 10 minutes.

While it's in the oven, tip the jelly into a saucepan and melt it gently over heat till it's liquid. When the tart comes out of the oven, pour the jelly over the top. Leave it all to cool in the tin.

Look out for

Spandex and the City

by

JENNY T. COLGAN

Mild-mannered PR girl Holly Phillips doesn't think much of costumed vigilante 'Ultimate Man' – and after his superpowered antics leave her hoisted over his shoulder and flashing her knickers in the newspaper the next day, she's embarrassed beyond belief.

But when Holly's fifteen minutes of fame make her a target for something villainous, she only has one place to turn – and finds the man behind the mask holds a lot more charm than his crime-fighting alter-ego.

Can Holly find love, or is super-dating just as complicated as the regular kind?

Chapter One

When my brother was about eight or so, and I was fourteen, I took him (heavily bribed by our mother, who was raising us on her own, and had remarked several weeks in a row that if she didn't have an afternoon off to get her roots done and drink several margaritas, she was going to crash the car on purpose) to a superhero movie, and he didn't enjoy it one tiny bit.

He was an unusually literal child, and he came out scowling.

'What's up?' I said, finishing up the horrible blue candy he'd insisted that I buy him and then didn't eat. I was still calling it 'sweets'; hadn't learned to call it candy.

'The baddies,' he said.

'Yes,' I said.

'There were goodies and baddies,' he said.

Then he looked at me, blue eyes frowning in the freckled face which was so similar to mine. The freckles looked cute on him. I looked like Peppermint Patty. My sole goal in life at fourteen was to get enough of a suntan to join them all up. This is what dermatologists call the 'kamikaze' method.

'Yep,' I said, not really listening. There hadn't been nearly as many cute guys in the cinema as I'd hoped.

Vincent shook his head.

'The baddie kept doing an evil laugh, Holly,' he said. 'Like, he knew he was evil and he really enjoyed being evil.'

'Yes, he did,' I said. 'In case the horns and the fangs didn't give away that he was quite evil enough. And the poisoned tail. And all that killing and destruction that he did.'

He shook his head again, even more crossly.

'I don't think real baddies look like baddies,' he said. 'I don't think they even *know* they're baddies.'

And he wandered off to the subway ahead of me – leaving me licking blue sherbet off my fingers – and I never knew why that stuck in my head.

'No. Definitely not, absolutely not, totally no and also no way.'

'What do you mean, "no"?'

The bar was dark and pretty noisy, but anyone could hear my no, and I really wasn't enjoying Gertie asking me about absolutely every man in there over and over again, like some kind of singleton torture interrogation.

Twelve years on from taking Vincent to that movie, my freckles were under quite a lot of make-up, my sandy hair was ironed into submission, but I was still eating – or in this case, drinking – blue stuff.

Gertie was in one of her 'PIN HOLLY TO THE GROUND ON TOP OF ANY AVAILABLE MALE' moods, and all I could do was let her talk and drink her curaçao cocktail, mostly at exactly the same time.

I sighed and glanced again at her latest suggestion. He looked like a tree trunk had wandered into a bar by mistake.

'Oh, for goodness' sake. Look at the muscles! They're one, gross, and two, I don't think a gym bunny is going to be very interested in girls, do you? Come on, he's like all sculpted and stuff. Can you imagine? He probably eats nine raw eggs a day. And looks at himself in the mirror all the time. Oh, and you know – sleeps with men.'

'I can't believe you have a problem with handsome.'

'I don't have a problem with handsome. Handsome has a problem with me.'

'That's not true at all.'

'You never fancied the handsome one in the boy band, did you?'

'No.'

'You used to like Louis not Zayn, right?'

'Where are you going with this?'

I squinted once more at the man at the other end of the bar. He appeared to be all jawline. He looked uncomfortable, like he didn't know what he was meant to be doing there, and also faintly familiar. He caught my eye and smiled in basically a pretty cheesy way.

'Argh,' I said. 'Okay, oh God. Right, he just stared straight at me. And smiled! Weirdo!'

'The problem with you is—'

'Oh, how I love a game of "the problem with me is",' I said. Gertie was my friend, but she was also all loved-up and was buying a place with DuTroy in the suburbs, so she totally had the answer to everything all the time, telling everyone she knew that all they had to do was fall in love and behave exactly as she had. You can tell what good friends we are in that we can still bear to go out for a drink together.

'You have talked yourself into not deserving the handsome boys. Because of, you know, thinking about stuff too much. And complaining about your freckles. Which are cute, by the way. So you go for the less handsome guy, thinking they'll be an easier get for you, but they're not, because you know why?'

'Tell me.'

'Because you think they don't know they're not the handsomest guy. But they know what you're doing. Trading down. And that makes them furious and resentful. So they won't be very nice to you because they know they're second-best. And then it gets worse.'

'How does it get worse?'

'Because when we turn thirty, everything flips, and suddenly the geeky, weird-looking guys start making tons of money and growing into their looks while the big lunks all get fat and bald. So then the weird ones really are the hot ones, and all the women want them. And now they really *are* furious and out for revenge for all the times they got treated second-best when they were younger.'

'So what are you saying?'

'I'm saying that handsome guys are probably going to be nicer to you just because they're more basically confident underneath. Plus, added bonus: they're handsome.'

DuTroy was extremely handsome and he treated Gertie really well. I wondered if she had a point. After two years with a furiously nerdy cartoonist who always looked faintly disappointed in me – not of my job, or the way I looked, or what I was saying, but just gently overall – and a variety of interesting, moody, often horrible poets and beardies, I did wonder.

I snuck another glance at Mr Muscle. He smiled again, showing very white teeth.

'I think he's a serial killer,' I said. 'There is absolutely no other explanation.'

'You are wearing the red dress,' said Gertie. The red dress, it was true, was a definite hard-worker. I didn't have the lucky pants on – this was a night out with my best friend – but the dress was a definite sign of some kind. Gertie didn't get out much since she'd met DuTroy, which was why she was sucking down blue cocktails like she secretly just wanted a hosepipe plugged into the bar, and urging me on to the kind of bad behaviour she didn't get to do any more.

'Hmm,' I said.

'Well, go get more drinks,' she said. 'Stand close to him. See what happens.'

'ARGH,' I said. 'Is this what people used to do before Tinder?'

'Physically stand in places?'

'Physically stand in places,' I said. 'Yuk. Bleargh. Plus I love being single.'

'What, even the Sunday mornings?'

'Yes! No. Not the Sunday mornings.'

If I could get it together, I'd launch a breakfast club just for those Sunday mornings when you wake up alone and try to convince yourself you're enjoying it. And you go out to get coffee and sit and read the papers with all those other people also trying to pretend they're living in a commercial and love sitting by themselves on a Sunday morning being cool and drinking coffee. At the Breakfast Club, we'll all get coffee and read the papers, but in a kind of all-together companionable silence. Maybe. The problem is, if someone else ran a Sunday morning breakfast club, I would absolutely totally one hundred per cent not go.

I stood at the overcrowded bar. It was hot and incredibly noisy. He was just a foot or so away, nursing a fizzy water, I think, and looking around.

It occurred to me suddenly that he didn't look like a guy hanging around a bar – there were a few, and they were all pretending to talk to their friends, intensely involved with their phones, eyes casting around the room in a slightly suspicious manner. He was quite still. Observant, as if he was looking for something very specific. I swallowed, moving towards the bar. As I got closer, I realised he was gigantic, easily six foot five and built – not heavily muscled, but sinewy, strong. Nice. If I had a beard, I told myself sternly. And a penis. And testes.

He scanned the room, saw me again, smiled distantly.

The drinks were pulsing through me. And I *was* wearing the red dress. I made an uncharacteristic decision. I smiled right back. Although his hair was very black, his eyes were blue.

'Hey,' he said, and even though I was sure this was all

an absolutely pointless exercise, and I had no real idea as to what I was doing, I said 'hey' back.

The next second, he grabbed me and threw me across the bar.

LOOK OUT FOR

Jenny COLGAN

writing as Jenny T. Colgan in

Discover a most irregular love story . . .

Connie's smart. She's funny. But when it comes to love, she's only human.

As a brilliant mathematician with bright red hair, Connie's used to being considered a little unusual. But when she's recruited for a top-secret code-breaking project, nothing can prepare her for working with someone quite as peculiar as Luke . . .

'Quirky, funny and romantic' SOPHIE KINSELLA

WATCH OUT FOR
Jenny COLGAN

writing as Jane Beaton in

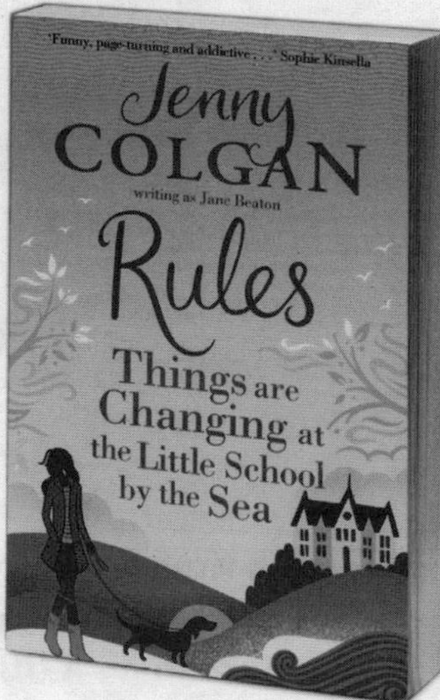

Escape to a beautiful Cornish boarding school by the sea with the wonderfully warm and funny *Class* and *Rules.*

'Funny, page-turning and addictive . . . just like Malory Towers for grown-ups' SOPHIE KINSELLA

'A brilliant boarding school book, stuffed full of unforgettable characters, thrilling adventures and angst . . .' LISA JEWELL

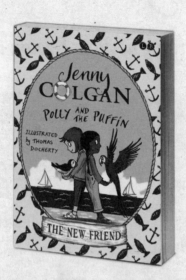

'A fun, warm-hearted read'
WOMAN & HOME

There's more than one surprise in store for Rosie Hopkins this Christmas ...

Rosie Hopkins, newly engaged, is looking forward to an exciting year in the little sweetshop she owns and runs. But when fate strikes Rosie and her boyfriend, Stephen, a terrible blow, threatening everything they hold dear, it's going to take all their strength and the support of their families and their Lipton friends to hold them together.

After all, don't they say it takes a village to raise a child?

Meet Nina

Given a back-room computer job when the beloved Birmingham library she works in turns into a downsized retail complex, Nina misses her old role terribly – dealing with people, greeting her regulars and making sure everyone gets the right books for their needs. Then a new business nobody else wants catches her eye: owning a tiny little bookshop bus up in the Scottish highlands. Out all hours in the freezing cold, driving with a tiny stock of books ... can Nina really make it work?

'A natural funny, warm-hearted writer'
LISA JEWELL

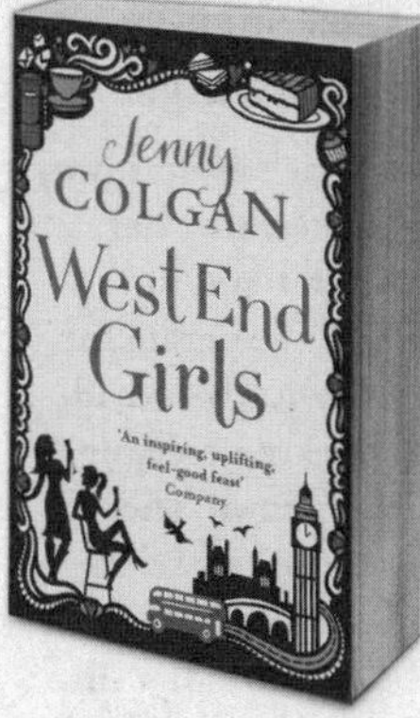

The streets of London are the perfect place to discover your dreams . . .

When, out of the blue, twin sisters Lizzie and Penny learn they have a grandmother living in Chelsea, they are even more surprised when she asks them to flat-sit her King's Road pad while she is in hospital. They jump at the chance to move to London but, as they soon discover, it's not easy to become an It Girl, and west end boys aren't at all like Hugh Grant . . .

Sun, sea and laughter abound in this warm, bubbly tale.

Evie is desperate for a good holiday with peaceful beaches, glorious sunshine and (fingers crossed) some much-needed sex. So when her employers invite her to attend a conference in the beautiful South of France, she can't believe her luck. At last, the chance to party under the stars with the rich and glamorous, to live life as she'd always dreamt of it. But things don't happen in quite the way Evie imagines . . .

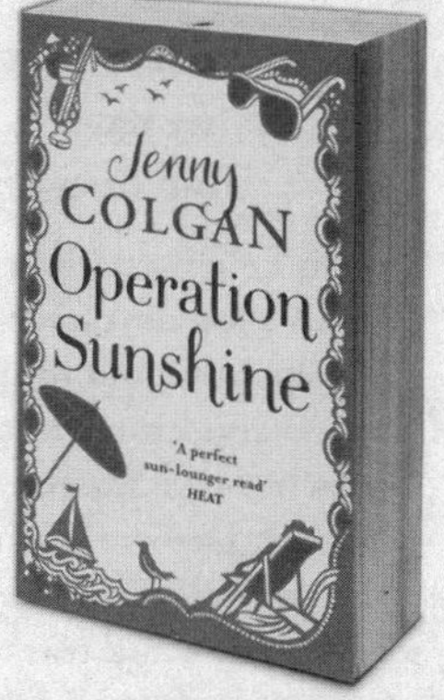

'Colgan at her warm, down-to-earth best'
COSMOPOLITAN

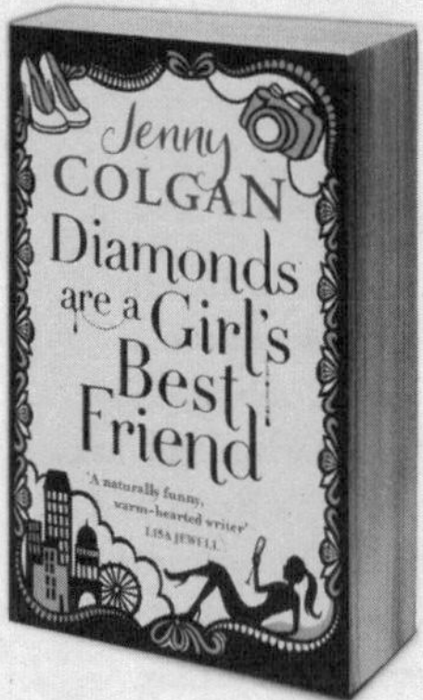

How does an It Girl survive when she loses everything?

Sophie Chesterton is a girl about town, but deep down she suspects that her superficial lifestyle doesn't amount to very much. Her father is desperate for her to make her own way in the world, and when after one shocking evening her life is turned upside down, she suddenly has no choice. Barely scraping by, living in a hovel with four smelly boys, eating baked beans from the tin, Sophie is desperate to get her life back. But does a girl really need diamonds to be happy?

A feisty, flirty tale of one woman's quest to cure her disastrous love life

Posy is delighted when Matt proposes, but a few days later disaster strikes: he backs out of the engagement. Crushed and humiliated, Posy wonders why her love life has always ended in disaster. Determined to discover how she got to this point, Posy resolves to get online and track down her exes. Can she learn from past mistakes? And what if she has let Mr Right slip through her fingers on the way?

Keep in touch with Jenny COLGAN

Chat with Jenny and meet her other readers:

/JennyColganBooks /@jennycolgan

Check out Jenny's website and sign up to her newsletter for all the latest book news plus mouth-watering recipes.

www.jennycolgan.com

LOVE TO READ?

Join **The Little Book Café** for competitions, sneak peeks and more.

/TheLittleBookCafe

/@littlebookcafe

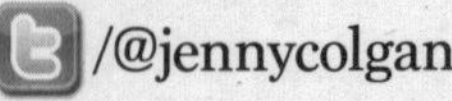

LET *Jenny* COLGAN

MAKE YOUR DREAMS C

You could escape

v

Find your perfe pectacular beachside boltho nor house, Boutique Retrea collection.

For details of the competition and how to enter go to

www.jennycolgan.com

For more information about Boutique Retreats: www.boutique-retreats.co.uk